STEEL DRAGONS MC BOOK THREE

DRAGON TORCH

C.A. RENE

DRAGON SCORCH

Edited by: ProofsbyPolly

Cover design by: Black Widow Designs Co

Paperback ISBN: 978-1-990675-56-0

For all Content Inquiries, please visit my website:
CONTENT WARNING | Careneauthor.com

Please read responsibly.

DEDICATION

To all the readers who live thousands of lives
through fiction, here's another one.

GENEVIEVE
BMW Motorrad Milano

PROLOGUE

"Tell me something, pretty Genevieve Varga." His voice is smooth like a finely aged wine, the tenor meant to set me at ease but fails.

"What could I tell you that you don't already know?" I brush my hair away from my face with my shoulder as he eats up my every movement with his eyes.

"After everything you learned here today,"—he leans forward, invading my personal space and making me cringe—"do you still love your daddy?"

8

PART ONE

2 Weeks Earlier

GENEVIEVE

CHAPTER ONE

"If you want to kill your own nephew," Malik drawls, "have at it."

Laith and more brothers come running into the room and they all stop short when they find their Vice on his knees with a shotgun to the head. "Give me the keys, Genni. We need Jaeger," Laith says as I keep my eyes on Quinton's uncle.

"In my pocket," I grit out. Standing about ten feet in front of Quinton on his knees with a gun to his head and Malik beside me, I tighten my hold on the gun in my hand, preparing to kill again if I need to. The thought of freeing Jaeger angers me, but maybe he could talk this man down.

"Vic's protégé is locked up?" Tazo raises a brow, the motion making him look eerily like Quinton. "What is happening around here?" He has a grin lining his lips as his eyes flick around the room, almost as if he finds all of this amusing. Laith is running off behind me after grabbing the keys as Tazo's eyes land on Malik. "What are you doing here in the

Dragon compound? Should I mark you as a traitor as well?"

"Don't fucking talk to him!" I snap and take another step forward.

"There's Wendy's fire," he breathes in awe. Hearing my mother's name has my heart pounding in my chest and my feet halting their advance.

"How do you know my mother?" My arm begins to shake and my finger starts to curl around the trigger as my voice strains with each syllable.

"Know your mother?" He lets loose a booming laugh before falling silent as his face morphs into a serious expression. "I loved your mother until your father killed her!"

"Shut up!" Quinton yells from his knees and begins to struggle as Cash tightens his hold on the back of his neck. "Stop with your lies!"

It all happens in an instant. The barrel of Tazo's gun is shoved roughly to Quinton's temple, and I run forward, screaming, "Quinton!" when a loud *bang* echoes around the room.

Everyone drops to the ground as I crouch, including Tazo, his gun no longer pressed to Quinton's head. Without thinking twice, I dart forward and throw myself on top of Quinton, his arms instantly coming around me as he flips us over and drags me behind the bar. My back hits the wood as Quinton crowds around me, his hands cupping my face and his eyes searching over me for injuries.

"I'm fine," I choke out as the commotion on the other side of the bar ramps up.

His eyes search over my face again, a look of frantic desperation shining back at me before he slams his mouth to mine in a brutal kiss. Then he grabs my gun, releasing me and standing slowly, his body still in front of me. It's not lost on me that he's putting himself in the line of fire while making sure I'm protected. I press my fingers to my mouth as my heart pounds against my rib cage.

"Where is he?" Quinton asks as more footsteps run into the room.

"Where's Genni?" Jaeger bellows, and my mouth dries out from the sound of his voice. It's hoarse and deep, but it's the fear wrapped around each syllable that has my lungs ceasing on my held breath.

"With me," Quinton answers, his voice softening a fraction but his body remaining tense as my gun is still pointed in front of him. "Where did Tazo go?"

I should rise to my feet and face Jaeger head-on, but I'm beyond exhausted and I don't have it in me to go another round with him right now.

"Someone needs to come clean up this man's brains because the flies will come in swarms soon." The voice has me gasping as I shove Chino out of the way and rush to my feet, looking over the bar at Delia Montez as she swaggers into the clubhouse. "Where's my girl?"

"Delia!" I exclaim as I hurry toward her, wrapping my arms around her shoulders. The hard barrel of a rifle strapped to Delia's back meets my forearm, and my eyes narrow in over her shoulder on the body lying on the ground, the hole where his face used to be making identification impossible. Cash will have to answer to my father now, wherever they are.

"Genni." Jaeger's deep growl has Delia locking up as she releases me, pulling her handgun from the holster at her waist as I turn around to face him.

"I don't like your tone," she *tsks* as she aims the gun at his head, the handle decorated with a green snakeskin. Jaeger's eyes flare with interest as he gives her a slow once-over then lands back on the gun, the look making my stomach flip.

"Little Montez." He sucks on a tooth as he saunters closer, his ruined cut flapping open around his waist. Pride crashes through me because I did that and watching him check out Delia makes me wish I'd just stabbed him in the heart. "Does your brother know you're out after dark?"

"Don't step any closer." Malik's deep timber sounds as he steps up to Jaeger, his gun firmly to his temple. "I'd threaten to piss on you if I wasn't so sure you'd like it."

Jaeger's jaw tics as he stares at me, his dark and bruised eyes filled with anger. "Call your dog off."

Laith steps up on Jaeger's other side and I hold my breath as I wait to see who he sides with. I was just between him and his brother not too long ago, but bile rushes up my throat as he stares at his twin, his own eyes filling with warning. "Brother—" He doesn't have a chance to finish his sentence before Malik is on him, his fist slamming into his face.

"Stop!" I yell and start after them, only to be yanked back by my ponytail, my back meeting Jaeger's front.

"Put down the gun, Delia," he croons as the two men I care about continue to fight. Then he bends and whispers in my ear, "This is what happens when you put two Pitbulls in a ring together." His words are nothing but white noise as I watch two men I care about hurt each other.

"Charles!" Delia hollers at Malik, her gun still trained on Jaeger, but since he and I are nearly the same height, it's trained on me as well. Only I know Delia would never put me at risk.

"Will you stop referring to them as dogs?" I snap at him as my head is pulled back, his mouth coasting along my cheek.

"Aren't all men though?" My muscles stiffen at his words, at the nearness of his body, and the firm grip he has on my hair. I could fight him off, make him submit or suffer broken bones, but I can't muster up the strength as I watch Laith land a hit to his brother's jaw.

"Let me go, Jaeger," I say with exhaustion-laced words. To my utter shock, he lets me go and walks into the fray to pull Laith away from Malik. Delia rushes forward to stand in front of Malik, her hand on his chest, stopping him from rushing Laith again. My eyes flick from one brother to the other and my heart cracks in half.

What am I expecting to accomplish here?

Malik has a busted lip, but his face is exuberant, like he's at a carnival on the teacup ride. Laith is looking a little more banged up as his chest heaves with the exertion of beating up his brother.

"Be glad Malik didn't use his gun this time, that's progress if you ask me." Quinton stands beside me, his hair messy from the events that have unfolded and his face drawn and tired.

"I didn't ask you," I snap. It's not lost on me that I shielded his body with my own without a second thought, but now that I am thinking, everything about him irritates me.

"I guess you didn't." He steps away from me and toward Jaeger, looking at me over his shoulder. "Did you really think they would all just fall to obedience because you were handing out your pussy as compensation?"

"Fuck you," I snarl, the sound hauling Malik's attention from Delia to me. "Are you feeling like a big man now because your asshole best friend is free?"

Malik's face goes from exhilarated to thunderous as he sees me facing off with Quinton. He takes two steps toward us before Delia grabs his vest, stopping him in his tracks. She knows this is my battle and there will be no respect earned if I have someone else fight it for me. Malik knows this as well and it's the only reason he's allowing Delia to stop him.

Jaeger watches the both of us with rapt attention, smartly keeping his mouth shut as Quinton laughs mockingly beside him, his arms spread wide. "Do you understand what just happened, Genni? Do you even know who that was?"

"Tazo Chino, your fucking uncle," Diego drawls as he steps into the clubhouse. The sound of his voice has me spinning on the spot and I nearly fall to my knees with relief.

He has a gun similar to the one Delia has, strapped over his shoulder, and his hair is windblown and framing his face in dark tendrils. He holds out his arms and I rush into them, breathing in deeply the scent of home. "I missed you," I murmur into his neck.

"Let's all cool off and have some drinks. We now have a common enemy," Chip calls out as he begins popping caps off beer bottles. "Unless we all decide to just kill each other and lose to that boomer."

"I'll take a whiskey sour," Delia hollers, slipping the gun back into the holster and striding to the bar with a smile on her face.

"Nice to see you again, gorgeous," Chip croons to her as she sits on a stool. "That's a big gun you got there, or are you just happy to see me?"

"Are you okay?" Diego pulls back and tips up my face with his finger under my chin to look me in the eyes. His finger drops as I give him a nod while I swallow down the emotion threatening to grip me in its cage. Heat hits my back as a familiar scent washes over me, and I let my head fall back to land on Malik's shoulder as his face pushes into my hair. "Looks like you're going to need stitches in that eyebrow, Charles," Diego groans. "And a few bandages on your lip."

"You should see the other guy." He snorts quietly into my neck, pulling a small smile to my lips. I look over and wince when I find Laith, Quinton, and Jaeger standing together. Laith is pretty battered looking and his right eye is already swelling shut.

"We need to find my uncle," Quinton quips. "He could still be in the compound."

"I sent some of your men after him when he fled the gates," Diego states as his arms tighten around me.

"You got that fancy gun on your back," Jaeger snipes. "Why didn't you shoot his head off?"

"Couldn't get a good shot." Diego shrugs, and I look over my shoulder to find Delia giving him a strange look. It is strange that Diego couldn't get the shot, almost unheard of. "I should look these two over." Diego sighs, changing the subject. "Do you think you can keep it civil?" he asks Malik who scoffs behind me.

"Not in the slightest," he retorts, and I turn to face him, my hand resting on his reddened cheek.

"Please, Malik." I give him a pleading look and his eyes soften.

"Fine," he mutters and then turns to look at his twin. "Let's go, Dimples. You're starting to look like the Hunchback," he calls out as Laith's hands curl into fists. "Mommy ain't here to patch you up this time, but Montez is a close second."

"Are you going to be okay with them?" I turn to ask Diego, my eyes on Laith as he stiffens with anger.

"I've got a few guns on me and they know I can use them." He is capable and his words relax me as he leans in and gives me a brief kiss. "Are you going to be okay?"

"I don't know if you noticed, but your sister is armed with a gun bigger than her. Is she wearing Kevlar?" Delia tips back her glass, draining her drink in one swallow, the vest hugging her chest.

"She's always had a flair for theatrics." Diego chuckles, then his eyes darken as he takes in Chip. "Make sure he stays the hell away from my sister. There ain't no way she's dating a Dragon." I nod and watch as he shoves Malik ahead of him and motions for Laith to follow, making sure to stay between the brawling brothers.

"Chin up, sis." Jaeger appears in front of me, his knuckle brushing along my chin in a mock punch. "Isn't this what you wanted? Hell's March and Steel Dragons coming together?"

His mocking tone and smug smile has my stomach knotting with anger as I stare him down. "I'm not your sister."

His eyes slip over my body in a slow, heated once-over and his voice drops as he says, "Oh, I know. I don't need reminding." Then he heads to the bar and leans on the top, grabbing a beer and chugging it down, his throat working with each swallow.

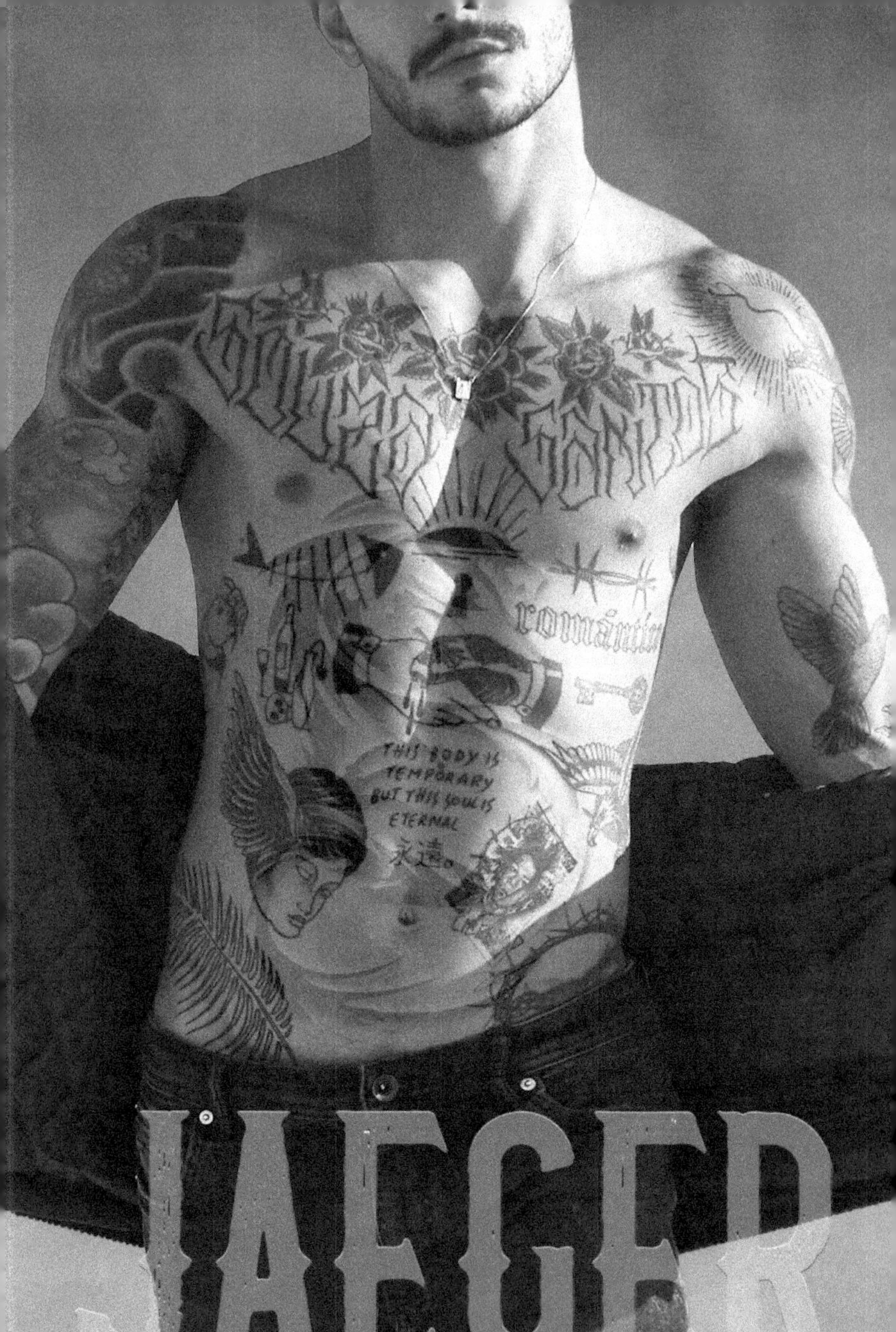

romântic
THIS BODY IS
TEMPORARY
BUT THIS SOUL IS
ETERNAL
永遠
JAEGER

JAEGER

Her eyes are on me as I drink the beer, hoping the bitter liquid quenches the thirst and settles my rattled nerves. It was bad enough running into the room and expecting to find my sister laid out, but to hear that Tazo was here in the club, his gun to my best friend's head is fucking terrifying. I'll admit it.

My eyes skip to Cash's body in the doorway of the compound, the top of his head completely blown off, then my eyes skip to Montez's sister as she sips a whiskey sour, her flirty eyes on Chip. She's looking comfortable in a fucking bulletproof vest with a gun strapped to her back, reminding me that Quinton's uncle could've rained carnage down on us today and I'm not sure why he didn't.

"We need to clean up Cash," I say to Quinton. "And then we need to discuss how the fuck your uncle wound up here tonight."

"We're not talking about shit until the others come back," Genni snaps as she steps up to the bar and downs a bottle of beer in one go. I won't even talk about how quickly my cock fills up at the sight of my fucking stepsister as she wipes the beer off her mouth with her forearm.

"Oh, dear sister,"—I give her my most winning smile as her eyes narrow on my face—"I wouldn't dream of it."

"Malik seemed well-acquainted with my uncle," Quinton murmurs as he brings a bottle of water to his mouth.

"He did," I hum as my eyes flick from him to Genni. "So tell us, *Prez*, what do you propose we do about Tazo?"

All voices quiet around us as her eyes meet mine, the challenge in them clear as her mouth curls upward. The sight of her like this takes my breath away because she's nothing like the sister I grew up with. "First, as your *Prez,* I'm going to order you to clean the filth up in the doorway. I've had enough dealing with the stench of piss and incompetence. Then when you and Quinton are done getting rid of the body and we have a bit of a rest, we'll all have Mass in Hell." I don't miss how she just combined the names of March and Dragons' meetings.

Delia whistles from her spot at the bar, her eyes on Genni are narrowed and filled with pride. She's not the only one because Quinton is looking the same as he reaches down to the front of his pants and shamelessly adjusts himself. I rap my knuckles on the bar and push off from the wooden slab. "Sounds good. Let's go, Chino." I clap him on the back, pulling his attention away from Genni. "It's as if Vic never died." My eyes slip back to Genni's as they round at the sound of her father's name. "And that's not a good thing," I add as I stride to a closet on one side of the bar. Opening the door, I begin taking out the thick, industrial rubber gloves and a tarp.

She doesn't know the things I do, I try to remind myself. She doesn't truly know the father she had, and I didn't either until right up to the very end. I won't hide anything from her this time. She wants to play President? Well, she'll have to hoist those big girl panties up and face every fucking thing I had to. Then I want to see just how well she'll be able to hide her disgust. My mother's face slips into my mind and I swallow down the grief threatening to spill over. If only I had known everything earlier, then maybe I could've saved her.

I toss a pair of gloves to Quinton, who is surprisingly compliant as he is quiet. He's also been patiently waiting for a few explanations, and I think it's the right time to lay everything bare, but if Genni thinks she will ever be President of my club, she's in for a shock. This is my legacy, and if given the chance, I can make it something greater than what it was intended to be.

Dragging my arm along my forehead, I collect the sweat as I watch what's left of Cash burn in the barrel behind the compound. Both Quinton and I have bandanas covering our noses and mouths because even the thought of breathing in a lungful of Cash has me on the edge of spewing.

We're sitting side by side on the picnic table, my ruined cut beside me and our feet resting on the bench as we watch one of the Steel Dragons originals turn to ash. The back exit from Medical opens and Malik Charles steps out, his face littered with bandages and bruises. The second he spots us, his mouth widens into a manic grin, splitting his lip open again as his tongue swipes to gather the blood. His eyes practically glow with murderous intent as he steps next to the barrel and leans on the wall, his head inclining to take a proper peek inside.

"Anyone else suddenly craving a well-done steak, charred to perfection on the grill?" His deep inhale followed by a contented sigh, has Quinton jumping from the table and lifting his bandana to projectile vomit across the grass. He never was one for the clean-up side of things. "Just me?" Malik looks around innocently.

Quinton retches again and then spits on the ground with a curse. "You are fucking insane," he growls at Malik. "Have a little respect for the fucking dead."

"Respect?" Malik falls against the wall and crosses his arms over his chest. "You two wouldn't know the meaning of the word even if the very definition of it was the tip of my dick and I smacked you in the face with it. Cash was never a true Steel Dragon."

"Cash was an original with Vic and my father—"

"And your uncle Tazo?" He smiles like the cat who got the fucking cream and I keep my mouth shut because, even though I can't believe I'm admitting this, I see his fucking point. "Tell me how they deserved such reverence."

"They didn't," I answer honestly, the bandana over my mouth softening the words.

The heat of Quinton's glare hits the back of my head as the door to Medical flies open again and screams float out from behind Montez. "Can you get back in here and help clean up the mess you made?" he snarls at Malik, then closes the door.

"What mess?" My brows crash together as the sly fucker smiles wide again, hauling more blood to the surface of his split lip.

"Kennedy was still in there recovering from my bullet to his shoulder. He wasn't too happy to see us back here and I may have stabbed open his wound to remind him who's daddy." Then he fucking winks and turns around to go back inside.

My head begins to pound as the club's seams begin to fray right in front of my eyes. Every dead Steel Dragon is now rolling in their grave as Hell's March members nonchalantly walk through our club. I'm supposed to have the reins, running my club with an iron fist and not standing by as our enemies claim this space as their own. This is all Vic's fault for making his daughter believe she had the power to change our dynamics, but it's also mine for sending her to Hell's March to begin with.

"This is so messed up," Quinton murmurs as he leans against the table, watching as the flames eat through the flesh of one of our brothers. "What the fuck is happening here, Jaeger?"

"There's so much I haven't said." I stare into the fire, my eyes burning from the lack of blinking and exhaustion combined. "That's about to change because everyone thinks they know the truth, but they don't know a fucking thing. If I have to live with this shit festering inside of me, then so will everyone else."

Quinton doesn't say anything further as we soak in the silence and watch as the dark smoke funnels up from the barrel and fades into the lightening, early morning sky. My body aches with the need to sleep, my head pounding from everything I'm trying to work through, and still, there in the forefront of my mind is Genni. I'm going to feel a sick, twisted sense of satisfaction when I lay everything out in front of her and watch the devastation soak through her features.

Pushing off the table, I grab my cut and leave behind the smoldering remains of Cash to walk around to the front of the compound in time to find Delia Montez walking out in her vest, flipping her dark hair back off her shoulder. Quinton stops beside me and she turns at the motion, lifting her rifle up and looking at us through the scope.

"Bang, bang!" she calls out, making me flinch as she drops the rifle back over her shoulder with a cackle. "See you pussies later."

VUITTON

QUINTON

I step out of the shower and wrap a towel around my waist, then grab another to dry off my hair. Even though I was in there for nearly thirty minutes, I swear I can still smell the stench of Cash's burning corpse on me. We haven't even hit the worst of what his death will bring yet because Mariam is nowhere to be found.

The steam from my too-hot shower billows out into my room as I open the door and head to my dresser. My finger brushes the eagle feather resting on its surface, the golden-brown colors stark against the black-lacquered surface. I've been too ashamed of myself to wear it lately, and every time I braid my hair and forgo slipping it into my hair tie, I feel the loss of its presence as if it weighs a thousand pounds.

Yanking open the drawer, I grab a pair of boxers and turn toward my bed to sit and put them on. As soon as my ass hits the mattress, the burden of the last few days presses in on me and I drop my boxers to the bed as I fall backward. I spread my arms along the length of the new bed, the blanket still stiff with disuse. This room isn't home anymore, not since I watched it burn with the wrath of a Varga.

I hear my bedroom door open and close and I tip my head up to find the Varga herself standing there, her hands behind her back and her body pressed to the door. She's dressed in a man's shirt, probably Malik's or Diego's, and her long legs are bare. Dropping my head back to the mattress with a groan, I stare at the ceiling.

"Not another nightmare," I plead to the too-white paint, brand new and not yet yellowed by nicotine.

"Am I the star of your nightmares, Chino?" Her voice is like velvet, thick and smooth, making my breath catch as I inhale.

"No, I'm the star of my own nightmares, Varga, you're just in every one of them with me." The confession has my heart stalling in my chest and my lungs struggling to absorb any oxygen. I am the sole reason I have those nightmares.

"I need to know where you went after you stormed out of here last night, and where your uncle found you." She sounds so much like the President her father was and another shot spears through my chest. Not even Jaeger has questioned me, if anything, he doesn't seem like he's even fucking present.

"Aren't we having Mass in Hell in a few hours?" I ask, repeating her words from earlier. "I thought I would have time for one more nightmare."

Her feet brush along the carpet as she comes closer, and I swear I can feel the heat of her satiny skin as she stands in front of me, but I keep my arms spread and my eyes on the ceiling. "Where did you go, Quinton? Where were you headed when I chased you out of here with the truth?"

She's talking about the video she played for the entire club of the night I took her virginity, the night I admitted I was falling for my best friend's younger sister and my President's daughter. The night I thought would be my last when they found out. "To Glitz," I admit, my voice hoarse with emotion.

"To her?" Her warm skin brushes my legs as she comes even closer. Her tone has changed as she gives me an insight into the vulnerable girl I once knew. "To Carrie?"

"I don't know." I shake my head, the motion making the ceiling blur. "Maybe."

"Is that going to happen every time we have a fight, Chino?" Her voice drops. "Are you going to try to hurt me by using Carrie?"

My head pops up as I find her standing there between my spread legs, her eyes finding mine. "What the fuck does it matter?" My brows come together as I stare at her with confusion. "Why are you here?" I sit up, my face nearly pressing into her chest. Her nipples harden with my proximity and she takes a small step backward, making me ache for the warmth she's denying me.

"Before we go into that meeting, before we sit in front of all the others, I need to know why. Why did you let them take me that night, Quinton? Why did you let Malik Charles walk right by you and dump me into a van?" Her eyes shine with unshed tears, but her face remains free of any other emotion. It's like she's wearing a mask, but her eyes are the windows to her broken heart.

Reaching out, I grip the hem of her shirt between my thumb and forefinger as I process what she's asking me. This is my chance to come clean, to admit to everything I have regretted for months. "I chose my family over you. I chose my club over the girl I fell in love with. I may have given you my heart, Genni, but this club is my family and it will forever own my soul."

"Did you know about his plan to give me to Barrett? To a man so sadistic?" Her eyes flare with hatred as her jaw tics.

"That wasn't the plan, Genni. Jaeger is all kinds of fucked-up, but that wasn't the plan. Bear was supposed to drive you out to the edge of the desert, give you the bag Jaeger packed with your things, and warn you to never come back. Jaeger was going to send his mother away somewhere safe before he did what your father asked of him, then take over the club." Every word is like a stone on top of my already dug grave, but it's been a long time coming.

"You're still protecting him," she snarls and tries to take another step back, but my fist seals around the hem of her shirt as I stand, dragging it up with me and holding her in place.

"I will protect him until the day I die. He is my brother, my *family*. You don't know the whole story. He put his hands on you, he fucking handed you over to the enemy, and none of those things are okay, but I know the person he is underneath all of that." I step in closer to her again, my face inches from hers as pain saturates her every feature. "You know the person he is underneath, and so did your father when he asked him to kill him before the cancer did."

She shakes her head as the first tear escapes her eye. "No."

"Yes," I grit out. "Vic told him he was dying of brain cancer and made him promise that if the time ever came to kill him before the illness did, then he was to do so without second thought."

"I don't believe that. My father would never—"

"Would never what? Ask his child to do something out of left field? Make them promise to fulfill a task he knew would haunt them forever? Did he not do that to you too, Genni?" Her eyes widen as she takes the moment to haul in a deep breath.

"My father was trying to protect me—"

"From himself, baby." Pressing my mouth to her forehead, I speak against her skin. "From the enemies he created and from the life he lived. It was a noble effort and I will always love the man as though he was my own father, but he was wrong. He took something meant for the son he raised as his own and promised the same thing to you. When will you understand that?"

Her shoulders fall as her body trembles on a sob, the movement loosening the towel around my waist. "What Jaeger did to me, how he handed me over to those monsters... How can I ever forgive that? He was my big brother, Chino."

"I don't know," I confess as my chest constricts. "I don't know."

My towel finally slips from my hips and lands at our feet as she takes that final step toward me, closing the tiny space between us. Flesh meets flesh, and we both groan at the contact. She's not wearing underwear under this fucking shirt. I harden instantly without a second's thought because that's the effect Genni has always had on me and always will, but this isn't right. Falling into bed with her again isn't an option, not until I've found a way to find redemption for what I had a hand in.

So I take a tortured step back and release her shirt before bending to retrieve my towel. "Sorry," I mumble as I wrap it back around my waist and look her in the eyes. "I'm sorry, Genni. For everything, but I don't think you should be in here right now. If you still want to talk after our meeting in a few hours, then we can."

I turn away from her because it's too hard to face the only thing I've ever craved and denied myself. She exhales a long breath behind me and then I hear her bare feet brush along my carpet as she walks away. The bedroom door opens and I press my hand to my stomach to stop the anxiety from toppling me when she says, "I'm sorry about the video thing, it was a low blow. I was trying to grab onto this club, my father's club, with both hands and that meant making you look weak." Then the door closes before I can even tell her she was forgiven the moment my uncle dropped me to my knees and pressed his gun to my head, the taste of death coating my tongue. It was at that moment I wished I had fought for her, loved her, *chosen* her. I wished I was a different person.

Looking over my shoulder to the spot where she was just standing moments ago, I inhale, dragging her lingering scent inside of me. It's time Jaeger spills everything he knows and leaves it all out in the open for everyone to make their own choices, and then I hope we can begin to heal. I drop my towel and forget about the boxers as I crawl into my bed with a groan. Those are all high hopes and where Jaeger is concerned, nothing is simple.

LAITH

CHAPTER TWO

My fucking head is *pounding*. I forgot how hard that motherfucker could hit. Turning my head to look out of the single window I have in my room, I squint when the sun hits my one good eye. It's nearing noon and I'm just now getting ready to sleep. Sleep has eluded me for a while and I have no idea when I last slept. Wait… yes, I do. It was the night I was awoken by V as she screamed through the nightmare haunting her sleep. The night I finally tasted her and made her mine.

Only she isn't mine, not completely.

Can a heart split three ways? What about four or five?

It's not just me, my brother, and Diego she looks at with desire. It's also Quinton, and I've seen glimpses of it between her and Jaeger as well. How could that even begin to work?

She's no longer across the hall from me in her stepbrother's bed since we freed him, and I'm once again feeling lost and alone. Was it just a brief fling, a quick taste of what I could've had if only I grasped it when I had the chance so long ago?

A soft knock on the door has me sitting up in bed and wincing from the agony in my head. The door slowly opens to reveal the woman who's claimed my thoughts, as if I summoned her here by sheer will.

"Hey, I came to check on you." V holds up an ice pack and some Ibuprofen. "Diego says you need to ice it and dull the pain."

"Thanks." I wince again as she rushes to the bed. "How are the rooms?"

"They're great, thank you for setting that up." She gives me a sidelong glance once she sits beside me and then cracks the ice pack.

"We had extra bedrooms built with the remodel. We're hoping to get more prospects." This mundane conversation is slightly awkward and it's because of me. I can't seem to get the image of her riding my cock out of my head, and yet I'm already mourning the loss of her.

"If we're going to make this work, you two will have to be civil." She finally breaks the silence as she hands me a bottle of water and two pills. "What do we have to do to make that happen?"

"Make what work?" I ask as I swallow down the medicine and let her press the ice pack to my eye, her face suddenly so close. Sucking in a breath, I let her scent seep through my chest as I soak in her features, seeing nothing but perfection.

"Did I assume wrong?" she whispers, her breath fanning over my face. "I thought we had something, or we could…"

She trails off as I continue to look at her eyes, the color like the night sky. "How?" My voice cracks as my hand reaches up to brush her hair behind her ear, nearly groaning when she leans into my touch.

"It's not conventional and it's certainly not easy." She looks up at me from under her lashes as my thumb strokes across her cheek. "I can't explain how each one of you fills the void inside of me. It was once a chasm, the depths raw and bottomless, but now it's sealing and you're a part of that."

"How does it *work*?" I reiterate as my mind goes over everything. "Does my brother know you're here? What does Montez think? How do they accept each other?"

"They know I'm here. I don't hide things from them, and it just happened. They realized they both wanted me and I wanted them back. It was an instant compromise because it meant we all got what we wanted. I don't know how they worked it out and how they continue to make it work, but it helps that they aren't brothers hell-bent on killing each other." There are questions in her eyes, the confusion swimming in their depths. My hand drops from her face as I take the ice pack from her and hold it to my cheek.

"What has he told you?" I ask as I watch her shift on the bed, drawing her legs up onto the mattress and sitting cross-legged. Is she wearing any underwear under the shirt I let her borrow?

"Not much," she admits, pulling my attention back to what she's saying. "And even if he did, I wouldn't divulge his side, like I won't do with yours, but he's damaged. He hides it under an aloof attitude, but there is violence simmering just beneath and I've witnessed it spill over. It's the same as mine and it can only come from a horrific betrayal." Her hand runs along my thigh, the soothing touch softening the sharp edges of her words.

"It boils down to what I suspect was postpartum depression, but I will never know for sure. When my mother had us, she was only nineteen and barely married to my father for a year. Their marriage was one of convenience, and when I think back on it now, I don't know if they ever truly loved each other or if he was even capable of it at all. He was cold, calculating, and quiet. He rarely spoke when he was home and it was almost as if my brother and I didn't exist when we were babies. My mother said it was because he worked a lot, but that was just an excuse. It was who he was, and it reminds me a lot of Malik." I drop the ice pack from my cheek and set it on the bed, grabbing V's hand in mine.

"Malik is none of those things," she tells me quietly. "He's protective, funny, and so fucking kind. I wish you could see what I do." Her fingers tighten around mine in emphasis.

"I've seen the way he is with you and you've experienced that side of him. I will admit, I was shocked with how much he expresses with you. It's not the brother I knew." As my chest expands with a breath, I will myself to go back in time and pull apart the memories I have tucked away. "He and I used to be close. We loved to be near each other as babies, going so far to only sleep if it was in the same bed. We loved motorcycles and ninjas," I reminisce with a chuckle, "which explains exactly why we both ended up in clubs. But my mother was mostly alone to raise two rambunctious boys and we were difficult, Malik more so. He had a rebellious streak that only grew the older he got and I was more concerned about my mother's failing health. She would sleep the days away in bed, leaving us to our own devices most of the time, and when my dad would come home, Malik seemed to gravitate toward him. They became close in their own way, and slowly, Malik began to change from rebellious to cold and distant." I release her hand to pick up the ice pack again and press it to my eye, praying the swelling goes down enough to see.

"He doesn't talk much about your parents," she says as she bites her bottom lip. "But he's been hurt by someone."

"Our mother," I confirm with a brusque nod. "She really didn't pay either of us much attention, but Malik would press every one of her buttons. Soon, she was slapping him around and locking him in bedrooms when it was time to eat. She left me alone because I was quiet and obedient, whereas Malik was cruel and filled with hatred."

"Do you blame him?" V shakes her head with a scoff. "No wonder he's so filled with anger. Your mother literally groomed you both to hate each other."

"I agree. She did do that. There was a lot of resentment from her toward Malik, and I believe it was because he reminded her more of our father than I did. When he died on September 11th, our lives changed. We learned he wasn't on a business trip at all, but that he was leaving on vacation with his much younger mistress. Our mother changed after that. We received a large sum of insurance money and we moved into a bigger home, and for a while, she was happy, but Malik was miserable. He began causing problems at school, fighting and being aggressive, and it was a common occurrence for him to be dropped off at home by a cop cruiser when we became teenagers." I drop the ice pack from my eye again and relief hits me as I'm able to open it a crack, the swelling having gone down and giving me a bit more sight.

"He lost the one person he could relate to," V gasps as she slaps a hand to her chest. "The one person he believed saw who he was."

"I saw him," I say quietly as that old guilt crashes over me. "I saw the good inside of him, but I couldn't stop what was happening under our roof. He didn't tell me. He didn't let me know until it was too late." Taking a deep breath, I stave off the emotion threatening to haul me under and steal my ability to speak. "She was hurting him, hitting him with the fire poker…"

The memory hits me in real time and I fall into a deep pit of agony.

Malik didn't show up to school today. Usually he's late because he rolls out of bed when he feels like it, but he gets here at some point, only to avoid our mother at home. But he's not here.

When lunchtime came and went, I knew something was wrong, I could sense it in my gut. So now I run along the sidewalk toward our house, my feet hitting the pavement in quick thuds, the impact resounding in my chest. I should've forced him to get up with me this morning, today of all days. September 11th's are always hard, but for our mother, it's like any other day. She doesn't feel the loss of our father like my brother does. If Malik confronted her or said something to her, I can only imagine how she would react.

Our house comes into view and I'm a little relieved when I find the driveway empty, no police or ambulance and their blinking lights. I rush up toward our front door and pause when I find it ajar, the sounds of my mother's screams filtering out around me. Her words are garbled from her sobs and my heart lurches up into my throat as I throw open the door and slam it behind me.

Malik's backpack is on the floor beside the shoes, one of the straps ripped, the edges frayed as if it was yanked off his back. I swallow through the cotton feeling of my mouth as another shout echoes to the front of the house, this time it's from my brother. Running toward the sound, my shoes squeak on the tiled linoleum floor, and then I skid to a stop in front of the den.

Our mother is standing over a trembling Malik with the fire poker held over her head as he screams again for her to stop. There's already a rip in his shirt over his shoulder, his blood seeping through the material quickly. She's going to kill him!

"Mom!" I scream as I dart forward and push her away from Malik, his eyes widening as our mother stumbles out of the way.

It all happens as if in slow motion. She stumbles away but her foot catches on the left end of the hearth, making her drop the poker and trip forward, her head connecting with the left corner of the mantle. The crack is loud and bounces off the walls around us, then she's crumbling to the ground, leaving a smear of blood on the stark, white stone.

"She died instantly and we were left orphans. He blamed me and hated that I intervened. It pissed me off that he wasn't thankful I saved him and he never acknowledged what I did was an accident. We were separated by the system and put into different foster homes, but before we parted ways, we had a terrible fight. I blamed him for everything, our whole lives being fucked-up. Even blamed him for Dad's absence, making it his fault the man never wanted to be around us. I blamed him for antagonizing our mother constantly, and then finally, I blamed him for that very last fight between them." I drop the ice pack to the floor, the contents already melted and warm. "He never forgave me and he vowed if he were to face me again, he would shoot me in the mouth and make me swallow every word I said."

Her arms wrap around my waist as she buries her face against my neck. "I'm so sorry," she murmurs, her warm breath heating my skin. "I'm so fucking sorry."

"He escaped from the car driving him to his foster home and I never saw him again until we came face-to-face in a shoot-out with Hell's March. There he was, standing in front of me, my own brother, and I nearly wept with tears. I was so caught off guard when his fist slammed into my face that I didn't have time to defend myself. I remember going down hard, and when I looked up to find him standing over me, there was nothing but hatred in his eyes. I thought he was going to kill me, and when he raised that gun, I made peace with it." My breath shudders as I tangle my fingers in her hair, twisting to pull her across my lap. She straddles me, her toned legs caging me in as I breathe in the scent of her hair. "He didn't though. He only made sure I swallowed every one of those words I spewed to him all those years ago."

Her tears soak my shirt and I press my mouth to the top of her head. "Is there hope, Laith?" she asks. "Will I have to choose?"

DIEGO

DIEGO

Genevieve finds her way into my bed as she does most nights when she needs comfort. I am the one who offers her peace when she's feeling overwhelmed or scared and I love that she trusts me to do that for her. She pulls back the blankets and slips in beside me, her cold feet settling against my legs.

"Everything okay?" I ask, my eyes still closed as her mouth drifts over mine.

"Tell me again." Her voice is raspy and my eyes open to find hers red-rimmed. She's been crying. I try to sit up, but she places a hand on my cheek to hold me in place, the touch instantly calming my growing temper. "It's okay. I'm okay. I just need to hear it."

I settle back into the pillow, my eyes roving over her stunning face as my heart swells. She's mine, and she owns every piece of my heart. Placing my hand over hers still pressed to my face, I smile and say, "I love you."

A sob escapes her lips as she burrows in against my chest, her fingers pressing into my back and her nails biting into the skin. "I love you, Diego. You don't know how grateful I am that you saved me."

"It was my job, sweetheart." I gather her in close. "But I'm happy I did."

"No. I mean *saved* me. Showed me what was worth living for, fighting for." She tips her head up and those blue eyes of hers look lighter coated in tears. "You have no idea just how much of my survival was because of the love and patience you showed me could exist."

Her leg drapes over my waist, her heel digging into my thigh and squeezing me in closer to the apex of her warmth. Her eyes grow heavy with want, but the lingering dark bags beneath them holds me back. I want her to rest, especially because we don't know what we'll be facing in the days to come.

She feels my hesitancy and drops onto her back with a huff. "Sometimes you love me too much."

"That's impossible." I chuckle against her temple, placing a sweet kiss to her skin. Skin that smells like Laith's soap. It doesn't bother me because I know it's what she's been using since she started staying here, but I bet it would irritate the fuck out of Malik.

After the shit he put me through today in Medical, I wouldn't mind seeing him irritated over his girl smelling like his twin brother. Malik holds his rage inside and lets it slowly leak out in small gusts every now and then. Like today, his anger boiled over for his brother, and even though I don't know what happened between them and Genevieve while I wasn't here, it's obviously weighing heavy on him. I didn't miss how Laith let him beat the shit out of him and only struck back when necessary.

"How long has Delia known how to be a sniper?" Her voice breaks apart my thoughts and I turn to find her facing me, her eyes filled with questions.

"Delia has known how to shoot for as long as I have. Our father was the club medic and assassin before he died. He taught us both how to use a rifle." I run my fingers along the skin of her cheek, dragging the calloused pads over the velvet softness.

"She never told me about your parents," she murmurs, her brows coming together in confusion. "And she lied to me about never having killed someone."

"Delia doesn't speak much about our parents," I confess to her. "And to tell you about the skills she possesses would also mean she'd have to tell you how she acquired them. Don't take it like she was hiding it from you, there's just a lot of trauma in the explanations. Delia has her reasons for being secretive and I've seen how close you've become. She may feel more comfortable talking to you now." Her face softens as she gives me a small nod.

"Being a kid in the club world is traumatic." She turns into me again, her body pressing into mine as her heat spreads over my bare chest. "It's almost normal to have a parent killed in a shoot-out or shot in the head by the son they raised as their own." Anger colors her cheeks red as her hand curls into a fist on my chest. "It's normal to experience loss, and we're all just supposed to carry on and pick up where they left off."

"We're certainly raised differently," I agree as I bend and kiss her heated cheek. "Danger is a lurking cloud over our heads, following us everywhere. We don't know the privilege of walking into the mall and shopping or sitting in an arcade with friends. There's always someone who can benefit from our kidnapping or killing. It makes us stronger though. We're built with extra armor to endure the risks."

"And to endure the losses," she adds as she tips her head back. "You gave me that armor. You and Malik."

I swoop in and claim her mouth in a searing kiss, the kind that makes your stomach flip and your toes curl. She's quick to respond, as she always is, and opens her mouth, allowing me to get that first coveted taste of her. She moans as I swallow the sound, its effect traveling to my cock as it quickly hardens. Genevieve throws her leg back over my waist, kicking the blankets off us both and lining up our cores. Her wet heat sinks through my boxers, telling me my girl has been walking through the corridor with no panties on.

I break away from our kiss and grab her chin, my fingers tightening into her flesh. "Are you not wearing panties?" Her mouth opens as her eyes widen, then she gives me a subtle shake of her head. "You thought it would be a good idea to walk around a clubhouse in just a shirt?"

"It's a long shirt," she supplies as a smirk coats her plump lips.

I reach down between us with my other hand to find her pussy soaking wet, her clit hard and begging for my touch. Instead of a soft flick of my finger, her cunt receives a sharp slap, the wet sound reverberating around the room. She sucks in a breath, preparing to scream, when I slip my hand up from her chin to cover her mouth. I soothe the sting with a tickling swipe of my fingers through her folds and over her clit, and just as those dark blue eyes of hers begin to roll back with pleasure, she receives another swift slap.

This is Malik's sort of thing, but I can't let it go unpunished. "You will never do that again, understood?" Her eyes fly open as my hand tightens around her mouth, shutting off any excuses she tries to give. "Nod that pretty head, Genevieve Varga, or else we can slap this pussy until she's red and swollen." Hesitation swirls in her eyes, wondering if a sore pussy is exactly what she'd like. Then her head briefly nods and I release her mouth.

"I don't have clothes here."

I growl at her excuse and pinch her pulsing bud between my thumb and forefinger. "Wrong fucking answer." Her head tips back with her moan as her hips jerk farther into my hand, her soaked core seeking relief from my cock. We have hours until we're meant to meet with everyone and discuss our plans, mere hours until more of Hell's March comes rolling up to the compound, and instead of sleeping, she wants to ride my dick.

I'm not going to tell her no. If this will set our nerves at ease, then why not?

My hand moves down over her chin and encircles her throat, her pulse beating wildly against my palm while my other hand drags her shirt up over her tits as her hands grip my wrist, her nails digging into my skin. I leave the shirt there before touching her body once more, my fingers stroking along both of her breasts, the pierced peaks puckering with my touch. Then I travel down over her stomach, dipping a finger into her belly button as her muscles quiver. She growls, the sound vibrating off the palm of my hand as her nails dig deeper into my flesh.

So impatient.

My hand finds her pussy at last and I spread it wide just as the door opens. "Are we cuddling?" Malik purrs and shuts the door behind him.

MUNK
MALIK
DIESEL

MALIK

My girl has her throat gripped in Montez's hand and her shirt tucked up over those delectable tits as he spreads her pussy just for me.

"Come on in, Charles," Diego huffs, his two fingers disappearing into our girl's cunt. Slayer's whole body begins to tremble as he slowly fucks her with his hand.

"Don't call me that. There are two of us now, and I refuse to be mistaken for a bitch." Pulling off my cut, I fold it on the dresser, then rip my shirt over my head as I kick off my boots, letting it land at my feet. Diego's chuckles get lost in Slayer's moans, making me hurry to undo my belt buckle. I drop my pants and boxers to the floor and climb onto the bed, my face landing in my girl's pussy. I suck her clit into my mouth as Diego continues to pump his fingers in and out of her, her scent wafting around my head. Taking a deep breath, I nearly bite into her tender flesh when I smell my brother on her skin.

"You showered in his bathroom?" The question is coated in a frustrated growl as I snap my head back, the sound more accusatory than I want it to be. Diego's fingers continue to thrust into her as he gives me a sly look.

"No." She leans up to look down at me, her eyes twinkling with innocence. "Everyone uses the same soap here."

A snarl leaves my throat as Diego snorts. "There's only one thing that will solve this, brother." He bites into his lip, making my cock jump at the sight.

"You sucking my dick?" I ask him, making Slayer fall back to the bed with a breathy moan.

"Yes, please," she gasps as she looks at Diego. He only shakes his head at her while a small smile plays around his mouth.

When his eyes skip back to mine, there's mischief shining in their blue depths. This is going to be good. "We need to mark her, Malik. Claim her," he explains, and something inside of me snaps.

Then his fingers begin to slam into her as they glisten with her arousal. "Claim me," she begs, not knowing what she's asking for as she rides the wave of euphoria.

I crawl up her body, trailing my tongue over the skin of her stomach, between her breasts, and then along the column of her throat as I settle between her legs. Diego slips his fingers out of her as I lick around the shell of her ear, then he grabs my cock in his hand to coat it with her juices. My balls tighten, my release hovering right there on the edge with just the touch of his hand covered in her sweet wetness. I drag in a breath, my eyes finding his as he continues to stroke my cock.

"Just making sure you're prepared," he says, his voice gravelly and deep. He releases my cock as I line myself up with Slayer's warm cunt, her eyes widening when I begin to push into her. Diego's wet fingers drag along my abs, then over my chest as I pick up speed and begin to pummel inside of her, the need to claim her only growing as the smell of my brother seeps from her very pores.

Her head tips back when my fingers grip the flesh of her thighs, forcing her to open farther as I finally work my cock to the hilt. Her neck lengthens as her chin points toward the ceiling, a loud whine escaping her. Diego's fingers are coated in her musk when he taps them along my mouth.

"Open," he demands.

Slayer's pussy clenches around my cock as I obey and open my mouth, accepting his fingers to glide along my tongue. The tangy taste of her fills my mouth as I suck his fingers clean, my tongue hitting every crevice as Slayer comes undone at the sight.

Her pussy sucks me in and holds me in place like a fucking vice as it pulses around my length, making me grit my teeth just to hold in my own release. Her cheeks bloom with a pink hue as Diego drags his fingers out of my mouth, and she watches as I lick every bit of her off my lips. "Like what you're seeing, Slayer?" I bend down and suck a nipple into my mouth, her nipple bar clicking against my teeth.

"God, yes," she breathes out as I bring my head back up in time to watch Diego grab her chin and claim her mouth in a possessive kiss. The sight of their tongues dueling has my balls tightening. I don't have much time.

I thrust into her two more times, then quickly pull out and grab my cock in my hand, aiming for her toned stomach. I decorate her golden skin with thick ropes of my cum, the fluid glistening along her abs.

She pulls away from Diego's kiss in time to watch me coat my palm in it against her stomach, then skim it upward and over her breast. Diego hauls off his boxers and swipes his hand through my cum, using it to coat his cock and then he's pulling her across his lap.

"Ride this dick," he growls as I come up behind her and grab her waist to guide her over his length.

"Fuck," she hums as she slips down over him, my cum and her release easing the way. My hands drag up over her stomach, then graze each rib, collecting my cum and moving it to her perfect tits once more. I grab them by the handfuls as she grinds on Diego's cock, his eyes hooded and mouth slack as he watches her.

"You smell like me now," I tell her as I massage my cum into her breasts. "Just as you're supposed to." Her hands cover mine as she moves her hips over Diego, her breathy moans like a soothing balm over the anger that's slowly receding as her scent changes. "Fill her cunt up, brother."

Diego grunts as he pistons up into her, his eyes firmly on our joined hands covering her tits. I watch as Slayer grinds her clit along Diego's piercing, her fervor moans growing louder in the small room.

"Fuck, I'm coming!" she exclaims as her movements become sloppy.

Diego's head arches backward as the sinewy muscles of his neck pulse with each jerk of his cock inside of her and Slayer throws her head back, her hair brushing my face as she screams his name to the ceiling.

Nothing in this world can ruin this moment. *Nothing.*

romantic
THIS BODY IS
TEMPORARY
BUT THIS SOUL IS
ETERNAL
永遠
JAEGER

CHAPTER THREE

Our rooms aren't paper-thin, but I swear I could hear her walking into Quinton's room and Laith's room. The rooms Laith put them up in are farther down the hall, so there should be no reason for her to be here. Except there is. She's pulled Laith into her weird relationship and I bet she's working on Quinton next. Hell, maybe she'll open her legs to my entire club and take over that way. If that's the case, I'll be out on my fucking ass in no time.

A knock sounds at my door and I sit up straight, my heart pounding through my chest. *She wouldn't come to me, would she?* I grind my teeth at my foolish reaction and get off my bed to open the door. Don't ask me why my stomach sours at the sight of my best friend though, as if I really was expecting Genni to be standing there. Keeping my face stoic, I quirk a brow in silent question.

Pathetic. I need to keep reminding myself that she's the enemy.

"Can I come in?" This is how far Quinton and I have drifted. He now asks for permission to come into my room, when less than a year ago we were fucking girls together in my bed.

"Yeah." Opening the door farther, I step back to let him in, noticing his braid newly plaited and missing the feather from his father. "What's up?"

I close the door as he begins pacing at the end of my bed, his fingers wrapping around his growing goatee. "My uncle being back is bad," he finally says as I sit on the bed and watch him.

"No shit." I nod and raise my brow. I know enough about Tazo, but to be honest, it came from a man I no longer trust. "He had a gun to your head, I would say it's bad."

"He'd have no problem killing me." He stops to look me in the eyes. "He wouldn't have any problem killing anyone in this club, but you didn't hear or see his reaction to your sister."

"What do you mean?" I perk up, my head tipping to the side. "Do you think they're working together?"

"Jaeger!" he exclaims, my name sounding like a curse. "Stop trying to find ways to make her the villain. That's your role. You are the fucking villain, not her."

There's no use denying it or trying to make excuses, so I let it go. "What was he saying to my sister?"

"That she reminded him of her mother, but it was the way he said it. Like he was in awe. Then he admitted to being in love with Wendy." I'm taken aback by his words as my mind scrambles to remember all the details my father told me about that man.

"He was fucking with you." I shake my head. "Vic was with Wendy. They had Genni for fuck's sake."

"I know!" He snakes his fingers through his combed-back hair, pulling strands free of their confines. "I know, but why say that? Why make that declaration? I can't wrap my head around it. Then to have Cash there at his side." He turns to look at me, his eyes wide. "Brother, there's something you and I need to talk about. I didn't get the chance because everything went to shit and fast, but I spoke to Cash just after he brought Genni to you here at the club."

"And?" Hearing Cash's name sends a shard of ice through my veins. He was the last original Dragon and he was my brother.

"He was talking shit about Vic and made Tazo sound like a saint, going as far as to suggest my father was a martyr for this club. He didn't sound loyal to the Steel Dragons, Jaeger. He sounded like you were put at the helm to further an agenda that's been set long ago." His eyes narrow on me with suspicion and I can't blame him, but I have no idea what the fuck he's talking about.

"I wasn't in with whatever scheme Cash and Tazo had going," I assure him. "I was working on my own agenda, one I started the night Vic asked me to kill him when the cancer took away his ability to hold his piss in. The night I realized the man who raised me had lied to me for most of my life, then expected me to do the one thing he was too cowardly to do himself. I wanted to get rid of the girl I thought was my little sister, but in reality, she sided with the man who betrayed me without a second thought. So no, I wasn't working for anyone. I was working for my-fucking-self." He links his hands behind his head and turns away from me, the back of his cut shining with the Steel Dragon emblem. "But there was something I did know about." He turns quickly to narrow his eyes on me once more as I shrug my shoulders. "Cash was in contact with Malik."

He drops his arms as his shoulders deflate and moves to sit next to me on the bed. "Is there such a thing as a loyal Steel Dragon?" He gives me a pointed look because I was just as guilty of cohorting with the enemy.

"You seem pretty solid." I nudge his shoulder with mine and get a small smile in return.

"Not really, Jaeger. I haven't wanted to admit it but I would turn for her. Leaving this place behind would be easy if that's what she asks of me. I tried to hold on to being a Dragon, to hold this club up to the standards it's always held, but now I understand it was all lies." I already knew it in the pit of my stomach that my best friend would one day realize his mistake in siding with me. Even back then, I knew that he was in love with my sister, but for some reason, he stuck by me, even when I orchestrated the worst scenario for her. He sees me as a brother, and not just the type you find when you join a club, a real blood brother, and I took advantage of that. It made me despise her even more for coming between us, but right now, I can't blame him for his apprehension.

"Before you make any rash decisions, just give me the chance to explain things. To explain everything." I grab his shoulder and squeeze, letting him know his words haven't driven me to hate him, if anything, it only further proves his loyalty to me. "Let's have this meeting with Genni and the March today, then we'll decide what's happening."

"Okay," he agrees as he stands from the bed. "I hope for your sake it all makes sense, brother."

"It may not be enough to sway everyone." I shrug my shoulders. "But it will be the truth. If my club wants to vote me into exile, then that's what will happen." I rise to stand as he makes his way to the door. "The Steel Dragons MC always came first for me, above all else. I tried my best to hold it all together when it started to crumble around me but, Quinton, it was crumbling long before Dad asked Genni to be President."

He pauses with his hand on the door handle, his head down and his shoulders hunched. It's not easy to watch your home burn around you, figuratively and literally. "I feel lost, Jaeger, and so fucking confused. And still, while I'm struggling to hold myself together, I can't even begin to fathom how she survived in the enemy's compound, her body at their disposal."

His words hit me in the chest as he opens the door and steps out, letting it shut with a quiet *snick*. I take a deep breath and let the anger that's always simmering just beneath the surface explode outward as I grab a bottle of beer from my dresser and smash it against the wall. Why is it not okay that Genni found herself behind enemy lines as the next President of an MC? It happens all the time to us and we're often tortured and killed for it. She fucking survived, and on top of that, she now has a taste of what it's like being President and the risks that come with it. How are there different rules for her because she's a woman?

When putting her in that position is supposed to negate those rules and make her an equal?

Did Dad think she would sit at the head of that table and tell us to risk our lives for her even though she would never have to do the same for us? That's not how it works. As President, you take the most risks as you protect your club by any means necessary.

Any fucking means necessary.

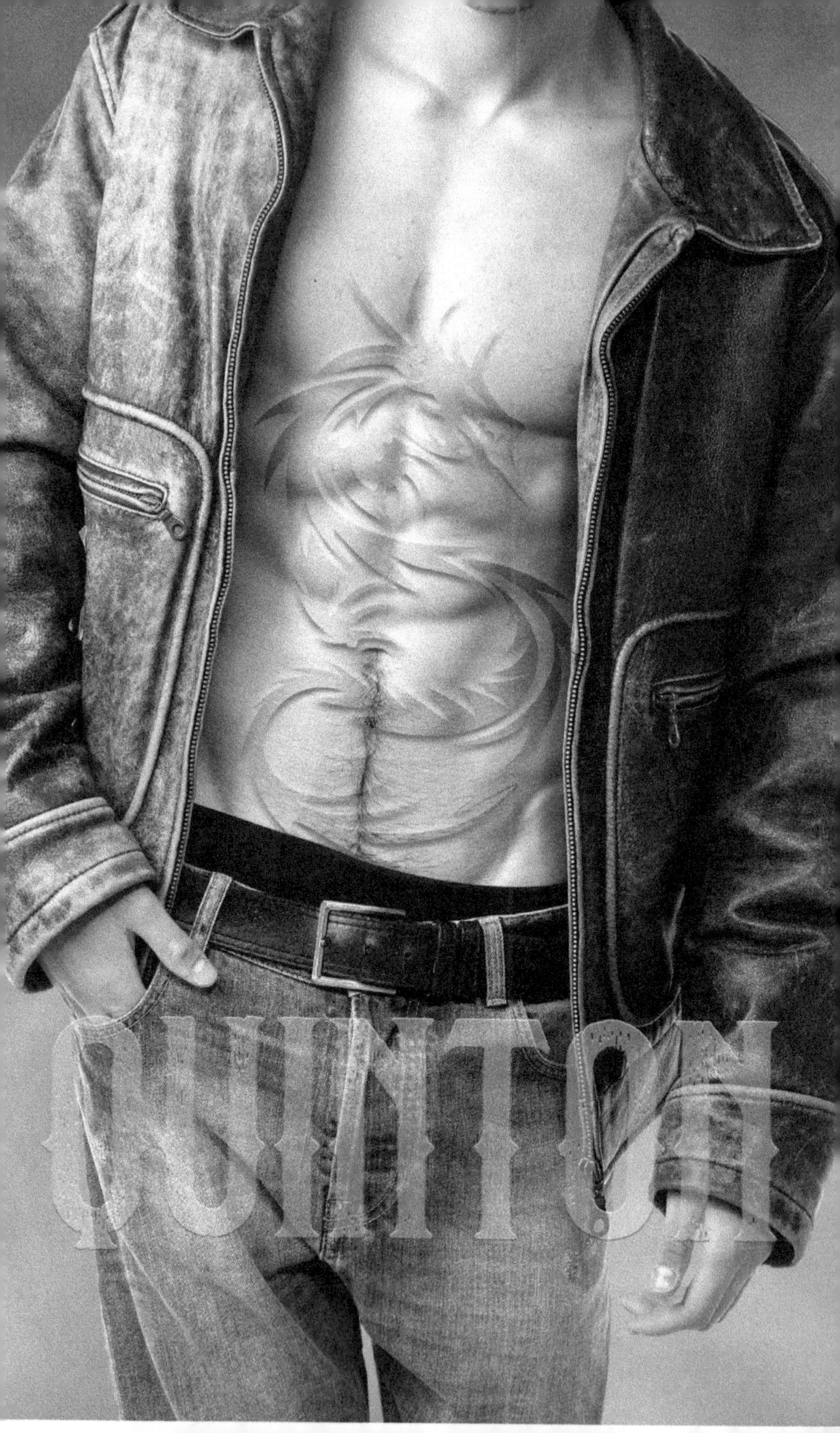
QUINTON

QUINTON

Jaeger's been abnormally reasonable. I haven't seen him this agreeable unless it's minutes before igniting a bomb. It leaves me feeling anxious about what's to come and the plan he has in his mind that he refuses to let anyone in on.

Because we can't be trusted. Even me because I don't think I could ever betray her again.

Most of us have turned on him, have begun to sway to the side of his sister and he can feel it. Why would he tell me or anyone else his plan? This is the stillness before the explosion, I just don't know what, or who, he's planning on destroying.

I rap my knuckles on the bar top and Chip gives me a nod, grabbing a bottle of water out of the fridge and handing it to me. "How are you, brother?" he asks as he leans on the bar, his blond hair falling over his forehead. "You holding up okay?"

I open the water bottle and take a sip, letting the cool liquid soothe my heated insides. "Things are too quiet, too easy." I look around the room and find my brothers tense but calm, like they're feeling the same thing.

"Change is coming and we can't stop it once it's started. Jaeger did some unforgivable things to his family and now it's all coming back around." Chip looks around the room, his blue eyes analyzing everything. "Knowing all that, I still don't think he's a terrible person." His eyes meet mine as a small smile ghosts his mouth. "Some would say he's the leader we were all expecting him to be. We are seeing things unfold in real time, but a leader is always ten steps ahead."

"Are you saying this was his plan when he handed his sister over to the March?" *And shot his father in the head while I stood by complicit?* "To have Genni bring both clubs together? What if they had killed her?" I shake my head as I try to wrap it around everything Chip is suggesting.

"There's no controlling everything when you make a plan, you just roll with the punches and hope you can force it down the path you want." He shrugs and pushes up from the bar, his eyes raking over the brothers in the room, pride shining clear from their depths."Look around you, Chino. Our club was on the verge of collapse when Vic was Prez and you know it. Majority of the brothers are too old to fucking ride and prospects weren't coming in as often. Now we're shacked up with Charles and Montez, the Vice and Enforcer/Medic for the March. Both fucking deadly. Not to mention Montez's sister is the one who saved our asses recently." He scratches at his newly shaved chin as he smiles. "I think we're stronger than we've ever been."

Chip's theory is fantastical in a way that frees Jaeger from the harsh truths of his actions and I've hoped for the same thing, but I know for a fact that none of it is reality.

He walks down the bar to serve an older brother some whiskey when Jaeger walks into the room. His cut is freshly oiled and roughly sewn back together, the President patch stark white against the dark leather. His hair is slicked back over his head and he has a cigarette tucked into his ear while his eyes rove over the room, accessing everything and everyone until they land on me. Dark orbs like black sand slip over me before he heads my way.

His steps are measured and unhurried as he swaggers across the room, as if he's a man without a worry. The mask he wears is one he's perfected over the years and one his President father taught him how to use. Nothing of what he's feeling is projected to any of his brothers and when he sits in the seat beside mine, he gives me a nod, further proving his nonchalance.

"Any idea when the March is rolling in?" I inquire as I watch him decline Chip's offer of a glass of whiskey. A little out of character for him.

"I think that's a question for their *President*," he replies, the corner of his mouth playing with a smile.

"I haven't seen her ye—" Just then the doors to Church open and out walks Genni, Malik, and Diego, their heads still bent together in conversation. "They're using our Church." I move to push off the bar when Jaeger puts his hand on my arm, halting me immediately as I swing my head to look at him with wide eyes. Why doesn't he give a shit? We should tell her that room is for Dragons only.

"Who cares? It's just a room with a wooden slab and some chairs." He looks over his shoulder at them briefly then turns back to face me. "Being a Steel Dragon is in our blood, not in that room."

His words stun me into silence as I feel her approach me from behind. It doesn't matter that her scent is off or that she keeps her distance, I can sense her as if she were right here in my lap.

"A handful of the guys from Hell's March will be in here in a few minutes," she informs us as Jaeger slowly turns in his stool to face her. I turn a little in my seat and nearly fall off the stool when I find her cut hanging over a tight tank top. It's clear she doesn't have a bra on and what's even clearer are the bars through each nipple. I swallow down my surprise and glance at Jaeger, his eyes firmly on her face.

"Sounds good. I'm just waiting on Kennedy to get over here from Medical. He's just getting dressed." Jaeger turns dismissively just as her hands hit her waist in contempt.

"He's not coming—"

"He's my Enforcer. He will be there." Jaeger's brow quirks as he finally scans her from head to toe, failing at being dismissive. "Looks like you've been back home." He motions to her jeans, black and ripped at the knees, worn like a second skin. "Those boots were sitting by the front door for a while."

"I sent Chip over there." She crosses her arms under her tits, making them strain against the thin material of her shirt. "I don't know when I'll be able to step foot back in there." My hardening cock suddenly deflates as agony flares through her eyes and I quickly look at Jaeger as he tips a shoulder.

"Suit yourself. I can send over your things to the March's compound." He turns back around and pulls his phone from his pocket, his fingers flying over the screen. *Heartless bastard.*

Genni opens her mouth to say something when the sounds of bike engines begin to rumble through the lot. Kennedy chooses that moment to enter the room, his face drawn with pain but his eyes filled with rage when they land on Malik.

"You son of a—"

"Kennedy." Jaeger's booming voice cuts off Kennedy's words, his tone filled with warning. "Let's take a walk." He rises from his stool and motions for the Dragon's Enforcer to follow him. They head down the corridor toward the bedrooms as my stomach flips. I used to be included in those little meetings, and now I'm left to the side. No longer a trusted advisor and just barely a Steel Dragon. I don't blame him, not after what I admitted to him earlier.

Turning back to the bar, I find Chip with his eyes on me as he uses a rag to clean the glasses. He offers a small smile but the look in their depths is akin to pity. I don't want anyone's pity and I'll take everything thrown at me because I deserve it for the decisions I've made.

The clubhouse door swings open and a Dragon Prospect stands there with a shocked look on his face as about five Hell's March bikers stand ominously behind him.

"Let them in," I call out and then turn around to face the others.

Jaeger and Kennedy appear from the corridor, Jaeger looking solemn as arrogance fills our Enforcer's face. *Great, they have some sort of plan in the works.* As Vice, I want to demand to know what's about to go down, but I don't really feel the position boasted by the patch sewn into my cut.

The five March members stride into the club and I give them all a close inspection. Bigger men, stronger men than the majority of our club's brothers, and when I look at Chip, he's scrutinizing them in the same light. What he said earlier is starting to make more and more sense. My gaze stops on one person in particular. He's tall and wide, like the others, but certain features have me looking between him and Jaeger. Does he see it too?

"Davis!" Malik comes forward to haul the guy in for a one-armed hug. "How was the ride over?" He wraps an arm around Davis' shoulders and leads him into Church, his head tipped to speak in hushed tones.

When heat sears across my face, I turn to find Genni standing beside Montez and her eyes boring into me. I can't tell what she's thinking by the expression on her face, but I'm thinking I'm about to find out.

GENEVIEVE
BMW Motorrad Milano

GENEVIEVE

I enter the room to find everyone standing, all of us looking to the other for direction. This is my club, handed down to me by my father, the previous President, but at the same time, it's not. These men follow my brother and look to him for guidance, and even though I've forced my way into their space, they don't recognize me as anything more than Vic's daughter.

"Let's take our seats." Jaeger steps forward and motions around the table. "Vices, Sargeants, Enforcers, take the first seats and whatever's left is up for grabs." I should've spoken up first, should have suggested that, but he beat me to it and now he looks like he's taking charge. Except, he moves to take the chair to the right of the one at the end and not the President's seat. "Genni." He motions to my father's old chair. I grit my teeth at the sound of that name, but I can admit it's getting easier to hear it.

I stare at the seat as my throat becomes thick with anxiety. It's a large chair to fill and the longer I question it, the more I feel unworthy. I fought for this and Jaeger is handing it over, albeit too easily, but I don't want it. Not until I understand everything about the man who once sat there. Something like doubt has been growing in the back of my mind and I find myself overanalyzing everything my father said and did in the months prior to his death.

My feet slowly take the steps around the table as everyone grabs a seat and my hand brushes the cool leather as I pull it out away from the table, taking a steadying breath as I sink into the cushion. Jaeger is on my right and Malik is on the left, next is Quinton on Jaeger's right and Diego on Malik's. The table then rounds out with Laith and Davis, then

Kennedy at the end. My eyes drop to the gavel in front of me as my skin suddenly flushes with heat and my chest tightens, almost unbearably.

Malik clears his throat, making me snap my head up to look at him. His face is still, save for his right brow slowly quirking in question as if to say, 'Pull yourself together.'

"Last night, we had someone come by the Dragon clubhouse with an obvious threat." I fold my hands onto the table and look everyone in the eye. "Tazo Chino decided it would be a good idea to hold a gun to his nephew's head inside his home, *our home*, without consequences."

"Fuck him!" Kennedy's fist hits the table, quickly followed by a wince.

"Finally, something we agree on." I nod at him only to receive a scowl. "I will admit, I don't know much about him, if anything at all, and an original who could've provided information found himself in the cross fire."

"Cash shouldn't have been killed," Kennedy growls, his knuckles whitening on the tabletop.

"He shouldn't have drawn his gun on Genevieve," Diego smoothly counters. "Would you like me to go into detail about what I saw that day from the outside?" Diego asks me, and I nod for him to continue. "My sister and I were situated outside the compound with our sniper rifles. I was on the roof of a building"—he points at the wall to his right—"across the street and Delia found her way past the club's defenses to position herself on top of your garage. We will discuss Club security after this."

"Indeed," I murmur as a few coughs sound around the room.

"Tazo did have his gun to Quinton's head, but both my sister and I felt the threat was minimal and we decided to hold our fire. I believe if he wanted Quinton dead, he would've done it instead of making an appearance at the club." Diego's eyes find Quinton's and a small smile plays on his mouth. "Besides, I'm not one to mingle in family drama."

"Word." Malik nods as he looks pointedly at his brother. My hand drifts up to my mouth as I try my best not to snort and look like a fucking teenager in the middle of a serious discussion.

"Family drama?" Quinton falls back in his chair, his long braid hanging over his shoulder. "I haven't seen that man since I was twelve years old. The threat was real and luckily he was distracted by Genni long enough not to pull the trigger."

"Praise be to God," Malik hums as I cover a snort with a cough. There was no holding back on that one.

Jaeger's eyes flick to me as I straighten, schooling my features. The dimple in his right cheek winks as he holds back his own smile, the sight veering me back to family dinners and us as rambunctious kids. Just the memory of Claire scolding us for being silly at the table has my eyes clouding over.

"Delia was quick on the trigger when she saw Cash suddenly withdraw his gun, his eye on Genevieve," Diego finishes and leans back in his chair. "Hell's March will protect our President with our very lives, if need be." His eyes are on Jaeger, the threat blatant in their blue depths.

Davis, Malik, and Laith all begin to drum their hands on the table in agreement as I slowly raise mine for silence. "Thank you, Diego. Now, with that out of the way, I need to learn everything about Tazo Chino." My eyes fall to Quinton as he straightens, his jaw pulsing as he looks around the table. "Quinton, what insight do you have?"

"He's telling the truth," Malik cuts in before Quinton can speak. "I don't think he knows a damn thing about the man he remembers as his uncle." It's clear Hell's March knows more about Tazo than they've ever spoken about and the thought has anger flaring in my chest. It's as if Malik can sense it when his eyes flick to me, his head tipping to the side as he says, "I was about to tell you about it at the bar before the man himself showed up."

"He was once a big player around here, someone who ran

a lot of the illegal side of club business. He's still around behind the scenes where he'd rather be, but an exiled brother and a couple of dead Presidents will bring him back out."

The memory of our conversation hits me quick and hard as I fall back, my body losing its tension. "You were talking about Tazo?" I ask him, and he gives me a brief jerk of the chin. "Okay, well, explain to all of us now."

"Tazo Chino was exiled when he shot at his brother and Vic stepped in to take the bullet." Jaeger leans forward, his attention rapt on Malik, the behavior not lost on me. "His being exiled birthed his need for revenge and that festered. Hell's March was soon created and he became a silent overseer, someone they went to for advice and who kept all the same contacts that the Steel Dragons had acquired over the years."

"Like the cartel," Quinton adds, and Malik nods.

"Yeah, and others besides them." Malik rubs at the growth along his chin, gathering his goatee in his hand. "A few years passed and Tazo became more than just someone our President went to for advice, he became Superior. Barrett and Bear did all his bidding because we were making money. A lot of money. Tazo knew every one of the Steel Dragons' routes for drop-off and shipments, he knew every deal you guys made, and when the time came, he thwarted it."

"Motherfucker," Jaeger growls and falls back into his seat. "No fucking wonder."

"No wonder what?" I question him as he looks down at his hands in his lap.

"Continue." He motions to Malik, completely ignoring me.

Malik looks at me, his eyes filled with questions and I give him a wave to continue. Trusting Jaeger to tell me the truth would be akin to shoving nails in my eyes anyway. I'd rather hear it from Malik. "Vic was becoming more and more desperate to recover from the losses his and his father's club were enduring. He'd just become Vice and had something to prove. He had somehow found out about a warehouse the March had acquired on the Arizona/New Mexico border and decided to blow it the fuck up." His eyes skip to Jaeger as a small smile works along his lips. "You weren't the only one who liked to blow things up. Only he never touched another bomb after that."

"Why?" I cut in, my heart pounding inside my chest. "Why didn't he touch another bomb?"

"That warehouse was for refugees fleeing from bad living conditions in South America, and we were providing asylum until we could get them to a safer place. Women, children, innocent people." My stomach sours as the room is blanketed in a humming white noise. My vision begins to blur as the voices around me fade into the buzzing in my ears. He couldn't have known what was inside those walls, he couldn't. Not my father.

No.

A hand grips my chin, the fingers biting into the skin of my cheeks as a voice tries but fails to penetrate the fog. Victor Varga, my hero, my father, a murderer. A mass murderer.

My body is shaken, the room jarring around me when Jaeger's face appears right in front of me, his eyes blazing with rage.

"Fucking breathe!"

romántic
THIS BODY IS
TEMPORARY
BUT THIS SOUL IS
ETERNAL
永遠
JAEGER

CHAPTER FOUR

Finally, she sucks in a breath just as Malik hauls me off her and Diego pushes in front of me. My fingers tingle where I had them gripped into her face and my body begins to tremble with a rage so fucking potent, I fear I will destroy this place before I've had a chance to reclaim it.

"Don't ever touch her again," Malik snarls before shoving me away.

"Maybe that's something you should've told her earlier," I snap at him as I stride back to the table. "You've had plenty of time to do so."

"He was trying to tell me before everything went to shit," Genni gasps as her elbows drop to the table and her face lands in her hands. I wish I could say I enjoy the feeling of her despair, but it only adds fuel to the rage billowing inside of me. This is what I was left with, and when I asked for Hell's March to drop her at the edge of the desert, it was to make this easier to deal with. How do you tell a Daddy's girl that her father wasn't exactly what she thought he was?

Now I have to watch her crumble under the pressure because she's weak when it comes to her father. Run the Steel Dragons and wipe my fucking sister off the floor when she eventually crashes. No fucking big deal.

She scrubs her hands down her face as I retake my seat, Diego standing behind her with a hand on her shoulder and Malik heading back to his seat. "Sorry," she murmurs. "Please continue." She pats Diego's hand, a direct dismissal before motioning for Malik to continue.

She has to know she looks weak, that her reaction portrayed that to everyone in the room, and it didn't help to have one of her boyfriends soothing her as well.

"It's only going to get worse," I warn her as I lean on the table and force her to look at me. "This life isn't unicorns and rainbows, it's death and torture. It's all a race to the top, to make sure you're the torturer and not the tortured."

"Shut up, Jaeger," she snaps, turning those dark blue eyes on me. The pain is reflected there, as I knew it would be. She couldn't rein it in if she tried.

"None of us are good men, not even the three or four you're humping." Malik growls from across the table as Quinton's hand digs into my arm. "We joined this club for the brotherhood, to be accepted despite what lurks inside of us. We're all fucked-up. We all have a need to do despicable things."

"And you think I'm good?" A slow smile works along her mouth, her eyes void of any emotion as she buries the pain from earlier. "You think I came back from the torture I endured as the same person who was forcibly taken as she kicked and screamed?" She's goading me, trying her damndest to make me feel something, but I'm not her, I won't let anyone in.

My eyes skim over her face, soaking in every feature and storing it in my memory to sit beside the younger version with pigtails hanging off her shoulders. "Yes." It's a lie, sort of. She still has all her feelings visible like an open book, but she's toughened enough to control them.

Her eyes widen a fraction before they roll into the back of her head with a scoff escaping her lips. "You're in for a horrible surprise." She turns back to Malik and waves her hand. "Please finish."

"After that, Barrett decided to retaliate and there was a shoot-out in the desert. Many casualties that day." His eyes skip to Quinton then back to me. "It's been war between our two clubs since then, and each battle only leads to another. There was no end in sight until Victor Varga approached Barrett for a cease-fire agreement."

"We all know about that," Genni says with a sigh, then her eyes land on the Steel Dragons side of the table, slipping down each of us until she stops on Kennedy. "There's something I've been meaning to ask you, Kennedy." Her lips tip upward in a ghost of a smile as her eyes narrow.

"You want something from me?" Kennedy leans forward with a wince. "After everything you and your *club* has done?"

Malik begins to rub his hands together as a sadistic look comes over his face. "If you can't play with the big boys, get on back to the nursery, *baby*." Then he blows him a kiss which has Kennedy shooting up from his chair with a hiss.

"I will fucking kill you!" Kennedy is nearly foaming at the mouth when Diego *tsks*.

"You ripped your stitches," the medic huffs. "You'll need to be sewn up again."

"You're getting jabbed more than a whore during spring break," Malik sneers as a few men around the room snicker.

"Knock it off," I growl at them both. "Sit down, Kennedy, before you bleed out." His eyes are aflame with anger as he looks at me, his body vibrating with the force of holding himself together. "He doesn't do well in crowds." I smirk and look around the room. "It's why he wasn't allowed to attend Mass before, but he's awful good at carving things up."

"That's not why I wasn't allowed into any Mass meetings,"

Kennedy groans as he sits back down, grabbing the bait just as we discussed before coming in here. He leans on the table so he can look at Genni, his jaw tight. "Vic Varga didn't like how often I questioned him, and I knew it was only a matter of time before the fucker killed me."

"What?" Quinton's head turns quickly to Kennedy as his brows knit together. I bet he's trying to remember those early Masses when we were just prospects. "I remember you being in Masses, I think."

"No, you don't, and you wouldn't have noticed me there anyway," he answers Quinton. "I would stay close to the wall, in the shadows where I belonged, until I became a bit of a nuisance." His eyes land on Genni's again as he shakes his head. "Your father was someone I looked up to, someone I thought hung the fucking moon, but after your mother died, he was different. I knew about the warehouse," he affirms as he looks at Malik, his top lip curling upward. "I was the one who was supposed to do it, but I don't fuck with bombs and refused." His eyes move back to Genni, softening just the slightest as he says, "It fucked him up. He kind of went off the deep end after that and we could no longer blame his spiraling on your mother's death. When I tried to keep him accountable, to question most of his decisions, he decided to cut me out completely. He told everyone I got drunk and told some club secrets, which never happened. He ruined my credibility in this club."

"As much as I'd love to take your word for it," Genni says, her fingers curling against the tabletop. "I will need something cleared up first. Finding out Cash was working for Tazo this whole time only makes this incident more suspicious."

"Out with it," Kennedy growls, his patience past the point of control.

"I saw you at a bar with Cash and Malik, who at the time I thought was Laith. What were you doing with a now-known spy for Tazo and a member of the Hell's March?" A hush circles the room as Kennedy's smile grows, his eyes moving to Malik.

"Why didn't you ask your man?" Kennedy finally sneers. "Or is he not trustworthy also?"

"I've told her what I can on my own, but I can't tell her other people's perspectives," Malik cuts in. "She knows why I was there that night and she knows exactly what I suspect happened. Now you tell her why you were."

The room falls silent, the heavy breathing of a few brothers the only sound in the crowded space. I remember this night in question. Laith told me about it and I questioned Cash. I have his side of the story.

"I followed Cash that night, the same way I had done many nights before. There was something about what was left of the *four horsemen* that didn't sit right with me. I knew he was talking to Malik and still, I kept it to myself because who would believe the brother who's not even allowed to sit in on club meetings? Besides, I wanted to find out more." His hand curls around the tangled mess of his graying beard as he looks down at the table with a sly look on his face. "I connected the dots that our drug runner, Junior, had been robbed by March prospects and Jaeger hauled in the kid for interrogation."

"Did you tell Jaeger about it?" Genni asks as she looks from me to Kennedy. "About how you were wrong to *interrogate* the kid?"

"Why would I tell Jaeger? He wasn't my President, but I told your daddy." The smug look on his face has me stifling a smile into my fist, because every doubtful expression crossing Genni's face was a mirror of my own when I found this out.

"You told my dad that Cash had been speaking to a March member and they stole from Junior? Are you saying he did nothing?" Genni's hand tightens into a fist on the table and I can only imagine she wants to smash it into Kennedy's face.

"Getting a clearer picture of your father now?" Kennedy scoffs as I hold up a hand.

"Hold on," I interrupt before Genni flies across the room to kill the man. "I have to remind you that this was around the time Vic was making his own deals with Barrett."

Genni continues to fume in her seat as silence hangs around us and Malik has the audacity to look bored as he says, "Cash was never a Steel Dragon completely. He always worked for Tazo."

"So he was playing you too, is what you're saying?" I smirk at him as he gives me one of his own.

"I didn't have a daddy hiding secrets from me." He leans on the table to look me in the eyes. "I knew who he worked for because it was the same man the March works for. Are you understanding now?" His smirk grows into a smile when I don't take the bait. "Cash was giving me info on how to hit the Dragons where it hurt, and that's all that mattered to me."

"After following Cash to a bar in town one night, I watched him go inside and stuck around for a bit to find out what he was up to. I already had a feeling he would be meeting up with the March. When Malik showed up, I followed him inside. I snapped some photos and sent them to Vic, then sat at the bar for a few drinks. They were sitting in a booth near the back with a few March Prospects and blatantly exchanged money and drugs. Immediately, I thought about Junior and what he told us happened to him." Kennedy's eyes meet mine and I lean back in my chair, knowing it's my turn to explain my actions.

"Junior was our chemical pusher. Coke, meth, heroin, and anything else you can make in a fucking lab. He had it all. Quinton had recently recruited him and he was doing well for a while. Then the product goes missing and I bring him in to find out what happened."

"To torture him," Genni cuts in. "You brought him in to torture him for something that he didn't do."

"How was I supposed to know that, sister?" I lean on the table and watch as her eyes darken with anger. I wonder if she hates being called sister because she's ashamed I'm her brother, or if it makes what we're feeling dirty.

"You listen to what he's telling you. He told you he was robbed by Hell's March." With her staring at me in anger and her jaw pulsing, she reminds me of our father. The sight has my teeth sinking into the flesh of my cheek as I fight his image in my mind.

"You would sing the same tune if you were under interrogation. You'd rat out anyone to live," Kennedy snickers. "If we believed everyone who came through our Slaughter Room, we'd all be dead." Genni shuts her mouth after that, her brows still furrowed in thought. We must look barbaric to her, but this is the MC life. She had a taste of it at the hands of Barrett not too long ago, so she must have some idea. "I approached the table where Malik and Cash were talking, the prospects having moved to another table." Kennedy's eyes meet Malik's as the psychopath clenches his fist on the table. "You were pretty fucked-up by that time, and when I questioned Cash about what was going on, he said it was all under Vic's orders. He laced your drink with the fentanyl you stole from Junior. How was I supposed to know the difference when I wasn't allowed to Mass?"

"Malik told me his drink was spiked," Genni supplies while the two men stare each other down. "And he was robbed, but he let it go. Or actually, Barrett let it go because he was about to receive a bigger payout." Her eyes clash with mine then, betrayal burning heavy in their depths. "Me."

Does it shock me that Barrett had plans to fuck me over as early as that? No, but now that I let everything sink into my brain, the timeline and course of events, maybe Cash set into motion my being double-crossed that night. There's nothing I can do about it now, even though I would love nothing more than to hear it from his own mouth, the brother I thought was loyal.

"Barrett wasn't pissed when you came back with nothing to show for stealing from the Dragons?" I ask Malik, my stomach suddenly bottoming out. It's all starting to make sense.

"Not even a little." Malik shakes his head before his eyes flick over to Genni. He's starting to piece it together too.

"Sounds like he had a backup plan," Diego surmises.

"Maybe something he put into motion that day," Malik

adds. "Barrett wasn't someone who let things go easily. Not without retaliation."

"Tell me everything about the deal you made with Barrett," Genni demands, and I want to deny her because she's nothing more than Vic's daughter, but I'm ready to finally let this shit go.

"Vic, Laith, Quinton, and I rode out to the cartel warehouse where the March had set up distribution. We knew the deal was tentative, or so Vic said, and we could sway them to work for us instead. We needed the money and a deal with the cartel would provide that. Vic also wanted to hit the March at the knees for thinking they could drive through our territory with their product, effectively destroying the treaty we had. I had already put out feelers, looking to have a meeting with Barrett because Vic was turning on me—"

"Turning on you?" Genni scoffs. "That's a little extreme."

"Is it?" I question her as I lean in closer. "Why? Because it's you? Because you were my little sister and not just some other brother in the club? How can you not see how much worse that is?"

Genni's throat works on a swallow as her eyes skip to the tabletop. Betrayal is a brick wall between us, both sides hardened with a foundation of mistrust. If I can understand what makes her hate me so much, why can't she see my side?

DIEGO

DIEGO

I want to step in and protect my girl from the words Jaeger is using as weapons against her, but I can't. She's now a President and has to deal with it on her own. The rest of us are only meant to watch and move the way she tells us to. It doesn't lessen the pain slicing through me though when her own agony is written all over her face.

"I guess we both have our own scars to deal with," she murmurs, a truce she's laying out for the time being.

"I guess so." Jaeger folds his hands together on the table and clears his throat. "That day at the warehouse, I knew I would be seeing a Hell's March member, but I was expecting it to be Barrett."

Quinton's head snaps around to look at his President, his brows furrowed together and his mouth set in a thin line. If this is the first he's hearing about it, then perhaps it's the truth finally coming out of Jaeger's mouth.

"Bear showed up with Malik and Diego, which surprised me because I didn't like having more people knowing about what I was up to. Exile and all that." He grins at Genevieve as she turns to look at me.

"Malik and I did accompany Bear to the warehouse. We were told Bear saw them on the surveillance set up by Jones. We weren't there when Bear and Jaeger spoke." Genevieve gives me a nod and turns back to Jaeger.

"He's right. Bear and I did have a talk alone. When I requested the meeting, they had no idea what I wanted to talk about because I wouldn't dare speak without having Barrett in front of me, but Bear was a close second. In all honesty, I wanted them to fuck up all Vic's dealings, make him look incapable as a leader and I would swoop in before he could announce Genni's position. I would give March a cut of all the jobs for compensation and we would all be winning, but Bear came with some news of his own and it pissed me off." His eyes dart back to Genevieve as his jaw works with anger. "He said they had been watching you sneak around with a March Prospect."

"What?" Genevieve exclaims, her face filled with shock. "That makes no sense."

"No?" Jaeger lifts a brow at her. "You were disappearing without telling anyone where you were, and when questioned, you said you were at the fucking mall." He looks around the table at each of us before saying, "My sister hates the mall."

"I had started training with Quinton," she mumbles, her hand running along her forehead.

"In secret," he counters. "In my mind, you were going behind our backs with the enemy and soon enough you would be at the helm of this club."

"Sounds like something Barrett would cook up," I cut in as I look at Malik. "But what was his end goal?"

"Yeah," Malik agrees as he runs his fingers along his jaw. "Sounds like a plan between Bear and Barrett, but it will be near impossible to find out now that they're both dead. Unless it came from the top." *Tazo.*

"It all made sense to me at the time." Jaeger shrugs. "So I was given a few days to decide how I wanted to deal with it and if a deal was still on the table. You continued to sneak out and I couldn't put a tail on you because I didn't want it getting back to Vic. I chose to believe them in the end because you were already plotting behind my back, so what would be one more betrayal?"

"Fuck," Genevieve curses, her fist hitting the table. "All you had to do was come talk to me."

"Same, though," he retorts as they glare at each other. "So, I devised a plan to have you taken and driven out to the edge of the desert, left there with a threat to never come back here. Bear agreed to the terms."

"Instead, I became a plaything for Barrett," Genevieve snaps, her chin trembling with the force to keep her emotions leashed.

"I didn't know that." Jaeger shakes his head and looks over at me and Malik, his face contemplative. "But did they?"

"I knew about it," Malik confesses. "When I heard there was a girl kept in the basement of the club, I figured it was the Varga Princess. I knew if she was there then either Barrett or Bear had had their fill of her. When I got to know her better, I wanted to figure out which one it was for sure, even though I had a good idea it was Barrett by some of the things he had said, and bury a bullet in their foreheads, but I decided to let her figure it out and not take away her choice of what to do about it. I already took away her choice when I took her on that deal you came up with. I vowed to never do it again." Genevieve's face softens as she listens to him, her eyes shining with gratitude. The three of us have hashed this out many times now, and even though Malik and I still feel like shit for what happened to her, there was nothing we could do about it.

"You should show her Vic's video," Kennedy suggests, an arrogant look coloring his features. "Let her watch her daddy's explanation for the shitstorm we are currently in."

"Video?" Genevieve's head snaps to look at Jaeger. "What video?"

My heart slams into my throat as I watch Genevieve stiffen, her whole body strung tight as she waits for Jaeger's reply. His mouth tenses as he rubs his temple, the indecision clear throughout his features. I don't for one second believe he's protecting his sister, in fact, I think he prefers to drag her along.

"Listen, you fucking parasitic worm," Malik growls as he leans across the table to look Jaeger in the eyes. "How much more damage do you want to cause? Because trust me, sweetheart, you're looking at a lengthy list of repercussions. We're not all sitting around here to make amends with you and your fucking club, we're here to protect Slayer."

A few Dragons bristle at his declaration and I nod my head in agreement because he's right. We're not here to make nice with the Dragons, we will never roll over for this club, but we will play nice right now for Genevieve.

"Show her what you have of *her* father," I demand as I flick open my vest to show the handle of my handgun. Genevieve's hands are curled on the table, the knuckles white as she tries to hold it all together. This is so hard for her, and to not be able to show exactly how she's feeling for fear of appearing weak must be taking its toll on her.

Jaeger reaches into the pocket of his damaged cut and pulls out a cell phone with a cracked screen. His cut is roughly sewn together, the two jagged edges overlapping in a botched attempt to repair it, and I wonder if it has anything to do with Genevieve. "Here." Jaeger slides the phone to her across the table, his jaw flexing with his restraint. I would almost think he wants to protect her from seeing what's on that phone, but he's a fucking master manipulator.

"Thank you," she murmurs and slips it into her pocket. Her throat flexes on a swallow as her eyes flick to me. She'll wait to watch it when she can fully sink into her feelings without fear of what is revealed on her face.

LAITH

LAITH

I've been taking everything in around me without saying much, piecing together all of the information I already had with new tidbits as they arise. The picture they're painting is becoming crystal clear. We were pitted against each other and Genni was the catalyst. I believe her being taken was meant to start a war just as the President of the Steel Dragons died, putting us at our weakest point.

"Genni wasn't meant to survive, was she?" I look up from the table and find my brother, knowing he will tell the truth when it comes to her. "She was supposed to die in that compound, right?"

Malik's eyes skip to Genni's as his jaw tenses and his hands curl into fists. "Yes. It looked that way when Diego found her."

I lean on the table and look around Quinton to Jaeger. "You had a hand in your sister's demise, but if it had come out that Barrett had killed her, what would you have done?"

Jaeger's black eyes meet mine as a fire ignites inside of them. "I would have no other choice but to call a war with the March, especially so soon after Vic died."

"Was murdered," Genni corrects as Jaeger turns back to look at her. "You murdered him."

"I did his final bidding, even though he didn't fucking deserve it after what happened to my mother. *Our mother.* She was murdered, her throat cut so deep her head was nearly taken off. He should've lived with that for however long he had left." Jaeger's words are laced with a deep hatred, but it's not for Genni. It's for Vic and I don't blame him right now. Genni swallows down whatever retort is on her tongue as her face falls with the mention of Claire.

"It's becoming more and more obvious that Jaeger was played by Barrett and used to run his agenda. I don't understand how Vic falls into all of this other than he was trying to protect his family before a vicious disease took away his ability to do so. Putting Genni in the President's position was risky, especially when it was already promised to Jaeger. He had to know that would bring about animosity." I rub my fingers along my chin as I speak my thoughts out loud. "Unless he thought he had more time to smooth it over with Jaeger and make him understand. Instead, Jaeger went to the enemy to solidify his position and Barrett saw the chance to claim us once and for all. We were at our weakest point and if it wasn't for Genni killing him when she did, we would either be dead or wearing Hell's March cuts right now."

The room falls silent until a Hell's March member steps forward from the back wall. His features seem familiar but it's not from seeing him before. Though I can't place who he looks like. My eyes skim his vest and find the Sergeant at Arms patch. He's important. "Barrett was my father and out of everything I've heard today, his reasoning sounds the most accurate." He points at me with a nod and then looks at Genni. "My father was cunning but he wasn't that strategic. He had always wanted to be the only club in Arizona, but he had no idea how to make it happen. That's why for years we fought with the Dragons to no end. No one gained the upper hand and we were always at a stalemate."

"So what were your father's plans, boy?" Kennedy snarls at him. "You're here, inside our compound, you owe us that much."

"Davis was never—"

"I don't owe you anything," Davis cuts Malik off as he takes another step closer to Kennedy. "My father and I hated each other. Hell, I had plans to take out the piece of shit until Genni took matters into her own hands. I never knew his plans or who he worked with, but if this Tazo guy was running Hell's March behind the scenes, then I would put my money on him being the strategist."

He's saying exactly what I've been thinking, and since Tazo's plans didn't pan out, he finally made his appearance, with his gun to his nephew's head. "We still don't know where Mariam is," I remind everyone, bringing their attention back to me. "She and Cash went to seek out Tazo but she didn't come back here with them. We need to keep an eye out for her in case she attempts to come back here as a spy."

"If she comes back here, I'll kill her," Jaeger snarls as Malik's mouth stretches with a devious grin.

"No. That would be a waste," I declare as I place my hands on the table. "I think we should let her come back. In fact, I think we should put out some feelers, looking for her, acting like we think she might be held hostage."

"I like where you're going, little brother," Malik chimes in as I bite into my cheek to prevent myself from snapping at his *little brother* comment. "Then we can get information out of her." He rubs his hands together maniacally.

"I don't think she'd talk," Quinton says with a shrug of his shoulders. "She was becoming suspicious of me before they went to Tazo. She didn't trust us."

"I didn't say we would be nice about it," Malik adds as a cruel smile lines his lips. This is the man I know well and this is the reason I was fearful of him and Genni being together.

"We're not torturing her," Genni states as she shakes her head. "Not unless we have proof that she conspired against us. I won't punish her for her dead husband's crimes."

"Fine. Jaeger can fuck it out of her." Malik's eyes shine with mischief as he looks at our President.

"Down," Jaeger murmurs with a cunning grin of his own as Genni huffs out a breath.

"You're sick." She pushes the chair out from the desk and stands, resting her hands on the table as she looks down at her brother.

"Luckily, you won't be here to do anything."

The room falls quiet as we watch her stare down her brother, his eyes never wavering from her face. "No," he mumbles. "I didn't think so."

"What's happening?" Quinton asks as his spine straightens in the chair.

"Jaeger Varga, you are exiled from the Steel Dragons Motorcycle Club from this day forward. You will leave these premises without your cut and your…" she trails off as she takes a deep breath.

"Branding," he finishes for her with a nod. "Those are the rules."

"No!" Quinton jumps to his feet as Kennedy mumbles something beside me. I can't piece together what he's saying though as shock tears through me.

Turning to look at the Dragon's Enforcer, I wonder why Jaeger's biggest supporter isn't fighting nearly as hard as Quinton is. Kennedy is sitting quietly in his seat as Quinton and Genni argue and everyone else watches with rapt attention. His hands are clasped together as though he's fighting to keep himself there, like he was told to keep his mouth shut no matter what.

My eyes swing back to Genni as her mouth tips downward. "I don't care about the branding, you can keep it since you were so obsessed with being a Dragon that you killed and betrayed your family for it." Jaeger nods and removes his cut, too calmly, before folding it on the table.

It dawns on me that he knew this was going to happen and his little talk with Kennedy earlier was probably a warning for him not to go off the rails. He's still plotting and planning for whatever outcome he's been working toward from the very beginning. My eyes find my twin's only to find him watching me as I continue to piece together a tightly woven tapestry of lies. He sees it all too, and just like me, he's keeping his mouth shut.

I won't deny that Jaeger deserves to be exiled, his actions toward Genni and their family were abhorrent, but he was also used. There is no right or wrong in this situation, every one of us is grappling with the ramifications of betrayal and trust isn't coming easy.

"Make sure you hit that gavel to the block," Jaeger says to Genni as he strides for the door. "Make your word final."

Genni hesitates for a moment, her eyes on her brother's back as she reaches for the gavel, her long fingers wrapping around the handle. She lifts it as his hand rests on the door, his eyes meeting hers over his shoulder. Then he gives her a subtle nod, the movement lost on anyone else who isn't scrutinizing the situation, but not me. The sound of the gavel hitting the wooden block jars me from him as I jerk my gaze back to Genni. She's standing there with her chin held at a confident level, her eyes free of any and all emotion.

A true President doing what's right for the club.

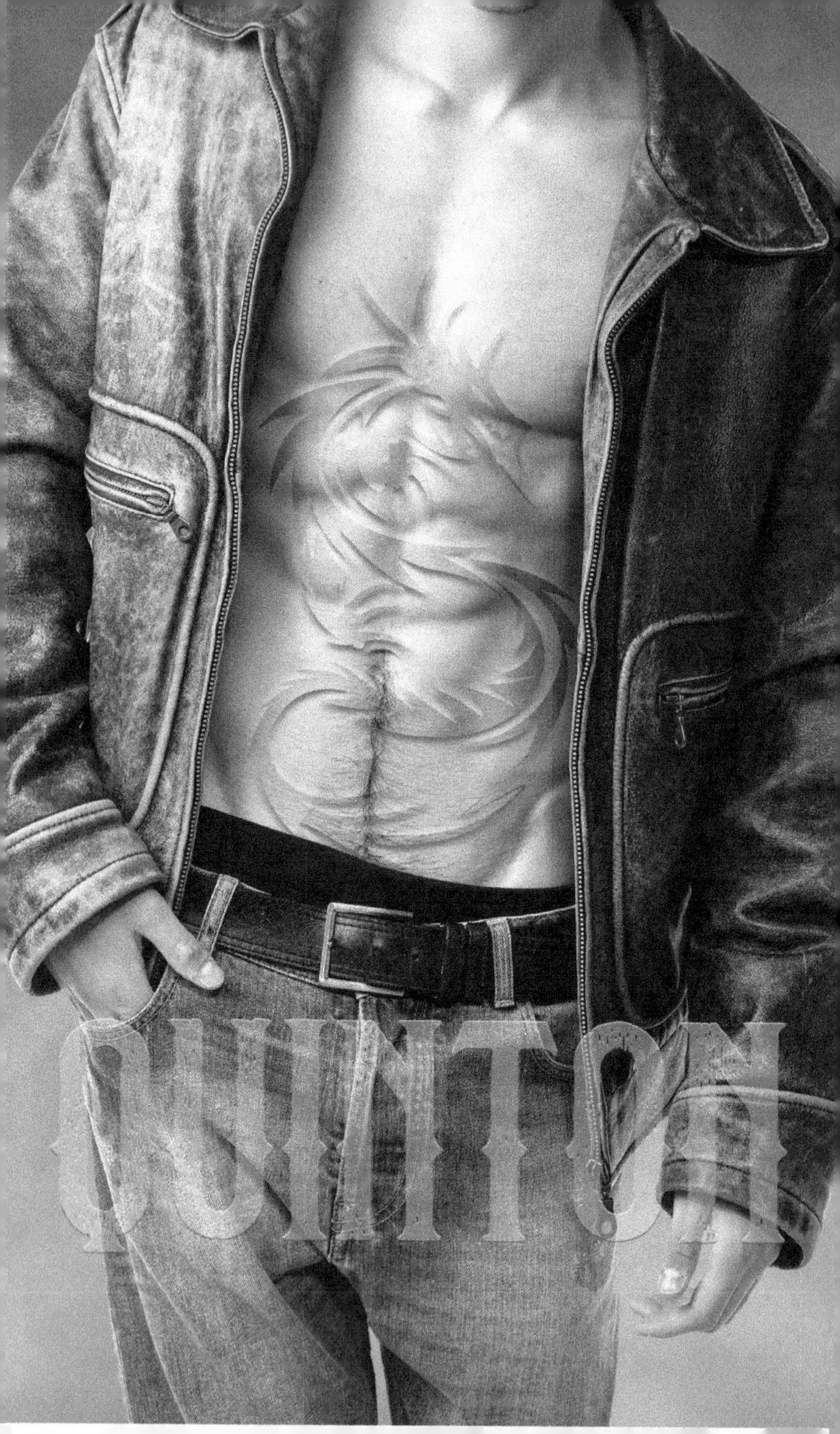
QUINTON

CHAPTER FIVE

"Don't do this!" I exclaim as I rise from my chair, my eyes begging Genni to be reasonable. "Exile is worse than death!" A few mumbled agreements circle throughout the room, but no one else speaks up for fear of attracting her wrath. She's a sister scorned and her sights are set on complete annihilation.

"Quinton," Jaeger says as he steps out of the doorway. "Be a good Vice to her and support her the same way you did me." He means to blindly follow her and stand behind her no matter what. Like now. I'm to accept his exile like I accepted her being taken. I nod because that was always the plan, his exile doesn't change that, and then I watch as he closes the door behind him, the *snick* like a final nail in the coffin.

"March," she continues as if she hadn't just sealed her brother's fate as her eyes roam around the room at the March members. "I need you to stay on the lookout for Tazo. He's under the impression that our club is his. If he comes around the compound for any reason, you are to inform me right away." She looks at Malik and Diego, giving them a sad smile. "I need you guys to head back there and take the helm." They both nod, although Malik looks slightly perturbed about leaving her here. "Davis, can you pull together resources and take note of the brothers here? Let's combine forces and spread them out evenly across both clubs. I want to make sure both compounds are protected." Her eyes land on Kennedy next, her hands on her hips. "Can I trust you to continue to be this club's Enforcer? I'd rather not exile every original member." She gives me a quick glance, making the hair along my arms raise.

Maybe I'm next. I stood by and did nothing to stop her brother's plan after all.

I turn to look over my shoulder at the door again as I slowly sit back in my chair, wondering if I should just leave and follow Jaeger. This club is my life and I have done things in its name that no person should, but right now, it's not feeling like home.

"I'm still here, aren't I?" Kennedy snaps back as Malik leans on the table and snarls across it at him. "Keep him away from me."

Genni's hand lands on Malik's forearm as she looks around the room, her eyes hard and her chin leveled. "I will give you all the same option I gave my brothers back at the March compound. You can leave without repercussions right now. I'm not the typical President, and I'm not my father by any means, but I will do everything in my power to uphold this club to the standards laid out by its founders. I'm fair and despite what you may have heard, I am fucking ruthless when I have to be." Everything she's saying is radiating from her very pores. She is so fucking strong and seems to have grown into her last name. "I will also lay my life on the line for every one of you if need be."

Shock rips through me when no one moves and not a word is spoken out loud. Every brother, young and old, is standing or sitting here and willing to follow the new leader without dispute. Even Kennedy, despite looking pissed off about it.

"Quinton." At the sound of my name, I turn to look at her, watching as she sits in her seat. "I'm going to need your help."

My first instinct is to scoff, to tell her she's a nobody here, but she's just proved that wrong. "With?" I ask as I swallow down every other retort that's resting on the tip of my tongue, a knee-jerk reaction after everything we've been through.

"Tazo Chino. I need any info you can find from your family." The thought of going back home to the Reservation and asking my mother about Tazo is terrifying. He wasn't just exiled from the Steel Dragons, he was forced to leave the family too. It was a double blow for him and my cousins haven't seen their father in years. "Do you know the full story about his exile here?"

"Tazo Chino was exiled because he put a bullet in your father," Kennedy cuts in, saving me from having to say another *I don't know*. "There was a big party thrown by your grandfather and he was announcing new positions to the brothers. Your father was already given Vice and he was preparing him as the future leader by giving him the task of announcing the brothers who would ride at his side. Vic and Dasan Chino were extremely close and all of us knew he would be made Sergeant at Arms. Everyone but Tazo it seemed." Hearing my father's full name is like a shot to my chest, and I can't help but slump in my seat. He's just been Chino for so long that it was easy to disassociate. "Tazo and Dasan weren't close brothers, kind of like you two." He swings his finger back and forth between Malik and Laith. "They were competitive and often squabbled amongst themselves, but jealousy was a factor in how they behaved. Dasan was younger than Tazo, but being that Dasan and Victor were best friends, it was clear who would be getting the position. Tazo exploded with anger when it was announced and tried to shoot Dasan, only Vic stepped in front of the bullet. Tazo was exiled, his branding cut and burned from his skin, and he was sent away. He and Cash were close though, and remained that way until Cash's death. That's all we know. If you're looking for secrets of any kind, you'll need to buy a Ouija board and contact your father."

I cover my mouth to seal in the snort as other brothers shift uncomfortably in their seats. "Thanks, Kennedy," Genni murmurs before turning to look at me once more. "Stay a few minutes?"

I nod as she slams the gavel to the wooden block, calling an end to the meeting. Everyone slowly makes their way out of the room as Genni rises and walks to Malik and Diego, both of them crowding around her.

"Whatever she asks you to do, I'll help you," Laith says as he gets up from his seat. "I'll wait for you at the bar. Then we'll head over to the Varga house to speak to Jaeger."

Shock has me tensing in my seat as I stare at Laith, trying to figure out just where his loyalties lay. Is it just with Genni? Or is he still a Dragon? "If we're caught speaking to an exiled—"

"I don't think I care," he grunts and raises his brow at me. "Do you?"

"What if she thinks we're betraying her?" The last thing I want to do is inflict more damage than I already have. My decisions when it comes to the Vargas have had detrimental effects on her. I can't live with any more guilt.

"Meet me at the bar," he reiterates before heading toward the door as Malik and Diego step away from Genni and follow behind him.

Genni moves back to the head of the table as the door closes, shutting us in here together alone. I can't help but feel slightly worried about what it is she wants to discuss. Will she ban me from seeing Jaeger? She has the right to demand that type of loyalty from her Vice, *from me.*

"Quinton?" Her voice pulls me out of my thoughts as she sits in Laith's vacated seat, turning to face me. She's not sitting in her father's chair and speaking to me like I'm meant to do her bidding. Instead, she's putting herself on my level, and by the look in her eyes, she's going to ask something of me, not demand. "I need your help with Tazo. I've just exiled your best friend, *your family*, but I need you to remain loyal to me and the club." She reaches out her hand to intertwine her fingers with mine, the soothing touch of her skin against mine settling the unease in my stomach. "You said to wait and have a talk after this meeting, and I'm here, hoping you haven't decided to turn your back."

"I would never turn my back on this club," I retort with a firm shake of my head as her fingers tighten around mine. My tattooed fingers are a stark contrast to hers when she slips our hands onto my lap.

"I meant on me," she murmurs, and I lift my head to look into her eyes. Her vulnerability is shining from the depths of those dark blues and my heart squeezes inside my chest. She's unable to trust me fully and I don't blame her. I've already decided to go behind her back to speak to Jaeger.

"What help do you need?" I ask as I adjust our hands to cradle them inside my other one. Turning my back on her is never going to happen again and I hope I can somehow prove it to her. It hurts that she has to clarify but I understand why.

"There has to be someone in your family who knows something about what Tazo has been up to since his exile." She releases a breath and drops her chin to look down at our hands as shadows dance under her eyes. She's exhausted and I can feel it seeping through her carefully constructed facade. "I can't expect you to uphold the rule of not associating with the exiled, especially since I didn't enforce the exile from the club *and* the state. I hate that I'm even saying this, but maybe he'll know something about it too."

"Jaeger?" She's talking about him, but I need to hear it confirmed from her mouth.

"Yes." She releases my hand and falls back into her chair with a heavy exhale. "I understand what you two mean to each other, you're family and he's my… family too." She hesitates and I can't help but wonder if it's because of the betrayal that she doesn't want to call him family or if it's something more. "I will find out what I can from the March and we can bring our info together after. Are you good with that?"

"Is he exiled forever?" I have to ask because right now it feels like he's more on a time-out.

"Exile is for life. I will not go back on that. Maintaining my position here as my father wanted means everything to me, and going back on an exile sentence would make me look weak." She runs her hand over her face, dragging her skin along with it. "Just trust that I have a plan, Quinton."

I open my mouth to tell her the last remnants of my trust were destroyed the moment she played that video in front of everyone, but I swallow it down because I don't know if that's true. I nod instead before saying, "Okay."

She gives me a soft smile and leans in, pressing her plush lips to my cheek. "Thank you," she whispers.

DIESEL

MALIK

Slayer and Chino step out of the room, their hands brushing against each other as they walk. I want her to be happy, and if she can forgive me for my part in her kidnapping, then she should be able to forgive him too. Whatever she decides I will be right behind her.

I turn back to the bar, giving them a little privacy as they talk, and watch my brother as he sips on a small cup of coffee. "You still drink those?" I scoff as I down the rest of my water and crush the bottle.

"Are you saying you remember what I drink?" He turns in his stool to look at me. "And here I thought you truly hated me."

My brows furrow with his comment as I think about exactly what I feel for my brother. "It was never hatred. You smothered me and stepped in when you weren't needed. I was treated like the unstable one and so I became him. You created me, Laith, you and Mother. Now you can reap the seed you sowed." Clapping him on the shoulder, I make his coffee spill from that ridiculous cup.

There are many things I remember about my brother, mostly because there was a point when I dreamed of killing him to avenge the family I felt he took from me, but I've come to realize that he was the family I was missing, not our parents. So I made sure to keep a mental list of the things he was good at and also what he was terrible at.

Diego comes back into the room just as Slayer and Chino approach the bar. "I cleared up Medical," Diego announces as he leans against the counter, smiling when Chip hands him a bottle of water. The guy is good at his job.

"We'll have to figure out a solution for that position soon," Slayer mumbles as she rubs her fist into her eye. She's exhausted, and I grin when I think about why.

"Let's have a game of pool before we all set off." I clap my hands and look at my brother, finding his eyes on me. "I pick my twin as a partner."

"You're not planning on shoving a pool cue in his eye, are you?" Slayer asks as she sits on a stool, her grateful gaze meeting Chip as he places a cup of coffee in front of her.

"Let's hope not," I muse. "You only recently became acquainted with his dick, I'd hate to cut your time short."

Slayer glares at me over her mug as Quinton begins to choke on fucking air. "How do you guys do it?" he asks when he finally drags in a breath. "How do you share without feeling possessive?"

"It just works," Diego replies while shrugging his shoulders.

"It's not something we can explain," I tell Chino. "You can either handle it or you can't." I'm not going to stand here and talk about my relationship with Slayer, it's none of anyone's business.

"You don't mind sharing her with your brother, who you hate?" Quinton sneers, his eyes flashing with jealousy.

"I know what I can handle." I smile wide as I flick my eyes between his. "But I can see what you can't."

"I'm right here." Slayer turns in her seat to face him. "If you have questions about my love life, direct them to me. Now kindly shut the fuck up about it."

"Noted," Chino grumbles right before I grab a hold of his vest and drag him to the pool table. He tries to put up a fight but soon realizes if I wanted to hurt him, he'd already be a mess on the floor. "What are you doing?"

"Playing pool. Diego will be your partner," I instruct as Diego's chuckle hits my ears.

"I hope you're good," Diego says as he grabs the triangle to gather the balls. "I'm out of practice."

Chino's eyes fall on my brother as he comes to stand at the side of the table, his brows knitted together as he gazes down at it. "I rarely witness Laith play, I would say we'll be fine."

I look questioningly at my brother as he continues to stare at the table, but he feels my gaze because he tips a shoulder up in response. "True enough. You two will probably cream us. Good thing I love a good creaming."

"Can you stop?" Diego moans as he positions the balls. Then his mouth tips upward as he leans his hands on the table, his eyes on mine. "Let's sweeten the deal. Winners get Genevieve between them for a night."

"He's gay." I point to my brother at the same moment Chino says, "I'm not sleeping with her."

"What the fuck," Laith snaps as Diego and Chino stare at him with confusion. "I'm not gay!" he stresses to them as they shrug their shoulders.

"I wouldn't judge you for it," Chino mumbles as my brother shoots daggers at me.

"Looks like we win either way," I inform Diego with a wink. We grab our cues as Slayer falls onto the couch beside us, her mouth quirking with a suppressed smile.

"Laith isn't gay," she says smugly. "And as for Chino, he'd love to have me again. Any way he could. Right, Quinton?"

"I'm not using you as a wager," Quinton growls as he crosses his arms over his chest, the cue gripped in his palm.

"No, just as a bargaining chip." Her counter has a whistle slipping past my lips as I line up the first shot, slamming the white ball into the others on a clean break.

A few of my March brothers gather around, watching us play as Davis sits on the couch with Slayer. He's grown into a true member since his father was killed, giving him room to breathe. This club means so much to him and I'm glad he accepted Slayer with open arms.

"It's creepy how identical you two are," Cory muses as he watches Laith and me.

"Watch out or I'll be putting your head on a spike like you did to Barrett and Bear," I retort, making him clutch his stomach and laugh.

"You should see their faces now. Eyeless and the skin like melting clay." He looks over his shoulder at Slayer, then back at me. "I like the way she thinks."

"Genni told you to put heads on a spike?" Laith asks as his brows come together.

"Don't forget," I warn him as I line up my shot. "Those men defiled her, over and over again." Crashing my cue into the ball, I watch as it sails into the solid and drives it into the pocket.

"My head should be there," Quinton mutters as he leans on his cue. I line up the next shot, and when I miss it, I motion for him to go next.

"If that's what she wanted, we would've done it. You need to let it go because as much as she still pokes you about it, she's long forgiven you." He leans over the table and lines up a shot with a striped ball.

"If you say so." His depressive attitude is getting to me and I'm close to shoving my cue up his ass to straighten him out.

"Stop acting like a bitch and man the fuck up," I snarl at his back as he straightens after missing the shot. "Start acting like a fucking MC brother and prove your loyalty to her." He turns to face me, his eyes flaring with violence. "There it is," I hum. "Don't make me kill you because your feelings are getting the better of you."

"Eight ball in the far right pocket," my brother calls out as I let a smile stretch over my mouth.

"Looks like he wiped the table with your balls," I snicker and step back. Chino rolls his eyes at the innuendo and looks over as Laith pockets the ball.

"Why don't you ever play?" he asks him, awe lining his words.

"Because I didn't want to make you little girls cry," Laith snaps back, his grin eerily identical to mine. The thought has my own grin dropping as I give him a once-over, my mouth pursing with irritation.

Does Slayer want him because he looks like me? Maybe I should show her just how adequate one of me is. I turn to do just that when Diego's hand lands on my shoulder.

"We all give her something different," he murmurs, as if reading my mind. "Don't cause a scene with both clubs here as an audience."

"Fine," I grit out as I continue to stare down our girl. Her eyes lift, as if sensing my gaze, and her brow raises in challenge. I snarl under my breath as Diego's chuckle only ignites the fire further. "She's taunting me."

"Punish her later. We have to get back to the compound and get into Barrett's office. We need more info on Tazo." He gives sound advice. This way I have time to figure out the perfect punishment. My eyes flick back to my twin's as he stands close to Chino, both of them murmuring about something. I'll include him too, he's deserving of a lifetime of punishment.

"I'm going to make a list." I shrug his hand off my shoulder and stride over to Slayer, reaching down to grab her shirt and hauling her to her feet. She smiles as her eyes become hooded, snickers floating around our heads. "Call me later," I demand before slamming my mouth to hers.

She moans and melts into me, unperturbed by the rough handling. She's so fucking perfect. When we part, she sucks in a breath and nods. "Okay."

Diego shoves me aside to kiss her gently, the differences between us so stark at this moment. I guess we do all give her something different. "Call us if you need anything," he tells her, placing another sweet kiss to her mouth.

"Let's go." I grab his collar and drag him backwards out of the club, raising my hand in farewell as I swing open the industrial door and release Diego. "Are we paying a visit to Jaeger first?"

"Nah, let Chino and your brother deal with that," Diego says as he grabs his helmet off his bike. "You and I are going to have a chat with Delia. Maybe a few of the clubs she deals with in Nevada will know a thing or two about Tazo. I'll call and find out where she is." He pulls his cell phone out of his cut's pocket as I snort.

"She'll be with Ajani." His eyes narrow on me as I pull my helmet on, giving him my best shit-eating grin. "I'll put twenty on the fact that they've been sharing a bed."

"What?" he exclaims as I start my bike, the roar drowning out any further questions.

GENEVIEVE
BMW Motorrad Milano

GENEVIEVE

Dragging my palms along my cheeks, I wipe away the tears as I take a deep breath, trying to clear the heaviness in my chest. Then I place the cell phone on the bed beside me and curse out loud. He made the video while he was at the cottage, and I'm sure it was the night we were there together. Jaeger must've found his phone in my father's cut pocket the night he killed him. Victor Varga had secrets, I always knew that, but I didn't realize to what extent.

How do I trust a man that held so much inside? Why would he hand me a legacy he knew I would fail at? He put so much faith in Jaeger to uphold his demands and take care of me, never once thinking it would all backfire. The betrayal still feels fresh, but I would be lying if I said I didn't understand why he did it. I never quite understood what it meant to hold the President title, but now I do and I wouldn't give it up without a fight either.

The overwhelming urge to drop by my childhood home has me sitting up in bed, my eyes moving to my house keys on the side table. Jaeger is probably there, but I don't care. I miss my room, my bike, and the place I shared with the family who once surrounded me with love.

I get dressed as the exhaustion recedes once more. I want to go home. Grabbing the keys from the table, I head out to the main room, finding Laith and Quinton with their heads tipped together in conversation. Without a means to travel, I'll have to convince one of them to bring me to my house, knowing they'll protest because they want me safe at the club and out of Jaeger's reach. My gaze swings from one to the other, weighing who would be the easiest to convince.

"Laith." At the sound of his name, he turns to look at me over his shoulder, a small smile working over his lips. "Could you give me a few minutes with Chino?" He looks at Quinton then, his brows falling slightly as the smile drops.

"Yeah, sure. I should get some sleep anyway." He stands from the stool and comes to stand in front of me, his hand lifting to cup my cheek. His touch is so gentle in comparison to Malik's and my reaction is the same as need tears through me. He leans in and kisses me, his tongue seeking entrance as I moan into his mouth. His other hand snakes around my waist as he hauls me in flush to his body, all his hard ridges molding with mine. I could kiss Laith forever and still, it wouldn't be long enough. "Good night," he whispers when he pulls away, his lips glistening.

"Good night." I press my fingers to my mouth as he walks away, watching his ass bunch in his jeans.

Quinton clears his throat, forcing me to turn back to look at him, finding envy in the depths of his hazel eyes. My heart hurts for the man who took my virginity, but it explodes for the girl who gave it to him as he stomped it under his foot. There are so many things we need to overcome if we're ever to be together, and right now it feels like a mountain we have to climb.

"Could you give me a lift?" I smile at him, trying desperately to hold in the pain of everything he's done. Regret lays heavy in his eyes, nestled beside the envy, but he has yet to really express it besides saying he's loyal to Jaeger.

"Where?" he asks as he gets up from his stool. I look around the room, finding members on the couch and at the pool table, and a few more sitting at the bar.

"Can we talk outside?" I lead him to the door as the memory of him kneeling in front of it with a shotgun to his head resurfaces. We may have a mountain to climb to reach our destination, but I'd rather climb for the rest of my life trying instead of living without him.

We step out into the brisk night air and I tip my head back to look up at the starry sky. There was a time when I wondered if my father was looking down on me, but now I want to scream to the heavens, asking what the hell he was up to.

"Where do you want to go?" Quinton asks again as he walks toward his bike. He's at the head of the line now that the spot beside him is empty.

"My house." He turns and gives me a puzzled look, his hands landing on his waist. "Please."

"Which one?" His head tips with the question, but his eyes narrow like he already knows the answer.

"I want my bike, and I want to sleep in my bed—" I begin as he shakes his head. "You owe me, Quinton."

"I owe it to you to not put you in danger again. Jaeger was calm today, too fucking calm, and I have always referred to that as his calm before the storm. There's no way I'm leaving you there with him." He looks determined, I'll give him that, but the longer I look at him, the more his shoulders relax. "Why?"

"I told you why," I say as I stride by him to his bike.

"Genni, he's volatile and dangerous. He won't be reasoned with," he warns as he comes to stand beside me. "I can't live with any more regrets."

Placing my hand on his chest, right over his pounding heart, I smile up at him, the touch reminding me of our warehouse training and puppy love. It makes my heart clench with nostalgia and I wish I could just transport us back to that time. "I promise never to blame you for whatever happens tonight. It's an order from your President, you must do as I ask."

He exhales a long breath as his heart races against my palm. "Fine, but you call me if anything happens. Not Charles or Montez. Not even Laith. You call me." It means he'll be close by. It's a compromise

I can work with.

"Okay." I nod as he grabs the helmet off his bike and hands it to me. Then he swings a long leg over the bike and sits on it to start it, waiting patiently for me to get on behind him. It's been ages since I've pressed my body to his back and wrapped my arms around his waist. I wonder if he's thinking that too as I finally sit behind him.

My hands rest against his hard stomach as I settle on the seat, the muscles beneath my palms flexing at my touch. The ride to the house is quick, almost too quick, and when he pulls into the driveway, I take another deep inhale of his scent, storing it inside my chest.

I pull the helmet off my head as I look up to the second floor, the curtain in my parents' bedroom moving. There's no way he doesn't hear us, I just wonder if he realizes it's me and not one of his former brothers. Getting off the bike, I hand Quinton his helmet as he puts it on his head. "I'll be at Glitz. It's not too far from here and I'll be right back if you call."

"I can take care of myself," I tell him as I cross my arms over my chest. "Are you going to look for Carrie?" My jealousy is a consequence he will have to deal with until I'm over what he did to me the night he took my virginity. The night he fucked Carrie right after me.

"No." He shakes his head with a ghost of a smile on his face. He knows he's struck a chord. "I have to pick up the money from Trevor."

"Oh." I drop my arms and give him a sheepish look. "Okay."

He shocks me by grabbing my shirt and pulling me to him, the smile growing on his lips. "Carrie doesn't matter to me, she hasn't for a long time." Then he surprises me further when he drags me down to kiss me softly. When he pulls back, his eyes are alight with questions and I do my best not to completely fold in front of him. We have barely begun to climb that mountain.

"I'll call you," I say instead, and he releases my shirt with a nod.

"Be careful," he warns and then begins to back out of the driveway. There's no need for the warning because it'll be Jaeger who has to be careful. I finger his switchblade I shoved into the pocket of my hoodie when I found it inside of his damaged cut. He purposely left it behind because it was a link to my father.

I pull out my keys as I walk by my bike. It's still sitting in the same spot I left it, the old oil stain beneath it a sore spot on the entire driveway. My fingers run along the handlebars as the last memory of me riding this bike hits me. It was coming home from the cottage with Dad and as soon as we turned onto our street, he knew something was wrong. *He knew.*

"The lights are out at our house." I point straight ahead and yell over the engine. "Not even the porch light is on."

Dad slows down and holds up his fist, a signal for me to stop, and when both of my feet hit the asphalt, an ominous feeling comes over me, leaving a bitter coldness in its wake.

"Dad?"

He still doesn't give me an answer as I slowly look up and down the street. It's too early for Claire to be in bed. The sun has just set and sitting there in the driveway is Jaeger's bike. He definitely wouldn't be asleep yet, unless they threw a rager at the clubhouse last night and he's still sleeping it off.

My heart beats against my rib cage as I close my eyes and will the memory to stop there. I've avoided this house for this very reason. I'm scared to relive it all and terrified that if I do, I won't come out of it whole. I survived it once, just barely, I don't think I can do it again.

With the metal of the keys biting into my clenched palm, I step up to the porch and drag a deep breath into my lungs. I hold it there for a count of ten and then slowly exhale it. It happens suddenly, without warning, as I slip the key into the lock, and I'm transported back to that night.

I force myself to move and scramble up the porch to find Dad staring at the front door. The red-painted, wooden exterior is cracked where the latch is, and the door is sitting slightly ajar.

"Dad—"

His hand snaps up, his finger hitting his mouth, warning me not to say another word, but I'm scared, and I'm afraid of what we're going to find when we open that door.

Dad motions for me to stand behind him as his hand grasps the doorknob, slowly pushing it open farther.

"Shit," he hisses.

I poke my head around his shoulder and look into the house, and at the end of the corridor, on his knees in front of the couch, is Jaeger. He's completely bound, twine wrapped around his legs and hands, and his own bandana stuffed into his mouth.

"Jaeger!" I scream as Dad rushes into the house, heading straight for his son.

"Fuck!" I hiss as I bang my forehead against the door. It's as if my mind has been suppressing the memories for too long, and now it can't hold back the force as my hastily prepared wall comes crashing down. I have to face them if I'm to grow the strength needed to lead, but the fear of drowning has me in a panic as my lungs fill with water before I make it to the shore.

Taking a deep breath, I turn the key and let the door swing open, my eyes scanning for any sign of Jaeger. For some reason, I thought he would be here, waiting for me, but the front foyer is dark, save for the glow emanating from the kitchen to the left. Straight ahead is the black leather couch and the red cushions sitting on either ends, still full as though the couch hasn't been sat on in months. Which could be true.

I take one step into the house and close my eyes, imagining Claire in the kitchen, cooking something amazing, the scent making my mouth water. I can imagine Dad and Jaeger out front, arguing over something as they work on their bikes, and I would be in the middle, torn about which one to join. Opening my eyes, I let the image fade because that's no longer reality. I won't lose myself to what-ifs here, not now when I have to stay vigilant. There's a monster lurking in these walls and I've come to vanquish it, and hopefully save Jaeger in the process.

He's my family after all.

I close the front door and take a few more steps toward the kitchen, my heart pounding somewhere up in my throat and my skin breaking out into a cold sweat. Once I step into that kitchen and face the worst of my memories, I can find Jaeger and conquer the beast within him.

On trembling legs, I take a few steps to round the doorway into the kitchen. The light over the stove glows, casting a yellow hue around the room and the counter surfaces that are free of any dishes. He hasn't been using the kitchen either, it still looks as though it was just cleaned yesterday. My eyes skip to the floor just beyond the island and I swallow back the whimper threatening to escape.

All I see is red fluid rolling from a large puddle in the kitchen, the island effectively blocking what I know must be Ma. I run in, screaming her name, my boots slipping on the blood pooling along the tile. I fall to my knees, and my phone flies out of my hand, slipping along the floor and sliding under the fridge, but none of that matters, because the beautiful woman who's raised me as if I was her own, who's loved me despite the fact that I didn't come from her, is lying face down in blood. So much blood.

"Oh no, no, no. Ma, please." My hands slip on the tile floor

as the blood oozes up between my fingers, and I sloppily crawl my way toward my mother. Just as I'm turning her around, I hear a shout from Jaeger down the hall.

"This is all your fault, you son of a bitch!" he screams at my father. "My mother was killed in the next room! I could hear her screaming!" he bellows, his words catching on his sobs.

"Don't be dead, don't be dead," I plead and beg, but as her stiff back hits the floor, I see the large slash across her throat and her eyes staring unfocused at the ceiling.

Falling forward, my hands land on the counter as I sob into the silence surrounding me. She didn't deserve what happened to her, just as I didn't, but the only difference was I was given a second chance. I can't waste it, and I'm here in her memory. I refuse to let her son waste his life too, she would want me to help him if I could. What he did to me was atrocious, but I can't bring myself to completely give up on him. His retaliation against me was unwarranted, but it was because of the rift my father caused.

Forgiveness for Jaeger is not even on my horizon, but the love I have for Claire trumps that. I am all that's left of our family and he will have no other choice but to face me. I will force him to hear everything I went through and then I will make him a proposition. I didn't lie when I told Quinton that I can't rescind the exile, but it didn't mean I don't have a plan.

"I got it from here, Ma," I whisper as I wipe the tears from my cheeks and take a fortifying breath. "Rest in peace."

I square my shoulders and walk out of the kitchen, knowing I have one more memory to endure before I head upstairs. The hardwood floor is completely cleaned, no remnants of blood remain, but it's as if it were happening again in front of my eyes.

Jaeger looks down at him as Dad clutches his chest, and I'm frozen to the spot, because all I can see is each of us losing our lives here tonight. But when Jaeger lifts his hand, the one holding my father's gun, and aims it down at my father's head, a scream gets lodged in my throat. My mouth gapes open, and my bloodied hands form fists, but still, no sound escapes. The only sound is my beating heart pounding through my ears as a chill skates down my spine.

"It's okay, Son." My dad looks up at him, his eyes soft and his face serene. "Do it." What is he asking him to do? Why is he giving up so easily?

My dad's voice is barely a whisper, but I'm so hyper-focused on him that I can hear every syllable. He looks as if he's on the brink of death.

"Take her," Jaeger says, his eyes flicking to look at me. "Get her out of my face."

Two men rush forward to grab me, one of them tossing me over a shoulder, and I fight with my fists pounding into his back. I scream, making my throat hoarse with garbled words and sobs. They go through the front door as I look up, just in time to see Jaeger fire a bullet into my father's head, his eyes on me the whole time.

My father told him to do it, he said it was okay for Jaeger to shoot him in the head. It all falls in line with what Jaeger has been saying about my father asking to kill him when the time comes. There's a clarity coating the memories now that I'm here in the place where it happened, and even though I can still feel the emotions of that night, it's a bit clearer now. Even though the pain wrapped in anger still lingers.

My hand wraps around the railing of the stairs as I take the first step, squinting my eyes as I peer up into the darkened second floor. He was in our parents' room. I saw the curtain move when I pulled up, but if he has the light still on, the door must be closed because it's pitch-black. I could call out his name but he wouldn't reply, and besides, we know exactly where the other is.

I get to the top and that's when I hear it, the heavy breathing, as if he's right next to me. "The prodigal daughter has come home." I turn toward the sound of his voice only to find his hand wrapping around my throat as he walks me back to the wall.

We've been here before. Exactly here, with his hand around my throat and his dark brown eyes looking into mine. Only this time they're missing the look of hatred I've become so familiar with.

JAEGER

CHAPTER SIX

She's here and everything about her is invading my senses. I had every intention of wrapping my hands around her throat and squeezing until her skin turned a pretty shade of blue, but the moment the pads of my fingers met her racing pulse, I was struck stupid.

Her breath fanning over my face is warm and sweet, and her skin feels like silk beneath my calloused hand. My mind blanks as I walk her back to the wall, leaning in to take a deep breath of her citrus scent. My nose skims along her cheek as she trembles, only this time I don't think it's from fear. I've been beating myself up about kissing her all those months ago but I think my sister enjoyed it as much as I did.

"Jaeger," she says, her throat working against the palm of my hand. "I need to speak to you."

I step into her body, pressing the obvious effect she's having on me into her lower stomach, my lips twitching when she gasps. "I thought you said everything you had to when you exiled me earlier." My words lack any ounce of anger, and my voice is deep and raspy, the direct result of my cock pulsing between us.

"Jaeger." My name is said through a moan as I pull back,

dragging my mouth along her cheek and brushing her lips as I do. There's nothing wrong with what I'm doing as we don't share blood, but we were raised as siblings for many years.

With that thought, I drop my hand and step back, turning to head toward my bedroom. "Grab whatever you came here to get, and get the fuck out."

"I came here to speak to you." She chases after me, and when her hand wraps around my bicep, I spin on her.

"Don't you think we've said enough to each other? You've gotten what you've set out to take from me from the very beginning. What more could there be?" My hand moves before I can give it much thought and I grab onto her hair, my fingers tightening around the dark strands. I drag her into me, searching her face for any sign of fear, but shock courses through me when I find her smug expression instead.

"I could break your arm in three different places with two very quick hits right now," she murmurs. "Not to mention how dangerous it is for you to have that already broken nose near my forehead." She's dripping with confidence and the longer I stare into her eyes, the more her threats become taunts.

"I could press you up against that wall again and spread your legs around my waist as I fuck your mouth with my tongue. How about that? You seemed to like it the first time we did it." I want a reaction, something to wipe that look off her face, but I'm once again outmaneuvered when she sucks in a breath and her cheeks are coated in a beautiful red hue.

"You do remember that night," she breathes out as she moves in just a little closer, her hands gripping my shirt at my waist. "I made up every excuse in my head and the one that seemed the most likely was you were too drunk to control yourself. Those names you called me, how you made me feel—" she spits out, but I cut her off with a laugh.

"And how did I make you feel, little sister?" I remember every gasp and moan I swallowed that night, and just the thought alone of my tongue in her mouth again makes mine water with anticipation. Her eyes slip to my mouth as my single thread of restraint begins to fray. Once that snaps, I don't care how many men claim her, I will be the only one to leave a lasting impression. A lifetime with them will never equate to one night with me.

"Let me go, Jaeger." She tugs on her hair and takes a step back, not yet completely out of my hold. "Our parents are rolling in their fucking graves." I don't care about Vic, I would pay big money to bring him back so he can watch me defile his daughter, but the mention of my mother has my hand dropping as I turn away from her.

My mother would hate for us to be like this. Not even touching on the sexual energy coursing between us, but she would hate what's happened to our relationship. What I did to ruin it. Mom didn't give a shit about club rules when it came to her family. We always came first even if she didn't for Vic and me. The club owns our souls and it always came first.

"Why are you here?" I ask as her steps fall in line behind me. I want her to leave so I can continue doing what I started earlier.

I pass our parents' room and head toward mine, but at the lack of her footfalls, I turn to find her standing in front of their bedroom door. "I could've killed you for what you did to me. There's no erasing what you put me through and there's no forgiveness for what I endured, but I'm beginning to understand the rift was caused by my father. I just can't figure out why." She turns her head to look at me as she opens their door, letting the wooden slab swing inward. "He couldn't truly believe you would take me as President lying down, but why did he risk your wrath against me? What was worse than having his two children hate each other?" She steps into the room and I follow behind her.

"Vic Varga had secrets," I grunt as I take in the destruction I've caused. His clothes are all over the room and his dresser drawers are turned over and pulled apart. "I'll figure them out if it's the last thing I do."

"Good." She turns to look at me, determination shining in her eyes. "That's what I was hoping for. I can't have you being a Steel Dragon and searching for answers. Do you understand?" Her eyes glimmer with unshed tears as I absorb what she's telling me.

"You exiled me so I would find out what kind of piece of shit your father was?" I ask, my head tipping to the side. In the end, she truly took everything from me and now I'm no longer a Dragon so I can do her bidding. Would it be wrong to say I feel a bit freer? Not that I would admit it to her because I won't hold back when it comes to Vic Varga any longer. It's his fault my mother is six feet under.

"*Our father*, Jaeger. Whether you like it or not, he was our dad, and yes, I need you to be the one to do it. We're the only two left with the Varga name and there's weight behind it. Find people who will talk and do it quickly." She turns back around and walks to his dresser to touch the picture of her and Vic when she was a kid. "I have two MCs to run and a psychopath to track down, it can't be me."

"You exiled me from the one thing that mattered in my life to become your gopher?" I scoff as my back hits the bedroom wall and my arms cross over my chest.

"I didn't die in that basement, Jaeger," she whispers as her hand falls back to her side and she clenches it into a fist. "But a part of me died after that, and I will never get her back." She turns her head to look at me and instead of hatred shining there, I find fear. "I don't recognize who I am anymore. I'm not the little sister who annoyed you because she wanted to hang out with you and your friends. I'm not the daughter who followed her father without question because she needed him to be proud. You destroyed her when you gave me up to the man who would kill her." She beats a fist to her chest as she sucks in a breath. "He killed that girl and now I've become someone I don't recognize. I became my own protector and I will do anything to keep what little of that girl is left safe."

"Fine." I swallow down the things I should say, the apologies that would sound apathetic on my tongue. The damage is done, and even if an apology is warranted, she deserves action instead. "I'll see what I can find."

"It has to be done on your own. You can't speak to a single Dragon," she presses, her chin lifting a little. She may think that girl inside of her is dead, but she's still there. She's just lying dormant and waiting for something to wake her up. *Or someone.*

"I got it," I snap and point to the door. "Now get out."

I can't let her weaken me, not now. Genni Varga has always been my weakest link, the one thing I could lose everything I worked so hard for, and I refuse to bend for her now. I agreed to her little exile reasoning and if she even attempts for more right now, I will finish what Barrett fucking started.

"I'm sleeping here tonight," she announces as she leaves the room and crosses the hall to hers. She pulls a cell phone out of her pocket and swipes her finger across the screen.

"Like hell you are!" I bellow. Having her here, this close for an extended period of time will be an agony I can't live with.

"Quinton?" she says into the phone, and my stomach flips with potent jealousy. She's calling him of all people? "I'm staying here tonight." She steps into her room and attempts to close the door, but my boot prevents it as she turns to glare at me. "No, he's here. He'll just have to deal with it." She kicks her boot out and slams the heel into my shin, making me stumble back with a curse as she shuts her bedroom door.

Instead of kicking her door in, again, I head downstairs to the living room and the small bar in the corner. I'm thirsty and need a drink, but it'll have to be whiskey because walking into that kitchen takes too much energy. I can't wipe my mind of the images from that night, and when I'm teetering on the edge of control like this, it's better to avoid them altogether.

An hour later and half a bottle of whiskey, I pull my phone out of my pocket and dial a person who can help. It'll be a shot in the dark, but I'm sure I can convince them to do it for her. The phone rings three times before their voice fills my ears with a groggy hello. I head up the stairs as I chuckle then say, "I need your help." Their sleepy cackle brings a grin to my own mouth as I open my sister's bedroom door, noting she didn't lock it. "It's for her," I tell them as I gaze in on her sleeping in her bed, her hands tucked under her chin. She's always slept this way. They mutter threats of bodily harm and then finally ask if she's okay. "She's here, sleeping in her own bed. She's fine, but I don't know for how long. So will you help me?" A long exhale coats my ear and I know I have them. "Meet me at the club, you know which one. Tomorrow night, 11:30." I hang up the phone without confirmation because they'll be there. They care too much about Genni not to show up.

I should walk right back out of her room because I am in no state to breathe in her scent, but I don't. Instead, I walk to the side of the bed she's sleeping on, my fingers running along the blanket she has pulled up under her chin. I fall to my knees in front of her, realizing the irony of doing so when I swore to her face I never would, and then I press my forehead to her pillow. I blamed her for so long, hated her with every fiber of my being, and still, my heart betrayed me. There's no way hatred can be born from nothing, love has to be there first.

"I'm sorry," I whisper as the armor of hatred begins to loosen around my heart. "You deserve to hear it but I refuse to say it to you until I've fixed what I've broken. I just hope you understand I can't protect you from your father anymore. We will learn everything together and I can only hope it doesn't crush you once and for all." I lift my head as her soft snores coast over my face and then lean in to press a soft kiss to her cheek. When she's still and serene like this, I can't help but give in to my heart's wishes.

The room spins as I rise back to my feet, my heart pounding harder than ever before. I will prove to her I'm worthy, that I've made mistakes but I'm not lost. Whatever it takes.

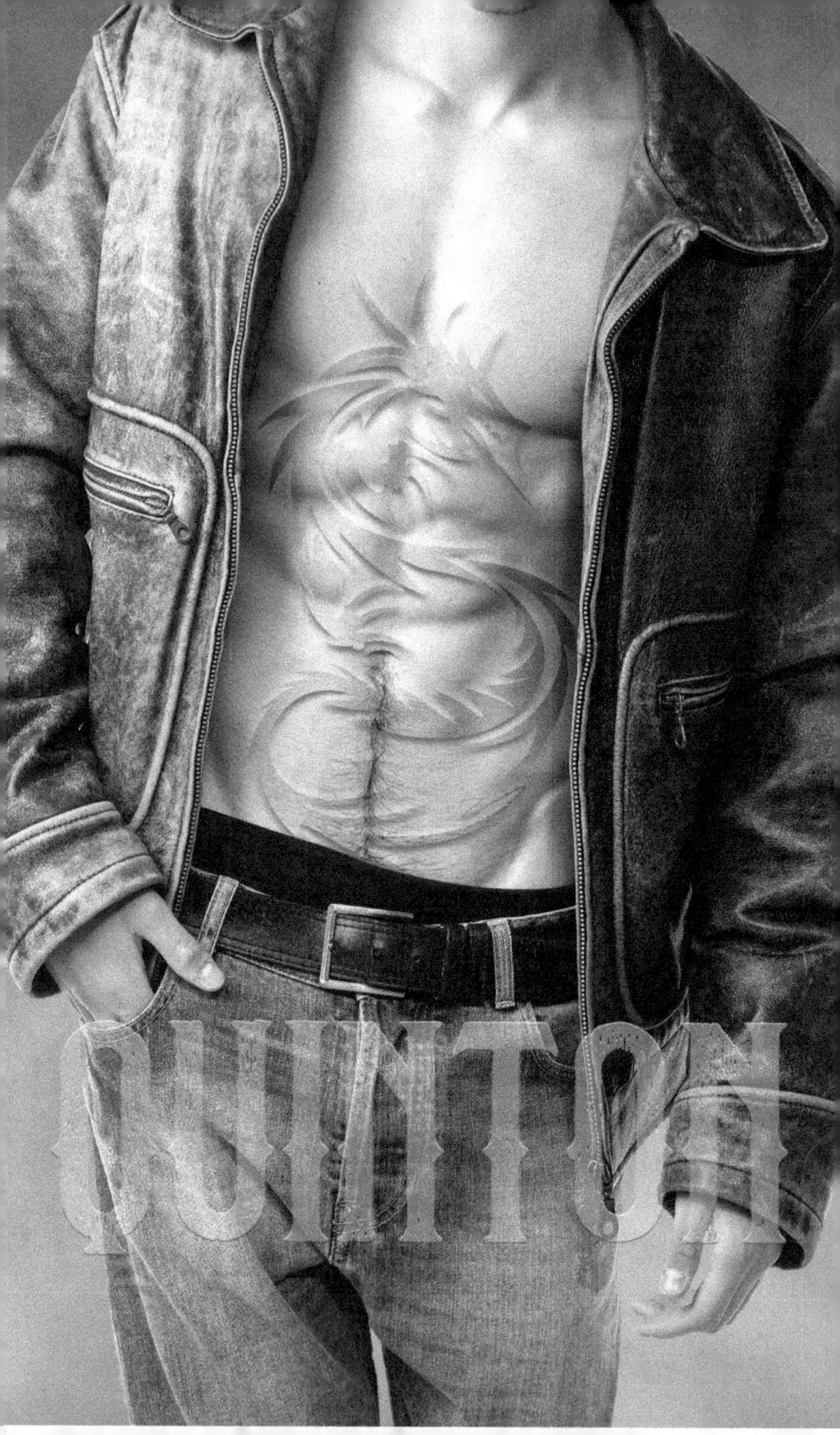

VUITTON

QUINTON

After receiving Genni's call last night, I didn't make it to Glitz because I turned around and went back to her house. I sat outside for a few hours, and when I was sure nothing was happening inside, I went back to the clubhouse to get some sleep. The ride to the reservation was going to be tiring enough, but then I had to add the trip I missed to Glitz afterward, which is going to make the day exhausting.

Once I'm out of the shower and dressed, it's about nine in the morning. I swipe open my cell phone and decide to text Genni before I leave. I fire off the message and brush out my hair when the phone pings with a reply. The quick staccato of my heart doesn't make me put down the brush, no, I hold it altogether, forcing myself to finish my hair before I pick up the phone to check her message. There needs to be restraint because I refuse to hope.

Genni: Everything is okay. I will be back at the clubhouse in a bit.

Me: I'm heading to the reservation. I'll see you later.

Genni: Thank you, Quinton.

I'm doing this for her, of course, but I'm also doing it for myself. There are things my mother knows, secrets she's kept for many years because she feared repercussions on the family or myself. Those secrets were big enough that when my father died, she begged me to leave the club, even offered to leave the reservation so we could escape the state. When I made it clear I was staying, she shut herself up tight, and I haven't been able to get her to speak about the things she knows. Today I'm changing that.

Tazo's family still lives on the reservation, and sometimes when I go by, I visit my aunt and two cousins. They never speak about the father who has abandoned them, but my aunt is a different story. She's been bitter for the last decade and has spoken out a few times about the abuse they endured. I think with her help, I can get my mother to talk.

I head out to the bar to find Laith sitting there, speaking to Chip in hushed tones. There has been a change in the atmosphere around the club since Hell's March has been here and gone. It's not a bad change. If anything, it feels something akin to hope. We were an aging club on the edge of disaster. We've lost two Presidents in a matter of months and now the head of the club is a woman. They're all drastic changes, but when I look around at the brothers, it looks like they're accepting it in stride.

There have been undercurrents of mutiny in the past few years, especially when Vic turned down a darker road for making club income. He was President though, so no one really spoke up. We just followed him blindly as we were slowly murdered and aging. Now looking back on everything, he didn't really have a plan to upkeep the club and it was all about bringing in more and more money. No matter how nefarious the means.

It's funny how you worship a person and choose to be blind to their faults. You're loyal and willing to kill in their name while they do despicable things. Vic was a stand-in father for me when mine died, I will never deny that. He treated me like a son and took care of me, but I can't tell if that was from the goodness of his own heart or his way of buying unwavering loyalty.

Then I think of Jaeger and how much he went through to one day become Prez, only to have his father pull the rug out from beneath him. I wanted to articulate to Genni why I stayed loyal to her brother, but the words never really came out right. They didn't do justice for what

I was, and *am*, truly feeling. Jaeger is my brother, regardless of blood, and I've seen what he has been through, both past and present. Vic didn't make his life easy, and there were many times he was put in situations that could have killed him, just so he could prove he was capable. I remember the plans he had to turn this club around and I was rooting for him to get to the position to be able to do it. He was so close and then Vic gave him one final impossible task. A task Jaeger failed.

A task I failed as well.

"Chino, come have a coffee," Chip calls out, pulling me out of my thoughts to find myself standing in the center of the room. I shake off the lingering feelings of guilt and head to the bar as Laith turns to watch me approach.

I take a seat beside Laith as Chip places a steaming cup of coffee in front of me. I nearly groan as I take the first sip, knowing I need the elixir to stay awake today. "What's the plan?" Laith asks as Chip heads down the bar to refill coffee mugs.

"I'm heading over to the reservation to talk to my mother and aunt. Just to let you know, Genni stayed at her house last night."

"What?" Laith nearly drops his coffee mug as he stares at me in shock. "Her house? As in the Varga house?"

"With Jaeger," I confirm and take another sip of my coffee.

Laith wastes no time pulling his phone from the pocket of his cut as I open my mouth to say it's fine. We're both stopped in our tracks though when a bike engine sounds outside, the rumble too high-pitched to be a Harley. We both scramble off our stools as a few other brothers beat us to the door, hauling it open and letting the bright morning sun in. They all crowd around the door as Laith and I shoulder our way outside just in time to find Genni parking her yellow Honda Superbird in her father's old parking spot. If there was a grand statement to be made, this would be it.

She pulls off her helmet and shakes out her hair, hauling a groan from the depths of my chest. Genevieve Varga is a vision in the Arizona sun as she swings her leg off the bike and stands to look over at us. She places the helmet on her seat and then shades her eyes with her hand as her hair blows in the breeze.

"Jesus," Laith mutters as I nod.

"Yeah." I reach down and adjust myself in my pants because there's no way the effect she has on me isn't obvious.

She comes toward us with her mouth in a firm line and her hair in waves around her shoulders. She looks rested, better than she has the entire time she's been here, but the ghosts of her past linger in her dark blue irises.

"Hey," she husks out as the brothers move away from the door and Laith steps in front of me toward her.

"Hey," I reply as Laith reaches out and touches her arm.

"Everything okay?" he asks, and I mentally thank him for being able to speak.

"Yeah, I think so." She shrugs and brushes her hair behind her shoulders. "I spoke to Jaeger last night, as much as I could before we were threatening each other, and I think I'm finally getting a plan together. What are you two up to today?" She looks between us as I turn to look at Laith.

"We're supposed to be doing a cartel run in a few days, I thought I would set up a meeting with them and see what I can find out about Tazo," Laith supplies as he gives Genni a once-over. "They've dealt with him in the past so I'm hoping they have something worth knowing."

"That's good." Genni nods as she looks at me. "When are you leaving for the reservation?"

"Now," I tell her as I scrub a hand down my face. "It's a long ride and I want to be back before dark."

"Be safe," she murmurs as we all awkwardly stand in a circle. I want to reach out and haul her into me, to breathe in her scent and feel her heat against me, but I don't know how or if I even should.

"I'll be inside," Laith says as he grips my shoulder, giving me a squeeze. "Be careful and call me if you need anything."

"Thanks, brother." I watch as he heads inside, waiting for Genni to join him, but when she doesn't make a move to leave, I turn and find her staring at me.

"You were right about Jaeger," she confesses as she looks to the side, her brows furrowed in thought. "He reacted as any Vice would when faced with his club being taken from him." She turns her head to look at me again as she bites her bottom lip. "I had just hoped he would react as my brother."

The need to touch her outweighs anything else, so I reach for her and pull her into my arms. She wraps hers around my waist as I dip my nose into her hair, breathing in the scent I've long committed to memory. "Why would he react as your brother when he doesn't see himself that way?" My words are muffled by her hair, but I know she can hear them. "I've seen the way he looks at you. I don't remember when he changed from big brother to… something else, but it happened."

"No." She shakes her head and tries to pull back, but I tighten my hold on her. Running from her feelings will only create problems, I should know. "It's wrong, Quinton."

My hand winds into her hair as I force her head back, making her face me. Her eyes are filled with confusion and that tells me no matter how wrong she thinks it is, she's feeling whatever it is brewing between them. "It's no one's business," I whisper as my gaze sweeps over her face and lands on her lips. They part under the scrutiny and her tongue swipes out to leave a trail of glistening moisture. How do I ignore that? How do I release her when she's prepared her mouth to be ravished by mine?

Backing her up until her ass meets the table, I step between her legs. The confusion in her eyes slowly fades as they begin to heat. No matter the damage I've caused to her heart, it still remembers me. I was her first, and yes, I fucked it up royally, but that doesn't change what we once were. I can get it back, I know I can. I just have to remind her of the moments we were falling in love and make a promise with each caress to never hurt her again.

Respect has to be earned, especially when I've proven I am unworthy of hers. Instead of devouring her mouth here where anyone could watch, I press my lips to her forehead and breathe her in. I don't want the brothers thinking her leadership stems from that sweet spot between her legs.

"I need to get going," I tell her and step back. She's leaning there with her eyes closed and her hands bracing herself on the table. When she opens them, I find a glimpse of the woman I trained so long ago. Vulnerable, scared, and confused. My heart cracks for the woman she used to be, but this gives me hope that she's still in there. "We'll figure all of this out. We'll be okay." It's a reassurance I can't completely stand behind yet, but it's a promise I'll make, even if it takes me to the grave.

"I have a feeling the man I grew up worshiping is not who I thought he was," she murmurs as she shakes her head.

"He was to you. He was a good father and he loved you. Just remember him that way. Anything else we find out bears no weight on the man who raised you to be who you are today," I reassure her as I tuck a tendril of her hair behind her ear.

"That's the thing, Quinton. The person I am today is because of him, and that's not something I want to remember. The things that happened to me to bring me to this point is something no father should ever put on his daughter." She stands from the picnic table and looks at me with a sad smile. "I'll survive it though."

"You will." I nod and take another few steps back. "I'll call you before I leave the reservation." Spinning around, I head toward my bike when she calls my name.

"Quinton!" I turn and raise my hand to my brow, shielding my eyes from the sun. "Call me when you get there too."

"Sure thing, Prez."

MALIK

"How was the trip?" I ask Cruz as he leans back in the chair, spreading his long-ass legs under the table.

"Drop was made and we got paid." He shrugs and then folds his hands over his abdomen. "Dientes Afilados gave us a larger cut for finding the contact." His eyes skip to Davis then quickly back to me, looking suspiciously like he's hiding something.

"What am I missing?" I look between them, my brow raising.

Davis' face lights up with a shit-eating grin as he turns to Cruz, his freakishly light blue eyes twinkling. "You can tell him, Cruz. Barrett is dead and Malik is on our side."

Cruz swallows as his brows crease, his demeanor telling me he's not quite trusting Davis' statement. "I'm still Vice here and in our President's absence, I'm acting President. So fucking out with it." I watch him closely for a reaction, knowing he's heard of who our new President is and how she acquired the position.

"Tell me a little about the new Prez first," he counters as he straightens in his seat. "I'm not saying shit if we have another psychopath who shoots first and asks questions later."

I understand why he's feeling that way, especially if he heard about what happened with Barrett and Bear and seeing their heads on spikes out front. "She was held hostage here and used by Barrett. Do you understand what I mean?" When he nods his head, I continue, "She was kept in the basement and left for dead when he had his fill. Diego saved her, got her out of there, and when she had the chance to come back and kill the man who harmed her, she took it. Bear pulled his gun too and she protected herself." I lean on the table and tap my hand on the wood. "She's fair and she's trained to act quickly. I won't sit here and tell you she's not dangerous, but she wants what's best for this club and she wants to turn it around. No more running drugs and guns."

Cruz's eyebrows raise in surprise as he looks at Davis, a small smile moving along his plush lips. "A woman President." He shakes his head with a chuckle. "This should be interesting."

"Don't underestimate her," I growl as my hand curls into a fist. "It'll be a sure way to have your head stuck on a spike too."

"I wouldn't underestimate any woman. I work with one who makes it her full-time job to assassinate assholes. I know just what women can be capable of." He glances one more time at Davis, prompting me to snarl before he exhales with a nod. "Davis and I have been running other jobs with Dientes Afilados on the side." When I open my mouth to ask where the revenue is, he holds up his hand to stop me. "Not for cash. They actually run a covert operation to save women and children from being sex trafficked. We've been helping out when we can."

"Knowing what our new Prez has been through at the hands of my father, maybe she would be down to make that an official club operation." Davis is practically vibrating in his seat and I can understand why. This is obviously something they are proud of and his assumption is most likely correct. Slayer's heart is too big to say no to such a thing.

"I will bring it to her. In the meantime, you can continue to help out but I need some ideas for legit revenue. We're dropping the cartel since they obviously rather work with the Dragons, and that's fine, we don't want them to know about our affiliation yet, and weapons distribution is dwindling down anyway."

"Rockz wants to open another tattoo shop and I've been busy as fuck at the shop. People have been going crazy for custom Choppers. I'll be hiring a few more guys," Davis supplies as I nod my head.

"I can link up with Dientes and get us into the mercenary

business," Cruz offers as I snap my fingers and grin at him. "We already know how to shoot, we might as well get paid for it."

"Those are fucking awesome ideas. Let's get some of the groundwork going." Barrett hated working with Dientes Afilados but he couldn't deny it was good money. "We can solidify that relationship now that Barrett is out of the picture."

"They had another bust-up with the Highway Knights a few weeks ago and asked if we would help them out a bit. I told Loqi I would run it by the Prez in the next Hell meeting. It would be a paid gig to show up with guns." The name rings a bell and I search my memory for why. When I come up blank, I shrug my shoulders. "Let me look into these Highway Knights and I will get back to you." They both stand as I lean back in my seat. "No more secrets, got it?" They both nod as they head out the door.

I reach into my cut pocket and pull out the ring of keys I found in Barrett's pocket before we burned his body. His office has remained untouched, but that changes today. Next, I grab my phone and call Diego. He made a stop into Medical to check if Ajani kept it clean and up to his standards, but I know he'll want to tear apart Barrett's office with me.

"Hey." I'm greeted by his rumbling voice, the tenor deep and sexy.

"You sound hot on the phone," I reveal as his chuckle hits my ear, the sound traveling to my cock.

"I'm hot regardless." I adjust myself in my pants, mentally making a note to get Slayer between us soon.

"That's true," I agree as I clear my throat, hauling another chuckle from him. "I'm about to head into Barrett's office. Wanna come bend me over his desk?" It's out of my mouth before I can stop it and Diego's answering laugh has my own mouth quirking upward.

"I'll come with you," he rasps, the innuendo hardening my cock further. "But I won't be sticking my dick in you in there. Who knows what bacteria is lurking on the surfaces?"

"So… you'll stick your dick in me somewhere else?" I fist myself through my pants as he *tsks* into the phone.

"If you figure out this whole Tazo thing, I'll bend you over for our girl to watch as a reward." My cock jumps against my palm at the deep suggestion in his voice, the rasp transforming into heated desire.

"That's the best incentive I've had yet," I tell him and hang up the phone. Just the thought of Slayer watching as I take Diego's cock inch by inch has me momentarily shocked in my seat. The three of us are combustible, but this would be a next-level explosion.

I leave the meeting room and walk down the narrow corridor to Barrett's office. I've never been in there and I will admit, I'm curious to find out what the fucker had been hiding. By the third key, I unlock the door and step inside, turning on the amber-yellow fluorescent light overhead.

The light illuminates a messy desk, clothes all over the floor as though he slept here on his small couch, and two safes in the corner. My eyes fall on the safes as I lean forward, my hands meeting the desk with a groan. How the fuck are we going to get into those?

Heat hits my back as a hand grips my waist. Diego would already be dead if I didn't know his scent so well. "I see what you had in mind," he growls as his groin brushes against my ass. "This is appealing."

"I like your idea of it being in front of Slayer." I turn to look at him as he takes a step back, his eyes hooded and his bottom lip nipped between his teeth.

"Yeah," he husks then clears his throat.

"Have you always been interested in men?" I ask, my curiosity getting the better of me.

"Honestly? No." He shakes his head and rounds the desk, kicking aside a pair of boots. "You?"

"I never really had the option." I shrug as Diego begins opening drawers. "See if you can find combos for those safes. Barrett was a fucking idiot. He must have them around here somewhere."

"On it."

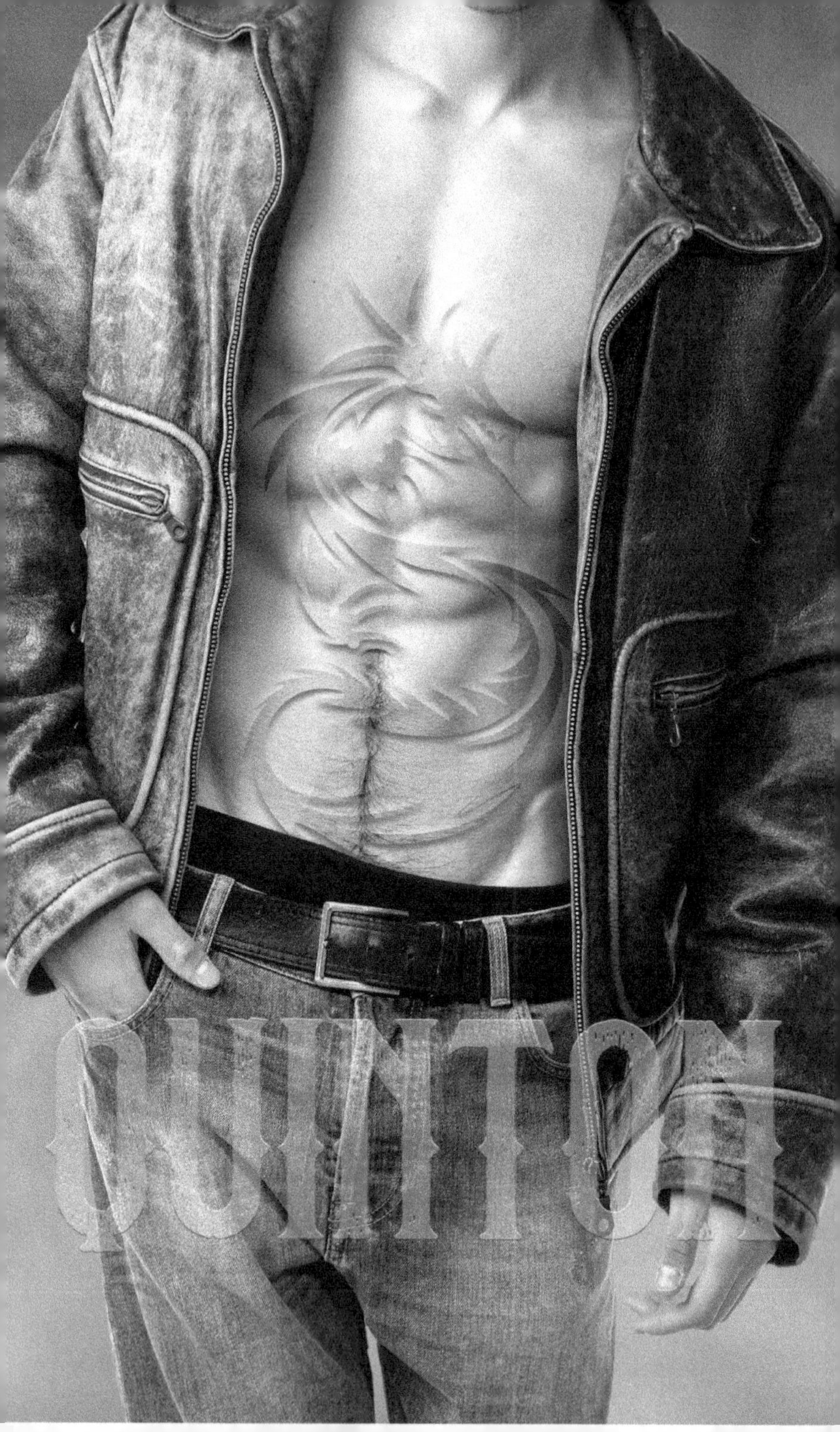
VUITTON

CHAPTER SEVEN

"Are you hungry, son?" Mom asks as she sits across from me at the table.

"No, this is great." I hold up the apple I swiped from the bowl on the counter. Being in my childhood home brings back a lot of memories of my dad and the many things he taught me. It was him who taught me how to hunt and be a sharpshooter from a young age and as I look around the home, all of those memories hit me full blast. It's why I avoid being here.

"Is everything okay at the club?" She rests her hands on the table, her knuckles prominent with how hard she works. She makes all the traditional clothing and shoes for the reservation.

Mom doesn't know much that goes on with the club now that Dad is dead. He was her link to the inner workings. Once he died, I stopped telling her too much for fear it would stress her out. "Vic died," I tell her as her eyes widen.

"How?" she whispers and leans forward.

"He had brain cancer." I decide to forego the details, not wanting her to think differently about Jaeger, especially when Vic planned his own death and the way it happened.

"Is my nephew here?" My Aunt Aiyana, Tazo's ex-wife, comes into the room, her face alight with happiness. "How long has it been since you came to visit me? I was beginning to fear those metal birds were keeping you away."

I put my apple on the table and stand to give her a hug as I laugh. "Steel Dragons, Aunt Aiyana." She pulls away from me and pats my shoulder before rolling her eyes.

"They wish they were Dragons." She takes a seat beside my mother and looks from her to me. "Why was I summoned? Is something wrong?"

I stare at the half-eaten apple in front of me and take a deep breath. "Tazo has returned."

"And Vic is dead," my mother adds on as my aunt gasps into her hand. "Yes, I know. This is what we saw in the fire so long ago." My mother reaches for my aunt's hand and I watch as they clasp their fingers tightly together, their knuckles whitening.

"What do you mean?" I ask and lean forward. "I came here to learn more about Tazo, hoping you could give me an idea of where he is."

"He is not allowed back here," Aunt Aiyana spits out, her eyes flashing with anger. "He killed his own brother for those Dragons and he was exiled from this reservation the same day. I am ashamed to have married him, especially when I found out about him and Awendela."

"Aiyana!" Mother hisses in warning. "We shouldn't speak of that." She looks around the room as if there are spirits lurking in the dark corners watching us.

"No, Catori." Aunt Aiyana pats their joined hands and then looks at me. "He should know."

"Know what?" I demand, my heart beating a mile a minute. I knew there were family secrets concerning my father and his brother,

Tazo. There was no mistaking the rivalry and competition between them, but the way they are looking right now, it's safe to assume this goes beyond bad blood. "Mom!" I exclaim when neither of them says a word, and she finally gives my aunt a nod.

"There was a reason we wanted you away from the Steel Dragons and we were ashamed when your father stayed, even after knowing what Victor Varga did to our family." She spits out Vic's name like it's poison and her face morphs into a grimace.

"What did Vic do?" I look between them, my mouth suddenly dry. I don't know how much more I can hear about Vic, the man I saw as a father figure. Why does it feel like I've been living under a fucking rock?

"Start from the beginning," Mother suggests as she stands from the table, releasing Aunt Aiyana's hand. "I will get you some tea."

"My younger sister, Awendela, was a free spirit. She didn't like to live by the rules and she broke them every chance she could. She didn't want to live on the reservation, and for as long as I can remember, she was always threatening to leave. When I married Tazo, she was eleven years old, and our parents were already dead. It was up to me to raise her and guide her into adulthood with the right beliefs. I can admit I failed." She drops her chin to her chest as she shakes her head.

I reach across the table and take her hand, hoping to ease some of her guilt. "It's okay, Aunt Aiyana."

"I was supposed to protect her from the males, prepare her for a perfect union, but your uncle had other plans." Again, that anger flashes in her eyes as she looks back up at me. "When Awendela turned eighteen, I began to bring the men over who would make the best match. They were hunters, worked for the Chief and Council, and would make proud husbands, but Awendela was stubborn. She didn't want to be married and she didn't want to live on the reservation. She caused me so many problems and I tried to have patience. Then one day, I woke up and she was gone. Her room was empty of all her things and it was as if she disappeared into thin air." Her eyes begin to water as I squeeze her hand

and she gives me a small smile in response as Mom comes back with a steaming cup of tea.

"Here, Aiyana. Drink this to help calm you." She places the cup in front of my aunt as I release her hand, my eyes finding my mother's face. She's looking back at me, her eyes relaying a message of sadness. It's clear something tragic happened to Aunt Aiyana's little sister.

"Sorry, Quinton," Aunt Aiyana whispers as she lifts the cup, blowing her breath along the surface of the hot liquid. "It's been so long since I've spoken of her." She takes a hesitant sip before placing the cup back on the table. "I learned that day that Awendela left the reservation with my husband to start a new life."

"She and Tazo were… together?" I admonish as I fall back in my chair.

"No." Aunt Aiyana shakes her head. "Awendela had no interest in my husband, she was at least loyal to me when it came to that. She used him to get out and when he found her a place to stay, she made it clear he was not what she wanted. I truly believe he would've left me and our two sons for her. I didn't see it then, but the signs were there. Tazo was obsessed with my little sister."

My stomach begins to churn when I think about an older Tazo preying on a young girl. "Did Dad know about this?" I look at Mom and she shakes her head.

"I don't know how much your father knew. I can say he and Tazo weren't close in the true sense of brothers. Tazo had a jealousy toward your father and it clouded his judgment. Dasan always tried to repair the rift between them, but Tazo never had any intention of repairing his relationship with his brother." My mother turns to look at my aunt, her hand moving to rub her shoulder. They've remained close over the years even though they share no blood. They're family and no matter the fact that their husbands are no longer in the picture, they still see each other as such. "Dasan did find out about Awendela when she began to show up at club meetings on the arm of a Hell's March President."

"What?" I exclaim as I straighten in my seat. "You can't be serious."

"Yes. My sister had a restless soul and she was always searching for thrills. According to your father, she was on the arm of a Steel Dragon President a few years later too. Victor Varga."

Awendela, my aunt's younger sister, was none other than Wendy Varga, Genevieve's mother. I tried to squeeze more information out of them, but they had nothing else. My aunt Aiyana said she never saw her sister again, and when they heard she died of cancer, she begged my father to bring her body home, but Vic wouldn't allow it. Instead, she was buried in a cemetery without her family present, and my mother and aunt could never forgive him for that.

I don't know anything else about how she went from Barrett to Vic, but that's where their dispute began. It's an age-old problem, men fighting over a woman, wars breaking out in the name of a sordid love triangle, and history almost repeated itself with Genni. Only somehow, she figured out how to share her affections.

I pull into the Glitz parking lot, hoping to make this pickup a quick one so I can get back and tell Genni everything I've learned. I get a pang in my chest when I realize I want to tell Jaeger as well, but it's club business and he's no longer a Dragon.

There's no doubt Tazo's ire only deepened when she chose Vic Varga of all people. We need to fill in the missing pieces of the story and then I'm sure we can figure out how to bring Tazo down.

I walk into Glitz and stop when I find Angel dancing on the stage. It's been a while since they've been at the clubhouse and last I knew, they were at the March clubhouse. Angel sways her hips along to a deep bass song as I bypass the stage and head down the corridor on its right toward Trevor's office. The sounds of the girls inside their dressing room fills the space as I head for the open door at the end of the hall.

"Quinton?" The sound of Carrie's voice has me stopping ten feet from Trevor's door as I turn to find her in a black silk robe, her arms crossed over her chest as she leans against the dressing room doorframe. "Long time."

"Where have you been?" I ask as I give her a quick once-over. There was a time when the sight of Carrie would have me straining in my pants and ready to go, but that's gone now. In its place is regret for how I've treated her over the years. She was just a warm body for me, someone I would use each night and forget about when the sun rose. It's shameful and disgusting.

"I went to Hell's March like you asked, but Genni was there and did you know she's now their President?" Her eyes are wide as she looks around, her spine straight with apprehension.

"Where did you go after that?" She left the March's compound with Cash, and I can only imagine they went wherever Tazo is. Suddenly it dawns on me, I have to tread carefully with Carrie if I'm to get the information I need and she could have what we're all looking for. Tazo's location. "I was worried about you," I tack on and swallow down the guilt of lying.

"Laith's crazy twin brother took both mine and Angel's cell phones while we were there and I have been too afraid to come by your clubhouse. I heard the March have been there." Her eyes soften as her teeth sink into her bottom lip. "Angel and I have been staying at a motel not too far from here, staying low-key. Cash was supposed to come back for us days ago and he never did."

"Are those the only places you went? Hell's March compound and a motel?" She begins to rub her hands up and down her arms as she looks down the corridor again and shakes her head. "No."

I'm standing in front of her in three strides, her back hitting the doorframe as she presses herself away from me. Fear flashes in her eyes briefly before she begins to relax. She's hiding something. "Are you safe?" I brush her hair back from her face and notice fingerprint-sized bruising along her neck and collarbone.

"Yes," she says as she gently pushes my hand away. "I need to talk to you. I did what you asked, I learned a few things about Hell's March. I can't tell you here. Would I be able to come by the club later when I'm off? I'll feel safer if you're there." I have to remember that she doesn't know about Genni being our President too, and if she does indeed know where Tazo is, I would rather get it out of her at the club since this one is filled with people I don't entirely trust.

"Of course." I nod. "Do you need me to come pick you up later?" She turns to look down the corridor as Angel appears, her face looking pale and thin and her body decorated with foundation-colored bruises.

"Angel and I will grab a cab later," she whispers and backs into the dressing room. "We'll be there around four."

I wanted to sleep tonight after the long ride, but I won't lose this opportunity. "I'll wait up for you." She heads inside as Angel brushes by me, her naked body glittering under the lights overhead. She doesn't say anything, but I don't even know if she noticed me standing here.

After I grab the money bag from Trevor and tuck it into the back of my pants, I head back out to the main floor. The music assaults my eardrums as I walk by the stage without even looking up at the naked female I know I'll find there. Maybe it's the guilt I've lived with for the past few months, but I can feel myself changing. Things I thought were priorities before are nothing more than an afterthought now.

I scan the room and stop short when I find Jaeger sitting at a booth, his hand wrapped around a glass filled with amber liquid. I'm off to the side of the room so he doesn't see me, but I head toward him anyway. We're not supposed to be talking but I can't help it. He's my brother.

Just as I'm nearing his table, someone familiar strides through the club, her heels reverberating over the music with the force of her steps. Her leather pants and jacket are paired with a white crop top and large gold hoop earrings, her hair straightened and hanging down her back. There's no question that she's headed for Jaeger's table, so I duck around a column and watch her approach. Her face is a mask of irritation as she slips into the booth, her jaw ticking as she looks at him with a raised eyebrow.

Why is Jaeger meeting up with Delia Montez?

romántic
THIS BODY IS
TEMPORARY
BUT THIS SOUL IS
ETERNAL
永遠
JAEGER

JAEGER

"Why the fuck am I here and not putting a bullet in your skull?" Delia growls over the heavy bass as I continue to feign interest for the stripper on stage.

"I've been exiled so I can complete a mission," I finally begin once she's seated. "I need to find out everything I can about Tazo and his connections." I turn to look at her and grin. "So I thought I would start with the one person who has many connections. The Viper."

"I don't know what you're talk—"

"Cut the shit, Montez," I snap as I take a drink of my whiskey on the rocks. "I saw your gun at the clubhouse. You know, the one you had pointed at my head? That thing is a legend. Green snakeskin handle, a one-of-a-kind commission used by the deadliest assassin known as The Viper. You slipped that day."

"I wouldn't say I'm the deadliest, The Reaper Incarnate is still up there on the list and running New York, not to mention Black Slaughter is still running some jobs up north in Whitsborough." She gives me a smug look as a server approaches the table. "Vodka soda," Delia tells her without taking her eyes off me. The girl walks away from the table as Delia raises a brow at me once more. "I did slip that day," she agrees as she settles back into her seat. "It was Genni and I wasn't thinking when I grabbed my guns and rushed to your clubhouse."

"Does she know?" I ask as I run my fingers over my goatee. "Does Genni know what you do for a living?"

"No." She shakes her head as the server comes back with her

drink, placing the glass in front of her before walking away. "I never had any plans to tell her. I wanted to be normal to at least one person in my life."

"Your brother is keeping your secret well then," I remark and take another drink.

"We both think Genni has dealt with enough death in her life, we didn't want to bombard her with more," she retorts, the jab not digging as deep as she'd hoped.

"I bet she would rather hear the truth than be *betrayed* again." That's what she should've went with because the fact that I killed her father isn't what keeps me up at night, it's her screaming my name as Malik Charles hauled her away.

"I'm sure she will have plenty of questions for me the next time we see each other," she murmurs as she brings the glass to her mouth to take a sip. "What exactly do you need from me? And keep in mind, I'm only doing this for Genni. The moment you fuck up, and we both know you will, I will put you down like the dog you are."

"Noted." I roll my eyes and settle back in the seat. "Tazo has been surviving over the years without an affiliation with the Dragons, but he founded and ran Hell's March. Are you able to find out where else he has his claws dug in?"

"Why?" She leans on the table and hits me with her light blue stare. "Why not find out where he's staying and kill him?"

"I need to know what he and Vic Varga were involved with. There are things we don't understand, that Genni doesn't understand, and I want to learn everything before we kill him." My hand curls into a fist as it rests on my bouncing leg. "Something feels off about this entire situation, and I won't rest until I have the answers. Then I'm blowing him the fuck up."

"Ah, classic Jaeger move." She taps her hand on the table and then slides out from the seat. "I will put out some feelers and get back to you." She gives me one final scathing look before saying, "I'm watching you too, Varga. Don't even think we're partners or working together either."

"I wouldn't think of it," I drawl as she walks away, leaving behind a nearly full drink. It's still hard to believe that she's one of the most deadliest assassins and I don't think I've fully absorbed that she's the one who trained Genni. It makes sense now how she kicked my ass in that basement.

I leave a fifty-dollar bill on the table and get out of the booth, my eyes scanning the room as I stretch. I saw Quinton here earlier and I bet he's on his way to rat me out to Genni and tell her that I was here meeting up with Delia.

It's no secret and I have nothing to hide, but Delia and Diego might. I'm not sure how Genevieve will feel knowing she stayed with the notorious Viper assassin. I grab the cigarette I have tucked behind my ear and head outside, stopping as soon as I'm through the doors to light it. My eyes drop to my bike parked to my left and then around the lot. Looks like Quinton left, which only tells me he's trying his best to be a loyal dog to make up for turning his back on his girl.

His girl.

I nearly laugh out loud at the fact that my best friend was fucking my little sister and he did it while looking me in the face each day. Then my stomach quickly sours as I begin to imagine him between her legs, coveting her as if she belonged to him. She never belonged to him though and she never will. Genevieve Varga belongs to no one.

When I get home, I curse under my breath at the sight of the yellow bike sitting in the driveway. She's here again and I fucking hate it. It's messing with my head and I'm forgetting all the reasons why I can't stand her.

I head inside, preparing myself for a battle because that's become the norm with us, but instead, I'm hit with the scent of a home-cooked meal. My heart squeezes inside my chest as I think of Ma. The door swings shut behind me, the banging sound seemingly echoing around the house.

"Jaeger?" Genni calls out, her voice crashing into the memory of my mother and washing it all away. Grief is something new to me and I haven't quite mastered how to control the highs and extreme lows of it. "Come here." She's in the kitchen, obviously, but what she doesn't know is that I can't go in there, not without preparing myself for it. I can count on one hand how many times I've crossed the threshold into that room since that fateful night.

I stand in the doorway and find her in front of the stove, stirring something in a large pot, my mother's apron covering her clothes. I wait for the anger of seeing her here in Ma's space and in her apron, but I shock myself when a grin grows along my mouth. I stay at the entrance and lean against the wall, crossing my arms over my chest. "What are you doing here?"

"I live here," she replies, the answer making me straighten as I shake my head, the smile falling from my lips.

"No," I protest as she scoops a meatball out of the pot with a large wooden spoon and advances on me. "No, Genevieve."

"Yes, Jaeger. This is my house and I didn't leave by choice. I was *forced out*." I open my mouth to protest further but she sticks the spoon in front of my face and demands, "Try this."

"Is it laced with poison?" She bumps my lips with the spoon as she rolls her eyes. Even if it is poisoned, the scent has my mouth watering and giving in to her as it slowly opens.

"If I wanted you dead, Jaeger, I would've done it in that basement," she reveals as I chew into the tender meat, the flavors hitting my tongue in an explosion of spices.

"Same," I confess as I groan around the food in my mouth.

"Go up and get cleaned up. Ma wouldn't want you in her kitchen smelling like booze and whores," she *tsks* as she heads back to the stove.

She's right, Ma would hate that, but Genni's got it wrong this time. "I had one drink, and trust me, it's been a while since I've touched a woman." I don't know why I need her to hear that and when she continues to look into the pot, her throat working on a swallow, I continue, "There isn't anyone right now."

For fear of looking like more of a fool, I back away from the kitchen and head upstairs, my boots hitting the wood in loud thuds. I will never admit this to her, but having her here breathes life back into this house. Before it was shrouded in the memories of death and no matter where I looked, I was reminded of the things I did and put into motion.

I head toward my room but stop short in front of our parents' room, the door still open the way I left it and Vic's clothes strewn all over the floor. At first, it was something cathartic to do while I worked through my overwhelming grief and it felt great to take it out on his belongings, but then it became a search for his secrets. He had them, he's just hidden them so well.

I stride into the bedroom, kicking aside a pair of his jeans as I stand in the center of the room with my hands on my waist. The love he had for Genni's mom was never a secret. He told my mother that his heart was forever sealed six feet under with the woman, but that she could have what was left of his soul. For a man who loved a woman so much, there are no signs of her having ever lived in this home. He had one photo of her at the clubhouse in his office, but she's looking out over the water at the cottage, her face looking forlorn.

Where are her things? What happened to all of her belongings when she died? A rush of anger comes over me as I head into the closet, my heart pounding inside my chest. His side is completely destroyed with clothes all over the floor and hangers hanging empty along the rod. My mother's side is still pristine as if she just pressed and folded everything a few hours earlier. I run my fingers along the blouses, the soft silks and satins reminding me how I would cuddle into her stomach when I was a kid. A sharp, stabbing pain hits me in the chest as I grab an armful of her clothes and press my face into them, trying desperately to smell her.

With her scent nearly gone, another bout of anger hits me and I kick out my boot, slamming it into the wall beneath her clothes, the dull thud echoing beyond the Sheetrock. A crack sounds and when I crouch down, I see I've kicked a false wall. It's a piece of wood painted white and nailed in place, mimicking the rest of the closet.

"What have we here?"

GENEVIEVE
BMW Motorrad Milano

GENEVIEVE

It's been quiet for the last fifteen minutes and Jaeger hasn't come back downstairs. Maybe this whole thing was stupid, coming here and making him dinner, hoping it would somehow repair the decimated remains of our relationship. Am I a fool to even try?

I stare at the full bowls of food on the table and throw my apron on a chair. I'm an idiot. Stalking out of the kitchen, I don't even care that the food is left out on the table, I just want to close myself off in my room and sleep in my bed again. Last night was one of the best nights of sleep I've had in a long time. What happened in this house hasn't been forgotten by me, but this is the only home I have ever known and it's good to be back. Regardless of if my murderous stepbrother sleeps just down the hall from me.

A *bang* sounds from the second story just as I reach the stairs, and I stop as my breath gets trapped in my throat. What is he doing? I slowly take the first few steps and pause again before reaching for Jaeger's knife, which is tucked in my back pocket. I won't be caught unaware in this house again.

When the silence continues, I slowly walk up the rest of the stairs, the knife held out in front of me. If he jumps out at me now, he'll only have himself to blame for the stab wound to his gut. The second level is dark, save for the warm glow of light slipping out from under my bedroom door. I close my eyes and hear Malik's voice in my head.

When your eyes are useless, open your ears and your nose. Smell the danger, hear the sounds around you, and remain still. Don't make any sudden movements.

I open my eyes and press my back against the wall, letting the dark slowly come into focus around me, and that's when I see him. He's standing in the darkened alcove of the hallway between our parents' bedroom and the bathroom. His chest is barely moving with each breath and his eyes are like swirling pots of ink, completely black and unsettling.

We don't say anything, we don't move, we just stare each other down from either side of the corridor. Minutes tick by, I don't know how many. Two, five, ten? And when he finally breaks the silence, I flinch at the sudden sound.

"Are you going to kill me with my own knife, Princess Varga?" he says my name with a sneer, the sound tightening my stomach with anger.

"Were you lying up in here in wait for me?" I fire back. "Hoping to catch me off guard?" My hand grips the knife handle tighter, the metal biting into my palm.

He pushes himself off the wall and takes a few tentative steps toward me, his lips pressing together in a thin line before his tongue slips out between them. I watch as he wets his lips, the sight making my core clench and my stomach flip with disgust.

Jaeger is my brother.

He didn't feel like your brother outside the clubhouse all those months ago, especially not last night either, something whispers in my mind as my pussy begins to throb with the memory of him between my legs as he ravished my mouth.

Jaeger takes a deep breath as a wolfish grin spreads across his mouth. It's almost as though he can smell me, smell the way my body is reacting to him, but that's impossible. His hand flies out and wraps around mine holding the blade between us as he steps into the pointed edge. I can feel the resistance give a little as the tip sinks into his flesh, blood blooming quickly through his white T-shirt.

"Jaeger!" I hiss as I try to draw the knife back, our eyes still connected. His is filled with something that looks strangely similar to remorse.

"This is what you wanted, right?" His voice is low and deep as his dark hair hangs over his forehead, giving him an almost boyish look, but there's nothing boyish about the man standing in front of me, piercing his flesh without flinching. "To make me pay for the mistakes I made? The mistakes I made in your father's name and the ones I made because of him?" He drops his hand from mine as his eyes scan over my face.

I relax my elbow, making it bend and releasing the blade from his skin. "Mistakes, Jaeger?" I tip my head to the side as I drop the knife to the floor so I can cover his wound with my hand. My forehead creases as I mull over his words. "Is this an apology for what you did to me?"

"Look at you, Genni," he breathes out as he steps into me again, trapping my hand between our chests. My other hand presses to the wall beside me as the heat of his body washes over me. "You're so fucking strong, your potential stretched and reached beyond what you could have ever imagined. You've killed without remorse, you've been to Hell and basked in the warmth of fire and brimstone." I can't tell if he means a word of what he's saying or if he's just taunting me again. "I did that for you," he whispers in my face as his hand slips into my hair, the touch starting out like a caress until his fingers close around the strands. "You're who you are today because you survived my revenge."

My anger is swift and volatile as it crashes through me, but I don't give him the satisfaction of digging my nails into the tender flesh of his cheek. This is why he's doing this, trying to bring out my ire, because he's still trying to live with what he's done and pain helps him sleep at night. My eyes flick down to the bloodstain growing wider around my hand on his chest and my heart fills with anguish. He doesn't know how to forgive himself because he's never done it before. "It was your fault," I agree with him, my words soaked in pity as I move my hand down over his pec and stomach, stopping when I curl it around his waist. "Are you going to need to hear that every day for the rest of your life? Does it feed your irrational self-loathing?"

Jaeger presses all of his weight against my body, forcing me into the wall, and drops his face to my neck, his hand yanking my head to the side. "Feel that?" He bucks his hips forward, pumping his cock into my lower belly, the hardness stealing the retort sitting on my tongue. "That's what your heartache feeds." The hand not in my hair trails fire down my arm and thigh, slipping to the back and gripping the flesh, forcing it around his hip. We've been here and done this before, and even though I should push him away, I press my hips harder into his. It's his turn to gasp, his hot breath coating my cheek as he pulls back to look into my eyes, the dark orbs drenched in surprise.

"That's right, brother," I taunt him as I reach up to run my hand along his cheek, his body vibrating underneath my touch. "I'm just as sick as you." Then I slip my fingers around to the back of his head and drag it forward, claiming his mouth with mine. If he thought he had the upper hand, that he could torment me with the attraction I feel for him, then he's wrong. I not only became tougher these last few months, but I've faced all my truths.

I want Jaeger Varga, the brother I was raised with, the one who ripped my heart from my chest and consumed it with a ravenous appetite.

The kiss is brutal in its intensity, nothing like our first. This time, I'm battling him instead of freezing with surprise. It's my tongue that demands entrance into his mouth and it's my hips rotating against his in time with each thrust of my tongue. I can feel him losing all logical thought as his body becomes an instrument, ready to play a tune only I recognize the notes for, a perfect weapon I can use against him.

Just as his cock is pressed against my pulsing pussy, I rip my mouth from his and slam my fist into his cheek. He drops my leg as his hand reaches up to touch the tender flesh with surprise, but he doesn't have the time to process it because I've crashed my body into his, attacking his mouth once more.

Another one of my truths? I'm not ready to forgive. He's created this monster, so now he'll have to learn to live with it.

Regardless of the resentment I feel toward him, my body is

primed and begging for his touch. It's a sick war inside my head, and I'm not sure which will come out the victor in the end.

His body is tense as I'm sure his face is pulsing with the hit I dealt, but soon enough, his hands are gripping my waist, his fingers biting into my skin as he hauls me into him farther. The kiss loses its ferocity though as his hesitancy wins out, and I pull away to take a step back.

The bruise on his face is already forming as his fingers meet the skin, a wince lining his features. "I guess I deserved that."

"Did you?" I ask as I walk backward to stand next to his discarded knife. Jaeger is unpredictable and I can never guess how he's going to react. "What for?"

A small smile grows along his face as he shakes his head. "For thinking I could ever stand having my lips on you, for thinking I could spread your legs and sink into your wet cunt as if you didn't try to take everything from me. Thank you for reminding me, sister." Then I watch as he slips back into our parents' bedroom and shuts the door.

That reaction was predictable and I'm beginning to think I've figured him out. Now I just have to be patient until I can get into that room without him around and find out just what he's hiding.

DIEGO

CHAPTER EIGHT

After pulling apart Barrett's office, we still haven't found a code for the safes, but we have found something of importance. It's a file containing Malik Charles' information. His house he owns in Phoenix and the elderly couple he rents it to, a list of women he's been known to frequent, and finally, all the missions he's been on in the last few years. Those missions had come from Tazo and not Barrett.

"Have you tried calling him?" I ask as Malik falls into the large leather chair behind the desk. "Maybe it's as easy as that. He gave you Vice, he made it so you couldn't be removed or touched in that position, and he's been the one handing you missions."

"Of course I tried to call him." Malik scrubs his hand down his face and exhales heavily. "I tried the same night he held a gun to Chino's head then disappeared. I saw the way he looked at Slayer and I was scared for the first time in my life." He tips his head back to look at the ceiling, his wavy hair moving around his face. "It's disconnected. I can't even tell you how long it's been like that either because I hadn't been keeping in touch as often as he liked."

"Have you ever met him anywhere?" I sit in the chair on the other side of the desk, dropping a pair of pants to the floor once I search the pockets.

"In the desert or an abandoned warehouse parking lot. Never where he was staying." Malik straightens and looks at me, his eyes finally reflecting the apprehension I'm feeling. "He's going to want her. Diego, I saw the way he looked at her, and I feel helpless to stop it. She forces us away and we can't say no because she's our Prez. Did we fuck up with that?"

"No." I lean forward and place my hands on the desk. "She's right where she belongs and we need to trust that we've trained her to be capable of taking care of herself. What we're doing right now is keeping her safe."

"My chest feels tight," he moans as he rubs it with his hand, his eyes closing with a wince. "It's been that way for months. I swear to the Heavenly Father, if I die because I finally found the woman I want to be with, I will terrorize every angel up there."

"You're in love with Genevieve," I tell him as he looks at me in complete shock. Falling back in the chair, I chuckle at his expression. "Did you think you wouldn't be capable?"

"Trust me when I say no one should be the receiver of the type of love I am *capable* of giving," he murmurs as he stands, grabbing the folder with his information in his hand. "Barrett was an idiot because there's a piece of paper in here with a mission, written on a motel notepad."

"Seriously?" I stand with surprise, my brows quickly falling with confusion. "I didn't notice that."

"That's why we make a great team, Montez." He comes out from behind the desk and claps his hand to my shoulder, the touch soon becoming a gentle massage. "Let's go ask Jones to do some tracking. It's a franchise and I know about three off the top of my head in Phoenix alone."

"That's a good idea. Surveillance for the past couple of days shouldn't be hard to comb through." He drops his hand and heads for the door as I follow him out.

"Not hard," he agrees with a shrug of his shoulders. "Just *a lot.*"

"Did Tazo ever explain why he made you Vice?" I ask as I follow him down the hallway toward Jones' room.

"He wanted me to kill my brother and infiltrate the Steel Dragons." He exhales a breath and stops in the corridor, turning to look at me, sadness lurking in his hazel eyes. "I was given the perfect opportunity to kill Laith twice, but I couldn't do it. When I shot him in the face, I told Tazo he flinched at the last second and the bullet hit his cheeks instead of his temple. He bought it but I was on thin ice and running out of excuses. Killing the only blood relative I have left was something I struggled with. Laith's actions changed my life, but I don't think he deserved to die."

We continue walking again and when we approach Jones' door, I grab his bicep to stop him. "Why did you agree to it then?"

"Because I missed having a family and that's what the March became for me. No matter how fucked-up this club got, I wanted to belong somewhere." His confession comes easy, as though he's come to terms with it all, but it has my throat swelling with emotion, making it difficult to swallow. "I never belonged with Laith and our parents."

"You belong with us now. Me and Genevieve. Okay?" His brows crinkle together as he looks down at the floor in thought.

"I don't think I've ever truly belonged to anyone, not even the March." He looks back up to me and gives me a wicked smile. "No take backsies."

"No," I assure him as I roll my eyes. "Just don't think you're dragging me to church." I drop my hand from his arm as he laughs.

"I haven't been to church yet either. Not until my sins on Earth are complete." His fist raps against the door as I chuckle.

"So, we're all going straight to Hell," I muse as Jones calls out for us to come in.

"Without our foreskins and baptized by the sweetest pussy." He opens the door as a deep laugh rushes from my mouth. It feels good to be happy, to share this feeling with the impending doom at our backs. "Jones! We need your help!" Malik bellows as he steps into the smokey room.

Jones looks like he's been on his laptop all night and smoked a pack of smokes doing it. "No shit," he mumbles around the butt in his mouth as he hunches over a laptop at his desk. "What is it now?"

Jones is in charge of moving funds for the club, and sometimes, moving funds from others into our accounts. "Can you get surveillance feed from this motel?" Malik opens the file in his hand and sets a piece of paper beside Jones.

"Which one?" he asks, his eyes still on his screen.

"The nearest three to us. We'll start there." Malik and I stand behind him as his long fingers fly over the keyboard, the screen blinking with lines of code. "Get a couple of guys on the screens. We have a specific person we're looking for," Malik demands as I pull out my cell phone to call Ajani.

"Hey, man." He sounds groggy like I've woken him up from sleep. He hasn't been resting much since I've been away and it has a lot to do with watching my sister and Medical here at the club.

"You sound like shit," I remark as his deep chuckle coats my ear.

"I've been picking up your slack at the clubhouse and your sister is a handful." Guilt slips along my spine, making me feel like an asshole when he laughs again. "I can hear your shame bleeding through the phone, Diego. We're fine, everything is okay." I release the breath I was holding and nod as I swallow down the need to ask if he's sure. I know Ajani, he wouldn't lie to me.

"I need to fill you in on some shit. Are you able to come by the clubhouse? Bring my sister." His deep exhale has my eyebrows crashing together, waiting for what he has to say.

"She said she had another mission," he grumbles, and I huff along with him. My sister has a side of her I can't be hypocritical about. She likes to watch bad people die, the ones who do sadistic things to others and think they're out of reach of the law, and she does it in the most painful way. I worry about her, but I also understand all too well her need to release the darkness that builds inside of her.

We're both still working through the trauma of our parents' deaths, but we travel different roads to do it. Yes, I kill when I need to and I'm an excellent sniper, but I would rather heal the sick and help the wounded. Delia needs to watch the light fade from a person's eyes as their soul carries on to Hell. It's her way and I don't interfere, but I fucking worry each time she's on a *mission*.

I wanted her to be the one to train Genevieve because there's no one more cunning than Delia. I've watched her take out grown men with her fists, knees, teeth, whatever she can, and she does it with ease. That's the kind of instinct I wanted ingrained in my girl after she endured the basement here.

"I'm heading in now," Ajani says, breaking the silence, and I snap back to reality. "I'll bring coffee."

"Bring Malik some whiskey and holy water." I snicker as his heat hits my back and his mouth presses in close to the phone at my ear.

"I've been a bad boy, Ajani." His rasp makes my cock thicken as Ajani laughs through the speaker. "Right, Montez?" Malik pumps his hard cock against my ass as I swallow down the groan threatening to spill.

"Always trouble," I grit out and hang up the call, stepping away from Malik before Jones realizes what's happening in his room. This is his space and us getting frisky in it can't be appropriate. "Let's go over that file—"

"Nah." He slaps the file to my chest and I grab it before it drops to the floor. "I need to pay a visit to my girl. Seems I got more sinning to do tonight."

Jones chuckles just as Malik adjusts his hard cock in his pants before heading to the door, his swagger heavy, then he swings it open and disappears.

172

LAITH

LAITH

"Thanks for coming," Quinton says as he stares at a glass of whiskey before bringing a bottle of water to his mouth to chug. "I've tried getting ahold of Genni, but she's not picking up her phone.

I grab the glass of whiskey and down the contents, making Quinton's brows hit his hairline. "I'd rather it be me than you. What's got you on the verge of breaking your sobriety?"

"The things I found out today. I'm still having a hard time piecing it all together." He signals to Chip for another bottle of water and taps the glass I drank for a refill. "I just need it in front of me," he explains with a shrug. "It makes me feel like I'm looking my temptation in the eye, but it's under control. I need something to be in control."

"Okay." I nod, knowing I won't let him drink it anyway. There's no way I'm letting him return to the mess he once was. "What have you learned?" My heart pumps in my chest when I give him a once-over. His face is pale and his eyes a little too wide, like he's having trouble processing what he's been told. I don't like that and I'm fighting every instinct of leaving here to find Little Varga and make sure she's safe. President or not, she's still mine.

"I went to visit my mother today to find out about Tazo, and my aunt came by, his *ex-wife*." Chip places the bottle of water on the counter and eyes the glass as he pours the whiskey.

"Tell me you threw this in the face of a handsy brother," he rasps, and I choke back a laugh. Quinton chuckles as he shakes his head, the sight calming my nerves a little.

"Laith drank it. Don't worry," Quinton assures him as Chip gives me a nod.

"Do you need anything, brother?" He drapes a towel over his shoulder as he places the whiskey bottle back on the shelf behind him.

"I'm good." I wave my hand and watch as he shuffles off to refill another brother's drink before returning my gaze to Quinton. "What did they say?" I probe him as he eyes the glass, his mouth tipping downward.

"Vic Varga wasn't the man we thought he was. He had more secrets besides brain cancer and a plan to betray his son." He scrubs a hand down his face and my stomach flips with his words.

"Are these facts? Or the ramblings of pissed off women?" When he gives me a scathing look, I raise my hands in surrender. "I have to ask."

"Tazo left the reservation after being exiled with his wife's younger sister, Awendela." His brow is lifted as if he's just dropped a bomb, but none of it makes sense to me.

"Look. That's some twisted shit to be doing to his wife, but how does this prove Vic had secrets? I'm not connecting the dots." I down the second glass of whiskey because I have a feeling this is about to blow my mind, especially with the way Quinton's chest is heaving.

"Awendela!" He throws his hands up with frustration and looks around the room. Our brothers are playing pool, fucking Bunnies, and having a good time, but Quinton's teetering on the edge of a mental breakdown. If I didn't know he was so in love with Genevieve, I'd find him an STD to sink himself into for the night. The curable kind of course. "They called her Wendy for short, Laith." My head snaps back to him as the world around me fades and white noise plows through my ears. I've only ever known of one Wendy around here.

"Vic's wife?" I mutter as I shake my head with confusion.

"First, she was with Barrett," he tacks on nonchalantly as if my head isn't already imploding. "Then somehow, she made her way to Vic. From Tazo, to Barrett, then to Vic. I don't understand how. My mother and aunt weren't told of the events that took place after she left the reservation because club business was never brought to them, but my dad would've known. He and Vic were best friends. Cash most definitely would've known, but he's dead. Everyone with answers is dead. Except for Tazo."

"Barrett to Vic?" I'm staring at him as I try to clear the ringing from my ears. "That doesn't make sense."

"Chip, refill this glass, please," he calls out as our brother gives me a look before grabbing the bottle. He has questions in his eyes but remains quiet as he fills the glass and heads back down the bar to give us privacy. "It does when we think of everything. The rivalry, the hatred. Maybe Vic seduced Barrett's Old Lady and made her his. I don't know, man. The only way I'll get answers is by finding Tazo and asking him myself, but first, I want to tell Genni about everything I've learned." He's planning on putting himself in front of his uncle's gun again in search of information for the club and Genni, and I can't let him do that.

"You won't be seeking out Tazo on your own. We do this together, as a team. We all grab him and bring him in for questioning. That's how we'll get our answers, right here in the basement." When he shakes his head, I grab his shoulder and give it a squeeze. "Don't bring Genni more pain by losing another person she loves."

His face winces with pain, as if he truly believes he's unworthy of her love, and there's nothing I can do to reassure him. He has to forgive himself for the things he had a hand in and let Genevieve prove he's been forgiven. "Why are you here? Let's head over to Jaeger's, that's where Little Varga is staying."

"I told Carrie I would meet her here, and she's an hour late," he mumbles and looks toward the door before glancing around the room. A few girls from Glitz are here partying with the brothers, but it's clear that Carrie and Angel aren't.

"Why are you meeting with Carrie?" I growl as I swat him on the back of the head, forcing him to look at me. "If you want our girl's forgiveness, you need to keep your dick in your pants."

"She was with Cash when he met up with Tazo, her and Angel both." He looks at me with wide eyes and then scoffs, "She might know where Tazo is staying and we need that info. You should've seen her tonight, brother. She looked scared to even be talking to me."

"It's clear she's not coming. We need to go talk to Jaeger and Genni. He's exiled, but he's the only one who lacks empathy. He'll see things clearer." I grab his vest to haul him off the stool when he shakes his head again.

"I can't leave in case she shows up. She's the key to Tazo, Laith, I can feel it. You can head over there first and I'll come as soon as I can. I trust you to tell Jaeger everything I told you." I drop my hand from his vest and groan because I'm worried about Carrie's motives. She had strong feelings for Quinton, but it never stopped her from opening her legs to any brother who showed interest.

"Okay," I give in and push away from the bar. Then I grab his glass of whiskey and hand it to a brother walking by before giving Quinton a stern look. "No more alcohol on the bar in front of you. Got it?"

"Yeah." He waves me off and takes another sip of his water. "Don't worry, I don't have any urge to drink. I need a clear head for this shit. I'll call you with an update when I have it." He glances at the door again, the tension in his shoulders betraying the stress of Carrie's no-show.

"Call the club and speak to Trevor," I suggest. "He'll tell you what time she left." He nods as I walk by and pat him on the shoulder. "See you later." He lifts his hand in farewell as I head outside to my bike.

The night sky twinkles with stars as I stand and look out toward the gate. An ominous feeling comes over me as I watch the Prospects both walking the perimeter and sitting up on the roof. After finding out how easily Delia got over the wall and into our compound, we upped the security, but I still feel like we're being watched.

I can't help but curse our former leader for the mess he made and left us to clean up. Victor Varga was a man I looked up to, held in the highest regard for how he treated each one of us, but I can't ignore the problems piling up around his ghost. This club, him included, were the family I so desperately needed when I found myself at their gate, begging for a chance to prove myself. I was fifteen with nothing to my name, but he took one look at me and welcomed me with open arms.

It eased the distrust I had for people and the jaded way I felt about family. Now I stand here in the happiest home I have ever known and feel like it's all built like a house of cards, one hard blow and it'll all come crashing down around me.

I leave the compound and head toward the Varga home, the unease inside my stomach growing. I didn't like the idea of Genni shacking up with her psycho stepbrother, but I also couldn't insist she stay away from her family home. She deserves to be there as much as he does, and Jaeger is going to have to accept that. They're family, even if they've been testing those limits lately.

I'd be a fool if I said I didn't watch the lines being blurred between them, that the hatred they thought they felt was only a mask covering the truth. Jaeger's been fighting it for a while, his threats to any brother looking at his sister was more territorial than protective, but I also thought it would never be acted upon. Until I heard Genni's account of what happened the night I found her inside our compound.

The house looks empty when I pull into the driveway, save for the soft glow of the kitchen light. It's late and they may be sleeping, but this can't wait. I pull my cell phone from my vest pocket and dial her number, smiling when her soft voice filters through to my ear.

"Hey." She sounds like she's tired but not sleeping.

"Are you home?" I ask as I look up at the second story. The last time I was here, I remember finding her spotted with bruises, unknowing they came from Jaeger. It was the day I found out she could shoot.

"Yeah. Was that you who pulled up in the driveway?" I can hear her walking around and then the porch light comes on.

"It's me. Can I come in?" The driveway is empty save for her yellow bike.

"Of course." The door opens and she stands there in the light with just a long T-shirt on, her nipples hardening with the breeze.

"Fuck," I hiss and get off the bike, discreetly tucking away my growing erection. I walk up to her and pull her into my arms, my lips landing on the crown of her head.

Her arms wrap around my waist as she sighs, the sound bleeding with stress. "Jaeger's not here and I can't help but wonder what trouble he's gotten himself into."

"He's real good at taking care of himself," I assure her as she pulls back and leads me into the house.

"He's been hiding something from me and I think it's in my parents' room. I tried to get in there today, but he's locked it. I could break it down but I figure I'll wait and give him the benefit of the doubt until I confront him. I'm scared it's about my father." I open my mouth to tell her that's why I'm here when the rumble of another bike sounds from up the street. "Maybe that's him," she says as she heads back to the door.

"Good," I grunt as she moves to open the door. I quickly grab her hand and pull it away with a shake of my head. "Just because it's a bike doesn't mean they're ours."

"You're right." She steps back and exhales. "I know better. I've just been on edge."

"Understandable. I'll take care of whoever is outside, then we'll have a chat." She nods and heads into the kitchen as I hear the bike pull into the driveway.

MALIK

I reach up to pull the helmet off my head and realize I forgot it back at the clubhouse. *Evel Knievel moves*. The house looks quiet save for the two bikes sitting in the driveway. One belonging to a Steel Dragon and the other belonging to my Slayer. Jaeger will hate to see me in his house again, especially since the first time went so well for him.

I walk by the bike and pause when *Charles* inscribed along the gas tank catches my eye. The wrong Charles is inside with my girl and he's about to get a bitch-slap to the cheek. No unsupervised visits until I'm sure he's potty-trained.

The door opens before I even step up to the porch and his eyes widen when he takes me in. "Bad dog!" I wag my finger at him as I take one step up to his level. "No dogs allowed in the house."

"The fuck is wrong with you?" He rolls his eyes and steps back, his body tense and preparing for a fight. I guess it makes sense after telling him I hate him and shooting him in the face.

"Do you really want to know?" I lean in close to him and plaster a wicked grin on my face. "Is that something you're willing to face, little brother?" He swallows thickly, his face filled with guilt as I shove past him and into the house. "Slayer!" I call out and grin maniacally when I hear her squeal. Then I take off my boots and take a few steps when her voice hits me.

"I missed you!" she exclaims as she climbs me like a monkey, her arms winding around my neck and her legs hooking around my waist. "Where's Diego?"

"He's not my keeper," I grunt as my nose lands in her hair and I take in a lungful of her sweet scent. My very own tonic for my soul. Fuck that, that's not right. My soul has long escaped the hell of my body, but she's replaced it. Slayer *is* my soul.

"I asked because I thought we were having an impromptu meeting." She giggles into my neck, her warm breath sending a message to my balls. They like warmth and a good bathing in vagina-happy juices.

"Sorry, Jesus, I need to fuck my girl," I mumble as I head to the stairs. "Where's your room, Slayer?"

"First door on the right," she husks out as her tongue swipes along my jugular.

"Come on, little brother," I call out to Laith. "This is the only way you're getting my girl. Supervised!" I'm halfway up the stairs when he stops at the bottom, his huff of annoyance like a shower of icy water. I turn to look at him as Slayer continues to lick my neck like a melting popsicle.

"I thought we could discuss things." I swear he's got the brain of a fucking toad.

"*I thought we could discuss things,*" I mock him as Slayer chuckles again. "If it weren't for your pretty face, I would assume you were dumped on our parents' front porch as an infant. You can stay down here and play I Spy by yourself." When his boots hit the floor in loud *thuds*, I snicker and whisper into Slayer's ear, "He never was any good at that game."

"What are you saying to her?" he asks as we reach the top of the stairs and start for Slayer's room.

"I told her about the time it took you over half an hour to find your dick," I answer as Slayer cackles over my shoulder. Then I kick open her door and step into her room.

"That was impossible to guess!" he yells out, rushing the rest of the way up the stairs. "You told me to look for something like a bald cat!"

I press my mouth against the shell of Slayer's ear and say, "He should have known I was referring to his pussy." I toss her onto her bed as her laugh reverberates around the room, and I have to admit, it's contagious. Especially when Laith comes ambling inside, his face a mask of irritation.

He opens his mouth to say something stupid I'm sure, but I hush him with a finger to my lips, then jut my chin toward my girl. His eyes widen as he takes her in on the bed at the same time I turn back to look at her. Her cheeks are flushed as her lips still carry the ghost of her mirth along their plush shape. The T-shirt she's wearing is now twisted up around her waist, and my Slayer is wearing a black thong, the material nearly nonexistent.

"Looks like we have a mission, little brother," I announce without taking my eyes off those panties. "Both of us need to find our way between those luscious thighs and make sure that pussy is purring as it should be."

Laith grunts as I reach into the pocket of my cut and take out the tube of lube I grabbed from my room at the club. I didn't think I would be sharing this moment with an asshole, but the two of them and I make a team. I throw the lube on the bed and remove my cut and shirt, folding and placing them on top of her dresser as Laith does the same.

Slayer hooks her fingers into the tiny strap of her panties and hauls them down over her thighs, the sensual show hardening my cock, making it press painfully against the zipper.

"What if Jaeger comes back?" Laith mutters toward me as she flicks the panties at him, the fabric hitting his chest and then bouncing to the floor. He's so far gone, I don't think he's blinked away from her pussy.

"He can watch," I snap and undo my belt buckle as Slayer runs her fingers through her pretty cunt. "You can too," I add on before dropping my jeans and boxers to dive onto the bed, planting my face between her legs.

Pushing her hand away, I feast on her pussy, sucking her clit into my mouth and teasing it with the tip of my tongue. Then I drive it into her heat, letting her sweet nectar fill my senses. She's the best thing I've ever tasted and the best thing I've ever had. The moment she begins to stiffen, those long legs of hers stretching over my shoulders, I draw back and lick my way over her mound and stomach.

"No, Malik," she whines as her fist hits my shoulder. "No teasing."

"Tell me what you want," I demand as I drag her shirt up and over her head, exposing her tits.

"I want to come," she growls, and I turn to look at Laith standing at the end of the bed. He's managed to get his shirt off and his jeans undone, but he's standing there like a deer in headlights.

I turn back to Slayer and suck a nipple into my mouth, my teeth nipping into the sensitive flesh. She squirms beneath me as she shoves my shoulders, trying to get me back where she wants me. I release her nipple and pop my head up to look into her adorably angry face. "Ask him to do it," I suggest, thumbing over my shoulder at my dumbass brother. "It's making me uncomfortable how closely he's inspecting my asshole."

"I am not…" he trails off with a sigh.

"Come here, Laith," Slayer commands, her voice filled with a President's authority. I roll off her, making room for him between her legs as I settle in beside her, excited for the show. I toy with her nipple as my brother sheds his pants and boxers, then crawls up between her legs. His eyes are riveted to her face and it's plain as day. He loves her.

Do I look like that too?

I want to feel bad for her, having the love of someone like me, but honestly, I rarely feel bad about anything. She knew what she was getting herself into and still, she chose me. My mother always said I was hard to love, but Slayer has proven her wrong. I should dig her back up just so she can be forced to witness it.

"Fuck yes," Slayer breathes out, and my attention is snapped back to my twin sucking her soul from between her legs. It looks sloppy and uncoordinated but she looks pleased. I'll let it slide because I'll be the best Charles brother in the sack.

Preening with self-assurance, I lean down and begin to pay her nipples some proper attention. Each peak is teased and sucked until the dusty rose is throbbing a bright red. Then her stomach flexes as her hands dig into my brother's thick hair, her scream battering the walls around us as she comes. He lifts his head, looking like the cat that got the cream, and grins at her, so damn proud of making her come.

I should smack her pussy juice right off his mouth.

Instead, I grab up the tube of lube and twist off the cap, my mouth tipping upward in anticipation.

"What's that for?" Slayer asks, her voice thick like honey.

"Your ass," I tell her as she gasps. I expect to find fear in her eyes, but when I turn my head toward her, all I see is heat. My cock swells harder as she licks her lips and continues to stare at the tube in my hand.

"Okay." She nods and pushes up to her elbows. "How do you want me?"

Laith groans at her willingness to be stuffed like a Thanksgiving turkey while I plan our positioning in my head. "Little brother on your back." I point to the bed as Slayer moves over for him. "Slayer, you ride his mini-frankfurter while I stuff this salami in your ass from behind." Her eyes widen as she looks from Laith's cock to mine, trying to determine whose is bigger.

I'm not checking out my brother's cock to find out either.

I get off the bed and head to my cut, pulling out a strip of condoms and throwing it onto my brother's chest. "Wrap the fuck up, you don't get to come in her yet." Slayer opens her mouth to likely protest, but one look from me tells her I need this. It's irrational but I don't care. I never claimed to be sensical.

She rips a condom from the strip and opens the foil with her teeth as she crawls between my brother's spread legs. I squeeze some lube into my palm as she glides the latex down Laith's length, his jaw twitching with the effort to keep it together. Little bitch is probably on the verge of spouting like a fucking fountain. Slayer looks at me over her shoulder, her eyes glittering with affection as she wordlessly asks me if she can fuck my brother.

I give her a nod as I continue to stroke my cock with the lube, knowing that watching her sink down over *him* will be worth it when I watch myself take her asshole.

She gyrates her hips as she takes him, inch by inch, and when she's fully seated, I kneel behind her and between Laith's legs. Then I press a hand between her shoulder blades, guiding her forward and making her ass more accessible as Laith begins to pump up into her.

She gasps when I squeeze the lube and watch it slip down her asscrack, her back tensing as she stops focusing on my brother and on the fact that I'm spreading her asscheeks.

"You have one job, little brother, and that's to bring your miniscule dick game enough to distract her while I get my cock in this pretty little hole. Understand?" His eyes narrow on me as his teeth bite into his lower lip, probably trying to count from ten backwards and fucking that up too.

His hands grip her waist, the fingers digging into the skin as he thrusts deep into her, making my Slayer drop her head forward with a loud moan. That's better. I spread her asscheeks and watch as Laith stretches her pussy, the condom creating a barrier between their skins. I need her to have something more for me just a little while longer. Then he can have her any way she chooses. This time though, I want to be favored for once.

I grip my dick in my hand, the lube all over my length and fingers as I line myself up to her puckered hole. I should prepare her better, work her out with a few fingers before I plunge in with my cock, but Slayer is like me. She enjoys the pain that comes with intense pleasure. I understand just what it means that she's even letting me back here, considering what she endured in the March compound, but I'm happy to replace that experience with a good one.

The head of my cock pushes against her resistance as my brother works his hardest to distract her, but the moment my head breeches that ring of muscle, her gaspy moan has me thrusting the rest of the way in. "Malik!" she screams as her fingers dig into Laith's shoulders. "Fuck!"

I can imagine the stinging pain riding along the current of pleasure. One enhancing the other.

My cock jerks as I feel my brother through the thin membrane, slowly pumping his dick into her, fearing she's hurt. He doesn't know her as well as I do and even though I take pride in that, she will want him to. So now I need to teach pin dick just how hard he can push our girl, and witness her giving it all and more back.

I begin to thrust into her, long, hard strokes of my cock as my fingers sink into the thick globes of her ass. She whimpers with each one, the sound walking a fine line between agony and euphoria. I'm a big man and this little hole has really been stretched to its limit, but she's taking it all so fucking well.

Laith reaches up to cup her face, his eyes filled with concern as they flick over her features, the sight making me release a delicious asscheek to reach forward and grab a handful of his hair. I yank his face forward, the motion nearly making him collide with Slayer as I lean forward, stalling my thrust inside of her. "She's stronger than you and I combined. She's been through worse and look at her now. Do. Not. Pity. Her." I yank his hair one more time when his eyes slip to her face again, the sharp tug bringing his eyes back to mine. "You want to be with her? Show her you can match her strength, that you can deserve her. Even if it's only for this short time." I release him with a grunt as Slayer pants, her heavy breathing hitching with a long moan when I begin to move again. "Now *fuck her*."

She pushes up from his shoulders and gives him a nod, my Slayer the warrior, and finally, he begins to fuck her. I can feel everything as he does by the widening of his eyes. His jaw pulses and his eyes harden as he tries and fails to stall his orgasm.

I thrust deep into her ass, forcing her to fall forward on top of Laith again with a whimper. His eyes roll back as he sucks in a deep breath, the veins along his throat pulsing prominently as he strains to hold off his release. I can feel his cock thicken further on the other side of the membrane separating us and know he's right there on the edge.

Just as he's about to release that breath, I pump into Slayer, making sure my brother feels every inch I'm feeding her, and then I release her hips to curl over her back, bringing my face closer to his over her shoulder.

One hand presses into the mattress as Laith narrows his eyes at me, suspicion lurking in their dark depths. Rightfully so, because in the next instant, my hand is wrapped around his throat, trapping the breath he was just expelling.

"Fuck!" Slayer cries out as her pussy milks his cock and her asshole tightens around mine.

His body jerks as his hand wraps around my wrist, pushing himself deeper inside *my* girl, *my* pussy. I tighten my hold and drop even lower, our noses brushing as his gaze flicks to Slayer, his eyes filled with apprehension.

"Don't you dare look at her. You look at me while you're coming." That sets him off and he does exactly what I tell him, coming as I loosen my grip on his throat. Then he sucks in a lungful of air as the tendons along his neck bulge.

I release him after and pull out of Slayer's ass, then remove her off my brother, letting his wet, cum-filled condom hit him on the stomach. She rolls over and lays on her back, her eyes hooded and filled with satisfaction. Her eyes skim down my chest and stop at my cock as Laith sits up and swings his legs over the bed. "You didn't…" she points out and trails off, confusion lingering in her tone.

"I will," I say as I crowd over her and nearly shoot my load when her legs automatically spread. "I want to fill this pussy up, baby." I nestle against her wet heat as the head of my cock probes her entrance.

"Yes, Malik," she breathes out as she nods, her pussy sucking me in like a greedy little whore. *My greedy little whore.*

I push all the way in and slowly drag my cock back out as Laith heads into the bathroom. Good, I want this moment with her, this claiming is ours only. I reach between us as her pussy tightens around me, the walls gripping my length. The thought of her cunt being filled with my cum spurs me on and I rub quick circles against her clit as my rhythm becomes more erratic.

"God, yes," she whimpers as I look down into her awe-filled face. This is Heaven, this is exactly everything the Bible describes as that sought-after kingdom in the sky. I've already found it.

I'm on the brink of my release, so I wrap my hand around her throat as the other works her clit, and her quick intake of breath tells me she's about to crash over that edge with me. Her legs wrap around my waist to drag me in closer as I plow into her, my cock hitting so deep. The second she clamps down around me, my eyes explode with stars and I fill her cunt up. Spurt after spurt of my cum shoots into her and I drop my forehead to hers, breathing in her sounds of contentment.

"I love you," she says to me, making my heart flip inside my chest. "So much, Malik Charles."

"You own me, Genevieve Varga," I declare as I press a kiss to her nose. "My heart, my soul. You own me." For me, love means nothing. It's a frivolous thing that's given and taken away, but to be owned, to give your entire existence to someone? That's the epitome of finding your person. I pull out of her and point my finger at her face. "Don't move."

"Okay," she whispers as her eyes fall shut and a small smile forms around her lips. The bathroom door opens just as I drag on my boxers.

"I should get her a towel," Laith murmurs as I look at my girl's leaking pussy.

"No need," I growl and lean forward, gathering my cum slipping from her entrance. "She'll hold it in." Then I push it back where it belongs. Deep inside of her. She mumbles something unintelligible and then a soft snore comes from her mouth. I turn to look at my brother over my shoulder as I pull my fingers out. "You need to earn this. Be a man and follow her, no one else. Your Steel Dragon brothers are nothing compared to her."

He nods with understanding as I suck my fingers into my mouth and turn back to look at her. Our combined releases explode in my mouth as I continue to watch her sleep. She has to be number one for all of us or I will remove the weakest links.

Laith begins to dress as my phone rings from my cut on her dresser. I get up and dig into the pocket and see Chino's name flashing on the screen. He could be a weak link I'll have to get rid of, especially if he continues to cry for his ex-President like the bitch he is.

"What?" I snap when I answer on the next ring.

"We got him."

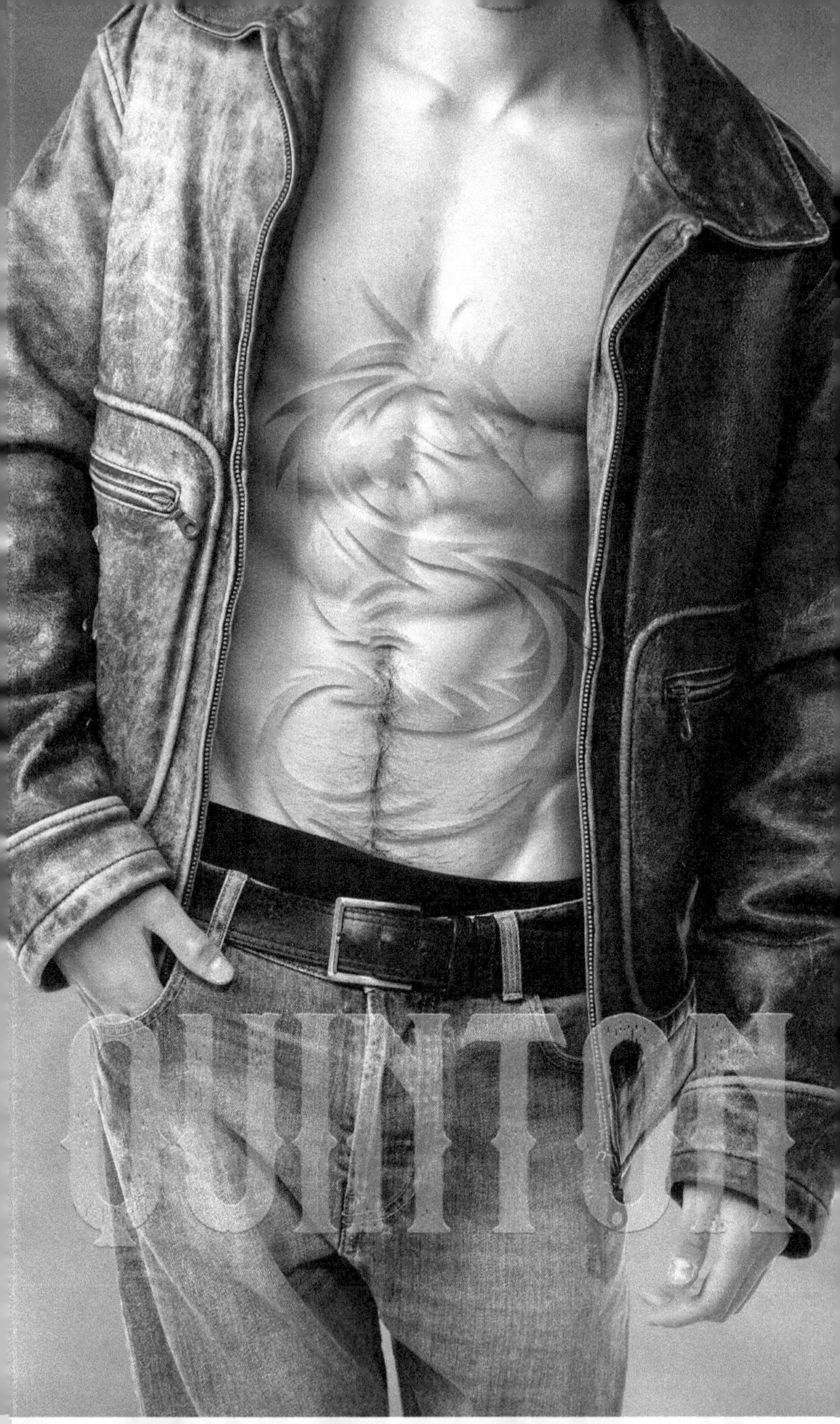

VUITTON

CHAPTER NINE

I wait another half an hour and when Carrie still doesn't show, I head over to Glitz. The club closed an hour ago but Trevor will still be there doing final counts and locking shit up. Carrie may still be there too. I can't get the look of her fear out of my head. Something was wrong and the fact that she didn't show tonight tells me that.

The parking lot is empty, save for Trevor's car parked near the entrance when I pull up. I try to rack my brain for any memory of what Carrie drives, but I come up blank. I may have been fucking the girl off and on for years, but that's all I ever knew about her.

I drop my helmet to my bike seat and unlock the door to head inside. The club looks completely different when all the lights are on and the music is off. The heat from lust-filled men and women is long gone and the interior now has a cold feel to it after the night crew has cleaned away the debauchery. As I head down the corridor, I stop beside the dressing room and look inside, just in case she's still here, but that too is empty.

Trevor's office door is open a crack and I can hear the *tap, tap, tap* of his fingers hitting the keyboard inside. We really lucked out by grabbing him up. He's loyal to his wife and none of these girls can sway him from the money he'd rather be counting.

"Hey, man," I say as I knock on the door.

"Chino." He looks up at me with confusion. "What are you doing here?"

"I came by looking for Carrie. She was supposed to meet up with me at the clubhouse and didn't show. Was everything all right tonight?" Trevor writes something into his ledger and then leans back in his chair, slipping his pen into his mouth.

"Everything was fine from what I could tell." He shrugs. "They got a ride home from Dan. I would've done it but tomorrow is the end of the month and I got thousands to wash." He motions to the ledgers in front of him. "You know the way the girls get, she probably just changed her mind."

"Could I get Dan's number? I just want to know where he dropped them off." I pull out my phone and swipe open the screen.

"No need," Trevor replies, making me look up at him from my phone. "I know where they're staying. Like I said, I usually drop them off." He rattles off an address of a motel off the highway and I give him a nod of appreciation.

"Thanks, man. I just want to check in on her." I move to leave the office when he clears his throat, stopping me in my tracks.

"We hear a lot of things over here and recently it's come to my attention that Jaeger has been exiled and his sister, Vic's daughter, has taken over. Is that true? Should I be worried about my job?" Trevor has a family and his life is stable, no matter what his job is and who he works for, so I understand his fear.

"You're fine," I reassure him. "The club is going through some changes right now but you're not one of them. Neither is this club or the shit you do for us, okay?"

He gives me a nod and straightens up in his seat, bending back down to pour over the ledgers. The Steel Dragons would be fucked without him and I refuse to let him worry when he has every right to. I don't know what the future of the Steel Dragons is right now, but I do know we need to take out the threats.

Tazo Chino is a threat and I think he has his claws buried so deep into our club that no one ever fucking had a clue. Except fucking Cash.

I'm hoping Laith is filling in Genni and Jaeger right now, and the fact that I haven't received a phone call is strange too. Once I have Carrie in front of me and see for sure she's okay, I'll head over to the Varga home and find out what the fuck is going on. I handed Laith a bomb and I should be hearing the effects of its explosion by now. Especially because it's about Genni's mom.

It still feels unreal to me that my aunt, by marriage, is related to Genni. Just when I think I've heard and seen it all, life smacks me on the back of the head and says, *hold my beer*.

The motel Trevor told me about is a popular franchise with many locations in and around the Phoenix area. It's the same one I would find my father at some nights when he was too wasted to go home but respected my mother enough not to be tempted by the Bunnies of the club. Just the thought of him has my heart clenching inside my chest. I worshiped the man and now all I can think of is him knowing that his sister-in-law's baby sister was a club pass-around. What made him believe that was okay? Was it because they saved her from Barrett? I can only imagine the monster he could've been, especially after what he did to Genni.

It's pitch-black when I pull into the grocery store parking lot across the street from the motel. The sound of my engine would be distinguishable to anyone familiar with bikes, and Carrie is a fucking expert by now. It's not the only reason I'm being stealthy. I also believe she could be being held against her will. What if Cash placed a safeguard with them before he showed up back at the compound? There are too many factors in play and the sight of fear in Carrie's eyes was enough to tell me her situation is not the best.

I walk across the street, the area around me quiet with the night until I step onto the walkway leading to the motel office. The rooms are off to the left-hand side, and from that direction, heavy bass pours from a room. I'm not sure which one, but to me, it sounds like a clubhouse party. I'd walk over there to find out which room it is, but then I look down at the cut I'm wearing and think better of it. Maybe coming here alone was a bad idea.

The office is closed and there's no one sitting behind the desk, so I turn around and head toward the sounds of the party. I stick to the shadows, letting my hunter instincts take over as the music grows louder. It's odd that no one has complained and it's even more strange that security isn't banging the door down. Who the fuck runs this place and where are they?

I find a picnic table off to the side of the building, the trees around it giving it ample coverage while still providing a perfect view of all the units. I sit on the table, letting my feet rest on the bench, and pull out the joint I rolled earlier from my pocket. I can feel myself getting exhausted and I can't succumb to it yet.

Once the spliff is lit and my lighter is dropped back into my pocket, I lean back and wait. It pays off because a few minutes later, a door opens and the music becomes louder as it rushes from the opening. A few men step out, both of them in cuts, and they lean against the second-level railing to light cigarettes. I sit forward and squint at the name on the back of the cut nearest to me. Highway Knights. It sounds familiar but I don't know where their charter is out of. It's not here in Arizona though.

I can't tell what they're talking about but seeing other MCs here in Arizona is giving me a bad feeling. The second a club drove past our borders, we used to hear about it, and now we're in the dark. This can't be good. I pull out my phone to call Jaeger when the music spikes again. I look up to find the door open once more, but this time I nearly fall off the bench from the scene in front of me. There's Carrie, not a stitch of clothing on and looking completely wasted as she laughs up into the face of the very man we've been searching for.

Tazo Chino is here, in front of me.

Instead of calling Jaeger, I scroll through my phone book to a person I know is crazy enough to take my uncle on and hit send.

It rings a few times and then he answers with an irritated growl. "What?"

"We got him," I say to Malik Charles. "I found where Tazo is staying."

"Do not do anything on your own," he tells me, his voice low and dangerous. "Get the location and get your ass here to the Varga house." He hangs up just as my uncle guides Carrie back into the unit, the other bikers following close behind.

Carrie is working for Tazo.

THIS BODY IS
TEMPORARY
BUT THIS SOUL IS
ETERNAL
JAEGER

JAEGER

Being in that house and smelling her flowery scent everywhere was getting to me. I needed to be in a quiet place so I can decipher what the hell it is I found. I grip the old leather-bound book in my hand as I sit on the rock across from the Steel Dragons compound. It's comforting to see it even though I can no longer walk past its gate. I feel like I've lost the only home I've ever truly known and I've been floating aimlessly through the days.

The things I found in that closet were never meant to be seen again and Vic probably would've discarded them had his life not been cut short.

I don't know the contents of this book, but I would wager they're explosive if Vic had them hidden behind a false wall in his closet. There was a box of belongings but this was right there on the top of the pile and I grabbed it before Genni could come nosing around again. I locked the room behind me but I don't trust the cunning of my stepsister so I replaced the wall in the closet too.

My cheek smarts with just the thought of her and I grin as I reach up to touch the bruised flesh. She's toughened beyond anything our father or Quinton could have ever taught her, and even though she may hate me forever for it, I helped create that. This bruise is like a trophy.

I open the book to the first page and look at the name written in perfect cursive, slanted from corner to corner. *Wendy*. This book belonged to Genni's mother, Vic's first love. I always wondered why evidence of her around the house was sparse, and now I know why. He had it hidden away in the wall. Maybe his grief was so potent that he had to put away everything that reminded him of his wife, except Genni was an everyday reminder.

I turn the page and begin to read the writings of Wendy when she was younger than Genni is now. If I wasn't completely sober right now, I would think I was tripping.

Today is the day. I have been planning this forever and finally, Tazo has given in. I can leave the reservation and finally experience life beyond its confines. I'm not trapped here, but my sister wants me to marry so badly and I'm just not ready.

I may have used Tazo's obvious affection for me to my advantage and I would be lying if I said I wasn't worried how he will react when he realizes I don't actually return his feelings. He's an old man and I am too young to commit to anyone. But men are easily manipulated when they think with the little head between their legs. My sister will be devastated when she figures it all out, but I need her to believe I was sleeping with her husband so that she never tries to look for me. I need her to hate me.

Tazo has been exiled from the Steel Dragons but he's assured me he has created a new club. Hell's March. It sounds more badass than a bunch of dragons. He's being kicked off the reservation for trying to kill his own brother, and his revenge is taking me with him. I don't care what I am, as long as I leave and never look back.

I'm not a piece of meat to be sold to be paraded in front of men and my sister will learn that the hard way. A woman doesn't have to be married to be great.

Genni's mom is related to Tazo by marriage and therefore, Genni is related to Quinton by marriage too. I laugh out loud, the surprised sound carrying on the wind. I wonder how Quinton will react when he finds out and a part of me can't wait to watch the devastation on his face. There's no blood shared, like myself and Genni, but ours isn't the only taboo relationship now.

No, we don't have a fucking relationship.

I shake that thought from my head as I flick through the pages until I find the change in her penmanship. The cute little swirls she used to use have changed to deep scratches, the paper indented with each stroke of the pen.

I'm pregnant. I was only supposed to endure him for a year, those were the conditions, but he has a dark side to him when he drinks too much. I've fallen victim to his depraved fantasies a few times too many and now I'm carrying the consequence of my actions.

I left the reservation for a better life and I trusted Tazo to help give me it, but that was my greatest mistake. I was nothing more than a prized possession to be sold off to the highest bidder. That so happened to be Barrett, President of the Hell's March.

He's handsome enough with his jet-black hair and tall stature, but he's cold and detached.

I was seeing the end of the agreement, the light at the end of the tunnel, until I stared at the two lines that appeared on the test this morning. I need to get away from here but I can't do that with a child. I don't even want children, or to be married. I just wanted to be free.

My heart begins to pound in my chest as I read those words. Wendy is pregnant here. Is it with Genni? Is Genni Barrett's daughter? I find my answer when I flick through a few more pages to find red ink pressed so hard into the page, it's ripped in a few places.

He's taken me away from my baby and says he's saving me. There's no saving me, not after everything that's happened. I want to be with my child, I want to go back to Hell's March. This man, this new President, believes he's giving me a better life, but I don't want to live. Not without my child.

I can still hear the cries when I close my eyes at night, and when I wake up, I walk outside the cottage and stare out at the lake, wishing I could just continue walking until my lungs fill with water.

But I can't because one day we may be reunited. Me and my baby.

I should close this book right now and race back home. There's so much that Genni needs to know but I can't seem to stop. A few pages later and I can feel the despair with each jagged stroke of her pen.

He says I will never see my baby again. The child is tainted with the evil of Barrett, but he works himself between my thighs each night with the promise of filling me with another. He wants a Dragon to be his heir and he wants me to give it to him.

If I had any fight left, I would claw out his eyes and fill the sockets with the shards of my broken heart. But I don't. I no longer care about living or breathing, and I don't care when he fills me up with his release and leaves me again.

It's lonely here in this cottage with nowhere to run. He has me guarded by Dragons, all of them with guns and leering eyes. What they don't know is, I don't run because I've accepted this fate. It's my curse to live because of what I did to my sister and her family.

I stand as the breeze comes, flipping the pages to one of the last entries.

He's got his wish, I'm pregnant with a Dragon heir. Each time I feel it move inside of me, I want to fling myself into the water and let it claim us both. I can feel this little one's life will be difficult, filled with tragedy. Forced to live the sins of its parents.

He's tried to come visit me a few times since he found out about the baby, but I threatened to shoot him in the head if he ever tried to fuck me again. He knows I would find a way to make it come true, and I've been telling him he'll one day die with my bullet through his skull.

I never want to lay eyes on another biker, or smell the scent of worn leather again. I long for the reservation and the dinners I would prepare with my sister. I miss my family, and every day I endure this life because I deserve it for what I've done to them.

Victor says Tazo is still looking for me, and if I stay here in the cottage and behave, he'll never find me. I'm not scared of him anymore, once he finds out I'm pregnant with yet another child, I'll be nothing but used up goods.

The final page is only a few lines, but reading them makes me long for the girl I was raised to love as a sister, but craved as much more.

She has his eyes and hair, but her face is mine. I laugh into the empty cottage as I hold her in my arms because she's not the heir he wants and he'll never get another chance.

That small passage jars my memory and brings me back to a point where my entire world imploded as I stood listening to a conversation I was never supposed to hear. How could I ever forget that day?

"Those are going to kill you," Genni snaps.

"Your mother said it would be a bullet to my head," Dad says with a chuckle. "I believe her predictions."

I slap the book closed as an envelope slips out from the back. I bend to pick it up before the breeze takes it out of my reach. My ass meets the wooden bench as I lift the unsealed flap and pull out what looks to be a birth certificate.

The first name doesn't mean much to me but the last name is one I'm familiar with. Brown. Barrett Brown was the sadistic President of Hell's March who found himself at the wrong end of Genni's gun. Genni has an older sibling and I wonder if she's even met him or spoken to him.

I tuck the envelope back inside and tie up the leather straps of the diary to keep it together. After settling it safely back inside the compartment of my bike, I put my helmet back on and start the engine. I need to get home and tell her all of this because the picture of the past is becoming clearer. Victor Varga made the plans he did because he never wanted Genni to be caught in the crossfires of Barrett's revenge. She was the daughter of the woman who was his first, so says the Property of Cut sitting in that box.

No wonder Barrett was so eager to have Genni and it all makes sense why he made that bogus deal with me for her. He defiled the girl who looked like his one-time Old Lady and left her for dead as revenge against the man who took his Old Lady from him.

If only Victor Varga told me the entire story from the beginning, I would've understood. I would've protected her at any cost, but instead, he was too afraid of what the truth would do to his reputation. His ego earned him a bullet to the head and put his daughter in the hands of the very man he fought to keep her from.

I still can't believe he kidnapped Genni's mother, it seems so out of character for Vic, but then again, if she looked like Genni, I can understand the temptation to have her. I fight it every day.

The driveway is full when I return to the house and my heart jams up into my throat when I realize they're having a meeting without me. Of course they are, I'm nothing but an Exiled. I contemplate backing out when another bike engine sounds on the street. A few minutes later, Montez pulls up with his sister, a passenger with him.

"What's going on?" I ask as I scramble off my bike. I left her here alone, could she have been taken again? Maybe by Barrett's son who is only finishing what his father started? "Where's Genni?"

"She's inside," Montez answers as he gives me a cautious look. "She called this meeting."

"I have information too." Delia gives me a pointed look and I nod, knowing I made the right decision asking for her help.

I'm about to back out of the driveway when the front door opens and Genni stands there in a pair of dark jeans and a white tank top, her pierced, pebbled nipples on display.

"That's a crime," Delia huffs out as she gets off Diego's bike, then turns to look at me. "Imagine being that hot." Her knowing grin has my already hard cock jerking in my pants.

"Jaeger!" Genni calls out. "Get in here! I've been trying to get ahold of you for the past hour!"

She has? I watch as Delia and Diego walk through the door, the latter leaning in to kiss her before he passes. I cut the engine of my bike and take off my helmet, her eyes still boring into me from the front door. I pull my phone out of the pocket of my leather jacket and swipe open the screens, seeing notifications for her missed calls. *Little Sister* is what I have her saved as and my throat clenches with emotion. It's been a while since she's called or messaged me and seeing her contact info there is reminding me of everything that's changed.

"Jaeger!" she calls out again. "We need to get started."

I'm holding them up, but there's something I need to change and it can't wait. I delete Little Sister and quickly change it to Princess, feeling slightly better about it.

I get off the bike and grab the book from the compartment before making my way to her as she crosses her arms under her perfect tits. "Took you long enough."

"We need to talk first," I murmur as I stand in front of her, my body aching to close the last few inches. "Alone."

"What is it?" Her eyes shine with worry as she looks into mine and I reach out to tuck a piece of her hair that's escaped her messy bun behind her ear.

"It's in our parents' room." Her eyes harden with realization and she gives me a nod, then leads me into the house.

I walk by the kitchen with my head down as I normally do, but the chatter coming from it has me pausing to look inside. The table is filled as everyone talks, and I can't help but think Ma would've loved that. I've been avoiding it because of the horrific memories but I need to let that go and remember the hundreds of others of us as a family in that room.

Quinton's eyes meet mine and he gives me a subtle nod, the look of concern evident in those hazel depths. He can feel it too. We're on the cusp of war and I'm fucking terrified of losing the one thing I once gave away so frivolously. Her scent swirls around my head as I turn away from the kitchen and find her standing at the base of the stairs, waiting for me. I take off my boots and motion for her to lead the way, then follow her to the second level.

"I'm fucking scared to find out what you've uncovered," she confesses in a whispered voice. "I don't want to hate him."

She stops in front of their door as I stand beside her, reaching into my pocket with my free hand to grab the key. Her eyes skip down to the diary in my other hand, her brows crinkling together with confusion. "You'll have to separate the man who was the President of the Steel Dragons from the man who was your father. They are not the same, Genni." It's the only advice I can give her and I hope she has better success with it than I have.

I open the door and motion her in first. She heads to the bed and sits as I hold out the diary to her. "This is now yours. Read it, but first, there's a box of things in the closet." I head into the closet and pull down the wall to drag out the box, the Hell's March cut sitting folded right on top. I carry it out to her and place it at her feet before bending forward and placing a kiss to her forehead. This is going to be a hard blow to withstand and I need her to understand that even though we have bad blood between us, this is something she can lean on me for.

"I left something on the bed for you too. I don't know if you want it or not, or if you'll want to burn it after reading this, but it's yours. It was always meant to be yours." She turns to find our father's cut lying on the bed. The worn leather cracked and faded in spots from age. There on the right breast, I sewed back the President's badge I ripped from my damaged cut and removed Vic Varga from beneath it. If she wants it, I'll sew her name beneath it.

"Thank you," she whispers as her fingers run over the leather, the tremor in her hand evident.

I leave the room as she opens the leather-bound ties of the diary and her gasp is like a shard of glass to my heart. She's in for a wild ride.

I close the door and head back downstairs, the sounds of chatter dying as my footsteps fill the space.

As soon as I walk into the kitchen, I'm pounced on by Malik. "Where is she? What have you done now?"

"I didn't do anything but find the last of Vic's secrets. She's learning about them now, so we'll wait for her before we begin any discussions." I lean against the wall just outside the kitchen as silence descends over us.

I'm ready to bury everything.

GENEVIEVE
BMW Motorrad Milano

GENEVIEVE

I don't know how long I've been sitting here because I've lost all sense of time. My mother's diary sits beside me on the bed, along with Davis Brown's birth certificate. Davis, Barrett's son and my Sergeant at Arms, is my half-brother. Now that I think about it, he and I do look similar.

My father's cut lies at my feet, having been thrown there the moment I learned he kidnapped my mother to save her, but became a monster to her instead. Reading about how he forced her to become pregnant in hopes she would bear him an heir made me irrational with rage.

Now that I'm coming down, I try to remember the words Jaeger said. I need to separate my father from the President of the Steel Dragons, but it's so fucking hard. He wasn't a rapist, not the man I knew. He loved my mother, it was there in his features whenever he spoke of her, and he cared about Claire, he treated her like a queen. So this man I read about in my mother's diary is a complete stranger.

Maybe he changed when he became a father. I've heard stories of men saying that happened to them and it's the only thing I can think of that even remotely explains his behavior during my mother's time and then mine. I do believe he took her from Barrett to save her and then became enamored himself. My mother was a beautiful woman and even without knowing her personality, I would bet she was irresistible, but none of that gives a man permission to force himself on a woman, and that's exactly what he did.

He did to my mother what Barrett did to me. Sounds like a

justified revenge. The bile rushes from my stomach without much warning and I expel it all over the cut at my feet. My father wanted me to be President of the Steel Dragons so that I would be given the best chance of avoiding Barrett's wrath. Instead, his scheming only served to hand me over to him on a silver platter.

What happened to me in that basement was a repercussion of my father's actions in the past. *Karma.*

The bedroom door slowly opens, the creak hauling me out of my sickening thoughts. I look up to find Delia standing there, her curly hair is up in a messy bun on top of her head and her face looks drawn, like she hasn't slept in a while.

"Can I come in?" she asks, her voice soft and soothing, but she's neither of those things, is she? Delia is also someone who hid her life from me.

"As long as everything you say is the fucking truth from now on, Delia," I warn, my words raspy from the bile scorching my throat.

"I will tell you everything you need to know about me, but there are limits to that," she explains as I wave her in. "What's happening?" She looks down at my father's cut with my vomit pooling on top of it, and then to the diary open on the bed.

"What do you do for a living?" I ask her, avoiding her question. She sits on the bed beside me and expels a breath.

"I'm an assassin for hire," she reveals and looks down at her clasped hands. "The Viper. That's what I'm called. I like to use poison but I also have a sick love for guns," she explains further.

"I asked you in the basement to teach me how to kill someone, and you said you didn't do that," I remind her. "You lied to me."

"I did." She nods and looks at me with eyes filled with regret. "You were my first real friend and I was scared that if you knew what I did, you would become like everyone else. I wanted to be normal, to have a normal relationship with you, even if it was for only a little while.

I knew I wouldn't be able to hide it from you forever, but those first few weeks meant everything to me."

"I wouldn't have judged you, Delia." I shake my head as I rub a hand over my throat. "You could've helped me—"

"No," she spits out, the word ripped from her mouth. "No. I wasn't going to teach you how to kill because I knew you needed to heal first. Trauma manifests differently in people. Take for instance me, the girl who enjoyed kicking bullies' asses and had a fascination with death. My trauma manifested into something dark, and now I need to do what I'm doing to avoid becoming a monster. Your trauma was forcing you to become stronger, to be the best version of yourself and you deserved that. I could tell that moment in the basement would determine how you coped and I wasn't going to lead you down a darker path. I wish I had someone do the same for me when I was struggling in the dark." She brushes the tears off her cheeks and chuckles softly. "There are people who would kill to find out what it is that makes me tick."

"What turned you into an assassin?" I'm completely engrossed in her story, knowing it's taking a lot out of her to tell me. If this friendship is as important to her as it is to me, then she needs to be honest with me.

"My mother's suicide, then my father's suicide when he found her." Her words are filled with anguish, each syllable laced with agony. I don't push her further, instead, I wrap an arm around her shoulders and rest my head against hers.

"Why do the kids of the MCs suffer the most?" I ask as she scoffs sarcastically.

"Because we carry on the burdens long after they die blissfully, never reaping the consequences of their actions." She says it so perfectly, everything I'm feeling, and I straighten.

"Delia. I need to be the one to end what my mother started. I have to be the one who goes to Tazo." She twists her head so fast to look at me, her denial ready to spill when I continue, "Don't you see? It's me he wants and with the training that you and the others have given me, it could be me who ends it."

"What did your mother start?" She tips her head to the side as I give her the rundown of the contents in the diary, including the fact that Davis is my half-brother. "Shit," she hisses when I'm through. "That's fucking crazy."

"Do you understand why I should be the one to go to him? He's been looking to get revenge on my father since the day he stepped in front of his bullet meant for Quinton's dad. The bad blood between them just continued to grow and he won't go away until someone pays for what was done to him." I stand, ready to head downstairs and tell the others my plan. Then I grab the diary as Delia stands too, her hand scrubbing down her face.

"You think you should die for the idiocy of those men?" She looks at me like I've lost my damn mind, and it makes me laugh, which only has her eyebrows reaching for the ceiling.

"No, Delia. I'm going to make sure he dies for what he did to my mother, and I won't be alone." She deflates a little with relief but stiffens again when my hand lands on her shoulder. "The Viper will be there with me."

"Fuck," she grumbles.

"So you're going to kill him?" Quinton asks as he leans on the table. "It'll be nearly impossible with the Highway Knights there with him."

We've all brought together our information. Quinton with Tazo's location and seeing the Highway Knights, Delia with more information on the sadistic behavior of the Highway Knights and what they like to do to women and children, and me with the diary and Davis' birth certificate. I've told them my plan and none of them thinks it's a good idea. Well, Jaeger hasn't said anything yet, he's still standing outside of the kitchen with his arms crossed over his chest.

"I want to do it for my mother. To finally put her soul to rest." Malik is notably quiet, his only opinion was no when I suggested I head over to the motel to confront Tazo.

"Can't we do it together?" Diego asks as he runs his fingers along the scruff on his chin. "You and my sister are no match for the manpower he has over there."

"That's the whole point. I want him to believe I'm coming to him after learning of my father's actions and offering to join forces with him to take out Jaeger and the Steel Dragons. He doesn't know about his exile." I turn to look at Jaeger, who still hasn't moved from his spot against the wall, but he's at least watching me. "Delia will wait for my signal, having killed his sentries, and come to get me out."

"You think you can pull this off?" Laith asks her, his eyes filled with doubt.

"It doesn't matter if she can or not. It's an order from your President." *Finally, he speaks up.* "It's your job as a club to make sure you support her in other areas. Be prepared for war because that's what's going to happen if Tazo is assassinated."

"I'm going to call Los Dientes Afilados for backup. They can be here in the next few days." Delia stands from the table, grabbing her phone out of her sweater pocket.

This is becoming all too real and I'm not going to be the type of President who sits back and watches her brothers battle for her. If I am to run these clubs then I have to be willing to die for them.

A yawn rips from my mouth, telling me I've barely had enough rest to do this tomorrow. I push back from the table and stand, leaning my hands on the surface. "I need to sleep, but we can reconvene here in the morning. Diego and Malik, please get the March ready, and please don't say anything to Davis about what was said here tonight. I want to tell him myself."

"Of course," Diego murmurs as he, too, stands and comes around to my side of the table. "We'll have the brothers ready for your call. I'll be back here in the morning." He grabs my face with both hands and steals the breath from my mouth in a soul-searing kiss. Malik is next, and by the look in his eyes, he's feeling murderous. He keeps his thoughts to himself though, which is a shock, and wraps my hair around his fist to drag my face to his. He still smells like me and the scent has my core pulsing with the memories of what we did earlier.

They're both gone just as quickly, their bike engines filling the night with their roaring purrs. Next, I turn to Quinton and Laith, both of them looking at me with similar expressions on their faces. They're terrified of leaving me to do what I'm demanding and yet they don't have a choice.

"I need you two to get the Dragons ready. My Vice and Sergeant at Arms need to be a united force to lead them. Can you do that for me?" I can tell they both want to beg me to reconsider, but Laith is the first out of his seat.

"Whatever you need, you know we'll make it happen." He gives me a sweet kiss, such a contrast to his brother, and it makes me feel so damn lucky to have them both. "I'll see you in the morning?"

I nod as my throat thickens with emotion, making speaking difficult. Then I watch him leave, his cut moving with each stride. I need them to be a team because their strength together will be invincible.

"I don't deserve it," Quinton says, drawing my attention as his chair scrapes along the tile. He stands and comes toward me, my first love, the one who will forever own my innocence. "But I need you to promise me you'll come back. I need more time to earn back your trust. I need more time to show you I love you." My breath gets trapped in my throat as he stands in front of me, his hazel eyes pleading. "I fucked up too many times. I was never worthy of your love, but I think I can be. I just need time to show you that. Genni, please promise me."

I rise to my tippy-toes and wrap my arms around his neck, pressing our foreheads together. "I promise," I whisper. "I've been waiting for you to show me how you feel. I've been waiting for so long."

He swoops in to seal his mouth to mine, his lips so familiar as if they've been imprinted on mine from our very first kiss. His fingers slip into my hair, the tips pulling me closer as his tongue seeks entrance to my mouth. I kiss him like I did that very first time in the warehouse, with love and a little trepidation. Quinton has the power to decimate my heart and I would be lying if I said I wasn't scared. He feels different, yet completely the same, and it makes my heart swell for him.

He pulls away and turns on his heel, unable to meet my eyes as he leaves the house, the closing of the door making me turn my head to the fifth man who's carved out a piece of my soul, but he's no longer here. I should've known better than to think he would be the next one to stand in front of me and beg for my safe return.

This is Jaeger after all.

Calloused hands drag along my thighs, sweeping my T-shirt upward. They're smoother than Malik's and Laith's, but rougher than Diego's. Quinton could've come back to send me off with a proper goodbye, but he's serious about being worthy of it first.

That leaves one person, and even though I've fully woken up, I'm afraid to open my eyes. The second I do, I fear he'll retreat like a skittish cat. We've been playing this game of touch and regret, and I don't want to wake up and have his touch turn quickly to disgust. I want to enjoy it just a little while longer.

"You're awake," he husks out as his mouth nears my stomach, his breath coasting over the skin as his tongue dips into my belly button.

I cautiously open my eyes and lift myself up to my elbows to peer down at Jaeger, his dark hair tousled over his forehead as his black eyes watch me with intensity. "What are you doing?" My voice is raspy with sleep as he trails his tongue upward, moving my T-shirt until it rests over my face, obscuring my view of him as he pushes me back down to the bed. "Hey."

"Don't move that," he warns as his fingers run along my panties, the tips pressing into the damp fabric. "I can feel how badly you want this, sis. The moment you disobey, I'm stopping."

"Okay." My voice breaks as I sink into the shield my shirt provides. He's giving me an out to feel him without the visual reminder of who he is. I've loved Jaeger as my brother, but that shattered the night he killed my father and handed me off to the enemy. It's broken our relationship down to the foundation and we're faced with two options: rebuild our sibling connection or forge this sharp blade of lust in the hottest depths of hell.

I'm going for option two, and I think he agrees when his fingers slip inside the waistband of my thong and rips it from my body, hauling a squeal from my mouth.

The sting of the fabric cutting into my skin is instantly soothed when his nose runs along the seam of my pussy, his deep inhale bringing heat to my cheeks. "I've dreamed of this," he murmurs, the hot breath of his confession mingling with my arousal. "I'm too ashamed to admit for how long."

My stomach flips as my hips lift, bringing him closer to my core, begging for his mouth. "Jaeger," I moan as he chuckles, running his nose over my wet flesh once more.

"I know you as well as I know myself, and I needed to come in here and give you a taste of what we could be, just to make sure you come back." I spread my legs wider as his shoulders settle under my thighs and his fingers open my pussy.

"Are we really doing this, *brother*?" I taunt him as his laugh hits my thighs a moment before his lips do. It's a gentle press of his mouth to my skin, but it sends a current of electricity straight to my clit.

His answer is to flatten his tongue against the entrance of my pussy and drag it in a slow, agonizing path to my clit. I scream his name at the sudden touch as my hips buck off the bed once more. "You taste like my greatest sin, Genni," he rasps, the sound of his voice filled with awe. "I'm ready to go to Hell for just one sip."

I wish I could reach down and grab his head to guide him exactly where I want him, but my shirt is preventing me from using my arms so I let them rest above my head on the pillow instead. "Jaeger…" This time my voice is filled with warning as he chuckles again, pressing an arm over my lower stomach.

"Hang on, baby, I'm about to eat you alive."

His mouth suctions to my clit as he uses his tongue to circle the hardened nub, making stars dance behind my eyelids. When I squirm from the overstimulation, he presses that arm down harder and continues his assault.

Jaeger slips his finger inside of me, curving it to drag along that sensitive spot as he lashes my clit with his tongue. My pussy begins to pulse with the telltale signs of my release, and I let myself go, coming hard on Jaeger's tongue. I squeeze around his fingers as he laps up every drop of my orgasm and then he pulls away, taking his warmth with him. I shake through the aftershocks of the intense orgasm when he pulls my shirt back down.

He's standing over me beside my bed, fully dressed but looking pretty proud of himself, his mouth and chin glistening with my release. "I know what your plan is, it's something I would've done too, but I can't let you do it alone. I called Delia and she'll be here in a few minutes." My heart pounds behind my rib cage as I stare at him, unable to form an excuse. He's right, I planned to leave in the very early morning before anyone could try to talk me out of it. "Be careful and remember,"—he leans down over me, his face so fucking close—"come back so we can finish what we started."

"Okay," I whisper as the front door slams shut downstairs.

"Time to go," he says and heads out of my room, never giving me a backward glance.

There's no way I'm not killing Tazo and getting my ass home if that's what's waiting for me.

PART TWO

Present

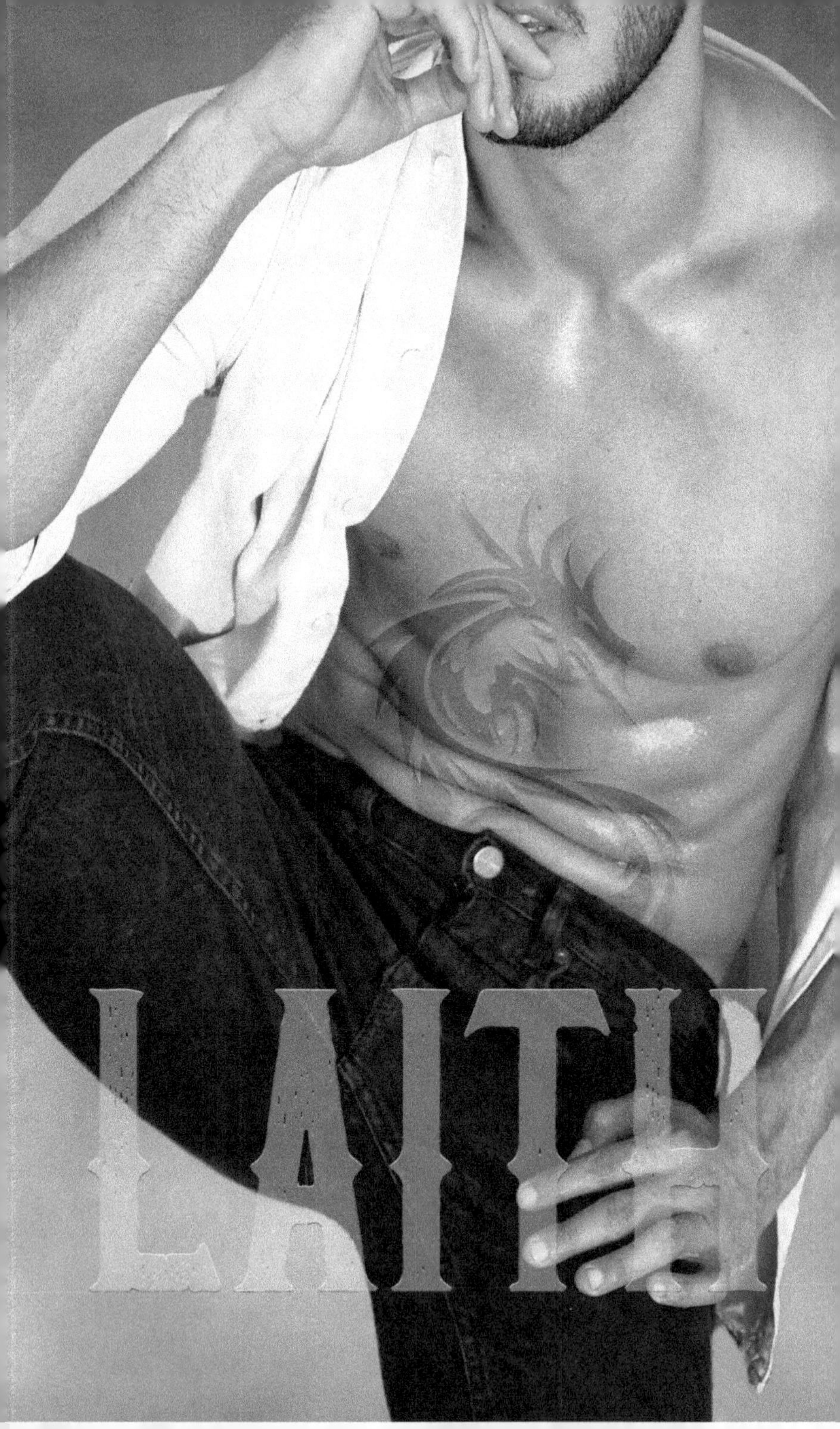

LAITH

CHAPTER TEN

I asked Delia a few days ago about the pastries Genni likes, and even though we are literally on the brink of war, I want her to have the things she enjoys. Our time here isn't guaranteed, even more so now that we have death breathing down our necks.

It's still early, the sun having barely risen, but I can't sleep anyway. The clubhouse seems empty without her, or maybe it's just me. I'm desolate without her touch and scent. I've fallen harder than I ever thought I would, and it doesn't even bother me that I have to share her. Half of her men are my enemies, sworn enemies, but I will fight alongside them to keep her protected. That's how far gone I am.

I'm not going to deny myself the person who makes me feel something for the first time in a long while. She's it for me and I don't care that she's not bound to just me. It's clear that the others each give her something different, and the way she is with me is unique. When we're together, it's like I'm her only.

It's not for everyone to understand and that's a good thing because our relationship isn't for everyone. It's for us.

I turn into the driveway and cut the engine, seeing Jaeger's bike and Genni's side-by-side. It was nice of her to let him keep it, even though he was exiled, and the fact that he's still allowed to be in Arizona is telling of her character. Genni's not always ruthless, or unnecessarily cruel to prove her position. She knows when to be compassionate and when to pull the trigger. She is the perfect President.

The house is dark still and I wince when I realize how loud my bike must have been. Hopefully, she's had enough rest because she'll need it for later. I hate the thought of her confronting Tazo, but I'm comforted knowing we'll all be there. No one will hurt her again, I'll kill before I ever let that happen.

Pulling off my helmet, I hop off the bike to place it on the seat, then open the side compartment to pull out the pastries. When the butter and sugar scents hit my nostrils, I groan as my stomach rumbles. I don't know when I last had a proper meal, and I would assume the same for the rest of us. It's been full-throttle since Tazo held a gun to Quinton's head and it's not showing any signs of slowing.

The last time we had anything remotely dangerous happen was when we had to fight the March for territory, the fight that had got Quinton's dad killed. Just the thought of casualties has me looking up to the second story of the house and wishing we had the means to keep her out of harm's way. The only way that could ever be accomplished though would be to defeat our enemies, and we need to listen to her plan to do it.

The front door opens as I step up to the porch and I find Jaeger in a pair of low-slung sweatpants, his chest bare and his hair dripping with sweat. It's clear he was working out.

"Come on in," he growls as he holds the door open wider. "We might as well get this over with."

"Get what over with?" I ask as I walk past him and into the kitchen.

Setting the box on the counter, I turn to find him leaning against the wall just outside of the room. I noticed this last night too. Jaeger has been avoiding coming into the kitchen. I know what happened here, and in my own experience, trauma builds a wall to help us avoid a room stinking of death. Especially when that stink was once your mother.

"Genevieve's not here." I blink a few times as the words reverberate in my head. I couldn't have heard that right.

"Say that again?" I step up to the sink and begin opening cabinets, looking for plates.

"She's not here, Laith," he reiterates as I finally find the cabinet I need.

"What do you mean? Where is she?" I turn once more and face him while holding a small stack of plates.

His eyes skip from the ceramic in my hands to my face, concern for the dishes clear in their depths. "Put those down." A sudden wave of anxiety hits me and I can't seem to suck in air as I place the plates on the table. Then I grip the back of a chair as I prepare myself for what he's about to say. "She left about an hour ago with Delia to confront Tazo."

His words make my head spin as I storm past him while grabbing my phone from my pocket. "You didn't think to call us as soon as you found out?" I bellow, my voice bouncing off the empty walls as he grabs my bicep, forcing me to face him. The urge to punch the smug look off his face is strong, but I still have some warped sense of respect for the man who was my President for a short time and also my brother for many years.

"She wanted it this way. We have to respect her. You can't storm off and haul her back. It'll make her look weak to both of her clubs." I ignore him and shrug out of his hold as I bring up my brother's contact. He's just crazy enough to burn this house down with Jaeger in it.

"Just because we fuck the same girl doesn't mean we're besties." His sleepy voice fills my ears, taking away some of the ringing.

"You need to get over here to the Varga house and bring everyone else. Genni is missing and Jaeger here knows exactly where she is." His breathing picks up on the other end of the line as rustling fills the speaker.

"Tell him I'm about to redecorate the fucking walls. I think blood red will look nice." Then he hangs up as I slowly turn to face Jaeger, his face filled with boredom as he leans against the wall.

"My brother seems to have outdone you with the crazy. Be prepared for him to cut you open," I warn as Jaeger rolls his fucking eyes.

"She left all her pussy men a note so you wouldn't burn the town down for her." He points to an envelope on the kitchen counter. I must've missed it when I was looking for the plates. "Her plan is a good one. If we all went with her, I'm sure we would've fucked it up."

"You sent her into a lion's den!" I snap, my body rigid with anger as I try to restrain myself from strangling him. "She's alone!"

"She's a fucking lioness!" he screams back, making me snap my mouth shut as he shoves off the wall to stand rigidly in front of me. "Genni can handle her-damn-self! And she's not alone. She has Delia with her. The Viper." I can't fault him for not giving a fuck, he gave her up once already. It's us I blame, the four men who claim to care so much about her. We left her here with him and this is the consequence.

"If anything happens to her…" I trail off as my words get trapped in my throat. I can't even think of that right now because I need to come up with a plan. By the time everyone gets here, we won't have much time to discuss things. She's already in the clutches of a madman who was once obsessed with her mother. The woman she looks so much like.

My heart beats against my rib cage as I haul open the front door and stagger outside to drag in a lungful of cool air. We were so stupid to leave her here. None of us was the wiser last night as she practically shoved us out the door. No one suspected the woman who had done this before when she left the March compound to confront Jaeger.

I turn to look over my shoulder at Jaeger, who's watching me with a blank expression on his face. She ran to him too. This is her savior's voice, the one telling her she's disposable but we're not.

"We don't fucking deserve her." Turning away from him, I growl into the rising sun.

"Now you're beginning to understand," Jaeger mumbles as he steps outside beside me. "But it's time we became worthy."

DIEGO

DIEGO

I'm already out of bed and nearly dressed by the time Malik hangs up the call with his brother. We ended up in Genevieve's bed together last night, both of us missing her but not able to find the words to express it. It felt good to have his body heat and breathe in her lingering scent on the pillows.

The ominous feeling I had leaving the Varga house last night now makes sense. She was planning to leave in the middle of the night and take my sister with her. "I'm going to kill them both," I snarl as I grab my cut off the end of the bed and shrug it on. "I'm going to wake up Ajani because I swear they were the last to go to sleep last night."

"Are you trying to say the Viper has a curfew?" Malik scoffs as he gets dressed. "She comes and goes as she pleases."

"How are you not freaking out?" I turn on him as he pulls on his cut, shaking his head with a small smile. The sight of his smug face has my hands curling into fists. "She's with the man who sold her mother to a psycho with plans to retrieve her after a few years."

"Slayer has been through worse men, Montez. Her brother handed her over to said psycho to be tortured and she survived. She's faced down monsters, fuck, she does it with us daily. She's not our Old Lady, a female to protect, she's our President." He slips on his boots and brushes by me, his saunter lacking any urgency.

"You literally said you would paint the walls of that house with Jaeger's blood," I throw back at him, my hands brushing through my hair. "I didn't say she wasn't capable. I just hate the secrets."

"Finger painting in Jaeger's blood is a delightful Sunday activity." He gives me a cheeky grin over his shoulder before stepping out of the room and heading toward the kitchen. "And you know as well as I do that presidents have their secrets. They do not have to inform their minions of their plans, just our parts in them," he continues as I follow behind him. "Call Jones and get eyes on the motel Quinton told us about. Then let's put the boys on standby. We may ride out today."

We find Ajani in the kitchen, drinking a coffee as I send over a text to Jones, knowing the fucker rarely sleeps. "When did she leave?" I look at Ajani.

He looks at me over the rim of his cup, his eyes heavy with exhaustion. "Around two hours ago," he mumbles before taking a sip. "I tried to stop her but she said it was for Genevieve and I wasn't going to stand in the way of that."

It's come to my attention that Ajani and Delia are closer than they lead on. He's my best friend and I try my best to ignore it because I want Delia to be happy, but I fear for his heart. My sister has tried to run from her demons until they overtook her, and now she revels in their darkness. She's not Old Lady material and I don't know how to tell him that.

"Thanks, brother," Malik says as he pats him on the shoulder and takes the coffee cup from his hand to sip. "Oh, that's vile." He winces and hands it back as Ajani chuckles.

"I'll head over to the compound and have the brothers ready on standby. With only one patient in the last couple of days, Medical has been quiet. I need a little action." The glint of excitement shines from his eyes and I would be right there with him if it wasn't because of my girl. "You've seen her at her worst and you've witnessed her growth to who she is today. It's normal to be worried, but Malik is right, she can handle herself," Ajani affirms with a nod. "And she does have your sister with her. I can only imagine the carnage that will surround them."

"Let's head over to the house," Malik cuts in as he heads for the front door. "I want in on this carnage. Slayer is being a hog."

I give Ajani an exasperated look as he chuckles and takes

another sip of his coffee. "She'll be okay, Diego. This is what she was trained for."

We arrive at the Varga house about fifteen minutes later and my stomach tightens when I find Genevieve's bike sitting in the driveway next to Jaeger's. I know they took Delia's car though, which still has a tracker on it from the last time she was taken. Jones says it's parked on a side street not too far from the motel and he's promised to keep an eye on things. There hasn't been much movement at the motel, but he's got two of his drones flying overhead. So if anything pops off, we'll know about it. That has to be enough for now. She's our President and we can't fuck with her plans unless she commands us to do so.

We head inside to find Laith pacing a line into the kitchen floor, setting off the urge inside of me to do the same. Malik's hand lands on my shoulder, as if he can sense my inner turmoil, and he gives it a squeeze. "Little brother, is this a new line dance you're practicing?" he teases Laith. I can't help it, a grin works its way along my mouth as Laith faces us with a relieved look.

"We need to ride out now. I told Quinton to get over here as soon as possible but he's taking too long." Laith rushes forward, the relief brief as his features harden with panic and the vein in his neck nearly vibrates with his heart rate.

"Where's Jaeger?" Malik asks as Laith points to the ceiling.

"He's been up there all morning. He won't help her, he thinks we should wait for her to do what she's got planned instead of interfering. It's like he truly doesn't give a shit about her." Laith's eyes fill with fire as his jaw pulses before he resumes his pacing.

"He has a point," Malik says before I begin to pace alongside Laith. "She's the President. Would we have been this worked up for Barrett, or in your case, Vic?"

"It's not the same and you know it!" Laith exclaims, stopping his pacing and stalling me in my tracks. "She's our—"

"I know," I reassure him with a nod. "She is our girl, but she's also our President. We need to come up with a careful plan. One where we're there for backup if she needs it, but also gives us the assurance that she's safe." I can relate to his panic. I was feeling the same this morning when we received his call, but now, I'm trying to envision it as a club tactic.

"Okay." He thinks over my words before expelling his breath and then sits at the table in front of a box of pastries, his face landing in his hands.

"Is this for us?" Malik asks as he lifts the lid. "Well damn, little bro, you shouldn't have." He reaches in and grabs a pastry, taking a large bite and leaving icing powder around his mouth.

"I didn't. They were for Genni," Laith grumbles as he reaches in next and grabs one. "Not for you."

"Well, blessed be to Jesus for providing me with Slayer's breakfast. More for me if she doesn't want any," he says around a full mouth as Laith gives him a scathing look.

Just when I think I'll have to push my way between them, I hear the distant rumble of a bike on the street and exhale a breath. Finally, Chino is here.

Thuds on the stairs have me poking my head out of the kitchen to find Jaeger completely dressed and looking freshly showered. He has on a leather jacket, the sides bowing with what I know are guns, and a pair of sunglasses.

"Where are you going?" I ask as he turns to look at me, his brow curving over his glasses.

"Last I checked, I was exiled. I don't answer to a club and I don't need to be doing club shit. You guys enjoy your little mass in my kitchen and be thankful I'm letting it happen here." Then he opens the door and slams it shut, disappearing outside.

"Was that Jaeger?" Laith calls from the kitchen as Quinton's bike pulls into the driveway.

"Yeah," I answer as I continue to eye the door with shock. "He left. Said this is club business and he is no longer a part of it."

"He ain't wrong," Malik adds.

No, I guess he isn't.

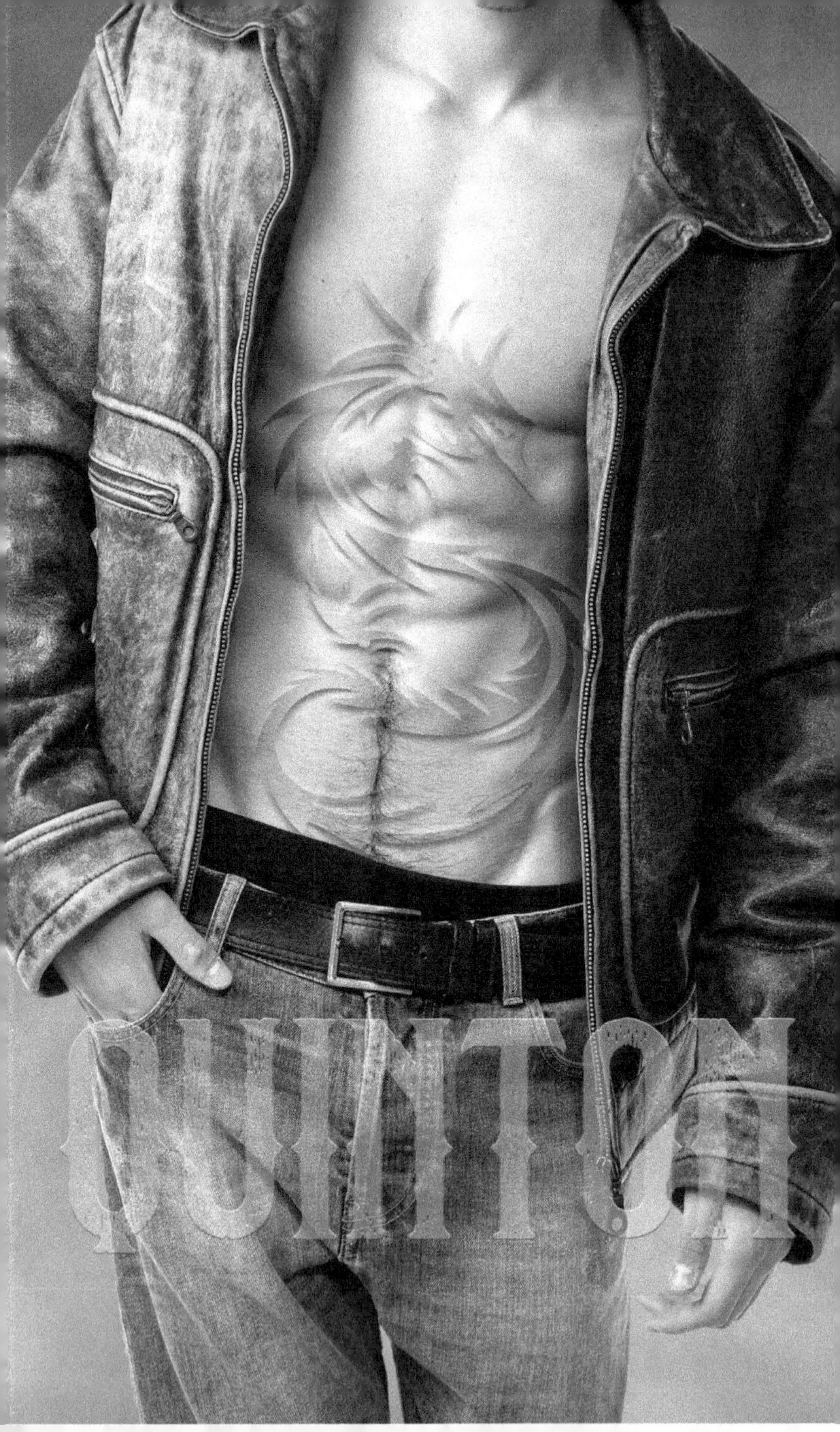
QUINTON

QUINTON

I pull into Jaeger's driveway to find him coming out of the house, looking like he's heading out. I park beside his bike and cut the engine as he stands in front of me, his glasses hiding his eyes.

"Are you leaving?" I ask him, aghast. "Your sister could be in danger."

"She's not my sister, Quinton, just like she's not your cousin, okay?" I swallow down the retort of it being through marriage, but he is in the same situation. Kind of. "And yeah, I got something to do."

"We need to move Genni out of Tazo's hands." I stare at him, trying to find the man I once saw as my brother. Has he slipped this far?

"Sounds like club business." He. Fucking. Shrugs. "I got shit to take care of. Your brothers are waiting for you inside."

"I stood by you!" I scream as I get off my bike and throw my helmet to the grass. "I stood by you when you gave her away, when you shot Vic, when you were a fucking asshole. Not once did I waver. You were my blood!" The anger swells inside of me, the force of it stealing my rationality. I can't believe he's become this shell of the man he once was. There's no amount of excuses that could make him become this monster.

Genni is the only family he has left.

"That all sounds like a you problem." He straps on his helmet as he straddles his bike and then guns the engine before pulling out of the driveway and speeding down the street without a single backward glance.

"Chino!" Laith calls out, but I can't turn my eyes away from Jaeger's retreating form. My chest ceases as I drag in a breath, the air getting trapped in my lungs as my stomach sours. He just turned his back on me like I was nothing, as if he had somewhere better to be than here. "Come on, man! We need to get to Genni!" The sound of her name snaps me out of my thoughts, but it doesn't relieve the anger. As soon as my girl is back safe with us, I'm taking care of the exiled Dragon.

I hurry inside to find everyone crowded in the kitchen and around Malik's cell as they speak to someone on FaceTime. "It's their tech guy, Jones," Laith explains. "He's got drones on the motel."

"Some of us should head over," I say, making Malik and Diego turn their heads toward me.

"That could set him off." Jones' voice crackles through the phone. "Tazo's got sentries set up around the perimeter of the motel and the surrounding streets. He's also smart about not coming outside. He knows we've got eyes on him. It makes sense that the girls would be in conjoining rooms."

"Chino, what room was he in when you last saw him?" Laith turns a laptop around to face me, the color a bright pink. Must be Genni's. On the screen is a street view version of the motel, the picture pixelated.

"There." I point to a part of the screen. "Second floor."

"Did you see that, Jones?" Malik asks the redhead on the screen who has a burning cigarette hanging from his lips.

"Got it." The movement of his lips has a large ash spilling from his smoke as he squints his eyes and taps furiously on his keyboard. "I have a drone hovering in that spot. No movement, but that doesn't mean shit. I'll let you know if anyone goes in or out. Stand by in the meantime."

The screen goes dark as my heart pounds in my ears. "Is he telling us to stay here and wait?" I ask with confusion. "We need to rush over there! He could've… What if he's…?" I can't help it when a choked sob tumbles from my mouth. "She's already been defiled because of me,

I can't let it happen again."

"Do you think that would kill her? Do you think she's that weak? Barrett fucking her for days wasn't what nearly killed her. It was the no food or water for over a week. She's stronger than any of us and she can endure anything." Malik's words are shocking as I stare at him and the expression of pure pride on his face, my mouth hanging open. He can't mean it would be okay if she's raped again.

"What he means is,"—Diego steps up beside him, patting a hand to his chest—"As long as she's alive, everything else can be dealt with. I don't think he wants to kill her, he's had plenty of opportunities to do so."

"Like the time he brought me to the compound with a gun to my head, AND YOU DIDN'T TAKE THE SHOT! He could have been dead right now! We wouldn't be dealing with this." Everything falls silent around us, the sounds of our breathing the only noise.

"I couldn't kill him." He and Malik share a look before he turns back to face me. "We need to know who he's working with. If he dies, that information dies with him."

"There are more than just Tazo and his little minions," Malik snarls. "He runs bigger things and we had plans to topple that tower long before Slayer came around. We can't deviate now."

"She'll come back with the info we need, then we'll start burning down his empire from the bottom up." Diego gives me a smile before he turns to speak to Laith. Malik keeps his eyes on me though, his knowing look making my shoulders slump.

"This must've always been the plan, for her to go to him on her own terms. She knew the risks, but we were all supposed to discuss it ahead of time. I would've preferred an extraction plan if need be, but she one-upped us and took Delia with her. It just means we have to have a backup plan for her, just in case. She left because she knew we'd be capable of getting her out if she's kept for too long." Malik's hand grips my shoulder as he gives it a firm squeeze. "We won't let her die."

"Okay." I exhale the pressure in my chest and rub my hands together to keep myself busy. "So what's the plan?"

"She left us a note," Laith tells me, throwing the envelope at me. "She wants us to combine the clubs, to make the transition easy and ensure everyone is getting along."

"How long does she plan to stay with Tazo?" I scoff. "We've been enemies for years. Combining clubs isn't something we can do overnight." I pull out the sheet of paper and read my name amongst the others in her perfect writing.

The guys are right. She's expecting us to pull off a miracle. "You and Laith head over and prepare the Dragons and I'll go prepare the March. This is what VPs do. Diego will wait for an update from Jones. Let's have this meeting tonight."

"Tonight?!" I exclaim, crumpling the page in my hand and tossing it back on the table. "The club is fucking fragile right now with Jaeger gone and Genni moving in. They won't take well to this."

"Or," Diego cuts in, "they're ready for a change. Give it a shot and be really positive about it."

"Be really positive about it," I mimic as I turn on my heel and stride to the front door. I can only imagine what Kennedy will say. "Make sure you call me with any updates."

It's hard to walk away from what's going on with Genni and my instincts are telling me to ride over to that motel and demand she be given back. It's my family who's holding her hostage, if she's even held hostage. I don't know what her plan is and exactly what she's doing, but I have to follow her instructions in the note. She's my President and I need to treat her as such when she demands it.

GENEVIEVE

CHAPTER ELEVEN

I was surprisingly calm when I walked up to an MC member and told him who I was and who I was there to speak to. The shock on his face was immediate as was his quick grab to my wrist before he hauled me up a set of stairs.

The place was exactly how Quinton described, and when the biker pounded on the door, the sounds seemed to rival the beating of my heart inside my chest. With no time to turn back, I was ready to look the man who ruined my mother's life in the eyes.

Now my hands are bound behind the chair I'm sitting in, facing Tazo who's sitting on the bed across from me. Our knees touch while he gives me a creepy smile and his fingers toy with the beard hanging from his chin, the sun hitting his golden skin as it shines in from the open blinds. "I know my nephew has been poking around at the reservation. I have eyes and ears everywhere. He must've come back with a fantastic story." Tazo believed me when I said I came here to beg him to stay away from his nephew and offer him the two clubs in exchange for Quinton's safety.

"Tell me, Tazo, exactly what it is you think Quinton has told me. I want to hear your version," I reply, my voice as sweet as sugar despite being tied up.

"You really do look like your mother," he breathes out and gives me an admiring look. "But I can tell you have a backbone, well, you would have to, wouldn't you?"

"Why would I have to?" I give in to his asinine questioning, needing to know everything he has to say about the woman I will never remember.

"To be able to shoot two men right between the eyes? POW!" He holds his fingers to his head like a gun and mock-shoots himself, the maniacal look in his eyes giving insight to his state of mind. "Your father is in there too… Unfortunately."

It's the perfect segue into asking him to tell me about what happened to my mother and I wonder if he meant it that way. With a pleading look, one I hope he thinks is genuine, I beg, "Tell me what she went through, what my father put her through."

"Awendela was a flirtatious girl, even at such a young age, she knew how to speak to a man to get what she wanted." The way he's speaking about a child makes me sick to my stomach. "She wanted to live her life free, and as she got older, becoming ripe for fucking and babies, she knew that meant being strapped to one man. She didn't want that. My wife was adamant though, Awendela needed to marry because we couldn't look after her forever. Aiyana had her hands full with our sons and had no time to be chasing her younger sister out of the beds of young men. Trust me, pretty Varga, she was in multiple men's beds. Just like you."

"I guess the apple doesn't fall too far from the tree." I shrug, his innuendo about my sexual prowess not bothering me in the least. He can think me a whore all he wants, it wouldn't change how many men frequent my bed.

He tips his head back with a booming laugh, and I can't tell if it's fake or not. Then he looks back at me, still chuckling and shaking his head. "To think, a few of those men are mine." His smile falls from his face and his eyes shine with mischief. "Two men who work for me and do everything I tell them to."

He's speaking about Malik and Diego, and even though they do follow all his orders, he doesn't know that they've told me everything they know. They're my men now. "Oh?" I tip my head to the side. "Kind of like Cash too? Before his head was blown apart?"

"Cash was my true brother, even after your grandfather and father exiled me, they couldn't split us up. They thought he was loyal to them, but he was loyal to me. He told me every run they had planned and it wasn't hard to insert myself. Poor Victor Varga couldn't figure out why his plans kept getting fucked with or how that warehouse was filled with women and children when it was supposed to be empty." He gives me an evil grin, the sight making my stomach clench with nausea. This man truly tried to ruin my father's life.

"And what? My mother was another ploy you put in my father's path? A distraction?" I spit out the words, my anger bleeding through every syllable.

"No." He chuckles again, his eyes flashing with unresolved anger. "She was never meant to be Vic's and she didn't want to be either."

The thought of the possibility of my mother being in love with Barrett, my rapist, makes me feel ill. "I can't believe she wanted Barrett."

"No, but she knew what she had to do in order to leave the reservation and not be dragged back later. She had to marry, and coincidently, Barrett needed an heir. Their union was one of convenience on both sides. In fact, Barrett was fairly good to her, even when she would hold a knife to his dick before she gave in. Your mother agreed to become Barrett's Old Lady in exchange for her freedom, it was a price she was willing to pay. It was only meant to last for as long as it would take her to get pregnant and have the kid. Then she was leaving and never looking back. Your mother wasn't the maternal type." The opinion he has of my mother means nothing to me. I don't trust him. He looks so damn proud of himself, but he hasn't explained just what he's gotten out of the deal.

"Where did you come in? You seem to be very intimate with their bedroom details. Was that your end of the bargain, you got to watch?" Once again, I have him laughing his ass off, the sounds bouncing off the walls around us.

"What did I receive out of the deal?" He leans forward, his arms resting on his knees as he gives me a smarmy look, his fingers brushing my legs as his hot breath fans my face. "Barrett's brother used to run the cartel your daddy's club liked to distribute products for. Barrett begrudgingly killed his brother for me and I stepped into his shoes. You see, I own the cartel, I own Hell's March, and I own the Highway Knights." My mouth runs dry as I try to swallow down the fear skating up my throat. This is so much worse than we ever thought. "I made Malik VP in case Barrett ever got the idea of stepping out of line. That crazy motherfucker would shoot him without a second thought, and even though he may be loyal to your pussy now, he'll come crawling back to me when you're dead."

I can't find the words to continue our conversation, and as I look around the room, I pray Delia finds a way to get me out of here because we didn't have time to form a concrete plan. She just told me to leave it to her, but Tazo has no plans to ever let me go, not that I thought he would. He wants to kill me and put his men back in line.

"Now back to the story," he croons as he leans back on the bed, giving me some space. "I was enjoying our conversation. Where was I? Right. So your mother gets pregnant and she has a son, which made Barrett happy. I don't want to think what would've happened if it was a girl. You wouldn't be here if it was. It was hard for your mother to walk away from her son, she grew to love the brat and decided another year with Barrett would be bearable, if only for her son. She was planning on running away with him and I let Barrett know that it might be a good idea to get her knocked up again." I look at him with shock as he nonchalantly retells the story of my mother's imprisonment. "He took my advice and became a little paranoid if you ask me. He was sure someone in the

March camp was helping her leave, so he thought he would weed them out. I'm sure your men have told you stories about Barrett, about his trigger-happy finger?"

I shake my head, unable to form words as he laughs and leans back farther on his hands.

"He decided to take Wendy to a Dragon drop one day, to strike some fear into her about what would happen if she tried to leave. It ended up being your father that day and he had caught on to Barrett's involvement in thwarting his runs. They came head-to-head in that desert, and it was the first time your dad laid eyes on Wendy. Of course, Barrett had her leashed that day, as he did most days." He runs his fingers along his throat and gives me a wink. "It was a pretty collar, all sparkly and pink. I can't speak for how your father felt about Wendy, if it was love at first sight as you women like to say, but he made it his mission to save the young girl Barrett was holding hostage. A few months later he succeeded."

"How did he take her?" I breathe out, my heart beating so loudly, I'm sure he can hear it. I begin to clench and unclench my hands behind my back to keep the blood flow moving. The twine is tied tight with no possibility of getting out of them.

"I may have had Cash tell him where he could find her and when the best time to take her was. See, your father trusted Cash with his life, not knowing the man was my brother first. Barrett was paranoid, like I told you, so he didn't keep Wendy and his son at the compound in case the person she was secretly working with would try to come for her." The proud look on his face is warranted and I hate to admit it. He was exiled from the Dragons and vowed his revenge and he got it by working the strings of both clubs. Even my father who thought Tazo was long gone, instead, the man was planning his fate from the very beginning.

"You fed Barrett's paranoia so that Wendy could be taken by my father, didn't you? It was better to have an unhinged leader than one who could rival you for the club ownership," I snap, my patience wearing thin the more he tells me of this twisted story.

"Actually, no." He shrugs as a small smile works over his mouth. "Barrett's Medic, the man he relied on to keep everyone alive and well, was actually the one planning to rescue Wendy. It had nothing to do with me."

"Diego's dad?" I whisper as my heart warms inside my chest. He was good, just like Diego is.

"Jorge Montez had a tender heart and loved to save things that should be left to die. Sound familiar?" It does. This is exactly how Diego is. His father would be so proud of him. "But his meddling brought him and his family some trouble. I decided his insubordination needed to be met with harsh consequences, so Barrett and I hit him where it would hurt the most. Sofia Montez."

"Who?" The name is not familiar and I've never heard Diego say it. When Tazo's face shines with delight, I know I'm about to be destroyed.

"Sofia Montez was the love of Jorge's life and she was considered too soft to be an Old Lady. Regardless of that, Jorge loved her and had two children with her. He tried to keep them separate from the club but I wasn't letting that slide. Especially when his son grew up to become a prodigy surgeon. That's why Cash was so important to your daddy and his club. Barrett was told to keep Jorge in line, but he was failing." The dark look in his eyes deepens as his pupils dilate. He's enjoying this, retelling me all the evil things he's accomplished, but they're only serving to make me sick.

"Let me guess." I put some snark in my voice to cover the sickness threatening to spill from my throat. "You taught him a lesson."

"I think I taught him a generational lesson, to be honest." His grin turns wolfish as he lowers his voice as though he's teaching me something important. "I hired a Highway Knight assassin to get rid of Sofia, but to make it look like a suicide. She wrote a note and everything, telling Jorge how miserable he made her for years and how she wished she never had his children."

There's no holding it back this time, I let the acid burn its way up my throat and expel it to the carpet at my side. It's becoming more and more obvious that I am meant to die here. If he's spilling all of this to me with such ease, it means he plans to kill me and I will never be able to tell Diego and Delia that their mother never wanted to leave them.

"Don't get sick now. I haven't finished your mother's story. It gets better." His eyes sparkle with delight at my obvious discomfort and I want nothing more than to kick him in the face, but my ankles are tied to the chair as well. "After Jorge offed himself because his wife hated him, Wendy was truly left alone, until your dad played the knight in shining armor." He stands from the bed and walks to the small fridge to grab a bottle of water, making sure to drink it in front of me, as if I haven't felt thirst so bad I thought my blood was turning to dust. If he thinks I'll show weakness after a few hours without water, he's delusional. "He was something of a bomb specialist, your father, and he bombed the March compound to create a diversion, then stormed inside to *rescue* your mother. Vic took her as she fought him and screamed, screaming for her baby who was crying in the crib, but your father didn't give a shit. He just wanted her."

I can't imagine my father doing that, leaving a child behind, but the evidence is clear. Davis was raised by Barrett and Wendy eventually had me.

"He took her to his cottage and ignored her as she begged him to take her back to her son. Your father was the true monster of her story because just a mere few days later, he forced her to open her legs as he began craving an heir of his own." My heart sinks into my chest as he sits back on the bed, his eyes roving over my face.

"It's hard to believe anything that comes from your mouth," I finally say as he chuckles.

"Tell me something, pretty Genevieve Varga." His voice is smooth like a finely aged wine, the tenor meant to set me at ease but fails.

"What could I tell you that you don't already know?" I brush my hair away from my face with my shoulder as he eats up my every movement with his eyes.

"After everything you learned here today,"—he leans forward, invading my personal space and making me cringe—"do you still love your daddy?"

romántic
THIS BODY IS
TEMPORARY
BUT THIS SOUL IS
ETERNAL
永遠
JAEGER

JAEGER

The taste of her still lingers on my lips as my tongue slowly drags across them, making me hard for the fiftieth time since I left the house. I wanted to be out of there before any of the guys showed up, but I should've guessed they would be over early, like panting fucking puppies looking for scraps of food. Not that I can say much, I've become that way too. I just don't show it like they do.

Loving someone is the equivalent of having a weakness. I learned as much when I listened to my mother's last screams of mercy.

The decisions I've made up until last night have been based on my emotions, my raw anger, and I've suffered from them. It was time to make a change. So I called Delia and told her to be back at the house in an hour, giving me enough time to crawl into bed with Genevieve and tell her about the first decision I made based on logic. After I tasted her, of course. I can no longer hate her for what our father did, and it's time to face the fact that I would've done the same if I were in her shoes. We both lived our lives just wanting to make him proud.

I haven't apologized for the scars I've given her, even if it wasn't my blade that created them. My part in her trauma could never be swept under the rug or forgotten, but that doesn't mean we can't move on. I'll make sure I've earned it before I ever have her in my arms again.

She thinks I'm sitting at home with her men, planning on how to bring the clubs together, but I'm exiled, and for the first time in a long time, I am fucking free. I don't have to think of my brothers or the club's reputation while I'm out and I don't need to worry about my cut attracting the wrong attention. My shackles have fallen off and I can walk unencumbered.

What's my first taste of freedom look like?

I pull into the empty parking lot of the warehouse and grin. It looks like I get to be Jaeger Varga, without Vice or President attached to it, and I can do whatever the fuck I want. Genevieve wanted me to be obedient like the others, but she'll learn the hard way that I walk to the beat of my own drum. Her father barely kept me in line, the club was my structure because I knew I had brothers depending on me, but right now? I'm doing exactly what I want without repercussions.

The warehouse is musty and stagnant when I walk inside, the dust floating through the streams of sunlight coming in from the windows twenty feet above my head. I pass by the cots we used when Genni blew up our bikes and club, then continue by the racks of mannequins and paper targets for shooting practice. This warehouse has been Dragon property for so long, and before it housed us when we were homeless, it was my sanctuary to tinker with what makes my blood quicken. Blowing shit up.

I pull open a set of industrial double doors and take in a deep breath as I look around. My equipment is just as I left it and I haul off my jacket to get to work. Genni said twelve hours, and if I haven't heard from her or Delia, I'm to lead everyone to the motel. She thinks I will bring solidarity to the brothers of both clubs, but I'm not doing that. As much as her exiling me felt like bullshit, I can't let her break that vow. The men would look at her like she's a typical female, someone who changes her mind on a whim. No, I'm not going to follow her instructions when those twelve hours are up. I have my own plans and I have a short amount of time to start them. I look at the time on my phone and hiss out a breath. Five hours down and seven more to go. It'll be tight but I can make it work.

Dragging my forearm along the sweat collecting at my brows, I fall back in my seat. It's not the most beautiful thing I've created, but it'll get the job done. I double-check the charge connection, the fuses, and then the C4 before testing the signal from my controller to the ignitor. The last thing I do is make sure it's properly attached to the drone. It'll be hard enough getting close without smashing it into the walls or roof, I don't want to damage the connections.

I'll only have one chance.

With a window of an hour left, my phone chirps with a ping. I swipe the screen to find Delia's name.

Delia: He's got her in his room on the east side. Room 37, second floor.

Before I can type out a reply, three dots appear on the screen.

Delia: The room is surrounded by Knights and cartel. He's running both from what I can tell. I can't get in without a distraction. I'm ready when you are.

Delia was stationed on top of an abandoned house's roof across from the motel the entire time Genni was inside, her sniper providing a view of the room where Genni is being kept. I knew it would be surrounded and I also assumed that if Tazo created Hell's March without being the visible President then he would probably have other groups under his thumb too. The cartel is a little surprising, but when I think back over the interactions I've had in the past with them, the signs were there.

It also reminds me of the *deal* I made with Barrett, which wasn't really a deal at all considering Tazo ran both of them. No wonder they fucking laughed at me. I was so eager to prove I could run a club and be its President that I never thought to look below the surface. Arrogance will get any man killed, it shows no bias.

I send Delia a thumbs-up, letting her know I'm in position inside one of the cargo vans used by the Steel Dragons and parked on the street across from the motel. Then I sniff my shoulder and wince at the stench. I had to jump into a dumpster behind the motel as soon as I got here to set up the drone, then wait for the Knights' patrol to pass by. I don't doubt the perimeter of the place is also under surveillance, but I took a risk that they didn't care about the garbage cage with the two dumpsters inside. It's been over thirty minutes since I climbed out of it and I don't notice an uptick in activity, not to mention the drone is still intact.

Forty-five minutes left. I bring my binoculars to my eyes as a Knight walks out of his room with a bag in his hand. Looks like groceries. He walks to room thirty-seven and knocks as two more Knights appear from the doors on either side of Tazo's. They all look at each other with a nod, their hands hovering over the guns at their waists. Delia's right, he's perfectly cushioned with men.

Tazo's door finally opens and he stands in the doorway with Genni squirming in front of him. He's using her as a shield. Her hands are tied behind her back, but otherwise, she looks fine. No bruising or pain in her eyes. They're filled with fucking rage though, not an ounce of fear as she snaps her teeth toward the Knight handing over the bag. I chuckle as I shake my head. She's not the same naive girl who thought my best friend could teach her how to shoot a gun and she'd miraculously know how to run a club of men. No, this woman who gives the men a taunting smile while saying something smug as the door closes is a fucking President.

I can't imagine that this is what Vic envisioned when he made his daughter President for her protection, but he better be proud of the daughter who's making the rest of us look like cowards.

Delia: Did you see that? Thirty minutes and it's time. Put

your diaper on, you fucking pussy.

A snort flies from my mouth as I drop my phone back into the pocket of my jacket and power up the drone. I didn't have a chance for a test run, but it wouldn't have mattered anyway since I didn't have time to fix anything. I just need it to fly twenty feet and drop onto the roof so I can detonate it.

The Knight who brought the food heads back to his room, three doors down from where Genni and Tazo are. My palms begin to sweat as I scope out the area to blast, hoping to contain it enough away from Tazo's room. Everything is lost if I blast everyone. Then I have to rely on Delia to slip in and kill Tazo to free Genni.

It's hard trusting something so important to another person, but I don't have another choice. My phone pings again and I pull it out of my pocket to find Delia's name.

Delia: Heading in.

She's a little early, but I don't blame her, I'm eager to have this over with too. She'll have to scale over the motel fence and get into position to run into Genni's room while the blast is ignited. It has to be perfect.

The drone is fired up and ready as I begin its ascent out of the dumpster and straight up to the roof of the motel. It's hard to decipher its surroundings on the small screen of the controller in my hand, but I've done this many times before. This time I have a lot more at stake.

I've always worked well under pressure though.

A drop of sweat threatens to drip into my eye as I move the drone into position, the landing the trickiest maneuver. It can't crash or be jostled too much because the connections could come undone or the fuse could ignite too soon.

Once the drone has crested over the roof and I can see its surroundings without squinting at the screen, I let out the breath I've been holding. The next thing is to get it to land without issue. I find the perfect spot when movement on the motel's perimeter catches my eye.

"Too fucking soon, Montez," I growl as Delia lands beside the fence and behind a set of trees. The sweat drips from my brows and hits the screen on the controller as I curse, knowing it's now or never. I don't have time to do calculations or estimate the blast zone. If I don't land and ignite in the next minute, Delia will be caught and Genni will be killed.

The drone stutters as I begin its descent, the jarring making me inhale quickly. "Please," I whisper as I continue to drop it. "Vic, if you're watching, do something good for once in your fucking life."

A few seconds later, the drone is settled and Delia darts out from the trees as a shout from above sounds. She's been spotted. I lift the cover to the detonator and murmur a plea to whoever is up in that sky to protect her.

Then I press it.

DIESEL

MALIK

"I got the heads down and they're burning in a pit," Cory says as he walks into the room, his eye on Rockz as he sets up his tattoo machine. "We're patching today?"

"Just Robby," I grunt as I sit with my head in my hands. We still haven't heard anything back from Slayer, and Diego says Delia's not answering her phone. I hate waiting and I fucking hate being useless.

I've become a fucking mule, a yes ma'am. Anger courses through me at the thought of sitting here, obeying orders when I've never done such a thing in my entire life. Cory leaves the room and I stand from the chair. Diego can do the fucking oath with Robby, I'm heading to that motel to rescue my girl.

Everyone turns to look at me as I storm from the Hell room and toward the bar. "Montez!" I bellow, watching as he turns on the stool. "I'm out. You can do the ceremony."

"What?" He scrambles from the chair to chase after me as I head for the door. "Charles! Wait!"

Shoving open the door, I tip my head back to suck in some fresh air. I'm sick of nicotine and stale whiskey-infused air, and I'm tired of fucking sitting around. "Sitting around here is driving me crazy. I need to go get her."

"We're not just sitting around. The guys are on a high, all of them willing to join forces with the Dragons to save our girl. You did that! It was your idea to do a patching-in to bring up morale, and it's working. They're all excited and for once happy to not be going to war with the Steel Dragons. They believed you when you said we would be unstoppable if we joined forces. I believed you too." He comes to stand in front of me, his light blue eyes filled with excitement. "She's going to be happy you did all of this for her."

"What if he... Tazo... What if he makes it so she... doesn't come back?" My body vibrates with tension as potent fear envelopes every muscle. Tazo is a ruthless asshole and I know better than anyone else just what he's capable of. Nothing is off-limits.

"We can't give up hope now. Delia would've called us if something didn't go as planned, you know she would. Let's go back inside to have Robby tatted and fitted with a new patch." Diego is like a rock, strong and true, withstanding any weather and surviving all calamities. Slayer is lucky to have him, fuck, I'm lucky to have him.

With that thought in mind, I grab the front of his cut and haul him into me, his chest meeting mine as he exhales. His surprised eyes dilate as I lean into him, his breath coasting over my face. "Thank you," I whisper just before I crush my mouth to his.

We've just installed new surveillance cameras all around the compound, and I'm sure Jones is getting an eyeful of this right now, but I don't give a fuck. I found my soul in Slayer but I think I've found salvation in Montez.

I slip my tongue into his mouth as his hands wrap around my waist, kissing me back with the same intensity. When we finally pull apart, he gives me a small smile and a nod, letting me know this is good, that he and I are good.

"Let's get Robby tatted and patched." He opens the door and gestures for me to head inside, my heart racing and my cock hard. The only thing that would make this better would be to have Slayer here with us.

Rockz covers the ram skull tattoo on Robby's shoulder as Davis removes his Prospect patch and replaces it with a *Member* patch. Usually, we'd have girls here and booze flowing, but we can't today because we have to be ready to ride out. All of us.

"Just got a message from Quinton and he says the Dragons are ready." Diego shows me the screen of his phone and I smile.

"She planned this, knowing it would take something as important as bringing her back to have us all work together. Cunning fox." Diego's face lights up with my words as he nods slowly.

"Yeah, I think you're right. She would think that far ahead." He chuckles and puts the phone away as soon as mine rings.

My heart suddenly slams against my chest as I pull it out of my pocket with unsteady hands. Jones' name flashes on the screen and I swipe it open, immediately putting him on speaker. "Jones?"

"Come to my room. Now." The click of him hanging up puts us both in motion as we run to the corridor and nearly skid by his bedroom door.

Diego jerks on the handle and we both stumble into his room to find him standing with his hands in his hair, the sight making me drop to my knees. "What is it?" I breathe out as Diego staggers to his side, his eyes on the screen.

"What's that?" he asks Jones as the man turns around to look at me.

"Someone made a firework out of the motel," Jones says, his words sounding garbled as though I'm under water. "Malik?" He drops his hands and comes forward, bending down so we're face-to-face. "Someone bombed the motel."

"Slayer?" I croak out as Diego curses.

"It's not near where she's being held," Diego cuts in and looks at me over his shoulder. "We need to ride over there."

His phone pings at that moment and he pulls it out of his cut as

I squint toward Jones' computer screen, seeing smoke and flames. Jones stands and heads back to his desk and I begin to rise. "What is it?" I ask Diego as he starts pacing and looking at his screen.

"It's from Jaeger. He's put us in a group chat called Gen's Dogs." In the commotion of hearing about the bomb, I didn't hear my own phone go off.

It's still wrapped in my hand from when we got Jones' call and I receive the notification for the chat on my screen. I tap it open to find one photo, a still shot of what's happening on Jones' screen and a single message.

Jaeger: You dogs better pray Montez's little sis can get her out.

"What the fuck?" I scramble to Jones' desk and look over his shoulder. "What is he talking about?"

Diego comes to stand beside me as Knights run from the building, but there's no sign of Delia or Slayer anywhere. "I think that's where Jaeger left to go this morning," Diego explains. "He was building a bomb. A distraction to get Genevieve and my sister out."

The group chat starts firing off with Laith and Quinton yelling at Jaeger about what's going on but as I look at the screen, I can't help but notice he's in here. One of the dogs.

Me: Look who's joined the pack. Don't step out of line or I'll rip out your throat.

GENEVIEVE

CHAPTER TWELVE

"Why would I lie?" Tazo asks as he stands from the bed. "What would I gain from it? Your father is dead, making you hate him doesn't benefit me at all. You say you're here to barter for my nephew's life, but truly I can tell you want to know about the woman who couldn't face you because you came from your father."

"What?" I rear my head back as he walks to the window and looks out through the blinds. "What are you talking about?"

"Vic Varga raped Wendy a few times a week until she became pregnant," he answers robotically, no emotion to cushion the blow. "He wanted an heir like she gave Barrett and he wanted it from her." He turns toward me, abandoning the window to continue his story. "She never saw the inside of his house, never spent a second off that cabin's property. Wendy was truly a prisoner of your *daddy*."

"She wouldn't have been a victim to anyone had you left her alone," I snap. "You said you loved my mother, but you were the biggest monster in her life." The anger pulses just under my skin, the heat spreading to the tips of my fingers as I clench and unclench them.

"I didn't force her to do anything. She wanted to leave the reservation and she agreed to be with Barrett. She had his child and then she agreed to stay until the kid was a bit older." He comes to stand in front of me, bending at the waist to look me in the eye. "It was your father who took her right to choose away. It was your father who forced himself on her, and it was your daddy who forced her to have *you*."

The gleeful look in his eyes only means he's gotten the reaction he was looking for. My face is numb as the blood rushes through my ears and my stomach rolls. My mother was forced to have me. I swallow it down and compel myself to remember what I endured in that basement and what I've survived. This man and his words will not break me, not when I rose from the ashes of true torment.

"There it is," he breathes out, his breath warming my heated skin further. "Wendy's fire. I saw it that day at the Dragons' Clubhouse and I was mesmerized. She really must've prayed for you to look like her every day of her pregnancy just to spite your father. I wonder, when he looked at you, did he feel remorse for the woman he destroyed?" When he doesn't get an answer from me, he straightens and sits on the bed, crossing his feet at the ankles. "I wonder if he felt her suicide every day he looked into your eyes."

I try my best to hold it in, but there's no stopping the flood once the dam breaks. "What?" I grit out through my teeth. "My mother died from cancer."

"Did she now?" He laughs, the sound humorless as his eyes flash with fire and he crosses his hands in his lap. "Is that what he has written on her tombstone? The one decorating an empty grave?"

"Empty grave?" I hate the way my voice cracks and how my breath leaves me in one rush.

"You were born in the middle of a thunderstorm, just after midnight," he begins, and I can't help the gasp that leaves my mouth because he's correct. "Cash helped deliver you, did you know that? No, of course not. It was a club secret. He said she glanced at you then handed you over to Mariam, begging her to take you away. She wanted her son and you reminded her of your father."

"No." I shake my head as the cursed tears slip from my eyes. I hate that he sees me like this, but when I look into his eyes, I know he's telling me the truth. My mother hadn't wanted me because she was forced to have me.

"Cash left her with some painkillers, the good stuff, while Mariam took care of you. She said she tried to persuade her to nurse and she refused, she tried to force her to eat but she didn't want any food. She wanted to die." The knots in my stomach grow the more he speaks and it's absurd the things he's saying but I can't bring myself to tune him out. "Your father didn't even come to visit you that first week, he was that disappointed about you being a girl. Didn't you ever wonder why there were no hospital pictures of you and your loving family? Every photo your father possessed of Wendy were all taken during her captivity at that cottage."

"Untie me," I snap as he chuckles and shakes his head.

"Don't order me around, bitch. You'll leave here in a body bag. I'll take your body back to the reservation and bury you beside your mother. Unmarked graves, but at least you'll be together." A knock sounds at the door and I exhale the breath I was holding to keep myself from screaming.

Tazo comes over to me and cuts the ties from around my ankles, making it possible for me to knee him in the face but I don't. I've lost my fight as all the new images of my parents float through my mind. He hauls me up out of the chair and sets me in front of him as he walks us both to the door. As soon as he opens it and I see the three men on the other side, I realize I'm a human shield. Fucking coward.

Tazo takes a bag of food from one of them as the guy leers at me, making me lean forward to snap my teeth in his direction. "Keep looking, bitch," I snarl. "I'll have your eyes as soon as I leave here."

"Bring Mariam to me," Tazo demands, then he pulls us back into the room before throwing me on the bed along with the bag and runs his hands over his hair.

"You're nothing more than an exiled Dragon who wishes he was my father," I goad him as he slowly turns to look down at me.

Tazo lifts his shirt and I nearly spit out the bile rushing to my mouth. His stomach is a mottled patchwork of skin, the same size as a Steel Dragon's branding. It's now been replaced with a large, multicolored scar. "I was once a Dragon and believe me when I say, I am much better off now." He lowers his shirt as the door between this room and the next opens and in walks Cash's Old Lady, Mariam. "She will corroborate everything I'm saying. She has no reason to lie to you." He looks at Mariam who's staring down at me with something close to pity.

"It would've been better if you died in the March's basement," she whispers as she rubs her wrists, and that's when I notice the red rings around them. She's being held here too.

"Tell her what happened to Wendy. Tell her about her mother's last few days," Tazo orders as he points to the chair I was in earlier.

Mariam sits in it as I sit up on the bed to face her, her face a mask of sadness and exhaustion. "Your mother was troubled, child. The things she endured, it makes sense that she lost her mind. She ended up overdosing on some pills Cash gave her for the pain, and Tazo came to take her away before Vic found out." She continues to rub at the red circles around her wrists as she looks at Tazo, her eyes shining with hatred. "But I made sure you were safe. I took you with me."

A sob is working its way up my chest, the pressure of it pressing against my throat. I will not give him the satisfaction of seeing me break down. "Thank you," I whisper to her as my vision distorts with tears. Then I take a deep breath before looking at Tazo. "I will kill you," I promise him as I struggle against the twine cutting into my wrists.

"With the skills I no doubt made sure you possessed," he fires back, stilling my movements. "That's right, Genevieve Varga, it was on my order that Barrett told Malik and Diego to train you. I wanted you to be strong for what I have planned for you. A man in the Highway

Knights has been waiting for an Old Lady, one strong enough to endure his… kinks. I promised him long ago that I would bring him someone, especially since he did me a favor with Sofia Montez. He may be a little old for you, but I'm sure you won't mind. Most women he's with don't last more than a few nights anyway."

These are his plans. He wants to send me off to some sadistic fucker who killed Delia and Diego's mother and made it look like a suicide while he takes over both Dragons and March. Over my dead body.

I open my mouth to tell him just that when the building rocks with a loud boom. I'm thrown from the bed, my head hitting the table, making my vision fuzzy, as the building continues to tremble.

"What the fuck is that?" Tazo yells as Mariam crawls over to me.

I try to sit up, but Mariam's hand lands on my chest as she shakes her head. "Don't move," she whispers as she peeks up over the bed. "This could be your chance. When you get out of here, you need to find your mother's cut."

"What's happening?" Tazo barks, jerking my attention from Mariam as a voice comes through what sounds like a phone.

"Bomb, Superior! You need to get out, the fire is moving fast!" The voice sounds frantic and my heart begins to beat with it. *Bomb?*

"Fuck!" Tazo hollers as he runs to us, finding both of us on the floor by the bed. That's when I smell it… smoke. At first, it's subtle, but when Tazo grabs me by the hair, knocking Mariam to the side, and yanks me up to standing, I nearly choke with how thick it is.

"No, Tazo!" Mariam scrambles to her knees. "Let her go, she's not going to bother you again, right, Genni?" She looks at me earnestly right before Tazo's boot slams into her face, making her head hit the bedside table with a loud crack then she crumples to the floor.

"No!" I scream and slam my head back into his face, making

him release me and stumble to the wall.

"You bitch!" he bellows and grabs for me, then stops to look at the ceiling in horror. I follow his sight to find the ceiling turning black with heat. "Fuck you," he spits out. "You can burn in here with her."

Tazo opens the back door and is immediately met with thick black smoke as he covers his face and disappears into it. That's when the heat sweeps in, telling me the fire is quickly spreading toward us. I drop to my knees beside Mariam, but I can't tell if she's breathing or not and I can't check for a pulse with my hands tied behind me. I don't have much time to get out before we're both burned to a crisp.

Standing, I begin to look around for something to cut this twine off when the front door is kicked open and a Highway Knight stands in the open space, his eyes wide with fear. My heart slams up into my throat as I realize he's here to take me, and I turn to look at the back door, now covered with black smoke, flames beginning to dance around the edges. If I run through that, I don't know what I'll be heading into.

A gurgling sound cuts into my train of thought and I turn back to find a knife sliding along his throat as blood sprays into the room, and when he falls to the ground, Delia is standing behind him.

Only this isn't the Delia I know. Instead, her eyes are blank, void of any emotion as they scan the room and then land on me. "Let's go," she grunts as she comes forward, her face covered in blood, the sight sending a spark of fear through me. She turns me around and I let her do it, telling myself this is my best friend as she saws through the twine around my wrists. "It's dangerous out there, so make sure you follow close behind me," she warns as the twine breaks free.

"I can't leave Mariam," I tell her and point to the side of the bed. I start to make my way to her when Delia grabs the back of my shirt.

"There's no time. She's dead." I find no sympathy in her tone, just robotic words lacking the feelings I know she possesses.

"I'm not leaving without her." I put my foot down and Delia blinks, irritation running through her blue eyes, the first emotion I've seen since she walked through that door.

She brushes by me and I follow her, shielding my mouth and nose with my hand from the smoke. Then we bend down over Mariam as Delia presses her fingers to her throat. Mariam hasn't moved an inch since she fell and when Delia turns her head to look at me over her shoulder, I already know the answer. Mariam is dead. Common sense tells me we can't bring her with us because she would only slow us down, but I was hoping she wasn't truly dead and we could wake her up.

"We need to get out of here now," she grits through her teeth and grabs my arm to haul me up with her. "Your brother dropped the bomb too close to your unit." She drags me out, my shock aiding her.

"Jaeger?" I mumble. We exit the room and directly to the left of us, I see the platform littered with bodies bleeding out along the wood. "Did you kill them?" Curiosity hits me while I look from the bodies to Delia, wondering what she looked like as she killed them.

"Walk faster, Varga," Delia snaps as she guides us to the stairs. We hurry down them and she drags me behind a bush just as three more Knights run by, not even looking around to spot us. "If they notice us, they won't hesitate to shoot us in the head." I stare at the side of her bloodied face, trying to find the girl I've gotten to know over the last month.

Only this isn't Delia Montez. I'm looking at the Viper.

romántic
THIS BODY IS
TEMPORARY
BUT THIS SOUL IS
ETERNAL
永遠
JAEGER

JAEGER

When I watch her emerge from that unit with Delia, I almost drop the binoculars with relief. I landed the drone a little too close to where she was being held and now the entire second floor of the motel is ablaze. Sirens sound in the distance as I continue watching Delia lead Genni off the property, the both of them climbing the fence and getting out without being seen.

I drop the binoculars to the passenger seat floor and put the van in drive, careening around a bend. I know where Delia has her car parked, but I'm not taking the chance. They can ride in this blacked-out van where they can hide out of sight until they're safe back at the compound.

Both of them are running toward me as I park on the side of the road and hop in the back to open the sliding door. "Get in here!" I scream, and they skid to a stop before jumping inside. I quickly shut the door and fall against the seat, breathing in the scent of blood and smoke. "Are you guys o—"

I don't have the chance to complete my sentence before Genni is on me, her arms around my neck and her mouth pressing to mine. My arms immediately wind around her waist as I pull her closer, my tongue swiping along her lips. She opens for me and I swallow her moans as I devour her, drowning in her essence. I've been fighting it for so long, whatever it is growing between us, and I let everything go as my hands find the globes of her ass to drag her along my—

"This is the epitome of a loving family," Delia fucking Montez says, breaking the moment before it even had a chance to start. "Don't show my brother because I don't want to give him any ideas."

I snort as Genni leans up to look at Delia over her shoulder, her perfect profile making me want to pull her back into my arms. "You're sick." She snickers and then looks at me. "Thank you for being here."

"I'm sick? I'm not the one making out with my brother—"

"*Step*," Genni and I say at the same time, her smile growing. The distinction has never really mattered to me before, but it does right now.

"Let's have everyone go back to your house and talk about everything we learned," Delia replies as she heads up to the driver's seat. "Don't worry, I'll drive so you horny siblings can make out."

"You saved me. You and Delia," she breathes out as the van lurches back onto the road. "I thought I dreamed what happened between us last night."

"Delia and I planned it out together." I shrug as I grab the front of her filthy shirt and pull her back into my arms. "And it wasn't a dream. I'll remind you again later."

This time when I kiss her, it's slow and searching, looking for the connection we once had and hoping I haven't completely decimated it. As much as I want her in my bed, I'd rather repair what I fucked up first. The rest is just extra I don't truly deserve.

The van jerks and we pull apart as Delia snickers. "Oops! Sorry! Pothole." It brings me back to the present with Genni looking exhausted and smelling of ash, and I give myself a shake. This isn't the time or place.

I wrap her up in my arms once more and press my lips to her temple as she curls into me. "You're so much stronger than I ever gave you credit for."

"Our father was a monster, Jaeger. What he did to my mother? The lies he told... I never truly knew him." Her words have me biting into my lip to stop the urge to stand up for the man she once idolized.

Who I once idolized.

"I'm a monster too," I say instead, making her gasp. "I did things I thought were right at the time but turned out to be disastrous. I'm not making excuses for him like I wouldn't make them for myself, but I would say remember how he was with you. That's who your father was for you, monster or not." I rub circles into her tense back, hoping my words will help her sleep better at night. I know what it is to be kept awake, wondering how I missed all the signs. "Men are weak."

She nods as Delia makes a sharp turn, making us both fall to the side. "Home sweet incestuous home!" she calls out, hauling another giggle from Genni. I'll tolerate it if she keeps getting the same response. We sit up as I open the side door and then I help Genni out of the van just as bike engines sound from up the street. "I sent my brother a text," Delia explains as she looks toward the noise.

I pull my phone from my pocket as I get out of the van and open the group chat, chuckling when I read their frantic messages to come back to the house for their girl. *Our* girl? Maybe?

The look on Genni's face, as she turns toward the sounds, has the rift I created between us widening. I step away, feeling like I'm imposing on something I don't belong to, and make my way to Delia who's standing on the porch.

"You smell like a barbeque," I quip as I take my keys out of my pocket to unlock the door. "And a mosh pit."

"You smell like a pussy-whipped bitch," she retorts, then starts to laugh as I look at her with a raised brow. "Didn't think you'd be here, huh? I bet you thought you'd be fucking strippers and Bunnies forever, letting the STDs collect like trophies."

"Shut up." I roll my eyes, only to have her throw me into the brick wall before her forearm is against my throat. It was just a matter of time before they began threatening me, but I will admit, I'm surprised Delia is the first. I thought for sure it would be Malik or Diego.

"You have this one chance. Just one. If you fuck it up, if you hurt her again, I will fucking castrate you, then kill you." She pulls back, not waiting for a reply because she doesn't need it. It's a threat and it's one I appreciate. I don't doubt a single word she's said. Delia would kill me with relish. I wouldn't be surprised if she was hoping for my failure just so she could pump me full of venom and witness my death.

She waits patiently as I unlock the door and then she heads inside as I turn and find Malik nearly dropping his bike to get to Genni. She begins to giggle when he lifts her into the air and twirls her, her hair flying out around them. It looks like something out of a romance movie and my heart stutters in my chest. Am I jealous? I don't know. A part of me wishes I could make her squeal like that with just the sight of me, but that wouldn't be authentically us. We've been fighting each other for years, as most siblings do, and when she blossomed into a young woman, I was fighting myself more often than not.

I avert my eyes and step into the house to give them some privacy, knowing Diego won't be too far behind. Then there's Laith and Quinton who will also be looking for a reunion. A happy little pack. I wasn't lying when I called them dogs but I would be lying if I said I didn't want to be a member.

"She's pure goodness." Delia steps out from the kitchen, cutting off my path to the stairs. "She's not like you or me. That heavy cloud you got over your head will always be there, trying to battle her sunshine, but you need to let her shine, Varga. Don't storm on her, because she doesn't deserve it, not after everything she's been through. Because of you." Her finger presses to my chest and it's like a bullet to my heart.

"I know, Montez." I can't help the crack that sounds when I speak or the way my breath catches and I have to suck in air. They're all signs of weakness, of emotion, but I don't have the strength to hide it anymore.

"Come in the kitchen and help me make her some food. I doubt she ate." She turns and when she notices I haven't followed her, she looks back at me, her brow raised.

"I can't go in." Another crack in my voice, another dent in the armor. "That's where… My mother was… I can't."

"I know." Delia walks back over to me and grabs my arm. "Conquer it and be strong for her. You need to face everything that happened and the things you had a hand in so you can forgive yourself. You won't be able to accept her forgiveness if you haven't accepted your own first." She drags me into the kitchen, and once my feet hit the tile, I nearly crumble.

"Sounds like you have experience," I croak out as I grab the countertop for support. My eyes look out of the window to find all four men fawning over Genni.

"Sure, with the concept, but I still have some work to do yet." She begins to open the fridge and whistles when she finds it empty. "You really can't come in here, huh?"

"No." I shake my head as she pulls out her phone.

"Pizza it is."

DIEGO

DIEGO

I sit on the side of the bed as Genevieve sleeps and the world around me explodes. She dropped some bombs of information that Tazo told her, and it changed everything for me and Delia.

Tazo had my mother killed.

She didn't commit suicide and the despair Delia and I have been carrying for all these years suddenly feels like it's for nothing, but it's not for nothing. Someone killed our mother and now my sister has fallen off the deep end.

Delia has been the Viper for a while, the *job* giving her an outlet to release the pent-up feelings of being inadequate and a burden. We've always believed our mother didn't want us, that the life she had with our family was something she resented.

Now Genevieve has turned everything we've ever believed on its head, and I know Delia is feeling guilty about hating our mother for most of her teenage and adult life.

I brush the hair back from Genevieve's face and exhale my breath. I'm relieved she's home and safe, but me and Delia aren't the only ones dealing with heartbreak. After hearing what Tazo, Barrett, and Vic did to her mother, my heart imploded for Genevieve. It took me sitting here and playing with her hair for her to even fall asleep, that's how torn up she is.

Malik left to go back to the clubhouse. He's intent on interrogating everyone to make sure Tazo doesn't have any spies, and Laith and Quinton have gone off to do the same.

"You can go if you want." Jaeger's voice disrupts me from my thoughts as I turn on the bed to look at him standing in the doorway. "I know you're probably worried about Delia."

"I am," I admit as Genevieve stirs in the bed, mumbling something in her sleep. "She's devastated and that's scarier than her being angry."

Delia didn't stick around to listen to much else after Genevieve told us about our parents, and I fear she's gone dark. I've tried calling and texting her but my messages aren't being read and my calls are going straight to voicemail. She's turned off her phone, something she rarely does. Her phone is an extension of the persona she created and she leaves it on in case a job comes up. I also need it to be able to track her, to know she's exactly where she says she is. It's the only way I can tolerate her lifestyle.

"She's tough," Jaeger says, a dark chuckle leaving his throat as I turn to look at him again. "What she did today, the way she had men dropping like flies, was fucking impressive. I don't ever want to be on her bad side." He shakes his head, his hair dropping over his forehead. "But the look in her eyes when she found out tonight was all too familiar."

My stomach flips when I remember the vacant look in her eyes as she stood from the table and said she needed some air. A second later, I heard Jaeger's van start up and I rushed to the window just as she was pulling out of the driveway. "I'm sure she'll return your van," I mutter, unable to think of anything else to say. This is the man who hurt the woman I love. He hurt her so badly that she completely transformed herself into V so she could learn to cope with the pain.

"It's Vic's." He shrugs. "She could blow it up for all I care. I know you probably want to find her. Genni is okay here with me." I hear what he's saying but all I see in my mind is the broken girl I found in the March basement. Is she safe here with him?

"It's fine. I'll call Delia again in the morning." I stand as he takes a step into the room. Ajani is out looking for her, but I really wish I could be too. I know her spots and I would think clearer if I was out there with him. Then I look down at the woman who owns each beat of my heart and know she needs me more.

"I wouldn't trust me either," he continues, lowering his voice as he takes a few more steps into the room. I hate that he's here in her space, but I also saw the looks they were sharing downstairs when they got back. Something happened between them. "All I can do is swear to you that I never want to hurt her again."

"Why did you do it to begin with? And don't say some shit about being betrayed. She was your sister." I say *was* because it doesn't sound right after witnessing the way they've been acting.

"Because I'm fucked-up. No, I'm not better now, and no, I may never be better. She was taking the most important thing from me and I wanted her fucking gone. That's the truth." It is. I can see it in his eyes, and I appreciate that he's not pulling at excuses.

"So if nothing's changed, why would you even think I'd leave her with you?" I sit on the end of the bed as he looks at her, his eyes softening, then he looks back at me.

"I didn't say nothing's changed. The club is no longer the most important thing to me. She is." It clicks for me then. The reason he walked away from the club so easily without putting up a fight and why he raced to her side when she was with Tazo. She's his priority now.

"Right." I nod. "Okay." I stand from the bed once more and walk back to the front before bending down and kissing her forehead. Then I look at Jaeger as I straighten to my full height. "You will tell her to call me the second she wakes up."

"I'll text everyone in the chat." He holds his hands up. "I promise."

"She has this ability to heal. Even when you think you're too far gone and there's no saving what's left of you." His eyes narrow on me as he crosses his arms over his chest. "Ask Malik."

With one last look at my girl, I head out of her room, Jaeger close on my heels. "Let me know when you find Delia. I'll be sure to tell Genni."

We head downstairs and I sit on the bottom one to haul on my boots as Jaeger stands across from me. "I know how strange this may seem. To most people, she's probably out blowing off steam, but I saw her. She was empty."

"I get it." He pushes off the wall as I stand and head to the front door. "You know her best and she's lucky to have that. She won't be feeling as alone as she would if she had no one." I can tell he's referencing himself and even though I want to argue with him and tell him he had someone, I need to find Delia first.

"Thanks," I mumble as I step out into the night, my skin beginning to pebble with the static energy surrounding me.

She's going to be immersed in carnage when I find her.

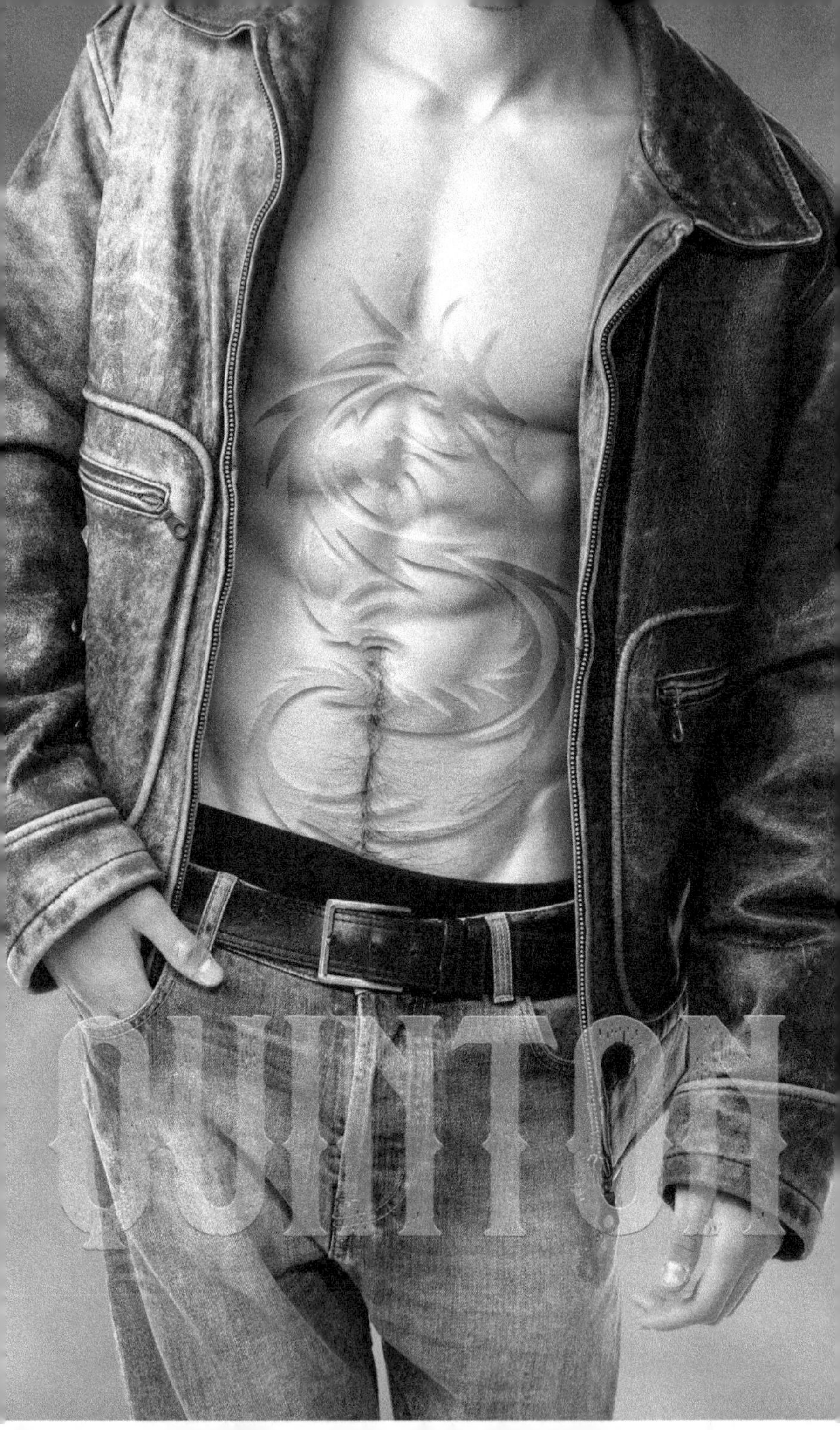

VUITTON

CHAPTER THIRTEEN

Laith looks ready to keel over as we rise from our chairs, waiting until the brothers leave the room. Kennedy stays seated in his chair, the hole in the shoulder of his cut showcasing the bullet he took.

"Joining forces with the March is like a spit in the face," he groans as he drops his face into his hands. "Everything we've worked toward is fucking crumbling to the ground." He looks up as Laith and I retake our seats, knowing we're in for a long meeting. "I'm not sexist or whatever." He waves us off before we can call him out on his bigotry. "But a woman leading the two most powerful clubs in Arizona? Have we lost our minds? It makes no difference that she's Vic's daughter, actually, it makes it worse. That man started this shitshow."

"I felt the way you did," I admit to him. There's no point in denying it, my brothers witnessed just how hard I fought against Genni taking over the Dragons. "She's better than Vic and she's better than Jaeger. We need a change and she'll be the one to do it. Look around us. Our brothers are getting older and no new prospects are coming to our gates. We're a dying club and the smart thing to do is combine us. We have a common enemy right now and we need to work together to get him out of Arizona."

"Enemy? He's our enemy, yes, but he created the March and the Highway Knights. Not only that, he runs the fucking cartel, Chino! Don't think for one second that the March is on our side. This is one big elaborate set-up." His eyes are blazing with mistrust as he sits rigidly in his chair. I can't fault him for his suspicions, they're valid, but I don't know how to explain the loyalty of the March without saying we're all with the same woman.

"Genevieve shot and killed Barrett and Bear without a second thought, then spiked their fucking heads on the front gates of their compound. Have you driven over to see it?" Laith asks as he folds his arms on the table and leans across while talking to Kennedy. When Kennedy shakes his head, Laith chuckles and continues, "I wish you did because when I saw it, the first thing I thought was, I never want to cross her. She had the brothers—Barrett's most loyal men—cut the heads off the bodies and spike it themselves. What do you think they were thinking?"

Thank god Laith has some brain cells still awake because it looks like he has Kennedy in deep thought as opposed to him arguing. "She's a woman," I emphasize, "but she's a leader and she'll put her life on the line for any one of us."

"Not me," Kennedy scoffs and leans back in his seat. "But I'll admit that she's gotten this far and that in itself is admirable. I also like that she fucking spiked their heads. It's something I would do and you all think I'm sadistic."

"They deserved it for what they did to her," Laith growls, and Kennedy shrugs.

"Sure," he says noncommittally. "I'm still here because this club has been my family, the only one I've ever had, and even though Vic treated me like a naughty kid, I love it here. I'll stay, but the second our values change, I'm leaving." He stands from his chair as Laith begins to rise.

"That's fair." Laith nods and sits back in his seat before Kennedy leaves the room, his cut swaying with his steps. "I'm fucking exhausted." Laith drops his head into his hands and lets out a groan. "I think I'm going to crash here for a few hours then go by to check on Genevieve. She's probably sleeping now anyway."

"Yeah," I mutter as he stands and looks down at me. "I'll get some rest too."

Satisfied with my answer, he leaves the room just as the brothers start up some music and a loud booming voice from one of them says, "Angel! You're back! Where's Carrie?"

I'm up and out of my seat quickly, my exhaustion long forgotten as I rush out into the main room. I find Laith standing near the corridor, his eyes meeting mine as his eyebrow raises. I give him a nod, letting him know I got this, and he turns to head toward his room, his shoulders slumping with fatigue.

"Angel!" I call out as she spins to face me, her face bruised and her lip busted. Shock tears through me at the sight of her and her battered face. "What happened?"

"Quinton!" she cries out and runs toward me, tears streaming down her cheeks. "You have to help me!"

She grabs the front of my cut as the party continues around me, the brothers too engrossed in the strippers and booze to care. I remove her hand and lead her into the Mass room before shutting the door and pulling out a chair for her to sit.

"What happened to your face?" I sit beside her and turn the chair to face her as sobs wrack her thin frame.

"He killed Carrie." My stomach drops with her words as my ears fill with a buzz. "I warned her not to believe him, that working for him would be dangerous, but she wanted to get back at you and the Dragons." I had my suspicions about Carrie the last time I saw her, but hearing how she wanted to get revenge on me and the club is disheartening.

"Get back at us for what?" Angel bites into her already split lip and winces as she shakes her head. "I can't help you if you don't tell me what's going on."

"Because of Genni. She was angry when she found out about you and her. Then Genni shows up as a President for the March. Did you know that?" She looks around frantically, her chest heaving. "Where's Jaeger?"

"How did she find out about Genni and me?" I lean back in my seat, trying to stay calm as a torrent of emotions rises inside of me. Carrie is dead because she was jealous, because she thought she and I had something worth turning to a sadistic man for help. I made her think that.

"Cash." She wipes the tears from her cheeks and hisses when she hits a bruise. "He told us all sorts of things. Carrie was really heartbroken about you though, and she was angry. I begged her not to do anything crazy, but the second Cash told her he knew someone who could help, she accepted. I knew it was a bad idea, but she wouldn't listen to me."

"It's okay. You're safe now," I soothe her as more sobs rip from her throat. "You can stay here, Angel. You don't have to go back."

"It's gone," she says with a hiccup before sucking in a breath. "The motel burned to the ground with Carrie inside. He caught her trying to sneak out a few nights ago and punished her."

My stomach flips. I can bet which night she's talking about. It's probably the same one I asked Carrie to meet me here at the club. "What did he do to her?"

"He punched her so hard that when she went down, she didn't get back up. I thought she was dead, so I dragged her into the bathroom and put her in the bathtub. I turned on the cold water and nearly screamed when she woke up. I swear I thought he killed her." She begins to wring her hands in her lap as she shakes her head. "He heard me scream." Her voice drops to a whisper as her eyes widen. It's as if she's reliving it all as she retells the horrific things that happened to them. "He came rushing back into the room, his face red with anger and his fists balled. Carrie saw him and she got out of the bathtub and ran for him as she screamed. He h–had a k–knife…" Her words end on a loud cry, the force of it bouncing off the walls as she falls forward into my arms. "He stabbed her in the throat and I watched her bleed out. Then he told me that if I made another sound, he would do the same to me."

"Fuck," I growl as her face drops into her hands.

"It was my fault because I screamed," she moans, her words muffled by her hands. "Then the fire started and I heard the guards outside of our door run away and I had to get out then or I would burn to death. I had to leave her there, but I know where he's staying." She lifts her head from her hands as my heart pounds in my chest.

"Where? Right now?" I clarify as she slowly nods her head, her eyes filling with tears again. "I'll set up a room for you so you can shower and rest. I'm sorry about Carrie but she would want you to live. She'd be happy to know you made it out of that fire." I stand up and motion for her to follow me, feeling bad that we don't have a medic on site to look her over. "How are you? Did you want to see a doctor?"

We leave behind the noise of the party and head down the corridor toward the sleeping area. "I'm fine," she says, her voice quiet. I look down at the top of her head as I lead her to one of the empty rooms. She looks so scared and alone, and I hate to leave her here.

"Laith is just a few doors down," I tell her as I open a room door and motion for her to head inside. "I'll bring you some clothes to wear from Jaeger's room and I'll let Laith know you're here. You're safe now."

"Here." She reaches into her pocket and pulls out a piece of paper. "This is the address."

THIS BODY IS
TEMPORARY
BUT THIS SOUL IS
ETERNAL
JAEGER

JAEGER

She's always slept just down the hall from me, but now it feels different. The girl I once thought of as an annoying little sister has become the woman my heart is thawing for. I'll be the first to admit that it's wrong. We were raised as siblings and honestly, that should have stuck.

The transition happened so smoothly that I'm at a loss for the precise moment I started lusting for her. Was it when she began to leave behind her little girl interests and beg for a bike to ride with me and my boys? Was it when she left behind the flowered sundresses and started wearing makeup? The only answer I have is that it happened well before I made that deal with Barrett.

I turn onto my side and look out of my window, the sun beginning to set. She's been sleeping since morning and even though I wanted to stay with her in her room, I forced myself to leave. This possessive attachment I've developed won't work with her newfound lifestyle of having a pack of boyfriends. Could I stand to watch her in the arms of another?

I haven't even had her for myself yet.

Yet.

Flipping the blanket off my body, I abandon trying to sleep and get out of bed. There's no chance of ignoring the pull any longer. I want to be beside her, I need to feel her.

The creaking of my bedroom door has me pausing, trying to listen for sounds of her being awake. When the house remains still around me, I head down the hallway toward her room. It's a creeping nostalgia as I pass our parents' room and I close my eyes to relive moments like this when we were younger.

Genni would have nightmares about dying of cancer because that's how she was told her mother died. She would cry and even though my room is farther down the hall, I would hear her because I'd leave my door open just in case. She would be sitting up in her bed, her pillow pressed against her chest as her midnight blue eyes sparkled with tears. I would crawl into bed with her and play with her hair until she fell back to sleep.

That was when I saw her as my little sister, but now as I walk into her room and find her spread out with her blankets kicked off, I see her as *mine*.

My nostrils flare as I inhale, my chest filling with the scent of her, and my feet move of their own accord to the end of her bed. The white T-shirt she's wearing has twisted up around her waist and the black thong is nothing more than a thin scrap of material between her legs. My mouth waters with the memory of how she tastes and when my knees hit the bed, all reason leaves me.

It's as if she senses me when her legs open farther and a soft moan escapes her mouth. Or maybe she's dreaming of one of her men, which in that case, I can't wait to interrupt.

Dropping between her legs, I lightly run my nose along her pussy, breathing it in through the barrier of her panties. She doesn't move an inch as I move up her body, my nose dragging along her shirt. The urge to rip her clothing off is overwhelming, but I tamp it down as I come face-to-face with her, the soft puffs of her breath hitting my cheeks.

Genevieve Varga is perfect. There's never been a doubt about her attractiveness, I've watched her blossom over the years. This perfection stems from the confidence she's recently acquired. The type that screams, *I can kill you in a few different ways.*

That's how I thought I would meet my end. I was sure she would kill me eventually and even accepted that it was deserved. Meant to be for me to die by her hand, but look at us now. Making love and not war.

Slipping my hand between us, I run my fingers along her heat, smiling when she sucks in a breath. I usually like my women a little more enthusiastic, but the appeal of taking her while she sleeps is all-consuming. My cock throbs and aches, not used to the slow approach. I pull my boxers down and settle between her thighs, pressing my hardness against her warm panties, then chuckling quietly when she gasps and arches her back.

I run my nose along the soft skin of her cheek, her flowery scent potent and thick around my head. My breath stutters in my chest as I hold it in, keeping her essence inside of me long enough for it to imprint itself on my soul. For most of my life, I feared my soul reflected my biological father's, that pieces of me came from my mother, but the rest was him. Dark thoughts and sadistic tendencies fed those beliefs, but now that I look down into Genni's soft features, relaxed with sleep, she really does have the power to heal.

Montez was right.

A part of me wants to bite into her plush bottom lip until she wakes up, hoping I taste blood, but then that quiet, sadistic part of me wants me to pull her panties to the side and slowly wake her up with my cock stretching her pussy wide.

When I jerk against her, I know I have my answer, so I lift off her and once again slip my hand between our bodies to hook my finger into her panties. My knuckle skims along her smooth skin, her heat now infused with her arousal. She squirms as she slowly moves toward consciousness, and I don't waste any time as I hold her thong to the side and line myself up.

Her eyes pop open as I work myself inside of her, her breath catching on a curse. Her muscles lock and her legs go rigid, her chest heaving with each breath. It's then I realize my mistake, my one of many. She was abused, probably forced to endure it when she was helpless to stop it. Kind of like now.

"Fight me," I taunt her as her eyes flick to mine, my cock now halfway inside of her. "Try to make me stop."

The fear emanating from her irises quickly changes to anger as I thrust the rest of the way in, my balls meeting her soaked flesh. She doesn't do what I expect her to, there's no screaming, but the hardening of her eyes tells me I'm about to experience some pain.

Her palm connects with my cheek, the sting spreading along my face as I pull out and slam back in. "How dare you just come in here and…" Her words turn into a long guttural groan as I pull nearly all the way out then thrust back in, quick and hard.

"And what?" I lean down and bite into her cheek as she hisses, her fingers slipping along my hair to yank my head back. "Tell me you don't like to be fucking forced, *princess.*" Her fingers tighten as she pulls on the strands of my hair, the pain flaring over my scalp. It only serves to make me harder, to make me want to continue to force her to take this cock.

"I was forced one too many times to *like it*, Jaeger," she grits through her teeth. "I won't let you do it too."

"Looks different from up here." I grin down at her as her pussy clamps around my cock, sucking me in, begging to make her feel good.

"Fuck you," she snarls as she butts her head forward. My hand wrapping around her throat and holding her back at the last second saves my nose. It's only just started to heal from her last assault.

"You are, baby. You're fucking me so well. Feel how good you take my dick." Her eyes sink into the back of her head as my words roll over her, her cheeks turning pink as I fuck her tight pussy. "Tell me how much you like to be forced."

Those blue irises land back on my face as they flare with anger once again, her thighs tightening around my waist. She jerks upward and bucks me out of her, knocking my hand from her throat and leaving my cock glistening with her juices as she shoves me onto my back. If she punched me in the throat right now, I would let her, but she shocks me as she straddles my waist.

"No one is being forced," she groans as her pussy sinks over my cock, inch by inch, dragging my heart over hot coals as my chest flares with a foreign feeling. She must find the fear in my eyes as she works her hips, her wetness slipping down to coat my balls. "Scared, Jaeger?"

"Take this off," I grunt while lifting her shirt up. I don't want to voice what I'm feeling, but the longer I hold it in, the more it burns a path from my heart to my mouth.

She decimates me when she whips the shirt up over her head and throws it to the floor. Her perfect tits bounce as she fucks me, those twin bars glinting from her dusty rose nipples.

The sounds of her pussy reverberate around us, each sucking noise hitting me in the balls as I bite into my cheek, trying desperately to hold in the release that's threatening to detonate. My fingers dig into the flesh at her waist as she continues to grind over me, finding her oblivion. She reaches up to grab her tits, her fingers pulling at the piercings as her pussy clamps around me, her walls tightening. "I'm coming," she pants as her movements become sloppy.

I let go as explosions burst from behind my eyelids and I come so deep inside of her as garbled words escape my mouth. She falls forward, her hair creating a curtain around us as she looks into my eyes, my cock still pulsing with my release. I tuck the hair behind her ear and lean up, seeking her mouth, but she draws back. "Gen—"

"Thank you," she whispers, cutting me off. "Thank you for giving that back to me."

"We're even." I sit up as she scoffs, the noise sounding cute as the thought makes me wince. *I think she's cute.* What the actual fuck is going on here?

"Even how?" Her arms wrap around my neck, the new position forcing my still hard cock deeper inside her. She bites into her lip and rolls her hips forward, whimpering when her sensitive flesh scrapes against my skin.

"For letting me in, for showing me how to forgive so I can begin to do that for myself." My words are muffled as I drop my face into the crook of her neck, breathing in a mixture of our scents.

The burning spreads in my chest again as I kiss my way up her neck to her cheek, my lips grazing hers. The soft velvet tip of her tongue tentatively strokes the corner of my mouth as I wrap my arms around her waist, dragging her against me and burying myself deeper.

"So good," she moans as she rises then sinks back down, my cum and her juices running down my balls to the bed. "Let's just do this for the next few days."

Then finally, her mouth is on mine, her luscious lips like sugar as I swipe through them with my tongue. Her fingers slip up the back of my head to grip my hair, forcing my head to the side so she can fully dominate my mouth. And I fucking let her.

She's bouncing a perfect rhythm on my cock when the sound of a bike engine pulling into the driveway interrupts, but she doesn't stop. I pull away from her mouth to tell her someone is here when she forces my head to her tits, wiping all logical thoughts from my mind.

The piercings through her nipples add ice to fire, and when I suck one into my mouth, she loses her momentum on a scream. I'm lost in her, completely oblivious to anything else until a throat clears.

"Sorry to interrupt, but we need to have a chat."

Genni gasps and looks over her shoulder as I release her nipple with a pop. "It better be important, Chino. You know how I get when you stop me mid-stroke." Irritation coats my words as Chino chuckles.

"It's usually to tell me to join in."

I can't stop the smile spreading across my face, and my cock pulses when Genni moans her approval.

Insatiable.

She snaps out of it though, long enough to ask, "What

happened?"

"I know where Tazo is."

MALIK
DIESEL

MALIK

I miss my girl. This is the longest I've been away from her and it's only been a day. Slayer tends to keep the dark clouds away with her eternal sunshine, but when she's not with me, I can sense the threatening storm.

Add digging through Barrett's things and it's a brewing natural disaster.

"This safe has his personal assets. Bank accounts, a house, and some bonds." Jones shuts the door and sits back on his ass on the floor.

"We'll give that to Davis," I tell him as I open the second one.

Jones whistles when we find the bags of powder and massive rolls of hundred-dollar bills. I haul those out, throwing them to the side, and grab the ledgers instead. This will be filled with our runs, where we picked up and where we dropped off, but the most important thing I want to see is where the money went.

The information ends up being in the fourth ledger, obscured by the many drops of weapons to the cartel. All except one delivery, three machine guns and ammo sent to an address that never appears again.

"Jones, can you look this up?" I point to the page as he grabs his laptop off the desk and lights a smoke.

He sits back on the floor beside me, his laptop in his lap as he types, his fingers tapping the keyboard. "It's a wood mill, but long gone out of business." He begins pulling camera feeds for the area but clicks his tongue when it comes up blank. "Definitely off the grid. Nothing like the motel."

"This is his place." I stand from the floor and grab my phone from my cut pocket. "Tazo has been chilling pretty close to the cartel this entire time."

"It's fucking smart. The protection along with the promise of endless money," Jones murmurs as he continues to dig for surveillance footage.

I try to call Diego first and groan when it goes to voicemail. He's looking for Delia because normal people are wired to care about their siblings. Not like Slayer and me.

Her number is next, and when that goes to voicemail, I can feel the first boom of thunder rumble inside of me. The next one I try is Chino and when he picks up, he gets an earful of my wrath.

"Why aren't any of you around your phones? Am I the only one looking for this cunt while you all beat your meat and moan about your parental issues?" My knuckles crack around my phone, the screen threatening to break.

"I found him," Quinton says, his voice sounding deep and husky. "I got an address."

"What one is it? Are you winded? Are you actually beating your fucking meat?" I snap, making Jones snicker on the floor.

"What? No!" He reads off an address and it's the same one we're looking at in the ledger.

"It's the same one I found. The area is dark. No cameras or surveillance. We'll have to go in on foot." A moan filters through his phone, the sound like a thread in the fabric of my soul, one I would recognize anywhere. "Are you touching my girl, Chino?"

It's got nothing to do with jealousy and everything to do with being left out.

"Not me," he chokes out and then clears his throat. "You should come by the house, and gather the others. We need to have a meeting."

"The type where clothes are optional? Because that's what it sounds like over there. Is that where Diego is? All four inches of his little cock inside my woman?" This time Jones falls onto his back as he chokes on an exhale of smoke.

"Not him either," Quinton murmurs as his footsteps reverberate through the speaker.

"It better not be my little brother, he's in time-out." I raise a hand to Jones and head out of his room. He'll make sure to take care of everything with Davis and I trust him to do it. Besides, I need to join all Slayer extracurriculars because I plan to ace them with flying colors while the others watch.

"Just get over here." The line goes dead and I slip my phone back into my cut. Sounds like Jaeger found his way into Slayer's bed, and if he's another one she wants, I won't stand in the way, but I won't make it easy for him either.

My eyes catch Rockz at the bar, his tattoo-covered arms folded on the counter, when my phone rings. Digging my phone back out of my pocket, I swipe it open quickly when I see Diego's name. "Did you find her?"

"No, but she did abandon Jaeger's van at a pig farm, which has me antsy as fuck." He sounds so fucking tired and dejected. After what we found out about his family yesterday, I don't blame him.

"Good place to stash bodies," I hum as I wave to Rockz and head outside.

"That's the first thing I thought of. It's Delia, so anything is possible. What are you doing? Are you outside?" The wind blows, freeing my hair from its tie as I stride for my bike.

"Our girl is fucking her brother while her ex, his best friend, watches. I'm missing out on the good shit and I'm not happy." His laugh crashes through to my ear, the sound deep and hoarse. "When are you coming back?" I can't help how deep my voice drops but there's something about a laughing Diego that makes my dick hard.

"Quinton messaged the group chat about finding Tazo, so I'm heading back now. I'll be at the Varga house in thirty." The sound of crunching gravel comes over the speaker as though he's walking on a dirt road.

"I muted that chat," I reveal as he laughs again, my dick throbbing at the sound. "Hurry back, I need you and Slayer in bed with me."

We hang up and my phone is back in my pocket before I'm hauling on my helmet. It's a complicated dynamic between all of us and Slayer. I'm content with sharing her but I'm possessive as fuck at the same time. So the thought of her getting dicked down by her bastard brother makes me both hot and bothered at the same time.

Fifteen minutes later, I pull up to the Varga home to find all the lights on, knowing I missed out on playing with her pierced tits. I park beside Chino's bike and hold back the urge to spit on it, knowing I'd take his tongue if he tried to pull that shit with me. *See? I'm growing up, Ma.*

My fingers glide along the bright yellow of her bike, missing when we would go for rides together but she'd be on her Harley, not this yellow thing.

As soon as I enter the house, hushed voices reach my ears from the kitchen. "I'm here to rebuke the Devil and his temptation, folks," I call out as I turn the corner to find Slayer, Jaeger, and Chino sitting at the table. "Do unto me as you would your brother,"—I hold my hands up toward the ceiling—"touch thine genitals while you serve your neighbor."

Slayer snorts and throws a Cheeto at me, the orange dust landing on my cut. "Penis be with you."

"And also with you." I nod as Chino and Jaeger smirk behind their hands.

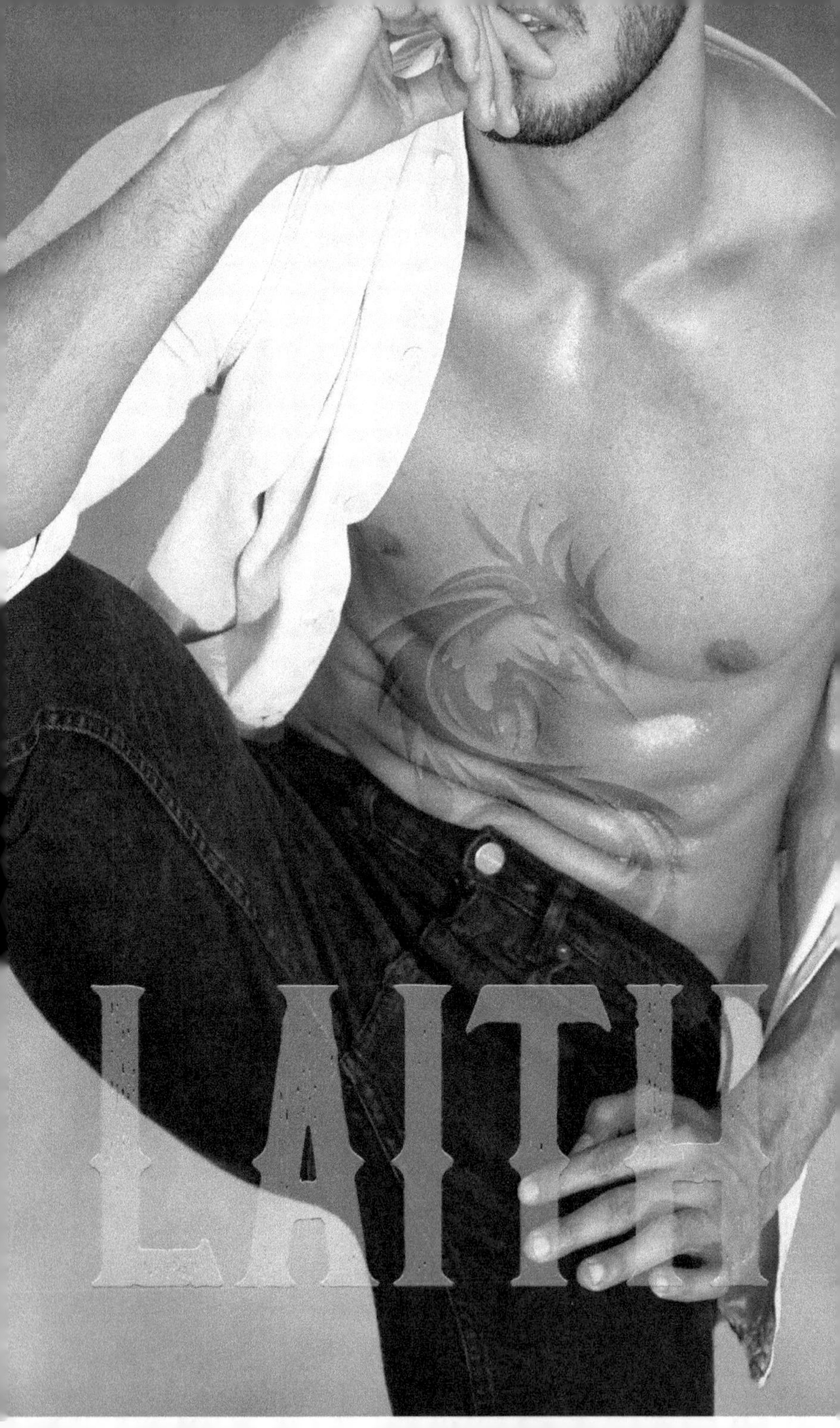

LAITH

CHAPTER FOURTEEN

My heart races as I sit up in bed, my fist pressed to my chest as my other hand slips under the pillow to grab my piece. I take a few minutes to regain my bearings, then a pounding sounds on my door.

"Laith!" The voice is familiar but I can't seem to place it. That's when I hear the rumblings of multiple bikes, as if my brothers are back from a ride. Only we didn't leave for one. "Laith! Hurry!"

Throwing the blankets off my body and grabbing my cut from the dresser, I call out, "Coming!" as I shrug it on.

Angel is on the other side of my door with fear emanating from her busted-up face. "They're here for me." Her body is shaking as I wrap an arm around her shoulders and look down the hall for Carrie. It's rare they're apart.

"Are you here alone?" I ask as I lead her toward the main room. It's clear the brothers had a party last night and only a few are left in here, either recovering or needing to be revived, so definitely no one rode anywhere, but there's no mistaking the sounds of bikes.

"Yes. Quinton said I could stay here. Now they're here to come take me back." She trembles as she presses a fist to her mouth. "I won't go back."

"Who's here?" I pull my phone out of my cut pocket to find a slew of notifications. Then I swipe open my screen to first see a text from Quinton.

Chino: Angel is sleeping down the hall from you. She had a rough few days. I'll tell you more later.

"Charles!" My head pops up from my phone screen to find Kennedy and a few of the brothers coming toward me. "I don't know where our President is, or the Vice for that matter, but we got a problem at the front gate."

"It's the Highway Knights!" Angel shrieks and burrows into my side.

"Go back to your room and lock the door. You're safe here," I assure her as I extradite her from my body. I don't have time to figure out what she's talking about.

Thankfully, she does as I instruct and runs back down the corridor, slipping into an empty room and slamming the door.

"Is it the Knights?" I ask Kennedy as I follow him through the main room. Brothers are coming out of their rooms or rousing from the couches, adjusting guns to their waists and preparing for a fight.

"I don't think so."

We open the door and the sun hits me full blast in the face. I've slept for over twelve hours. There's activity beyond the gate, and when I shield my eyes from the sun to look that way, I find at least thirty bikes.

"What the fuck?" I rush over to a few of my brothers who are standing at the gates as they talk to men I've never seen before.

"Laith,"—Chip leaves the gate and heads my way with a confused look on his face—"they call themselves the Dientes Afilados out of Nevada and apparently, Delia Montez has asked them to travel all this way to help us against Tazo." He looks back over his shoulder toward the meanest looking motherfucker I have ever seen. "That one is the leader, Papi Loco, and he's demanding to speak to the President."

The closer I get to the gate, the more I see of them. "Let them in!" I call out. If they were sent here to help us as they claim, there should be no reason to leave them baking out in the sun. "Chip, I think you need to clean that bar up from last night. We've got quite a few of them." Chip claps me on the shoulder with a chuckle, the excitement rolling off him in waves.

"It's like the good ol' days of blood and whiskey." He rushes inside as the rest of us make way for the bikes rumbling past us.

Their cuts sport a shark mouth emblem, the teeth dripping with blood, and it fits because they exude a bite first and ask questions later vibe. It also gives me hope that we can beat Tazo and come back on top with Genni bringing us all together.

The first thing I do is pull up the group chat on my phone and fire off a message. I don't want the Dientes to feel threatened if I'm making a phone call, but the guys need to hurry their asses over here. Especially Genni. She's our President after all.

The men hop off their bikes and stretch, all of them looking about the size of tanks. Then a van pulls in with their emblem on the side as Papi Loco comes to stand beside me.

"Weapons, ammo, and about enough C4 to blow Arizona off the map, if that's what you want. When Delia beckons, we come running. She's done a lot for us and we're forever in her debt." His voice is gruff with age, the sound reminding me a lot of Vic. When he pulls out a pack of smokes and lights one, the nostalgia hits me in the face.

"Our President will be here soon. I'll get you guys set up with rooms in the meantime. Our bars are stocked and we'll have some barbeque going. You guys must be starving." I nod to a few brothers to set everything up, then turn back to Papi Loco as he takes a drag of his cigarette with a grunt.

"We hear you've been having some trouble with Tazo and the Knights." I turn at the sound of the voice and find a younger version of Papi Loco. "I'm Loquito, Loqi for short." He holds out his hand and I give it a firm shake. "I'm Vice of the Dientes."

"Laith Charles, Sergeant at Arms. Trouble is an understatement," I grumble and look around the lot. "How do you know Tazo?"

"We don't know him personally, but the Knights have been a thorn in our side for quite some time. They like to traffic women and children and we like to fuck them up for it." He bounces a little on his toes, the manic look in his eyes kind of reminding me of Malik. "So even though the Viper is a good friend, we came here to kick their asses just a little more."

"We're glad to have you. They're also connected with the cartel and any help we can get is appreciated." I motion for them to follow me inside the clubhouse, standing out in the open with Knights and Tazo still on the loose is making me nervous. "Let's head to our meeting room and have a chat."

"Yeah. We need to come up with a game plan and fast. The Knights aren't known for their patience or finesse. They hit hard and it's always messy," Loqi informs me as we head inside. "Civilians and local enforcement don't hinder them either. They act untouchable."

"Until we decide to step in," Papi Loco rasps out, his tone dark. "Then we take out as many of them as we can."

The club is quiet when we step inside, the brothers standing around and staring down the newcomers with looks of distrust on their faces. It's hard to trust other clubs when we've always been at war with them.

"In here." My phone begins to vibrate as I lead the men inside Mass and I pull it out of my pocket to see Malik's name on the screen.

"Settle in, I have to take this."

I answer the phone to the sound of wind in my ear, "Yeah."

"We're on our way. Slayer is on her bike so she'll be there quicker. Do not discuss anything without her." He hangs up before I can get a word in and I growl as I shove the phone back into my pocket.

"Let me make them comfortable, brother," Chip says as he walks by me, a tray in his hand. Whiskey, shot glasses, and a few blunts are sitting on top.

"Good idea," I mumble, my irritation still fresh. My brother will always be a fucking prick and I either need to accept it or kill him. The latter is looking better and better every day.

The higher-pitch rumble of a bike coming into the compound doesn't sound like a cruiser. Malik wasn't joking when he said she would be here soon. The door opens and she struts in, the sun shining behind her, making her hair more mahogany than brown. Her face is free of any cosmetics and set in a determined expression, the hard glint in her eyes shining bright.

The cut she's wearing sports two President patches. One for Dragons and the other for March. She's wearing a black tank top underneath and a dusty pair of jeans, her heavy boots hitting the wood floor in loud *thuds* as she approaches me.

"What can you tell me in thirty seconds?" She flicks her gaze around the room, taking in our brothers and the newcomers in a scrutinizing scan.

"They were sent here by Delia. We have a common enemy in Tazo and they've been fighting the Highway Knights for dominance in Nevada. The president is an old man who looks like an asshole but sounds fair. His son is a little more laid-back but he looks insane." It's rapid-fire and even though her eyes aren't on me, she's soaking it all in.

"Do they know I'm a woman?" It's the first sign of reluctance she's given and despite holding back the urge to grasp her chin and force her to look at me, I lean in close.

"They're about to find out."

GENEVIEVE
BMW Motorrad Milano

GENEVIEVE

The club's quiet, a little too quiet, and filled to the ceiling with tension. Maybe I've finally sent them all over the edge with this latest addition of another MC.

When Laith sent the text message that this club had shown up at the request of Delia, I was out of the door and on my bike in an instant. My heart nearly worked its way out of my chest the entire ride here because I was so sure I would see Delia, but she's not here.

Disappointment hangs heavily in my chest, but I push it down. I've texted her, I've called, and I've left her voice messages, but I've been answered with silence. To say I'm worried would be an understatement because I know all too well what it is to think you know a family member for your whole life only to be punched in the gut with the truth later.

The distant rumble of bike engines sounds from outside of the club, telling me Malik, Quinton, and Diego have shown up. I asked Jaeger to come because he and I have clearly progressed in our relationship and I was willing to take the wrath of the club to bring him back. He said no, but he assured me that he would be there to fight each one of our enemies.

"Let's get this over with." The door to Mass is open and I stride toward it, each one of my steps small in comparison to the man who once ran this club. I don't ever expect to fill his shoes, and honestly, after everything I've learned, I don't fucking want to.

There has been no time for me to sit and digest everything I have been fed about my father because he has left me a war to win to save this club or watch it all crumble and every brother perish. At times like this, I despise him for leaving me this legacy. I want to go back to being blissfully ignorant as I once was, but then I think about all of their faces and the pride they display for this club. I could never go back.

So I lift my chin a few fractions, pulling myself up to my proper height and straightening my shoulders, readying myself to carry yet one more burden in the name of the Steel Dragons. I'm a Varga, and despite the man who gave me this last name and his actions, I will be the first to live up to what it should represent.

The voices drop to a hush, leaving the room completely still as I walk inside. My eyes quickly move over each man, both sitting and standing, in the room as I move to the head of the table without faltering and not once dropping my shoulders.

"Sorry to keep you waiting." My voice doesn't even sound like my own. It's as though I've embodied the callous behavior of my father mixed with the essence of my mother and the strength she passed on to me. I've become V once again and I embrace her like an old friend. It was nice being Genevieve for a while, but now I need to become the woman who had the guts to shoot two men in the head. "I'm sure Delia has filled you in on a bit of the situation we find ourselves in here." I don't sit in my chair, instead, I remain standing, placing my hands on the tabletop as I lean forward. Laith takes his rightful place to my right leaving the first chair open for Quinton.

"You're Vic Varga's daughter?" The president of the Dientes, his patch saying *Papi Loco*, places his elbows on the table and also leans forward. He's about the age my father would be now and he has the same weathered look on his face. He's handsome, in a rugged, cruel way, and there's a ruthless cunning shining from his eyes. His long, salt-and-pepper hair is tied back in a low ponytail and his matching beard hangs, the ends brushing the center of his chest.

"In the flesh." Just as the words leave my mouth, my guys show up. Quinton, Malik, and Diego storm their way into the room in a cloud of dust, leather, and mischievous smirks. Quinton takes his seat next to me while Malik and Diego sit on Laith's other side. I give them a nod and turn my head back to the President of the Dientes. "As you know, the Highway Knights and the cartel have been a source of contention, to say the least, for my club. Their leader, Tazo Chino, who likes to call himself the Superior, has been working effortlessly to destroy us. So to have you and your men here to lend us the much-needed numbers to win this fight is so very appreciated. If you ever need us to help you, we'll be there without question."

With that out of the way, I finally take my seat, waiting for someone to fill the silence.

"We heard about your father, he seemed like a great leader," the younger man next to Papi Loco says, *Loquito* is on his patch. "Our condolences. Do we have a plan of attack? Or are we flying by the ass of our chaps? Because we can do both." A few chuckles circle the room as I relax a little in my seat, despite Papi Loco's stare on the side of my face.

"We have a location but we're currently scouting it out to see if it's legit. I saw your van parked outside and took a peek in the back. Looks like you're well-stocked for what's coming. How often do you find yourselves at war with the Knights and what can you tell us about them?" Loquito's face lights up at my inquiry and it's him who leans forward.

"Last year, those Knights nearly killed me in a war over skin. They like to traffic women and children across borders and we like to fuck that up for them." A few of the Dientes hit the table in a drumroll beat as Loquito grins. "Kho and Khaine here have been hitting hard into their supply runs, taking out their source of income and mapping their routes for the skin exchange." It takes every ounce of strength to hold in the laugh threatening to spill from my lips as my eyes land on a set of twins. Where my twins are dark-haired and golden-skinned, these two are pale with near-white hair, making their monikers well-deserved. "Then Coin and Bank have been in charge of rescue and picking up the victims to be taken care of at our compound before sending them back home. Perc and Vico supply us with the weapons we need to gun down those motherfuckers whenever they're in sight. If this Tazo person is in charge of the Knights, I can only imagine the *product* he's distributing."

He falls back into his seat as the rest nod their heads, the information only making my stomach sour further.

"He trafficked my mother and he planned to do the same to me. So you can imagine just how personal this is. I want to decimate the asshole and I'm glad you are all here to do it with us." I motion for Malik to take over as he's the one with the information about Tazo's whereabouts, thanks to Jones.

He pulls out his cell phone and pushes it across the table, showing the satellite image of the warehouse where we believe Tazo is staying. "It's grainy and low resolution because this place is practically off-grid, but I think this is where we need to go to find Tazo and the Knights. The first problem? A cartel warehouse is about a mile up the road and I know the location well. He'll have easily a hundred men, if not more. He's got the numbers but his men aren't loyal to him, they follow him through fear."

"So we cut out the cancer at the source," Papi Loco growls as his hands curl into fists. "If killing this Tazo guy means we eliminate their leader, I'm all fucking for it."

"Let's do this," Malik says as he leans across the table, extending his hand to Papi Loco.

Papi Loco takes it in his and they shake as the rest of us pound our fists on the table. It sounds like a war drum, the heavy beat like a symphony of dread.

"But tonight, we party!" I call out as everyone cheers.

It's not my scene to chug back whiskey and fuck the Bunnies, but this is my club and I'll be here to celebrate what may very well be the last night for some of us.

"I'm worried about her," I admit to Diego as I down the rest of my beer. "She's never ignored me this long."

"She's not ignoring you, my love." He leans in and swipes the hair back from my face. "She's lost right now. I can sense it."

Chip places another beer in front of me and removes my empty, his forehead shining with sweat but his face radiant with happiness. We invited the March to join us since we'll all be fighting together in a matter of hours. Luckily, Rockz is helping Chip out behind the bar and I'm not missing the looks they're giving each other. It's clear there's some sort of attraction and it's taking my mind somewhat off of the impending doom.

"I'll kill that bastard for what he did to your family, for what he did to mine," I vow as I tip the bottle to my mouth and take a swig.

Heat hits my back and I take in a deep breath of rain and cedar. Laith. "Can we talk?" he murmurs in my ear, the sound like honey over my fraying nerves.

Turning on my stool, I find Diego and Malik in deep conversation, their heads close and bodies touching. I haven't been missing the looks between them either and I fucking love it. Then I'm facing Laith, and my heart melts at the sight of him. He's my gentle protector, the man who cradles my heart like it's glass, unafraid of showing me how much he cares.

"Hi." I smile at him as I reach out and take his hand.

He tugs me off the stool and leads me down the corridor toward the dorms. When he opens the door to his room, I'm hit with his scent, making my toes curl inside my boots.

"I wanted some time alone with you before tomorrow, if that's okay?" The bashful look he gives me makes me giggle as I grab his face between my hands.

"Wheneveryouwantmeisokay," I say quickly, my words running together with excitement as I wrap my arms around his neck.

He bends down to run his nose along mine, the touch a sweet

caress. "You're so fucking beautiful and strong. It drives me crazy." Then his mouth is on mine, the kiss lacking the gentleness of his hands as he drags them up under my shirt to haul me in closer. "I love you so much, Genni." There was a time when the sound of that name would send me into a spiral and becoming V was the only way I could tolerate life, but now, when any of my men say it with love, I want to hear it over and over again.

"Show me," I whisper as he slowly removes my cut while peppering kisses all over my face.

He folds my cut and places it on his dresser, then he's doing the same for his as his eyes meet mine in the mirror. The look quickly morphs from adoration to fire as he turns and grins. "Take your pants off and face this mirror."

The demand in his tone sends flames licking over my skin as goose bumps erupt in tingling masses. I kick off my boots and undo my pants, my fingers feeling like dough as I two-step my way out of each leg.

By the time I've disentangled myself from my pants and underwear, Laith is standing in front of me, his pants and boxers discarded and his hand stroking his large cock. *My large cock.* "Turn around and put your hands on that dresser, *Prez*, then spread those legs for me."

I sigh and do as he asks, my pussy dripping with anticipation. His hands grab my waist as he positions me where he wants me and I begin to tremble when his cock nudges my entrance. "Yes, Laith," I moan as I hang my head.

"Eyes up and on me, princess," he growls, and when I don't comply fast enough, his hand cracks against my ass cheek, the pain bringing my pleasure to life.

My eyes meet his as he pushes into me, his cock stretching me as my mouth falls open and the air rushes from my lungs. From this position, he feels larger than usual and when he bottoms out inside of me,

I swear he's the deepest he's ever been. "Shit," I hiss as I close my eyes, only to receive another slap to the ass.

He pulls out, achingly slow, then slams back in, nearly sending me into the mirror, but his hands on my waist stop me at the last second. He continues with that punishing rhythm as the sounds of my arousal permeate the space around us.

Laith releases one hand to grip my hair at the back of my head, his fingers tightening around the strands as he holds me in place. It's domineering and so fucking hot. "Come apart on this cock," he orders, my pussy beginning to pulse with his words.

Reaching down to the apex of my thighs, I begin to furiously rub circles against my sensitive clit. The combination of Laith's deep thrusts and my massaging of my clit sends me over the edge and I scream through the pleasure as my pussy milks his cock.

He's not too far behind as his strokes become erratic and his breath hits my shoulder before he falls over my back with a groan. His hot cum shoots inside of me as his jerking cock sends shocks of pleasure over me.

"I love you," he pants as I lift my head to find him watching me in the mirror.

"I love you too."

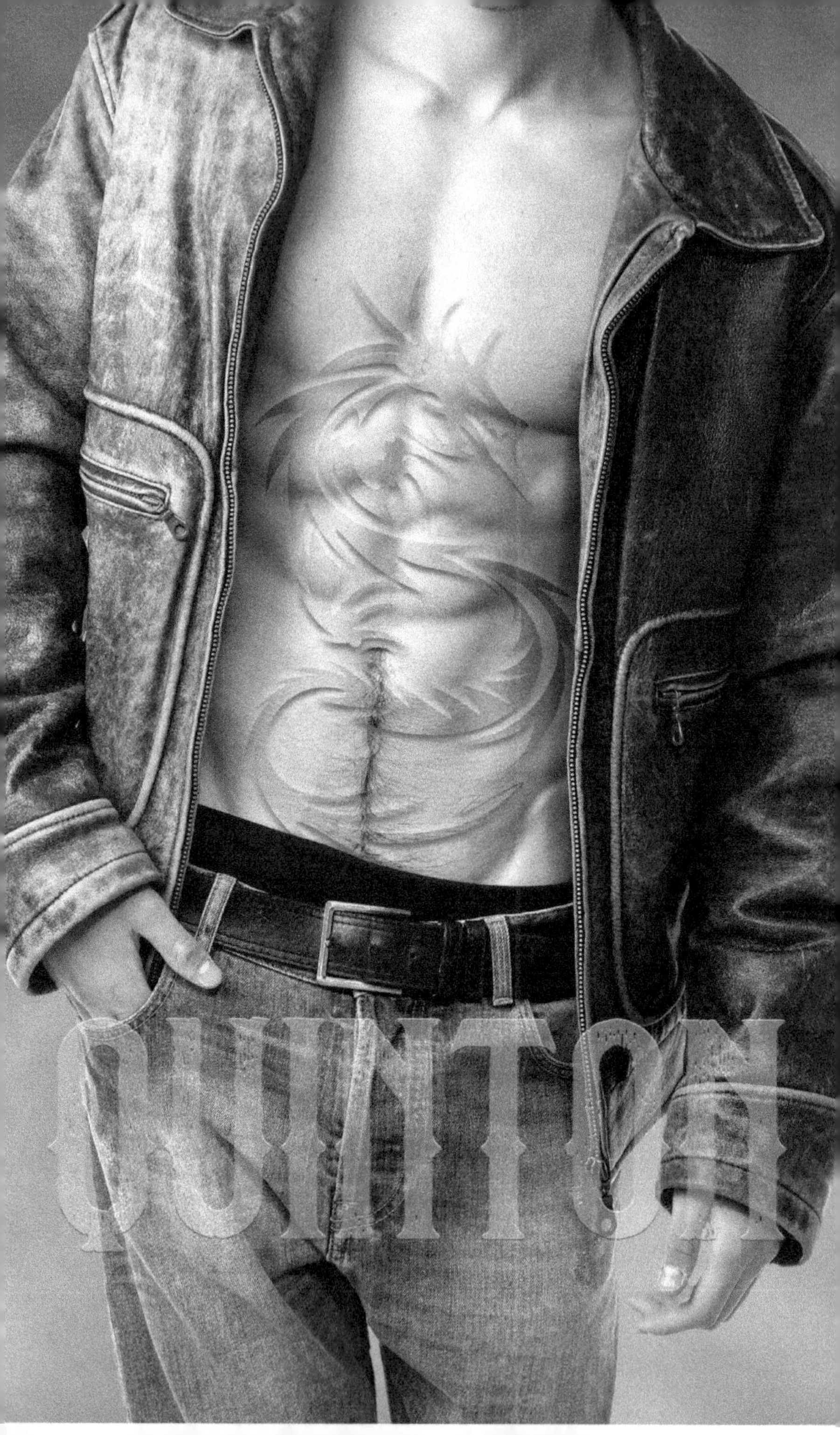

QUINTON

Jaeger: I'm ready to blow some fuckers up tomorrow. What are you guys doing? I bet the brothers are drinking and partying it up, huh?

Guilt swarms my insides as I read his message before looking around the room at the chaos happening. It's not the same without him, and even though we were reckless in the shit we did together, we were always at each other's side. Whether that was drinking or fucking.

I crush the water bottle in my hand and throw it down onto the couch. Everything has changed and I can't decide if it's for the better. The deceit and the sneaky ways our leader forced us to do shit is gone, but the brotherhood is also diminishing. Or maybe it's just me because when I look around the room, I see it clearly.

It's astonishing how well the March and Dragons are coexisting when not even a year ago we were shooting at each other. Genni did this. She accomplished something no other President could. Harmony.

It's as if my mind conjures her as she comes walking out of the corridor, her hair a little messy and her lips swollen. My cock jerks in my pants at the sight of a well-fucked woman. *My woman.*

Do we all think that? Does Malik or Laith look at her and see her as theirs? Is sharing really this easy?

My cock hardens as though it remembers exactly what it should be doing right now. It's an MC party and I'm stone sober, so I might as well indulge in the next thing I love doing at a party.

Pushing up off the couch, my phone pings in my hand and I look down at another message from Jaeger.

Jaeger: Make sure she's safe.

That's when the idea hits me and I grin from ear to ear as I type a message back.

Me: We'll be there soon.

Jaeger: We?

Ignoring the next ping that comes through, I stuff my phone into my cut pocket and follow Genni to the bar. I watched her walk off with Laith toward his room and she seemed a little more inebriated compared to what she does now. Looks like Laith's dick sobered her up.

"Wanna get out of here?" I sidle up next to her and twist a piece of her hair around my finger.

Chip snorts as he hands her a beer, giving her a knowing look. "She needs to be able to walk tomorrow," he says before he walks to the other end of the bar.

"Says who?" Genni scoffs as she lifts the beer to her mouth, but I grab the bottle and place it back on the bar, giving her a pointed look.

"I'll need you to at least stay on the bike." Slipping my hand into hers, I tug her off the stool and toward the exit, leaving behind the sounds of the party. I'm glad my brothers are having a great send-off for tomorrow, but there are two people I would rather spend my night with.

My best friend and my girl.

"Did you really make me leave a party to bring me home?" she scoffs as she gets off the bike. "I'm not that drunk, Quinton, and I want to be with my brothe—"

I pull her back to me and crush my mouth against hers to cut off her words. This is where I made love to her the first time, and if she'll have me, this is where I want to spend the night before we go to war.

With a sigh, she breaks the kiss and looks around the driveway, her eyes landing on Jaeger's bike. "This might be a little awkward because I had sex with him last night, or day, or whenever it was." She waves her hand over her head as I chuckle. "You guys already know I'm not monogamous, in case you're expecting me to choose. The love I have for Malik, Diego, and Laith isn't going anywhere either and neither are they."

"What about me?" I ask as I release her and stand from my bike. "How do you feel about me?"

"You broke my heart, Quinton," she admits, her words whispered and etched in pain. "Jaeger nearly broke me, but you finished the job that night." Both of us turn to look at the end of the driveway, reliving the moment Malik Charles came out of the house with her thrown over his shoulder. "I've learned to see it all in a different light now because I believe it brought me to Malik and Diego. That doesn't mean I've forgiven you and Jaeger, not fully anyway." She places her hand over her heart as mine implodes in my chest. "I'm trying, but the trust is gone. How do I know you won't do it again? That my life isn't something you two view as collateral for any agenda you're thinking up."

I open my mouth and then shut it as words escape me. How do I prove to her how much it killed me to have been a part of what happened to her? The months I was like a zombie afterward, nearly drinking myself to death? None of that would make an impact though because my pain didn't alleviate hers.

"I'm not saying any of this to make you feel guilty. It's just the truth. When I look at you and Jaeger, I still think of that night. Him shooting my father in the head and you letting Malik take me to the man who would torture me for weeks." She points to her temple and takes a step closer to me. "I had nightmares for months after, but do you know what hurt more than anything in that basement?"

I shake my head because I can't imagine anything hurting more than that.

"I lost my family." Her voice breaks as her hand drops to her side and her chest swells with the effort to hold in her sob. "Ma, Dad, Jaeger, and even you, Quinton. You were here with us almost every day, you practically grew up with Jaeger and me, and that night, I lost you all." The first tear skates down her cheek and she swipes it away with irritation. "So I found a new family. Diego and Malik brought me back to life, and then Laith came along like a soothing balm for the wound you two created. He was a link to the Dragons but he was willing to leave it all for me. He gave me back my worth."

She reaches up to wipe at my cheeks, clearing the tears I didn't know were there. "I've loved you for years," I admit to her as she looks into my eyes. I hope with everything that she sees the truth I've forced myself to hide in the name of my brotherhood with Jaeger. "Then I lost my father, and being a Dragon made me feel close to him. I was petrified of losing that. I clung to Vic and Jaeger who felt like a true father and brother to me, and that meant letting you go. If I wasn't around you, then I could ignore everything I felt for you."

"Until you had to train me." She smirks as my mind flips through our days at the warehouse. Right up to the first time I kissed her.

"I couldn't ignore it any longer." I wince and grab her hand. "You've always been inside my heart, but those days felt like a dream. I wasn't a Dragon and you weren't my President's daughter, but that wasn't reality, was it?" She shakes her head slowly, her hair moving around her shoulders. "I made an oath to your father and the club, and

I'm a man of my word. So when Jaeger told me you were planning to take everything from him, I stayed true to that oath."

"I know—"

"I'm not done," I cut her off and pull her close, wrapping my arms around her waist. "I've regretted that decision every night since and that only made me hate myself more because I was breaking the oath to my club." Her forehead presses to my chest as she exhales a long breath, her fingers curling into my shirt beneath my cut. "I want to make it up to you for the rest of my life. My oath is now yours, if you'll have it."

Her arms wind around my neck as she looks up at me, her eyes sparkling with tears as she nods. "Okay."

Leaning forward, I kiss her gently, her mouth tasting like the sweetest nectar I have ever consumed. When my tongue swipes along her lips, they open on a moan and I take advantage of the moment to slip into her warm mouth. She turns to putty in my arms, just like she did the first time I kissed her, and it's the first time I've felt true hope.

She breaks the kiss to gaze toward her front door, her mouth curving upward. "Did you bring me here so we can repeat our first time? With my brother?"

I wince at her words and she laughs when she sees my expression. "Please don't call him that."

"I've been hearing quite a few stories about you two from the brothers. That you would tag team the Bunnies. Or was it Carrie and Angel?" Her teasing tone does nothing to stop the embarrassment from heating my cheeks.

"Only when we were drinking," I confess with a roll of my eyes as she grabs my hand and yanks me toward the door.

"And are you two drinking tonight?" she inquires as she digs her keys out of the pocket of her cut.

"No. I'm not anyway." She turns to look at me as we stand on the porch, the light from the bulb overhead making her brunette hair look mahogany.

"Does this mean you don't mind sharing? That you'd be comfortable with my other relationships?" The hopeful gleam in her eyes has me leaning forward to press a chaste kiss to her mouth.

"Any way I can have you, Genni," I whisper against her lips as she softens, her tongue coming out to flick at my bottom lip.

"And tonight you want me between you and Jaeger?" She pulls her head back to look in my eyes as I nod.

"Yeah. That's exactly what I want." Her pupils dilate, the black nearly eating away all the blue as she bites into her lip.

I grab the keys from her hand and unlock the door to step inside just as Jaeger comes out of the kitchen, his hair a tousled mess on his head and wearing only a pair of low-slung pajama pants. It seems he's getting over the fear of that space. His surprised look moves from Genni to me as questions appear in his dark eyes.

"I'm going to text the others to let them know she's safe," I tell him as I hand Genni back her keys and move toward the living room, giving them space to speak. With my phone in my hand, I open the group chat and fire off a message.

Me: Slayer is sleeping between me and her brother tonight.

It takes a few seconds, but Malik is the first to reply, as I knew he would be. He's completely insane and he's crazy about her. I bet he was the first to notice her missing.

Malik: A mortal sin, how intriguing.

Laith: Make sure she gets some rest too.

Diego: I second Laith. We can't take chances for tomorrow.

Closing the chat, I slip my phone back into my pocket and turn to find Jaeger with Genni in his arms, her legs wrapped around his waist and their mouths fused in a passionate kiss. My cock swells at the sight and I take pride in what I've done here tonight. I knew I could help mend what Jaeger and I broke so long ago.

Jaeger breaks his mouth away from hers to trail kisses down her throat as she looks at me over his shoulder. "Are you just going to stand there all night?"

Her smug smile has me stalking toward them, my steps sure and my heart pounding. I stand at Jaeger's back, my hard cock brushing his ass as I grab a handful of her hair and lean in to kiss her, my tongue spearing into her mouth.

She whimpers and I pull back in time to see Jaeger's teeth release the sensitive skin of her neck. "Your bed or mine?" he asks her while I step back, her eyes meeting mine.

"Mine," she husks out, causing my cock to strain against the zipper of my jeans. She knows that's exactly where I want to be. In the same bed I took her innocence.

I wonder if she remembers what I said I would do to her when we were fucking at the clubhouse that night.

My cock jerks at the memory as we head up the stairs. She was so angry catching me in the room with Carrie and it only heightened my desire for her. She was a fighter, even back then, and I've never been so proud to belong to someone.

This goes beyond my oath to the club. I made a choice to become a Steel Dragon, but there was no consent when my soul fused itself to hers. I wouldn't change a damn thing, though.

Jaeger kicks open her bedroom door, his mouth once again on hers, and I follow them inside. The bed is rumpled from the last time I caught them in here together and the memory only has my cock aching more.

"Give me your belt," Jaeger says to me as he throws Genni on her bed. She giggles as she sits up and strips off her cut and tank top, her perfect breasts bare beneath.

"If you think you're whipping me with that, you have another thing coming. Delia may kill people with poison, but I kill them with bullets." She falls back on the bed and arches her back to remove her jeans, taking her panties with them.

My fingers pause on my belt buckle as I watch her, my breathing becoming heavy with want at her threat.

"C'mon, Chino," Jaeger snaps and pushes my hands out of the way so he can undo my belt for me. "Get it together."

He snaps me out of the trance I'm in, and I quickly remove my cut, dropping it on Genni's dresser and yanking my shirt up over my head. My jeans are now baggy without my belt and hang low around my waist as Jaeger turns and snaps the leather toward Genni.

She doesn't flinch or shy away, instead, she gives him a heated look, her mouth tipping upward in the corners. "What are you going to do with that?" she asks, her voice smooth as honey slowly rolling over my skin.

"I think you deserve a punishment," Jaeger growls as I undo my pants and let them pool around my feet. I realize my boots are still on when Genni sits up once more and those long fingers of hers glide down over her stomach, disappearing between her legs.

"I deserve to be punished?" She tips her head to the side as that hand of hers works furiously between her legs. "Are you sure about that?"

"That's not what I said." Jaeger tosses the belt onto the bed, the leather strap landing close to Genni's other hand, and both of our eyes follow the motion. "I said you deserve a punishment. Not that you would be receiving one."

"I don't understand." She pulls her fingers out from the apex of her thighs and Jaeger falls forward on the bed, grabbing her wrist and sucking the fingers into his mouth. She gives him a confused look, her head tilted to the side.

Once he releases them with a *pop,* he stands back up and drops his pajama pants, then turns around to face me, his cock standing just as hard as my own. "You're going to whip us with that belt and then we're going to fuck you to sleep."

"Us?" I ask as I finally free my feet of my boots, socks, pants, and boxers. Hesitation to approach the bed has me standing stark naked as I look between them. "What do you mean *us?*"

"I mean, it's the least we can do for reparations, don't you think?" With his back to Genni, he doesn't see her as she picks up the belt and rises to her knees on the bed.

I open my mouth, perhaps to warn him or reply to what he said, but everything stops in that moment when that strap of leather cracks against his ass. First, his eyes nearly bug out of his head as his mouth hangs open on a silent scream, second, I see the anger swell in those inky pools. "You wanted this," I remind him as I take a few steps toward him.

"I'm just seeking reparations." Genni snickers as she cracks that belt back down over his ass again. I'm not going to lie and say that his small whimper of pain doesn't have my cock jumping in my hand.

"Your turn, fucker," he grits out through his teeth, motioning me toward the bed.

"This wasn't my idea." I shake my head, my cock quickly deflating.

"Come on, Chino," Genni coos as she strokes the black supple leather. "Two strikes and then I'll let you fuck me wherever you want."

My cock springs back to attention as I take the few steps to the bed, my eyes on the belt in her hands. "Fine." I turn around to face Jaeger, leaving my ass exposed for Genni's whips when my eyes fall to the welts forming on Jaeger's ass. "Holy shit!" I hiss. "Hold on—" I don't have a chance to say anything else as the belt comes down on my ass cheek, the immediate connection of leather to flesh like an inferno on my skin. There's no stopping the high-pitched scream that erupts from my throat, making Jaeger fall backward on the bed with a laugh. "Jesus," I squeak out as my hands immediately cover my ass cheeks in an attempt to protect myself from yet another assault. My cock deflates once more as pain throbs along my ass.

"One more, Quinton," Genni coaxes. "This type of reparation works so well."

I move my hands to turn and beg for her to end this painful game, but she's quick and flicks that leather against my skin again before I get to plead my case. Another squeal escapes my lips and then I turn and grab the leather in my hands, ripping it from hers and throwing it onto the floor. "Enough!" I snap as she falls back on the bed, her pierced nipples winking at me from her breasts.

This isn't the Genni I had so long ago. She's not that sweet and innocent girl anymore. Now she's a woman and she's grown in the confidence of her strength and hardened in the experience of our betrayal.

Jaeger crawls over her legs as she spreads them wide, a devious smile coating her mouth. "I have to warn you," she husks out, "I was with Laith not too long ago."

Jaeger shrugs his shoulders and proceeds to run his nose up and down the inside of her thigh, the scruff along his cheeks grazing her pussy. "It doesn't matter to me," he reveals before spreading her folds and running his tongue from bottom to top.

With my cock hard once again, I crawl onto the bed and up her side, my eyes on those adorned nipples and my mouth watering for a taste. I suck one into my mouth as her back arches off the bed, my hand cupping the other as my fingers flick the bar.

She's squirming beneath us, her moans coupled with my heavy breathing and Jaeger's feasting like the soundtrack for my wildest fantasy. Jaeger and I have done this many times before but this time it's different. I am content and instead of chasing my own release, I want to make sure she's feeling good first. I wonder if Jaeger is thinking the same thing.

Releasing her nipple, I turn to find him lost between her legs, eating her with a concentration I have never witnessed from him. I guess that's my answer. He comes up for air a second later, his mouth lined with her juices and a smug look on his face.

"You're on the swings tonight," I tell him. "I'm hitting the slide." His eyes flick to Genni as she rises onto her elbows, giving us puzzling looks.

"Are we going to the park?" she asks, her cheeks pink and her eyes glazed.

"We love a play date." Jaeger snickers as he falls onto his back on the bed and pats his lap. "Come ride the swing."

"Oh," Genni breathes out as she swings a leg over Jaeger's waist and gives me a look over her shoulder. "Slide?"

"Head first into the dirt, baby." I give her a wink as her eyes clear of confusion.

"Lube is in the drawer." She points to the side table. "And take it easy. I'm delicate."

Jaeger wraps her hair around his fist and drags her down for a kiss while I open the side table drawer. With the tube in my hand, I kneel between Jaeger's open legs as Genni sinks down over his length, her pussy eating every inch as she hisses out a curse.

Coating my cock with the lube, I grab the discarded belt from the floor with my other hand and toss it to Jaeger. "Make sure she stays in place."

"What?" she asks as she turns her head to look at me, her eyes falling to my glistening cock. "Fuck, I missed that dick."

I smirk as Jaeger wraps the belt around her neck, making her buck forward on his cock. "Take it easy," he coaxes as he pulls the leather through the buckle and hauls her down to him, opening her ass for me. "Kiss me and don't move or this tightens." He yanks on the belt for good measure.

With one more thrust into her, Jaeger stalls and begins to kiss her as I grab the globe of her ass in one hand and guide my dick to her asshole with the other, my teeth sinking into my lip with the effort to hold in my moan.

As soon as I'm inside of her, I'll be lost to everything else. It's the effect she has on me and I've been lost without it all these months. "Take a deep breath," I warn her as she breaks the kiss from Jaeger but is unable to lift her head because of the belt.

"Get the fuck inside of me, Quinton. You have to know I was being sarcastic about being delicate." Her words have me working past the tight ring of muscle in no time, and then I'm sinking inside of her, the fit tight and nearly strangling my cock.

Once I'm all the way in, Jaeger gives her some slack with the belt and looks up at me with a devious smirk. "Seesaw, motherfucker."

That's how we work in tandem, like a fucking seesaw. He drops the belt completely to pull her up by the waist as she melts into a puddle of heated flesh and arousal, and I push further into her. When I pull out, he thrusts into her pussy, and then we're off in the perfect rhythm as her juices seep out of her.

Adding to the tight hold she has on both of our cocks, her moans of pleasure and whines of pain only bring me closer to that edge. Jaeger yanks her back down by the belt to suck on her neck and I take that opportunity to grab her waist and fuck her tight asshole with vigor.

The flesh around my cock becomes red as I slam in and out of her, my cock working Jaeger's at the same time.

"Fuck," he growls as she breaks the kiss to suck in a breath and scream, her pussy and asshole squeezing both of our cocks as she comes, fluid running out of her to soak the bed. "I'm going to fucking come so hard in this pussy," Jaeger announces, and a couple of thrusts later, I feel him jerking deep inside of her, his cum coating her insides.

She's trembling when I lift her off his cock and pull out of her ass, grabbing the belt to bring her back flush to my chest. I spread her knees open with my other hand, giving Jaeger a perfect view of his cum dripping from her pussy as I release the belt and lift her up to spear my cock through his cum and hers.

I fuck up into her, knowing I only have a few good thrusts in me before my load joins Jaeger's. Her head falls back to hit my shoulder, her moans filling my ear when I grab a perfect tit in my hand. "Tell me you love our cocks," I demand as I pull her downward by the tit at the same time I slam up into her.

"I fucking love your cocks," she breathes out, the velvet tone of her voice making my balls tighten and my breath to get trapped in my throat while I freefall into my release. Grinding up into her, I come so fucking hard that stars erupt behind my eyelids as I hiss out a breath between my teeth.

Our damp bodies meld together and my heart beats against her back, the tempo quick as I start to come down from the high I'm riding. A few moments later, I release her as she falls forward to lie beside Jaeger, the belt still around her neck and her thighs coated in both of our releases.

"Let's go to the park once a week at least," she mumbles before she drifts off to sleep.

DIEGO

CHAPTER FIFTEEN

Adjusting the scope on my gun, I run my eye along the line of men, *and women*, standing in the middle of the desert near the warehouse where Tazo is staying. We hit up the cartel warehouse an hour before the sun rose, only to find it empty. There's no doubt in my mind that everyone is inside the large warehouse we've been watching for the past few days.

This is it. We're about to fight in the biggest battle we've ever fought, and my anxiety has been running on high all night. It's going to be hard being the only sniper now that Delia is still MIA, and even though Quinton offered to set up his gun, I refused because I wanted him beside Genevieve. The more men who love her down there, the safer she'll be. I don't doubt for a second that any one of them would die in her place. Even Jaeger.

Sitting back on the roof of the Dientes' van, I count my mags once again. Twenty mags, each one with five bullets. A loud *boom* sounds in the distance, a signal for us to be ready. Jaeger rigged a bomb to the cartel warehouse with the plan to move the Knights and cartel out of the other warehouse without having to raid them or bomb them and hurt any women or children that might be inside. A whirring noise settles over my head, and I look to the sky to find Jones' drone.

"Montez," his voice sounds through my phone lying on the roof of the van, "they're moving."

"Roger that," I reply and fall to my stomach, settling the gun in front of me.

We parked the van about fifty yards from where my brothers and the love of my life are assembled and up on higher ground so that I could see the bigger picture. The role I'm playing is an important one, I know that, but I wish I was with them, fighting for our clubs and claiming back what's rightfully ours.

Tazo needs to be gone and it needs to be permanent. He was exiled once and that did nothing to keep him away. If anything, he grew an empire under all our noses and now we have to ensure it all falls to the ground, never to rise again.

I take a moment to think of my sister, hoping she's okay and that we all make it out of here today and see her again. My eye lands on Ajani standing at the front line, his hands hovering over the double guns at his waist, and I look for any sign of his worry. There's something between him and my sister, and I plan to force it out of him after today, if we live.

It's hard to be optimistic when death surrounds us every day. If we make it out of here, we'll value each day a little more, and that's something to strive for. Being a club without territory disputes is another.

I have every reason to take out Tazo myself, to shoot a bullet through his skull, but Genevieve begged me to let her do it, that she would kill him in the name of my mother and hers. I love her with every fiber of my being so there was no argument.

Clouds of dust kick up in the distance and I ready myself for the coming storm. After a few moments, the sound of rumbling engines fills the air and my brothers stand in a firm line across the road, all of them with their weapons drawn.

"This is for you, Mom and Dad," I whisper as my finger hovers over the trigger.

LAITH

LAITH

Genni shakes out her hands for the tenth time, the tension radiating off her like a thick cloud of anxiety around my head. I'm so attuned to her but so is my brother. Malik stands to her right and a little in front, his eyes darting around the place as the silence amps the tension.

The ground rumbles under our feet as Jaeger's bomb goes off, letting us know that phase one of our plan has gone smoothly. I exhale a relieved breath because that means there's now less of a chance that we'll have to raid Tazo's warehouse and potentially kill innocent people.

My fingers glide over the two guns at my waist, strapped in by an ornate Steel Dragon holster. It was a gift from Vic, the man I once respected and looked up to. I'll wear it today in his memory, not to honor him but to have a piece of him here to witness us put to the grave the war he helped facilitate.

Having the Dientes here gives us the much-needed manpower and an element of surprise against Tazo. He'll assume we joined forces with the March, but he'll be shocked to find the Dientes when they join us. The plan is to have most of them come in as a second wave, hopefully at a time when Tazo thinks he has us retreating.

Jaeger will be leading them.

He may be exiled, but he'll always be a part of us. He deserves to be here to fight for his club, his family, exiled or not.

"They're coming," Malik calls out as he points to the dust cloud in the distance. The ground vibrates a few seconds later as bikes approach.

The spikes thrown over the road about three yards ahead will stop those, and that's when the carnage will begin. I reach out and grab Genni's hand, making her turn to look at me over her shoulder. Her eyes soften for just a second as she gives it a squeeze, then I'm released as her shoulders stiffen and she brings herself up to her full height.

Malik looks around at each of us and when his eyes land on mine, he gives me a slight nod. My heart begins to pound inside my chest as he averts his gaze, the fear of losing him so potent. It's funny that I thought I hated him for so long, that the thought of him dying never affected me, but it does. He's my brother, the only blood I have left in this world, and I want to get to know him again.

I open my mouth to tell him something, but the emotion clogging my throat makes it impossible. The sounds of bikes crashing snaps me out of it and I grab one of my guns as distressed cries reach us. This was never a fight to surrender. It was always going to be to the death.

A guttural scream wrenches from Genni's throat as she runs forward, leading us all into the fray as our President, and I pray Diego has his sights set only on her. Every one of us could die today, as long as she's still standing.

Our brothers all join in and bellow with Genni, the sounds smashing into the enemies' screams. We find them up ahead, hiding behind the fallen bikes as smoke and dust add a screen over all our views.

The first pops have me diving toward Genni, but I breathe a sigh of relief when Malik drags her out of the way. We're all wearing Kevlar, but that doesn't protect us from head shots.

A few of the Dientes rush toward the bikes, jumping over the obstacles like it's an Olympic sport to take down the Knights they've been waiting to sink their teeth into.

A shot hits me in the chest and I grunt with the impact, my head swinging from the fallen bikes toward the fray. "It's fucking showtime," I growl as I lift my gun and run past the smoke.

One.

Two.

Three motherfuckers drop like a sack of potatoes and all of them with Knight cuts on. Where the fuck is Tazo and the cartel?

DIESEL

MALIK

"You've been hit, Malik!" Slayer screeches, her hand covering the graze on my shoulder.

"It's just a flesh wound!" I yell back as I drag her behind me. That shot would've hit her if I didn't push her out of the way.

Men are dropping around us and I would guess most are thanks to Diego keeping an eye on Slayer. I can barely fire a shot off before they fall to the ground with a hole in their heads.

"Quinton!" Slayer exclaims as she tries to dart toward the Dragon who's firing shots from both guns like he's in a Western. He's hyper-focused and I don't want Slayer distracting him.

"Shh!" I wrap my hand around her mouth and force her to duck behind a bike. "He's fine. If he takes his eyes off the enemies, he'll die. Understand?" She nods, her eyes wide and her breaths coming through her nose in wild huffs.

Releasing her mouth, I lift my gun and shoot at the Knight crouched behind the bike beside us, then turn to press my finger to my mouth. Slayer nods at my command to be quiet, but the second I turn my head again, she's up and running through the smoke, chasing behind Quinton.

Motherfucking females.

Chasing after her, I kill three assholes with bullets to the forehead, the spray of warm blood hitting my face is delightful. The last time I shot my gun at anyone was during a turf battle with the Dragons, but I didn't get the pleasure of killing anyone.

I catch sight of Slayer up ahead, running down the road past

Knights and cartel, and not one of them touches her. Looks like the cartel showed up so Tazo must be around here somewhere. My heart stops because that means they're on orders not to kill her, which also means Tazo Chino wants her alive. Jumping over fallen bodies, some March and some Dragon mixed in, I try to breathe through the panic threatening to engulf me.

There's no telling what that bastard will do to her to get back at her father.

I shoot the last of my bullets in the first gun, throwing it over my shoulder to the road as I grab the next out of my holster. Slayer gets farther away as I try my best to keep up with her when a body slams into me, knocking me to the ground.

My head connects with the pavement as my vision slowly fades to black. My attention was on Slayer and I didn't see this asshole coming. *Rookie move, Choir Boy*, I chastise myself when the cold press of a barrel hits my head.

I try to knock the fucker off, but my body isn't cooperating with my brain. I'm fucked-up.

"Get the fuck off my brother!" Laith's bellow has me fighting the fog a little longer and I move my head in time for the bullet to graze my temple. The burn is immediate as my head is knocked against the pavement with the impact. "Malik!" Laith screams as he shoots the Knight in the head, the dead weight hitting me like a ton of bricks.

I suck in a deep breath once the body is pushed off me, and then I open my eyes to find my brother staring down at me. My vision is hazy but I'd have to be blind not to see the frantic look in his eyes. It's exactly the same as the day he saved me from the homicidal wrath of our mother. "Fuck, you're a handsome motherfucker," I groan as he grabs my arm to haul me to my feet. "You need to get to Slayer. Tazo has a no-kill order on her." My gun hangs limply in my hand as I sway on the spot.

"She'll be fine," he snaps, dragging me to the side of the road, his gun up and ready to shoot. "Diego is watching her."

"If he gets to her, she'll disappear for good, Laith." Does he not understand the urgency? Has he forgotten what Slayer told us happened to her mother?

It's clear I got the brains from our womb-share and he got… the little dick.

"She can look after herself! You trained her! You have blood gushing from your head and if I don't find something to press against it, you'll be in trouble. Now shut the fuck up!" He sounds like me when he's angry.

"You're a c–cunt, but I'm gl–lad you're my brothhher." My words are slurring together as the world tilts around me, making the road rush up as I black out.

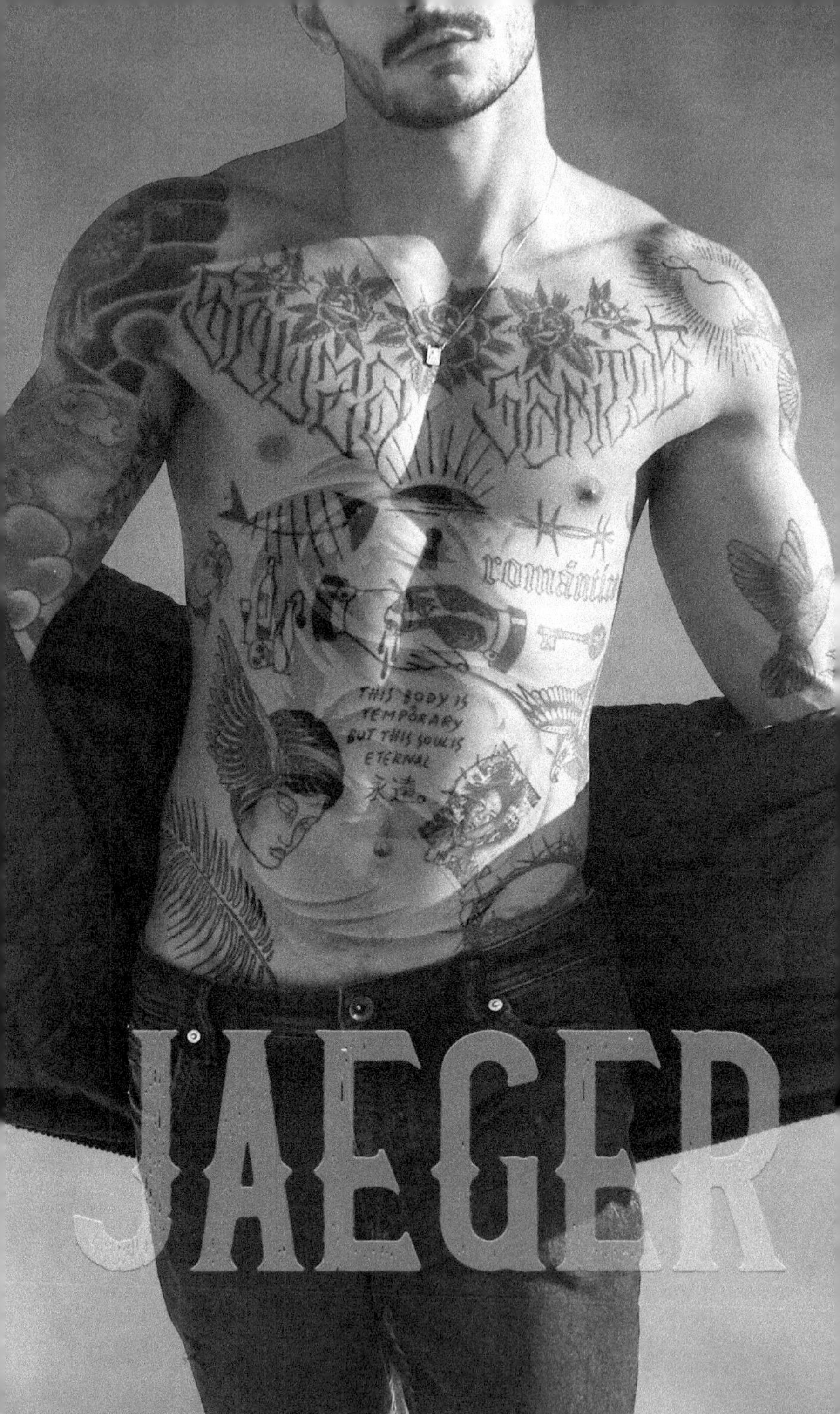

românia
THIS BODY IS
TEMPORARY
BUT THIS SOUL IS
ETERNAL
永遠
JAEGER

JAEGER

The area is pure pandemonium. I look around for any familiar faces as the Dientes run by me and straight into the fray. We're all wearing red ribbons around our biceps to differentiate us from the enemies, but as the smoke and dust fly around my head, I can barely tell who's who.

My first thought is where is Genni? She's brave enough to run into enemy lines with a gun and sheer will. The thought of her lying around here injured or worse has my heart pounding up into my throat. The irony isn't lost on me, it wasn't too long ago when I wanted her to disappear.

I slowly walk around the crashed bikes, the smoke billowing from a few of them a little concerning, and keep my eyes strained for long, dark hair. With my gun held straight out in front of me, I step around bodies, some my brothers, but most the enemy.

My steps falter when I look to the ground and find a familiar but discarded Dragons' cut, the emblem faded with time and the leather creased with use. I know whose it is before I crouch down and flip it over, the hole in the shoulder my first clue.

"Fuck," I snarl when Kennedy's Enforcer patch stares up at me, the blood splattered all over it painting a gruesome picture. So does the trail of crimson fluid leading toward the center of the battle. "Fuck, brother."

He was an asshole, but he was loyal to me and I hope he's okay. My fingers release the leather as a rifle bullet zips over my head. I turn quickly in time to find a cartel member falling forward, the top of his head blown away. Feeling like an idiot, I quickly stand and hold up a hand for Diego. Maybe the fucker really does want me to live.

Moving to the side of the road, I stay low as I move forward, my eyes skimming the bodies, praying I don't find her.

"Wake up, you piece of shit." Laith's panicked voice sounds to my right, well away from the road. "Don't you fucking die on me."

"Laith?" I call out as a shot goes wide, missing me by a few inches. "Fuck!" I crouch lower and head toward the sound of Laith's voice.

"Over here. Malik's been hit." My first thought is *do we want the fucker to live?* But then I imagine Genni's face the moment we tell her the psycho is dead.

"Where?" I ask as I find them in a low ditch, a puddle of blood forming around Malik's head.

"His temple. It's a graze but it won't stop bleeding. He passed out a few minutes ago." I find Laith with his hands against his brother's head, trying to stave off the bleeding.

"Head wounds bleed like a bitch," I tell him as I unstrap the Kevlar. "Here, take my shirt." I drop the vest to the ground and rip my T-shirt over my head. The nakedness doesn't bother me now, I've been feeling that way since the day I lost my cut, so it makes no difference.

Laith grabs my shirt from my outstretched hand, shaking with the fear I see reflected in his eyes. "Thank you."

"He'll be okay," I assure him. "God doesn't want him and the Devil would be too afraid he'd take over Hell. He's here to stay." Laith nods, his jaw flexing as he holds my shirt to his twin brother's head.

"Malik said something about there being a no-kill order on Genevieve. I think Tazo plans to take her." Laith looks at me earnestly as I run my eyes over the sand behind him.

"Fuck you!" It's Genni's voice that's carried on the wind toward me, making my spine straighten with a type of fear I have never experienced. More potent than the night my mother was killed.

"Go!" Laith spits out from between his teeth. "Go save her."

I want to tell him she doesn't need saving, that she's stronger than he or I will ever be, but instead, I rise to my feet and run, forgetting my Kevlar in the process.

Bodies lay strewn along the road, some of them my former brothers and others a mix of cartel and Knights, but I don't have time to stop and figure it out because my woman is in danger.

The woman I love.

I would rather die a hundred deaths than to ever experience her loss. I never want to live this life without her. Five cartel men are dropped from my gun before I run out of bullets, tossing it to the side when I finally come to where Genevieve is standing off in front of three Knights guarding Tazo.

Looking around, I quickly scan the area for anyone on our side and come up empty. It's me, Genni, and the enemies. A gunshot has me barreling toward her but I stop short when a Knight falls to the ground, her bullet nestled in his head.

"I only want Tazo," she calls out to them as her hair blows in the wind and the dust swirls around her body. "No one else needs to die today. Move out of the way." Her arms are dotted with blood and it looks like she has a bruise forming on her cheek, but at least she's alive.

I won't let him take her.

It happens quickly, but luckily for me, I see the imperceptible nod Tazo makes. Two men step forward from behind Genni, both in Knights' cuts and both of them large. Their sights are on Genni and it's clear to me they plan to take her. I can't let that happen to her a second time, not when I have the power to prevent it.

I don't have a weapon on me, not even a knife since I dropped it beside Laith and ran for Genni in a panic, but I do have my body and if I die saving her, then that's all that matters.

"Don't fucking touch her!" I spin around to find Quinton darting out from the opposite side of the road as he fires two shots, one going wide but the other landing a hit on one of the men behind Genni.

His gun continues to click as he pulls the trigger, but he's out of ammo. I don't think as I launch myself forward and slam into the other Knight. Genni's scream fills the air as a gunshot sounds out, and I knock my fist into the fucker's temple as I scramble to stand. My heart drops when I see Quinton writhing on the ground, his hand on his thigh, and the two men standing in front of Tazo taking advantage of Genni's distraction.

I rush for her as her gun is knocked from her hand and they each grab an arm, but just like the first time, I fail to save her. Tazo lifts his gun and shoots me, the impact knocking me backward as my knees hit the road.

"Jaeger!" Genni cries out as fire blooms across my stomach like flames eating at a trail of gasoline.

First I look at Quinton and the blood coating his pants, hoping they didn't hit an artery, and then I look at Genevieve. She struggles in their hold, her face a mask of terror and her screams turning hoarse.

My hands seal over the growing inferno in my stomach and warm blood oozes out from between my fingers. Being shot in the stomach is a rough way to go.

"Jaeger!" I look up at Genni and give her a shake of my head.

"I failed." The words are whispered as I fall to the ground, the fire moving along my limbs.

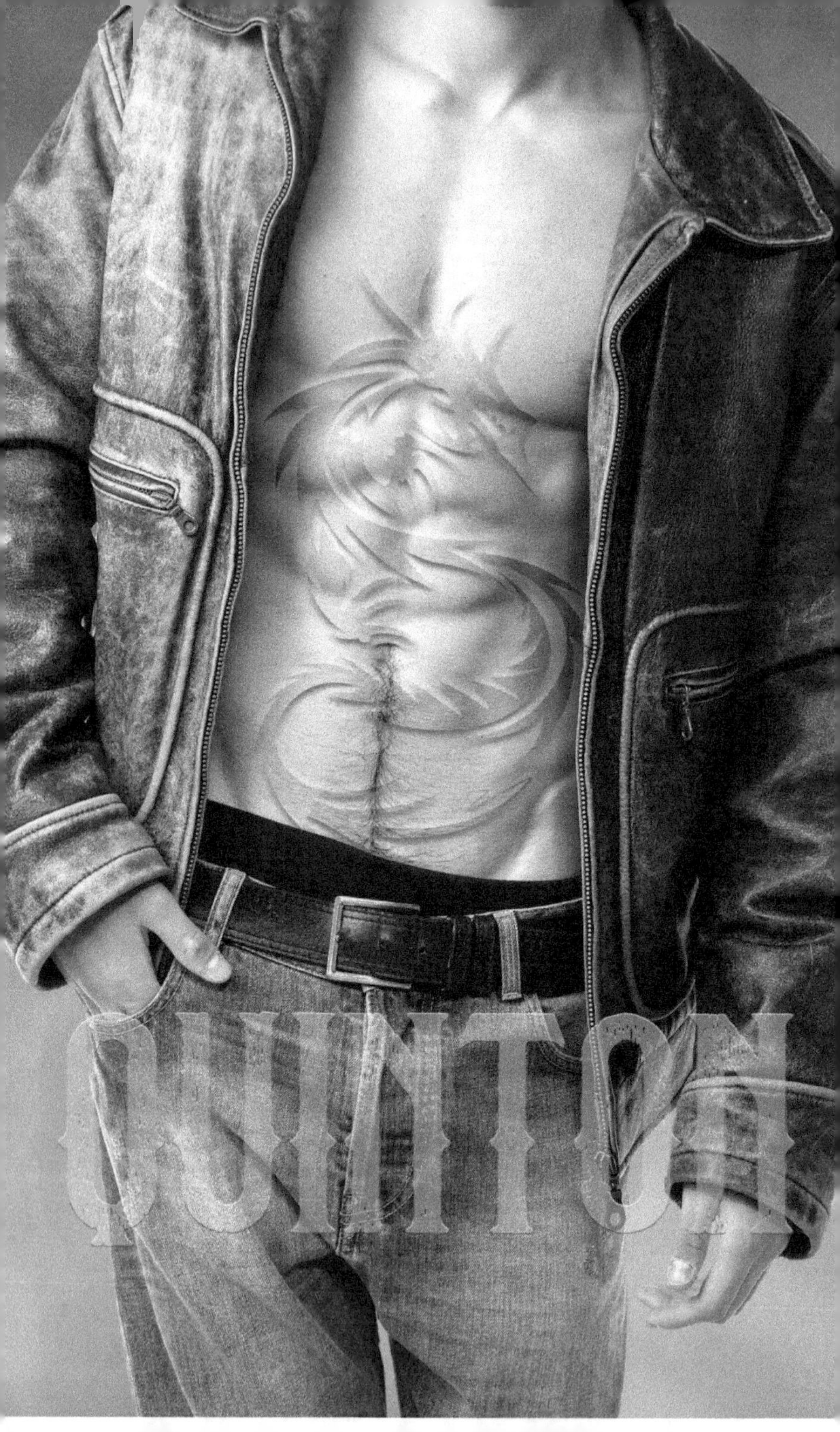
QUINTON

QUINTON

We're in a valley, too low for Diego's scope and the sandstorm isn't helping. I tried to save her, but I ran out of fucking ammo. We were supposed to have won already but it seems Tazo had more men than we expected.

He was waiting down here for a reason and I ran at him without thinking things through. Tazo has outsmarted us again and I feel like a fucking idiot.

The gunshot to my thigh is agonizing and from the loss of blood, I think the bullet nicked an artery. I can hear the rush of blood inside my ears as my chest aches with the heavy beating of my heart. The sky is cloudless overhead and all sound around me disappears as I take in the cerulean blue.

Today I'll meet my maker.

My eyes slowly fall shut as I'm jerked off the ground, large fingers biting into the skin of my arms, my body numb to the pain. Peeling my heavy eyelids apart, I take in the scene in front of me. Jaeger is lying face down on the ground, his body so still that I fear he's dead.

Genni is screaming at him to wake up, her cheeks glistening with tears as she chokes on her sobs. Then our eyes meet, those dark blues turning lighter as they fill with more moisture.

"Don't touch him!" she screeches, her voice cracking and hoarse. "Let them go. It's me you want!"

She's fighting for me, for us, offering herself up in exchange for our safety. Something we never did for her. The guilt still resides inside of me, like heavy chains, even when I can feel myself dying. There's no redemption for the things I let happen and wherever it is Jaeger has gone, I will soon join him.

I'm dragged toward my uncle as he stands with his hands clasped in front of him, the setting sun shining behind him, giving him a halo of light, and he's wearing a thin smirk, his eyes filled with glee at the carnage in front of him. The jostling ignites a flare of pain through my thigh, and I hiss out a breath to keep myself from crying out.

"You should've joined me, but you were a useless waste of air like your father." His words are hurled like shards of ice, each one sinking beneath my skin to settle against my heart. My father was a good man who loved his club and his family and it hurts to hear him disrespected like this.

The Knights force me to my knees, the impact making me cry out in agony as Genni bucks wildly in the arms of our enemies. Once again, I'm standing by while doing nothing as someone takes her away, but this time I don't have the strength to fight. "Don't touch him, you asshole!" she bellows, her words filled with rage. "I will kill you. Do you hear me? I will fucking gut you."

She goes still as my arms are released, but as I begin to fall forward, I'm stopped by a yanking on my braid. Tazo holds my hair in his hand as he slowly brings me back up to sitting, my head held in place by his taut hold.

"Did you tell your girlfriend here what this hair symbolizes?" He gives it another yank, making my head snap back. "It means strength, wisdom, and a connection to Mother Earth." He's speaking to Genni who's begun to fight, attempting to break out of the Knights' hold. "Do you really think your man here has all of that? After what he did to you?"

"Don't even think about it, Tazo." Genni's growl is low and filled with promise, but it's all lost on me when I feel the back-and-forth sawing along my braid.

My mind doesn't fully absorb what's happening as I force my heavy eyelids up and look my girl in the eyes. She's screaming at him to stop, her tears dripping from her jaw to rest against the Kevlar covering her chest. Despair crushes mine as shortened strands of hair hit my cheeks, but there's also a part of me that believes this is my punishment for what I've done and it gives me a chance to start over.

If I live through this.

GENEVIEVE
BMW Motorrad Milano

GENEVIEVE

The last rays of sun kiss his beautiful black hair, giving it blue highlights as the pieces come away from Tazo's blade. It's clear the old man is getting off on my screams for him to stop so I grit my teeth and hold it in. I stop struggling against the men with their filthy hands on me and I cease all fighting, watching as my boyfriend is degraded by his uncle.

Time stands still as single strands of his hair fly around his face, his eyes never wavering from mine. He looks tired, solemn, and in pain, but if I'm not mistaken, he looks resigned. There's no fight from him to stop what this man is stealing, no will to struggle against the blatant disrespect, and I know why.

Quinton thinks this is his atonement for his role in my being taken.

"Quinton." This time my voice is steady as my throat burns with the exertion to speak after screaming for so long. "I forgive you for everything, okay? I love you. I always have." My vision distorts with the tears welling in my eyes at the scene in front of me, but I refuse to let another one fall. "You don't deserve this. Fight."

"It makes my heart swell with pride knowing his father is probably turning in his grave," Tazo sneers. "I wish I could've done the same to him for following your daddy like a puppy. He had no strength and neither does his son."

I don't react to his words, there's no point. Tazo is a terrorist and he strives off the pain of others. I refuse to give him any more of mine. With my mother on my mind along with Delia and Diego's parents and Mariam, I relax my muscles, giving the impression that I've given up.

I'm nothing more than a weak, pitiful woman, right?

With Malik's training echoing in my head, I scan the area around me. We're in a valley, and the sounds of battle are slightly above us, explaining why Diego hasn't been firing any shots our way. As long as he's protecting the others, I think I can handle Tazo myself. My eyes sweep over the ground to Jaeger's body, the sight of his still and bare back making my heart flip inside my chest. He better not be dead.

Finally, I find a gun just inches from my right hand on the Knight holding me. Then my gaze swings back to Quinton as Tazo finishes cutting off his hair before releasing his head to hang toward his chest. I stave off the threats that want to pour out of my mouth because I don't plan on using my words any longer.

Tazo tucks the braid into the back pocket of his jeans and then snags his fingers into his nephew's hair, laughing with the Knight at his side. "Such soft hair."

"Genni!" The sound of Diego's voice gives me a small window of opportunity and I take it.

The Knights holding me turn toward the sound, their grips loosening just a little. Snapping out of their holds, I grab the gun at the waist of the one to my right and shoot him in the head, the blood and matter raining around me in a cloud of carnage. Spinning quickly, I shoot the other to my left, even though his hands are in the air in surrender. Too fucking bad, asshole.

Diego shoots the other Knight by Tazo's side who's grabbing Quinton and lifting him. I shoot the gun only to have the echo of an empty chamber and throw the piece to the ground. Diego stops with his gun aimed at Tazo but he doesn't shoot because the fucker has Quinton in front of him.

The right leg of Quinton's blue jeans is saturated with blood, the color a dark red and I swallow down the sob creeping up my throat. He's dying.

"Let him go and I'll let you take me," I offer as I slip my hand into the back pocket of my pants and touch the knife I slipped in there earlier. The very same knife my father gave Jaeger all those years ago.

"Do you think I'm an idiot?" He laughs, the sound echoing around the valley.

"Yes," I answer immediately. "You're the dumbest fucker I've ever met."

"Let him go, Tazo!" Diego calls out. "Your men are retreating, the few that aren't laying and bleeding out on the road anyway."

Tazo's reply is to place his knife against Quinton's throat, the tip sinking into the skin and drawing blood. Quinton's eyes find mine and he swallows thickly, making the knife dig deeper. It's right there, the urge to fucking panic and drop to my knees to beg, but that Varga pride is still potent as I stand my ground.

Quinton opens his mouth and licks his tongue along his lips before he mouths three words. It does nothing to alleviate my anxiety, especially when Tazo's knuckles whiten with his grip on the knife, his intention to use it clear.

With his knees buckling, Quinton starts to fall, the blade of the knife cutting upward as I start to run. Flicking open the switchblade, I scream as I get a firm hold on the handle. With one shot, just one chance, I need my aim to be true.

Blood pours from Quinton's throat to the top of his cheek, just under his eye, and the sight gives me all the strength I need to throw the knife. Handle over blade, it flips in the air as Quinton hits the ground, the air expelling from his lungs in a long, pained exhale.

It's mere seconds, but it feels like hours as the blade sails through the air. Tazo only has time to take one step back before the blade is embedded in his throat, all the way to the handle. His eyes widen as he drops his blade, his hands wrapping around my knife, then he sinks to his knees with a gurgle. I come to a stop, watching as the blood runs down his neck and over his shirt, the deep red spreading quickly.

"Genevieve! Diego!" Davis' voice has us turning as he comes running down the hill. "We have many brothers injured! We're loading up the van to drive them to the hospital."

"We need to get Jaeger and Quinton there!" I bellow as Diego drops down beside Jaeger, turning him over with a curse.

"He's alive, but it's not looking good." He looks up at Davis and shakes his head. "I need you to find Ajani."

"He's with Malik. He was shot."

Everything around me spins as the words hit my chest with the force of a thousand bullets. Malik, Jaeger, and Quinton have all been shot and it's looking like I may lose them.

My knees hit the dirt as I fall forward and throw up the bile from my stomach.

GENEVIEVE

CHAPTER SIXTEEN

2 Months Later

"What if they hate me?" I look into Quinton's eyes as he opens the passenger door of the rental car and grabs his cane. His hair now sits just below his ears, the ends kissing his jaws.

Being in an MC means we don't have many vehicles besides bikes and those aren't feasible when you're recovering from a leg wound.

"It would be normal, actually." Quinton laughs as he pushes himself out of the car and leans heavily on the cane. "My mother doesn't like many people."

"Great," I mumble as I smooth down my sundress and brush my hands over my ponytail.

Quinton tried to convince me to wear my cut but I didn't think it was appropriate to flash something that holds a different meaning for them. It represents the men who took one of their own and trafficked her out until she sunk deep into a depression and longed for escape.

I asked Davis if he wanted to join us today, but he said no. He wasn't ready to face the reservation just yet, not while he was mourning the things that happened to our mother.

These last two months, I've gotten to know my half-brother well, and even when I proposed he come with us, I knew he would say no. He craves space and silence when he's dealing with heavy emotions.

I, on the other hand, have learned to walk alongside my trauma, to hold it by the hand and lead it instead of the other way around. It'll never truly go away, but it no longer rules my life.

"Would you like to go to the burial grounds first?" Quinton asks, the sun shining into his hazel eyes, making the green more prominent. He now sports an angry red scar that runs from just under his right eye down to his throat, a constant reminder of what we endured.

"Yes." My hand slips into my dress pocket as I touch the envelope resting inside.

When I searched the box of my mother's things, I found an envelope in the pocket of her cut, like she knew I would find it one day. It was addressed to *Genevieve, my daughter*. It's been hard not to believe that she hated me because I was the product of something terrible and I wasn't enough to make her stay. I put myself in her shoes and even though I couldn't imagine leaving behind children, I also wouldn't want to live like that.

There is no resentment living inside of me for her, it's all love tinged with a sprinkle of what-ifs. My life wasn't lacking a mother because Ma took care of that and no matter how much I long for the mother who couldn't stay rooted in her desolation, I'll always be grateful I had Ma in my life.

Quinton takes my hand in his as we walk through the reservation. He waves to a few people standing on their porches, watching us as we walk by. Everyone is friendly and welcoming, and I can't imagine why my mother would ever want to leave. This place is like an oasis trapped inside a bubble, protected from the vile diseases of the outside world.

"Awendela's mother was a great healer here," Quinton begins as he walks slowly toward a large wooden gate. "She was a spiritual healer that many people would line up to visit. She was the daughter of the Chief and she was revered. I think that's where you get your instinct for leadership from."

My chest swells with pride for my ancestors and the important people they were. "Did they confirm she was there? That Tazo wasn't lying when he said he buried her next to my grandmother?"

"They found her and reburied her in a wooden coffin with a few of her belongings. My mother said they gave her a marker so we'll be able to find her easily." He opens the gate and holds it for me as I enter the burial grounds.

It's as if I've entered a place heavily inhabited by souls of the departed. Their presence is lingering in this space, their energy sweeping over my skin. Goose bumps rise along my arms as I shiver, the feeling of fingertips grazing my body. It's comforting to know they're witnessing my being here with them.

"I can feel them," I whisper as he guides me around wooden monuments carved by hand. "All of them are here and watching."

"Maybe you have the gift your grandmother possessed." He gives me a smile and my heart melts. "Here she is." He points to a newly carved marker, the wood still seeping sap. "I'll leave you be for a bit. I'm going to visit my father."

He hobbles through the grass toward the other side of the grounds as I sit on the grass beside the dirt of her grave. "Hi, Mom." My voice cracks and I clear it as I pull the letter from my pocket. The one I found in her cut from Mariam's last wish. "I have your letter here and I thought I would read it for the first time with you."

Tears slip from my eyes and hit the yellowed envelope as my heart gallops inside my chest. "My father might have been a monster to you, but he was a great dad to me. Still, I have to tell you that I sold the cottage and donated the money to a charity for women and children saved from trafficking. I did it in your name."

Awendela is decorated on the small headstone, and I wonder if she would've preferred Wendy. Or maybe that was the name of a woman who didn't want to live. My finger slips beneath the sealed flap, the glue coming apart easily after so many years. "I was happy to know you named me," I continue speaking as I take out the single piece of paper folded inside. "It's one thing I have that will forever be connected to you. Something terrible happened to me too, similar to what you went through, and I hated my name because it reminded me of a girl who couldn't save herself. Then I became a new person, adopting a new persona and wishing it would erase everything else that happened to me. Until I saw this envelope. I am Genevieve Varga and I will cherish the name you've given me forever."

The piece of paper is thin and delicate, the coloring a little yellow with age. It's hard to believe my father was planning to keep this from me, letting me believe my mother died of cancer. There's wanting to protect your child from the dark clouds, but a whole other thing when you yourself created them. He was afraid of what might've been written on this single sheet of paper, so afraid that he refused to open it himself.

Or… maybe he would've told me everything before he died.

It's all speculation at this point, but what isn't are the words written on this sheet. This is my mother's truth and as close to the truth of what happened that I'll ever get.

Hi, little baby in my belly,

The OBGYN came by the cottage today with an ultrasound machine and I was able to meet you for the first time. I'm getting close to giving birth... again, and I thought about whether I wanted to know what you were. Girl or boy.

A large part of me didn't want to know because I plan to escape this place, but a smaller part of me won out in the end. I had to know so I could give you a name. Your father won't be happy, but I used a black marker to write it on the wall.

Genevieve.

He'll be angry because you're not the boy he's been hoping for, but he'll be even more livid when he thinks we can try again. I'll be long gone.

If you do find this letter, please find my sister, Aiyana, and tell her I'm sorry for leaving and even though my life has been hell, I don't regret it.

I have Davis and you, little Genevieve, to show for it. You both will be my legacy for the future and I hope you find each other one day.

Please know I love you and we'll see each other again one day.

Love, your mother.

Folding the letter back up, I slip it inside the envelope and then back into my pocket. My heart finally slows down as I stare out toward the reservation, trying to imagine my mother here as a child. A feeling of peace comes over me and I relax as my eyes drift shut. I'm not mad about her passing, she had her reasons and I respect them, but I am sad that I will never know her.

At least I know she's resting in peace and that she truly loved me, despite not being able to stay here with me. My life would've been drastically different if she did live and I can't think of anything I would change about my childhood. It was perfect the way it was.

Quinton's steps sound behind me and I turn to find him slowly approaching, his face looking sad and distant. It's hard for him to come here because he was so close to his father and he misses him every day.

"Are you sure they want to see me?" I stand from the ground and brush the grass off my skirt. "They have every reason to hate my father and not want to meet his daughter."

He comes to stand in front of me, his hand that's not gripping the cane brushing the hair off my face. "You are the daughter of a woman they loved. That's what they'll be thinking when they meet you."

Taking his hand, I let him lead us out of the burial grounds as I look one last time at my mother's grave. She's happy here with her family, I can sense it.

Quinton takes me to a house with lush green grass and a garden of flowers out front. The exterior is painted a dark gray and the shutters a light blue. It looks welcoming.

I take a deep breath as we walk up the path, but we barely step up to the door before it's thrown open and a woman comes flying out, her graying hair billowing behind her. She gathers me in her arms and presses her cheek to mine as a sob wracks her chest. Her sorrow penetrates my shock and I close my arms around her. "You look just like her." Her words are filled with grief, the sound so familiar that I nearly lose myself in it.

"This is your Aunt Aiyana," Quinton murmurs as Aiyana pulls back to frame my face with her hands and scan her eyes over my features.

"You're so very tall." She laughs and runs her fingers through my ponytail. "That you did not inherit from your mother, but your face? It's like she lives within you." She presses her hand to my heart and I swear I can feel a presence.

"Aiyana, move aside so I can see her."

I stand to my full height as another woman steps onto the path, her head held high like a regal queen. This must be Quinton's mother.

"This is Catori, my mother," Quinton confirms as Aiyana steps aside and I take a few steps toward Catori.

"It's an honor to meet you," I whisper, my voice cracking with nerves.

"Come here." She opens her arms and I let her pull me in close, breathing in a scent so similar to Quinton's. "We are glad you came home to visit."

Home.

After spending the day at the reservation with Quinton's family, we pull into the March compound exhausted and stuffed with food. "Your mother must've thought I was malnourished," I groan as I fall back against the driver's seat. "I feel like I'm going to explode"

The compound door opens and Jaeger steps out, his Hell's March cut looking oiled and new. He holds his hand up above his eyes to shade them from the setting sun and smirks toward us, the look making my stomach flip.

Jaeger shines as an MC member and even though I exiled him from the Dragons, I never meant to take it from him completely. My plan was to offer him a position with the March and after having a Hell session with my brothers, they all agreed to accept him.

As their President.

We get out of the vehicle and he rounds to my side, his smile growing as he takes in my attire. "Is that a dress, Princess Varga?"

"Stop picking on me," I warn him. "Or I'll tell everyone how you fell to your knees and begged me to forgive you." He wraps his arms around my waist and hauls me in against him, his breath coasting along my cheek.

"I was shot in the stomach," he says with a chuckle. "But I guess you did have me on my knees like you promised, huh?"

"Every night." I pull back to smirk at him as he steals my breath in a rough kiss. I tighten my hold on his waist, only for him to hiss as I quickly pull away to lift his cut and inspect his shirt for blood. "Shit! I'm sorry." He's still recovering from the gunshot to his stomach after having spent three weeks in the hospital. The doctors said if it wasn't for Diego's quick thinking, Jaeger wouldn't be here today.

Thank fuck because I can't imagine a world without him in it.

"It's okay. Still a little tender." He kisses my forehead once I straighten to my full height, glad that I didn't harm him any further, as Quinton shrugs on his cut and shuts the car door.

The ram's skull emblem on his cut shines new as well as he slowly walks toward us. If Jaeger was made President of the March, it was only right to make Quinton Vice. It's what they've always wanted since they were kids, and it was never my intention to take it away from them.

"What happened today?" Quinton asks him as Jaeger links his fingers through mine to lead us inside.

"Rockz is setting up now. The brothers are excited about it." As soon as the doors open, my ears are assaulted by the sounds of heavy metal and the scent of liquor wafting under my nose. The reservation was like home in its serenity, but the clubhouse is also like home in its chaos. Both are a part of me.

"Are you doing a swearing-in today?" I look around Jaeger into the club, my face breaking out into a smile when I find my brothers.

Ajani is taking a much-needed break from Medical as he sips a whiskey at the bar. Since he accepted the club's Medic position, he's been running at full steam day in and day out. He says it's to keep an eye on the brothers still healing from our battle, but I know it's keeping his mind off Delia.

In front of Ajani at the bar is some gauze and ointment needed for the tattooing of a new member, and I tip my head in question. We already swore in three prospects a few weeks ago.

"That's for you," Jaeger whispers into my ear, and my heart stalls in my chest. "It's time you were made a true member."

It's something I've thought of often when I see the brothers with their tattoos on display, but I didn't bring it up for fear of being told no. Yes, I was once their President, but I had imposter syndrome for most of it.

"Come on, Lady Prez," Rockz calls out, his nickname for me having stuck after Jaeger was made their official President. "Where do you want me to stick you?"

"Watch it," Jaeger growls in warning, his hand tightening around mine.

Diego steps out from a corner of the room, his bright blue eyes like beacons to my soul. "What are you doing here?" I rush over to him and launch myself into his arms, a smile on my face.

"Malik told me to record this for him and then I'm under strict orders to bring you back to the Dragon compound." He shakes his head with obvious affection despite the sadness that lingers in his eyes.

"Did you speak to her today?" I drop my voice low so the others can't hear us.

"Yeah. She's not coming back anytime soon." He releases me and scrubs a hand over his face, his exhaustion hitting me in thick waves.

"You need rest, and we need to find you an assistant medic." Diego agreed to take the Medic position for the Dragons, a level up from the last man who held it if you ask me.

Delia has yet to reply to any of my texts, but she has enough sense to check in with her brother. It hurts that she's ignoring me, but I'm giving her the space she needs to heal. If she ever goes silent for too long, we'll hunt her down or anyone else we need to. I've given her the space, but my patience is running out. Soon I will take it into my own hands and find her to drag her back home where she belongs. Mourning by yourself is like standing in a crowd of strangers. The ghosts of loved ones past can't help you.

"C'mon, sis!" Davis calls out from the bar, his fist hitting the wooden top. "Let's get you tatted!" He's been doing well as Sergeant at Arms and it's been a smooth transition for him to become close to Jaeger and Quinton. "Put it on your stomach and we can match!"

My hand hovers over my stomach, the skin still healing from the Dragon branding ceremony last week. I was officially patched in as President, making Malik my Vice, and Laith my Sergeant at Arms. It was the same day we had a ceremony for the dead, including Kennedy, whose body was never recovered. He and I never really saw eye to eye, but I hope he's found peace.

"Shoulder blade," I decide as I undo the top few buttons of my dress to let the fabric slip down over my left shoulder. "I want to be able to show it off whenever I want."

The place erupts into raucous cheers as Rockz pats the bar top where he's placed a pillow for my head next to a tumbler of whiskey. "Hop up."

I sit up on the bar as my brothers all cheer and I lift the glass in a toast. "You guys gave me a family when I thought I had lost mine. You welcomed me with open arms and I am beyond honored to be sworn in as a Hell's March member. I love you all." I raise the glass as they all lift their drinks, then we tip them back, the burn scorching its way down my throat to settle its warmth in my stomach.

The girl I was a few years ago is long gone, her ashes settled somewhere in the Arizona desert, but I rose like a Phoenix with a fire to scorch anyone who threatens my family.

"Malik, can you see our girl?" Diego's voice hits me as I lay stomach down on the bar. Malik suffered two gunshot grazes and I count myself lucky that was all they were. He'll have fresh scars to add to the old ones, but he's here with me and that's all that matters.

"Yeah—"

"Move, brother. I want to see her." Laith's voice brings a smile to my face as I relax further. It's his effect on me, always calming my nerves. They still have their moments where they want to rip each other's heads off, but something happened during that battle and it solidified their relationship. "Genni, I love you. Is that a dress?"

"I love you too!" I call out with a chuckle.

"Slayer, make this quick and meet us back home. You hear me?" Malik's gruff tone coming through Diego's speaker sends tremors down my spine to settle in my stomach next to the whiskey.

Home.

Home isn't a place or a structure, it's the people who mean the most to you. Family is home, and I've finally found mine.

EPILOGUE

Slayer settles that sweet pussy over Diego's mouth as his abs flex and his cock jerks against his stomach. She's facing me as she rides his face, her clit piercing winking at me when Diego spreads her lips.

I got her into the parlor a month ago after begging her to trust me, and I only had to agree to one condition. She would let me pierce her clit, if I let her tattoo her name on my dick.

Best decision I've ever made.

My hand wraps around my cock, stroking along the jagged letters of her name, *Slayer*, as Diego's cock drips precum from the tip. My mouth waters as I fall between his legs, deciding to give Slayer a show. She always gets more turned on when Diego and I touch each other.

I grab his cock in my hand as he grunts into Slayer's pussy, his velvet skin heated to the touch. Leaning forward, I drag my tongue along the tip, collecting his precum and letting his salty taste coat my mouth.

Her moan is loud as she keeps her eyes on me, the Dragon branding on her stomach rippling with her movements. "Take all of it, Malik," she demands as she grinds down onto Diego's face. "I want to hear you gag."

I never disobey an order from my President. So I suck Diego deep into my throat, making sure to pay close attention to his sensitive skin. Clenching my muscles around his length, I begin to bob up and down, listening to him grunt from beneath Slayer.

Reaching underneath my chest, I find Diego's heavy balls, the heat radiating off of them soaking into my palm. I massage them as he thrusts up into me, making my gag sound around the room.

"Fuck, yes, Diego. Fuck his face." The sound of Slayer's wet pussy pressing down on Diego's face combined with my slurping his dick is like a hedonist's dream.

It takes no more than three thrusts before Diego's cum is spurting down my throat, and I swallow every drop before releasing him. Then I grab Slayer off his face and lay her on top of him, her back to his chest as I line myself up with her pussy and thrust inside.

"Fuck!" she screams as I pound into her, my balls begging for release as her walls clamp around me. "I'm. Going. To. Come." Each word is punctuated by a heavy pant.

Diego's fingers creep around her waist and slip down to her clit to grab the ring through the hood. Then he pulls on it before rubbing it into her clit, making her pussy gush around us.

"So fucking wet," I grunt as she tenses, her pussy pulsing before she screams through her release.

She clamps so hard around me as I work myself in and out of her, chasing the euphoria until I fall into the wave of pleasure, riding it out as my cum fills her.

Falling to the bed beside them, I take in a deep breath as Diego and Slayer hum through the afterglow of our fucking. It's always like this, explosive and electric, no matter how much time goes by. These two are mine and nothing short of death will ever part us.

"'*Give thanks to the Lord for he is good. His mercy endures forever.'"*

Slayer snorts as Diego chuckles. "Are you going to spout Bible verses every time you come?" she asks, humor thick in her tone.

"Every damn time."

THE END

SAD TO SEE THIS WORLD END? CARRY ON FOR A SNEAK PEEK INTO A BRAND NEW DUET!!!

HELL'S
VIPER
HELL'S MARCH MC BOOK ONE
C.A. RENE

PROLOGUE

The smell of iron hits the back of my nose, feeling thick in my throat as I swallow it down. My face is dripping with blood and when I lift my hands up in front of me, blood drips from each finger like a leaky faucet.

Humanity slips away more and more each day as I sink into the sessions of torture, drawing death out with long, enticing slices of my blade. The Grim Reaper and I have perfected our dance of death. He lets me twirl in carnage before sweeping in to steal the show with an epic finale.

Living a double life for years, I found balance in the crack that nestled itself between my two halves, but now I'm whole, no longer straddling the line of two personalities. It's freeing not having to hold back the desire for depravity and constantly proving myself worthy of the people around me.

"Viper!" His voice is like steel, cold and unforgiving, and so familiar it makes me turn on the spot.

My heart stirs as I take in his rich umber skin and autumn-gold eyes. The organ in my chest is trying to beat out a rhythm so deep in its muscle memory, working desperately to remind me of the song.

He tilts his head, showcasing the rapid flutter of his pulse at his neck, and holds out his hand. Long fingers and neatly trimmed nails that are capable of saving someone's life. I suck in a breath as my heart gallops faster.

Ajani.

"Everything is okay now," he says gently as he takes another step forward. "I'm here."

My body begins to tremble as the cold of the concrete under my bare feet sends ice through my veins. I blink to bring the room into focus, seeing the blood on the walls and the bodies on the floor.

Leather cuts lay discarded in tattered pieces on the floor, yet none of them belong to the man I seek.

"Can't leave yet," I grunt as I turn to the body I was just skinning. "Haven't found him."

"Delia, please!"

Delia.

Dark curls, cerulean eyes, and a weak nature filled with emotions.

I don't know where she is, she's no longer here.

I am The Viper.

For all book updates and social platforms, check out my website

ABOUT THE AUTHOR

C.A. Rene lives in Toronto, Canada with her family, where most of the year varies from chilly to frigid. Most days you'll find her wrapped in her many blankets in bed while reading or writing her next dark, twisted story.

Her stories boast of inclusivity and refusal to be conformed in any small box. Writing across genres is a hobby and drinking wine is a must… Or coffee … with a splash of Baileys.

ALSO BY CA RENE

The Whitsborough Chronicles
Through the Pain
Into Darkness
Finding the Light
To Redemption

The Whitsborough Progenies
Ivy's Venom
Carmelo's Malice
Saxon's Distortion
Gabriel's Deception

Desecrated Duet
Desecrated Flesh
Desecrated Essence

The Reaped Series
The Reaper Incarnate
Hunting the Reaper
Claiming the Reaper

Hail Mary Duet
Blue 42
Red Zone

Sacrificial Lambs
Sing Me a Song
Song of Tenebrae
A Verse for Caelum
A Harmony of Procellarum

Steel Dragons MC
Dragon Slayer
Dragon Strife
Dragon Slayer

Hell's March MC
Hell's Viper

The Phantom Chasers
Bedlams Playground
Silent Night Theme Park

Mimic
Festum Mors